Sunshine Blues

Sunshine Blues

sex, drugs & rock 'n roll, but the peace & love are dying

Printed in the United States of America
Rev. 2.27.2024

Bob Calverley
a Bob Calverley publication

Disclaimer

This is a work of fiction, a product of the author's imagination. Any resemblance or similarity to any actual events or persons, living or dead, is purely coincidental. Although the author and publisher have made every effort to ensure there are no errors, inaccuracies, omissions, or inconsistencies herein, any slights or people, places, or organizations are unintentional.

Cover photo courtesy of Shutterstock.com
Formatting by deboraklewis@yahoo.com
ISBN: 9798989267736 (Paperback)
ISBN: 9798989267743 (ebook)

Library of Congress Control Number: 2023920589

Sunshine Blues

1968

sex, drugs & rock 'n roll
but the peace & love are dying

Bob Calverley

PROLOGUE

July 1967, the Golden Triangle, Burma

"What's that?" A handkerchief dangling from his hand, Matt Doran pointed to a thatch-roofed hut a hundred yards away at the edge of the jungle. Then he slapped the handkerchief back over his nose and mouth to block the acrid odor of boiling morphine and ammonia.

Jettrin Juntasa, a burly six-foot-plus Thai man in his late thirties, seemed to avoid the question with one of his own. "Mister Matt, you wan go back hotel now?"

Doran mopped sweat off his face not yet sure what to make of Juntasa. The Thai had just taken over running the family business following the death of his father. The father had been brilliant, but so far the son hadn't impressed Doran. What Doran said was, "I want to see everything. Never seen how heroin's made."

In English almost as painful as the smell coming from the pots, Juntasa had just explained the process for making the sticky brown morphine base. After glancing at the workers hovering over the bubbling pots, his eyes shifted back to the hut. "Okay. But that not part of… ah, make-making..."

They picked their way around the pots and negotiated the grassy mud of the uphill slope leading to the hut. Doran kept patting sweat off his forehead with the handkerchief, thinking maybe he should have accepted Juntasa's offer to fly back to the hotel and its air-conditioning. The Thai couldn't speak English well, but he could fly a helicopter.

Doran stopped at a ragged straw mat hanging over the hut entrance and heard soft voices inside. "What is it, a dorm for your workers? You coulda just told me."

Juntasa laughed. "No, you see. Go, go in."

Doran entered. He found three women dressed in skimpy shorts, nothing else. Two sat on army cots while the third, older than the other two, stood drinking from a plastic cup. The older woman nudged the young girl nearest to her with her foot and the girl rose from the cot, one hand trying to hold her small breasts provocatively. She forced a smile, said something in Thai. He spotted a bloody bandage on one of her hands.

Juntasa, pushing through the door behind him said, "Them... girls for workers."

"What happened to her hand?"

"I cut off finger when she no fuck," he said. "I buy girl from family. Sometime girl stub... stubor..."

"Stubborn," Doran said.

"Stub-born." Juntasa pronounced the word slowly. "Make stubborn girl come here. If she still stubborn, I cut finger off. One finger. Then she fuck. Work all time."

The girl continued cupping her breasts, one at a time, with her uninjured hand as Doran regarded her, gaining some respect for Juntasa. What a good idea. Cutting off a single finger. It gave him an idea.

The girl couldn't have been older than Gloria, his fifteen-year-old stepdaughter, an incredibly stubborn girl whom he had whipped with a bamboo switch. And she still had the nerve to threaten him. He remembered that Juntasa's father, a man he'd known for almost twenty years, had once explained how he staffed his brothels with girls sold by poor Buddhist families. If cutting off a single finger cured a stubborn girl, maybe Doran should try it with his stubborn stepdaughter.

"Let's go back," he said.

Juntasa, one of the first officers in the Royal Thai Air Force to qualify as a rotary wing pilot, earning him the nickname "Colonel Whop Whop," flew them back in his personal OH-6 helicopter. They crossed the border into Thailand landing at a small, exclusive and discreet hotel. After a shower and fresh clothing, Doran felt comfortable sitting outside in the shaded patio while big slow overhead fans gently pushed air around him and Juntasa. They drank iced tea and negotiated a deal for their heroin venture. Soon, Doran discovered that Juntasa negotiated far less skillfully than his father. For many years, Doran had helped the Juntasa family invest, hide and launder the vast proceeds from their prostitution business. When Doran learned that the Juntasa family had started making heroin, he saw an opportunity for them, and of course, for himself. He did not think that the younger Juntasa fully understood the opportunity.

Did the Thai government know that Juntasa had begun selling opium and heroin in South Vietnam? Were the North Vietnamese or the Vietcong somehow involved? Most heroin came out of Laos, perhaps with the help of the CIA who fought the communist Pathet Lao in the Laotian Civil War.

Doran wondered if the younger Juntasa could manage such a dangerous game. But vast profits beckoned.

After an hour, and halfway through their second pitcher of tea, they reached an agreement and shook hands.

"One more thing," Doran said as Juntasa rose to leave.

"Xari ka? You want new boys?"

Doran shook his head. Juntasa had arranged for two boys to share Doran's bed.

"Would you be interested in acquiring another girl? A Western girl?" Doran asked. The negotiation had gone so well, he'd had time to think of other problems.

Juntasa paused.

"Blond," Doran added.

"Last year get blond woman for general. Friend of father. Trade Yakuza two Balinese girls for her. But she too old," he grumbled. Then he snarled. "Yakuza duck fuckers."

Doran strained to keep from laughing. Juntasa might struggle with English, but he mastered the swear words easily enough.

"You remember my stepdaughter? I believe you once saw her when you came to America with your father."

"Yes, young girl, beau-ti-ful face."

"She's fifteen now." Doran took a photograph from his shirt pocket, passed it to Juntasa. The picture showed his blond stepdaughter in a gym uniform. A photographer had taken it for her junior high yearbook. It hadn't appeared in the yearbook, but the photographer had sold a print to Doran.

Doran watched Juntasa's reaction to gauge his interest as the Thai studied the picture. "I sell her to you."

"Sell her? Why?"

"She spies on me. Knows too much about my business. Safer if she's over here." He knew the Juntasa family specialized in exotic sexual services and that many Asian men prized blond Western women.

Juntasa looked at the picture again. "She fuck? If she no fuck..."

Doran waved his hands like he didn't care, which he didn't. "She's a virgin."

"Virgin?" Juntasa gasped, unable to mask his excitement. "You sure?"

"Of course. But I trained her. She knows what to do."

Juntasa gazed at the picture for a long time, and Doran knew he had him. "What happened to the old blond woman?" he asked.

"I kill her," Juntasa said still staring at the picture.

Grosse Pointe Shores, Michigan

Gloria Doran stood naked in front of the full-length mirror in her stepfather's bathroom holding his small round shaving mirror in one hand, her back, arched and twisted, as she tried to see the marks on her back. Most of the stripes had scabbed over and the scabs had fallen off, but one stripe, deeper than the others, hadn't healed. Her brassiere kept irritating it, and it still hurt when she lay on her back. At least she no longer left bloodstains on her bed sheets.

It had been two weeks since her stepfather had whipped her. He'd return tomorrow from his overseas business trip. What would he do to her next? Whip her again? Or something worse? Gloria thought about going to the police. But her stepfather had beaten her stepmother Gina so badly she'd ended up in the hospital many times. The police never did anything even after the nurses called them.

Thinking about Gina almost made her cry because Gina had died in a traffic accident only three months ago.

"She finally got away," Gloria whispered. No reason to whisper, no one else in the big house but her.

She already knew what she should do, but would she really do it? She had to leave. Go to San Francisco. The Summer of Love. Find the hippies. Weave flowers into her hair. Play her guitar and sing. She started humming the Rolling Stones song, *Gotta Get Away,* as she padded into the hall on her way to her bedroom to get her guitar so she could sing and play the entire song.

Then she stopped. If she started playing her guitar, she might play all night, go to sleep and wake up no further ahead with her plan to run away. So she turned around and went into the spare bedroom. She found Gina's old suitcase and started packing.

-1-

(Six and a half months later)

February 1968, Rui Binh Base Camp, Republic of Vietnam

"Flight's in," Cartwright said. He pointed a spoonful of peach cobbler toward the mess hall's corrugated metal roof.

Jimmy Hayes, looking up at the ceiling, yawned as he listened to the helicopter roar. "S'only a coupla ships, not the whole flight."

After Hayes had reported in at the orderly room following his unusual ten-day trip back to the World, Cartwright, the company clerk, had stuck to him like airplane glue. Hayes strained to remember Cartwright's first name till "George" finally clicked into his tired brain. Crazy fucker wanted to fly on gunships.

"I've flown gunner on slicks four times," Cartwright said. Trim, stain-free jungle fatigues, unscuffed boots, his eyes open wide, a hopeful smile. Too nice for a gunship gunner, but a good clerk as far as Hayes could tell. At least he got your mail to you, a problem for the last clerk.

"Even went out on a night mission. Really fuckin' cool, man."

Yeah, right, sure you did.

Hayes brushed his breast pocket for cigarettes before remembering he'd stopped smoking. His girlfriend Gloria didn't like smoking. Luckily, he didn't think he'd smoked long enough to get addicted.

"Ask Grugel. He's the platoon sergeant," Hayes said. "But we don't take up tourists."

A little harsh, but Hayes didn't want to encourage Cartwright. He yawned, bone-tired after flying on airplanes and helicopters from Fort Dix, New Jersey, to Nui Binh Base Camp, tucked up against the Cambodian border where the Ho Chi Minh Trail snaked into South Vietnam on its way to Saigon. It had taken at least twenty-four hours, maybe a little more. The International date line always mixed him up. Though he'd shed the coat, the rest of his woolen dress green Army uniform stuck to his body like a big wet bathing suit. Same uniform he'd worn for his visit to CBS and Walter Cronkite. And tomorrow he'd be the crazy fucker flying on a gunship. Originally a gunner, he'd transitioned into a crew chief responsible for mechanically maintaining the helicopter. But crew chiefs also occupied one of the two door gunner positions. Hayes needed horizontal sleep lasting more than a few minutes.

Moments later four Headhunter gunship pilots banged through the mess hall door. The gun platoon, known as the Headhunters, was part of the 99th Assault Helicopter Company. Tired, dirty, sweating in their Nomex flight suits unzipped to let in air, the four pilots scraped chairs aside on their way to the plywood counter for food.

"I ain't unloadin' on kids and mama-sans. I don't give a shit if it's a free-fire zone," said a loud voice. Hayes stood up, tried to see who'd spoken. Sounded like Nesterenko.

"They moved the villagers out. The only dinks left were fuckin' VC." Again, Hayes didn't catch who had spoken.

"You call women carryin' babies VC? Jesus Christ, Moss, you could see the kids. They weren't fuckin' VC."

Moss? Hayes knew a pilot named Moss. Several months earlier, before he joined the Headhunters, Hayes had been the gunner on a slick piloted by Moss when the company flew into an ambush. The crew chief on Moss' and Hayes' aircraft, and a gunner on another helicopter, died. A few days later, Moss finished his tour and went home. Because of his steadiness under fire, the platoon sergeants transferred Hayes from slicks, helicopters that carried troops and supplies, into the Headhunter gunships.

"Is that the same Moss we had before?" Hayes asked, turning back to Cartwright who'd just risen to leave.

"Shit, I don't know. This fuckin' Moss is new, a CW2. Came in day after you left. Second tour. If he was ever with the 99th, it was before my time," Cartwright said. "I gotta get back and finish up a couple of things."

Hayes tried in vain to listen to the pilots arguing but they'd stopped shouting. Officers' ate in their own section of the mess hall separated by a thin curtain. Hayes didn't think he could barge in uninvited. A few minutes later, four of the Headhunter gunners and crew chiefs banged through the door.

"What the fuck's with you Mitchell? You suddenly don't wanna shoot nobody? Sheeit, you got Mr. Moss on my ass," Jesse Grugel, the platoon sergeant, said. Fred Mitchell, a lanky black crew chief from Chicago, headed for the counter. He picked up a tray, forked a pork chop into one of the compartments, splattering gravy on himself. Grugel followed him. "You were given a direct order to fire."

Meanwhile, the other two Headhunter enlisted men, Delaney and Kannegiesser, though not arguing, spoke loudly.

"Jesus, lotta fuckin' bodies down there," Delaney said. Another crew chief, Delaney looked dazed. Probably stoned, Hayes thought.

"Yeah man, they lit it up, regular Willy Peter barbecue." Kannegiesser, a gunner, spoke in a deep resonant voice at odds with his stooped posture and slight stature.

Willy Peter, short for the white phosphorus found in smoke grenades and other explosives, seared skin and started fires.

"Jesus Christ, Mitchell. Don't walk away when I'm talkin' to you." Grugel grabbed Mitchell's shoulder. When Mitchell spun around, the pork chop slid off his tray, landing on the floor. The two men looked at the pork chop, then at each other.

Mitchell dropped the tray, balled his fists. "I'll kick your fuckin' redneck ass."

Hayes rushed over to stand between them.

"Get outta my way," Mitchell said, pushing into Hayes while Grugel bumped him from behind. The sergeant tried to maneuver around Hayes, but Hayes shifted to stay between the two men.

"Hayes, we were startin' to think you were dead," Delaney said with a snicker. But he moved to stand beside Hayes. Hayes smelled the marijuana on his clothes. He and Kannegiesser had probably shared a joint on their way to the mess hall.

"C'mon, Mitchell. Cool it. It ain't worth a court martial," Hayes said. He felt the pressure of Grugel pushing against his back ease.

"I don't give a shit. Another two weeks and I'm outta this fuckin' war and the fuckin' army," Mitchell said.

"That's why you don't want to fuck it up now," Hayes said. "Tell me what's goin' on. I just got back."

Hayes guided Mitchell to the table where he and Cartwright had eaten.

"We were makin' a run. Fuckin' rockets wouldn't fire so we ended up goin' through the village down low. We're flyin' with Nesterenko and…" Mitchell stopped, swiped at the sweat on his forehead.

"Donaldson," Delaney said pulling out a chair. Kannegiesser plunked a new tray of food down in front of Mitchell, who nodded his thanks. With a sideways glance, Hayes saw Grugel talking to a pilot in front of the curtain to the officers' dining area. He recognized Moss.

Mitchell looked down at his food. "Maybe Grugel couldn't see 'cause most of the ville was on my side. We went through fast, but I could see. Grunts said they were receivin' fire, which was bullshit. Supposed to be all VC, but I ain't shootin' women and kids. The grunts fired the village so everyone was runnin' around, at least the ones the grunts hadn't wasted already."

"Yeah, a lotta bodies," Kannegiesser said.

"I guess Moss got pissed because we didn't open up. Fucker's acting commander till we get a lieutenant. Anyway, we fly back over the ville just as Moss was lining up to hit it with rockets. Nesterenko probably got in the way on purpose. He and Moss were arguing about it after we landed," Mitchell said.

"Yeah, I heard. They were still arguing when they got to the mess hall," Hayes said.

Moss and Grugel came over to the table to stand behind Mitchell. Had Mitchell seen them? Kannegiesser tried to catch Mitchell's attention to let him know, but Mitchell's gaze remained locked on Hayes.

"I ain't gonna kill women and kids," Mitchell said. "They can court-martial me if they want."

"You disobeyed a direct order, soldier, so we might do that," Grugel said.

Mitchell didn't turn around, kept his eyes on Hayes. "Go ahead. You wanna charge me with refusing to shoot women and kids, we'll see how that goes."

Mitchell sounded like he meant it. Hayes had always liked the steady Mitchell, a quiet guy who rarely caused trouble. Besides, Mitchell had seen the Paul Butterfield Blues Band in Chicago, one of Hayes' favorite bands.

"I think you may be right, Mitchell." Hayes remembered some things his Uncle Sepp had told him. "Those Nazis who murdered all those Jews claimed they were just following orders, but we executed them for it. There're some orders you shouldn't follow."

"Shut up Hayes. This is none of your goddamn business," Grugel said.

"Everyone shut up," Moss said. He looked at Hayes. A flash of recognition? Grugel opened his mouth to speak but changed his mind. For a moment Hayes heard the clink of knives and forks, nothing else. "I'm gonna talk to the CO. Nesterenko told me the same thing. I didn't really believe him. Now I'm not so sure."

"Yeah, but a fuckin' order is an order and—," Grugel started.

"Enough," Moss said. He looked at Mitchell, then Grugel. "Leave Mitchell alone. Both of you eat something. That's an order."

After a shower, Hayes lay on his bunk in a pair of boxer shorts, looking up at the dusty two-by-four rafters. Music from Kannegiesser's stereo lulled him toward sleep, and cool air wafted in through the open screened upper section of the hooch. He thought about the five men he'd killed back in the USA. Murder? For sure, but he'd murdered more people in the war. But was that murder? He didn't regret killing the enemy. Usually after killing anyone in combat, he felt elated at being alive. The fear and then the overwhelming sadness at the enormous loss of life came later. Almost every night, enemy soldiers he'd killed marched through his dreams. However, he felt no sadness for the men he'd killed in

America. They'd wanted to kill Gloria and him. He'd do it again.

The music drew him out of his dark thoughts. He tried to figure out the chords. Couldn't. Gloria could do that. She could do so many musical things better than him.

A beautiful melody, but strange words.

"...parsley, sage, rosemary and thyme." What the hell, a song about a recipe?

"Hey Kannegiesser, who's that on your stereo?" Hayes called.

"Simon and Garfunkel. *Scarborough Fair*. My sister sent me the record."

"Pretty song," Hayes said. For some reason, Gloria loved him. But would she still love him when he came home? He'd changed and not for the better. He'd gone from playing stupid amped-up love songs in a rock and roll band to murdering people with an ease that scared him.

He drifted from Simon and Garfunkel into his dead parade.

No rock and roll to save his soul.

-2-

Detroit Metro Airport

"Senator Carlton's at a prayer breakfast! He's a..." Gloria stopped herself from saying hypocrite. She didn't like the senator, but he'd been her late father's best friend. He and Mrs. Lincoln were the only two people around her that she knew. She didn't know either of them very well.

"Don't worry, child. He'll pick us up soon as it's done," Mrs. Lincoln said.

Gloria looked out a window at the cars gliding by outside baggage claim. Why couldn't they take a taxi? No sleep on the jet from New York. Too much to worry about. Almost seven months since she'd run away from home. Her life had gotten complicated. She counted to ten in her head to keep from snapping after Mrs. Lincoln's repeated questions about money and whether she'd slept with Jimmy in New York.

Does the woman think I'm pregnant by the Holy Spirit?

She and Jimmy, along with an Army policeman, had been in New York to talk to the FBI and CBS News. Gloria had asked Mrs. Lincoln to come along as a chaperone but hadn't expected her to take the role so seriously. Gloria, not the Army, paid for her trip and she'd hoped to cheer up Mrs. Lincoln. The woman's son Roscoe had been murdered, and her mother had died from cancer in the same week. Gloria had met Jimmy through Roscoe but hadn't met Mrs. Lincoln until after Roscoe's murder.

"We shouldn't waste money on a taxi. The senator promised to come for us," Mrs. Lincoln said.

Gloria sighed and said, "If I paid you rent, you think I could stay with you till Jimmy comes home? It's only six months. I've already been staying quite a few nights."

"How on earth could you pay rent?"

"Um, my father gave me some money before he… died. And Jimmy said he's gonna get some of his Army pay sent to me."

Mrs. Lincoln stared at her. "So that's how you can… How much did your… I guess it's none of my business."

Gloria brushed the pocket of the baggy maternity pants where she had almost four thousand dollars. She needed to open a bank account.

"I did like that hotel beauty shop," Mrs. Lincoln said, smiling, one hand lightly brushing the side of her graying hair.

Gloria thought her beautiful, the same smooth dark brown skin as as her murdered son, Roscoe. She must be about fifty, but looked younger. Gloria liked her first name, Frances, Frances with an "e." "Your hair's really nice. That shorter style's cool."

In their hotel room in New York, Gloria had heard Mrs. Lincoln softly crying in the middle of the night. For her son? For her mother?

"You know, just before Jimmy went to Vietnam, we recorded a bunch of songs in the garage with Roscoe. You were gone. Roscoe must have given those songs to the record company because Jimmy and me heard a couple of them on the radio. There must be a record."

Mrs. Linclon smiled. "Roscoe spent so much on all that equipment. Always said he would make a hit record some day."

"You think it's for sale in stores? My father said he was gonna to talk to the record company after they tried to cheat us. Maybe he did before he..." Gloria swallowed, the look on her father's face when her stepfather shot him flashing into her mind. But she forced herself to finish. "If they're selling records, we should be paid. Both of us. You should get Roscoe's share."

Mrs. Lincoln stood up, took off her heavy winter coat, laid it across their bags. "Senator Carlton thinks you should be in high school, and I quite agree. What grade were you in before you ran away?"

"I don't want to be a pregnant high school girl. No way."

She watched a taxi roll by outside. "Um, I need to get my driver's license. I've been driving without one for six months."

"Well, I remember Roscoe took drivers ed in school, so—"

"I need a license for identification, so I can prove I'm Gloria Doran."

"Oh."

"When I talked to the FBI in New York they got all upset when I didn't have any I.D. They only stopped bugging me when that Army policeman said maybe I should get a lawyer. Do you think I should get a lawyer?"

"A lawyer? What on earth for? That could be expensive."

"Um, I had to talk to a lot of police after my stepfather shot my father. I was right there. After that my stepfather took me to East Lansing. He was going to kill me…." She shuddered, the image of her father's face flashing through her mind again.

"Everyone knows he was an awful man, dear."

"I don't know about that. Those police in East Lansing still wanted to know who killed him. I didn't see it even though I was there. I… I, um, didn't see…."

She'd lied, almost exactly like she'd lied to the police. Jimmy had killed her stepfather. Technically, she didn't actually see him do it because she'd been lying face down on the ground. And the police never directly asked her if she knew who did it. They just asked her what she saw. She told the police serveral technical lies like that.

"Then in New York the FBI mostly wanted to know about my stepfather's money. Anyway, I'm worried I might have to talk to the police again."

"I don't see why you need a lawyer. You haven't done anything wrong, have you?"

Besides lying to the police? Did Mrs. Lincoln blame her for her son Roscoe's death? They both knew who'd murdered Roscoe, and they both knew the murderer had been looking for Gloria. The two never talked about the Mafia war that was on the TV news almost every night. Gloria wanted to forget it and thought Mrs. Lincoln did too.

"No, I haven't done anything wrong." Another lie. Every night she prayed to God to ask forgiveness for her many sins, which, in addition to lying, included fornication. On their last night in New York, she'd snuck into Jimmy's hotel room.

Mrs. Lincoln draped an arm around Gloria. "Let's hope you're done with the police, dear. Let's hope both of us are. You shouldn't get a lawyer unless you really have to. Lawyers are expensive."

They stayed silent for a few minutes. Gloria took deep breaths, pictured guitar chords in her mind until she felt better.

"You know, I might inherit money from my stepfather. He was an awful man, but he was rich. There's nobody else that's family. And my real father had money too. He wasn't married. I only knew my father for a few weeks but Senator Carlton told me he changed his will right before he..."

Mrs. Lincoln looked at her for a long time. "Do you want to tell me about your father?"

Gloria looked out the window again. She didn't want to talk about her father and thought the senator had probably told Mrs. Lincoln more than she wanted to disclose. The two of them outnumbered her, so she said, "I think I need a lawyer. Maybe a lawyer could help us with the record company too."

"Well, I don't know any lawyers, but the senator might know some."

A stirring inside reminded Gloria of her biggest worry.

"Do you think you could help me find a doctor? I worry about my baby all the time."

"Oh yes. Soon as we get home, we can call the hospital referral service. I know I have that number."

Mrs. Lincoln hoisted her legs onto the end of her suitcase, settled herself, closed her eyes. "Keep an eye out for the senator."

Gloria wished she had her guitar. She usually played her guitar every day for hours losing herself in music. She understood the relationships of guitar chords and mathematics too. So, she sat by the dozing Mrs. Lincoln trying to reduce her problems to numbers, trying to make sense of them. The most important number? Her age, sixteen. Made her a child to Mrs. Lincoln and Senator Carlton. Gloria saw herself as a teenager, a teenager with older people's problems.

"I have to grow up," she said, "fast."

-3-

Three days later, Detroit

"Kee!" Frigid air slapped Jettrin Juntasa's face and his spit sailed back to splatter on his cheek. He jabbed at the switch to make the car window go up faster. What had the radio said? Fifteen fucking degrees below zero, twenty-five-mile-an-hour winds, gusts up to… he couldn't remember, but remembered something else.

"Shit!" *Practice English, always practice.* "Shit, shit, shit!" But he already knew that word well.

After he wiped the sticky mess off his cheek with a wad of napkins, he blew his nose and crammed the last hunk of a bacon-and-egg sandwich into his mouth. Hot, salty American fast food. He looked outside at the snowbanks lining the street while he chewed. If he found the girl soon, maybe he'd go to Las Vegas on the way home. Get out of the fucking cold. No. He couldn't do that. When he got her, he'd have to guard her.

"Great Brahma on a bicycle!" He whacked the steering wheel. For a moment he tried to think of a way to stop in Las Vegas, groaned and picked up his new zoom binoculars. The day before, he'd wandered through Sears for a long time before he bought the binoculars, in addition to an excellent locking blade knife, which had already proven useful. No Sears in Thailand.

Juntasa leaned forward, braced his elbows on the dashboard, focused the binoculars on a brick house half a block away under a bright streetlight. Nothing. He marveled at the massive icicles hanging from the roof and shivered despite the heat blasting through the car.

Perhaps the girl had gone somewhere warmer. Made sense, but he dismissed the thought. Too fucking early to give up, despite the cold.

He started thinking about the warmth of Thailand. Both the king and the prime minister had suggested that he resign his commission in the Royal Thai Air Force in order to devote fulltime to the family business after his father suffered his first stroke. The American presence in Southeast Asia required many prostitutes.

About the same time, a Yakuza business associate explained ritual yubitsume, or finger shortening. A Yakuza cut off the end of his own little finger in a precise ritualistic manner and presented the severed appendage to his superior to atone for a mistake. Juntasa thought the Yakuza stupid, but intrigued, he put his own twist on the concept.

Whop, a finger gone, or maybe two fingers for he was nowhere near as precise as your average Yakuza. Soon, his legion of whores, madams, pimps and business associates, all took note that, with the father gone, the son would be obeyed. And his 'Whop Whop' nickname had taken on a new sinister meaning.

Outside, lights flicked on in the house. Juntasa snatched the binoculars and studied the new lights but saw nothing. He lit a Pall Mall.

He crushed out the cigarette after a single long drag because he didn't want to spoil the new car, a big fucking Chrysler Imperial Crown Coupe. He'd looked at Cadillacs and Lincolns, but the Chrysler salesman showed him how a small table folded out from the car's center console. The passenger seat swiveled around to face the table between the front passenger and the back seats. He'd never seen anything like it. He planned to ship the wonderful car back to Thailand and present it to the king.

He picked up a dictionary to look up a word.

"Swi-vel, swivel." He had to improve his English vocabulary. He read English better than he spoke it but he could feel his English improving. Years ago, his father had sent him to a school in California where he learned to speak English while studying American real estate. His father had wanted to invest in American property.

"Swivel, swivel," he said again.

What did an American do with such a clever table-swiveling-seat? After eating lunch in the car with a pretty waitress from his new Thai restaurant, Juntasa fucked her in the back seat, the heater thrumming at maximum capacity. The restaurant manager, who'd objected to Juntasa's desires toward the waitress, stood guard in the restaurant parking lot during a snowstorm to chase away anyone who might interrupt them. Juntasa, who did not consider himself overly cruel, allowed the manager to hold a dishrag against the remainder of the little finger of his left hand.

The restaurant existed to launder profits from Juntasa's now-defunct, heroin business with Matthew Doran. What fucking profits? He'd seen nothing, though Doran had bragged that their first shipment would make as much as a million American dollars. In newspaper stories he'd read in the Detroit Public Library, he'd learned of Doran's death, in addition to the deaths and disappearances of several leaders of the local Gargano crime family.

He bellowed, "Yet pet! Farang kee nok!" He thought for a moment. "Duck fucker. Bird shit foreigner."

Juntasa had come to Detroit to collect Doran's stepdaughter. Doran had sold her to him, took Juntasa's money, but had not delivered the promised girl. The debt did not die with Doran.

Movement caught his eye. Juntasa grabbed the binoculars, focused on two women in heavy winter coats coming out of the house. One, a big African, didn't interest him. He shifted to the other. Blond hair spilled over the back of her coat. She turned from the front door. He zoomed the binoculars to her face.

"Chi! Yes, yes."

Juntasa watched the two women plod through the snow toward the car. The blond girl thrust keys into the the black woman's hand. Then she stomped over to the passenger side and got in, slamming the door so hard he heard it inside the Chrysler.

They drove away. After ten miserable cold days, he'd found his property. Who could forget that face? The girl looked bigger than he remembered, bigger than her picture. The bulky winter clothing? The four years since he'd seen her last? Sixteen now, but the same beautiful face.

"Hn̄ā s̄wy," he said, "beautiful face."

On the way back to his hotel, he pondered how to take possession of his property.

-4-

Later that morning

"It's cold outside. Don't you want me to drive you home after your appointment?" Mrs. Lincoln asked. Following the early downtown meeting with the record company president, Gloria and Mrs. Lincoln had splurged on breakfast. The tiny restaurant, three booths and a six-stool counter, was located across from the elevators in the medical office building where Gloria had her doctor's appointment.

"No, I want to go to the library and read up on babies. It's an easy bus ride from here." Gloria waved a bus schedule. She hoped Mrs. Lincoln would leave soon. "If I have to, I'll take a taxi home. I can afford it."

"If you call, I'll come pick you up. Maybe I could change my mind about letting you drive." Relieved, Gloria smiled. They'd argued when Gloria asked Mrs. Lincoln if she could drive to the downtown meeting. She said that she should get familiar with the car in case of an emergency like something going wrong with her pregnancy. The real reason was she couldn't stand how slow Mrs. Lincoln drove on the freeway.

"You were right. I should get my license first," Gloria said. She regretted the childish argument.

"And you were right too, dear. If I'm not around, you might have to drive yourself."

Gloria nodded as Mrs. Lincoln reached for her coat. Then the older woman settled back in her seat, looked at Gloria with a stern face. "Fifteen dollars a week is too much for your rent. It should be ten, or maybe eight. With the money the record company gave me, I'm not so worried about money now."

"No, fifteen's fair," Gloria said. "I had to pay ten dollars a week, twelve at some places, just for a room in a house full of noisy students. And half the time I couldn't use the kitchen. If I left food in the refrigerator, somebody would take it. You'll let me use the washing machine, right? And maybe you can teach me some of your recipes. Before Jimmy comes home I want to learn how to cook better."

"Are you sure you can afford it?"

Gloria nodded. "We each got two thousand dollars, and this time the contract looks fair."

At their meeting, the president of the record company, Maxie Zimmerman, presented them with checks. He asked Gloria to come back for a photography session. He suggested that she practice with some of their musicians so they could send her on a short tour. The record sold well wherever radio stations played any of the songs, which was mostly in Michigan and Ohio so far. A tour could spread the music to more stations. The company had released a forty-five rpm single, already in the top twenty on one Detroit radio station.

"So are you going to sign the contract? They won't like it if I sign it and you don't," Mrs. Lincoln said.

Gloria glanced at the brown manila envelope containing the contract sticking out of her purse. "I'll sign but I need to send a copy to Jimmy. He has to sign too. I'm sure he will. The money part's fair."

She didn't say that she hoped to find a lawyer and have him look over the contract. While Gloria thought she understood the numbers, she didn't understand the rest of the dense wording.

Zimmerman's enthusiasm cooled after Gloria disclosed her pregnancy. He hadn't noticed because the table hid Gloria's condition when he entered the conference room.

"As long as the doctor says it's okay, I want to perform. I feel great. I can sing and play all the guitar parts."

But he said nothing more about a tour, or the photo session. Gloria also thought that Zimmerman might have been afraid of her late father. Several times, he mentioned that Clyde Bonaventure had called about the contract. He apparently did not know that Bonaventure had died or of his relationship to her.

In the coffee shop, Mrs. Lincoln seemed to read her mind. She asked, "So Clyde Bonaventure was your father?"

She nodded. Best to have it out in the open. "Yeah, he was."

"You're sure?"

"Yes. He showed me this old picture of his grandmother. I'm the spitting image of her. Maybe I can show you the picture some time." She hesitated but knew she should address the obvious issue. "So yes, that means I'm half black. My father said my mother came from Finland and was very blond but he didn't say anything else about her."

Actually, her father had said more. He'd told Gloria that her mother had been a prostitute.

"That must have been a shock," Mrs. Lincoln said carefully.

"Yeah, but you know, I feel a little special too. I think it makes me more authentic as a musician. Me and Jimmy like so many black artists."

Mrs. Lincoln started to frown, then smiled. She reached to squeeze Gloria's hand. "I've always felt that everyone needs to treat everyone else the same, no matter the color of their skin. When I first met you and told you about my Roscoe, I could tell you cared about him. That meant a lot to me."

Gloria smiled and squeezed back. "I don't know how I feel about being half black. How am I supposed to feel? I'm still Gloria, spoiled rich girl from Grosse Pointe. I haven't told anyone but Jimmy. Senator Carlton knows 'cause he was there when my father told me. He must have told you. That's okay. Oh yeah, I told Jimmy's Uncle Sepp too.

"I can see it now that I know," Mrs. Lincoln said, "but I never would have guessed. Even now, I thought there might be a mistake."

Mrs. Lincoln stood up and put on her coat. "You're sure you'll be okay? It's cold out there."

"I'll be okay. I'll call if I have to," Gloria said.

As soon as Mrs. Lincoln left, Gloria quickly got the attention of the waitress and ordered a hot fudge sundae. Still hungry after a breakfast of eggs, pancakes and bacon, she hadn't wanted to eat a sundae in front of Mrs. Lincoln who'd started a diet.

On Mrs. Lincoln's recommendation, Gloria had called Hutzel Women's Hospital and asked for a referral to an obstetrician.

"My son Roscoe was born there. So was Diana Ross of the Supremes," Mrs. Lincoln said.

The doctor turned out to be a young Polish woman, Emily Sadowski, whom Gloria liked from the start. Sadowski spent more than an hour examining and talking to her. Her long dark hair hung in a simple ponytail over a crisp white coat. A big mole on her cheek slightly marred the young doctor's face, which made Gloria like her more. Sadowski pressed Gloria about why she hadn't seen a doctor. Gloria ended up saying more than she'd planned, telling the doctor about witnessing the murder of her father.

"But I'd just found out he was my father and really didn't know him very well… um, he's… he was black. I saw him get shot. Then I heard on the radio later that he was dead," Gloria said. Then she told the doctor that her stepfather had also been killed.

After listening, the doctor studied Gloria for a long time before speaking. "I think you should talk to somebody about all of this, a psychiatrist maybe. That's a lot of trauma, especially for someone so young."

"Well, I've been talking to you… um, I like you. You're really nice," Gloria said. She felt her face flush. "Most of the time, it's hard for me to talk to anyone unless I know them. Better now, but before I ran away from home, I couldn't talk to most people. I'd get stuck, especially when I was scared.

When I was little that happened a lot, so I used to sing instead. Long as I can remember, I liked singing more than talking."

Again, the doctor regarded Gloria. "We can talk more. I'm just getting started in practice so I have open time in my schedule. But right now I must go to the hospital. So let's make another appointment for you."

After setting up a regular weekly appointment, Gloria wandered outside to the bus stop. Instead of the library, she rode a downtown bus and got off two blocks from where her father had lived. She took her time on the way to his house, examining the neighborhood.

"I wish we'd known each other longer," she said softly.

She shivered at the front door of the house. Here, her stepfather had murdered her real father. Lights on inside, who was there? The senator? Yes, probably him. Was he living there? At her father's funeral, he'd told her she would inherit the house.

She'd planned just to walk by the house, no more. She liked the orange brick, the leaded glass windows, all the polished woodwork inside, but didn't like the senator, Logan Carlton, who drank too much and consorted with prostitutes. At the funeral, he'd only snuck into the church after making sure no reporters saw him, a la-de-da state senator at a gangster's funeral, her father's funeral.

She pushed the doorbell button, heard a faint chime, footsteps clumping down stairs. The door opened to reveal Carlton, a frown on his face.

He stared until a puzzled smile loosened his tight lips.

"C-c-could I come in?" she asked.

"Of course." Carlton forced a bigger smile and stepped aside. She caught him stealing a glance up the staircase. "What are you doing here?"

What are you doing here?

"I'm not sure," Gloria said. Then she remembered the picture she'd told Mrs. Lincoln about. "I wanted to see those family pictures. Are they still here?"

They both heard a creak coming from above.

"Yeah, they're still here." Carlton glanced back at the stairs. "I don't know…"

His cropped kinky hair glistened with some kind of cream. She smelled his aftershave but no odor of liquor, thank God. Then she shifted gears in case he asked her to leave. "Maybe you can help me? I need to get a driver's license."

"Go to the state office and pass the test," he said. "Can you drive?"

"I can drive, but don't teenagers usually take a course at school? I'm not going to school."

"You should be."

"No, I'm pregnant. I don't want—"

"You need to finish school. I can get you into…"

Gloria turned to leave.

"Hold on, okay?" He took a step toward her and sighed. "We can talk about school some other time. About the license, I'm sure you can just take the test."

"I don't have anything to show who I am." She turned to face him again.

"What do you mean?"

"Well, I'm Gloria Doran, and the record company says I'm Sunshine on the album. But I don't have anything to prove who I am. Can I still get my license?"

"That's right. You have a record. It's on the radio. I only listen to the news, sometimes ball games driving to Lansing." He looked thoughtful for a moment. "How about your birth certificate? Don't you have one of those?"

Why hadn't she thought of that? But she'd never seen hers.

"It might be gone. My house burned down." Gloria had burned the house down in a fit of rage, something she'd never told anyone.

"Okay, I'm beginning to see the problem. C'mon inside." Carlton led her into the living room. He twisted back to look at her. "Maybe I can help. You're a good driver? You're sure you could pass the test?"

Before she could answer, Gloria heard the upstairs creak again, louder this time. They both looked up.

"Let me go take care of something. Wait here."

Carlton trudged up the stairs. Gloria took off her coat, laid it on the leather sofa, then went back to the stairs. She heard muffled voices before Carlton reappeared at the top of the staircase. A young woman with brown hair as drab as her face, dressed in jeans and a puffy blue nylon jacket, stood beside him. She took her time coming down the stairs, gave Gloria a curious look, opened the front door and left. What had they been doing up there?

"C'mon up. That was Judy. She's a grad student at Wayne State. She's helping me write a paper. More room to work here than in my little apartment. We get the estate settled, I might be interested in buying this place from you."

While he spoke, Gloria started up the stairs but felt her knees weaken halfway up. She hesitated, then took the last steps to the top.

Would she see blood? She wanted to see the pictures, not go into the room. She felt her face and armpits moistening with sweat and gulped a deep breath.

"You okay?" Carlton steadied her elbow and guided her through the door.

"Just got a little scared coming back here."

Inside, the room looked the same. No blood, nothing to show that a murder had taken place there. Two wooden chairs faced the desk with papers scattered around a green portable Smith Corona typewriter that she hadn't seen before. Maybe he was telling the truth about writing a paper. The woman had not looked like a prostitute.

On the wall opposite the door, Gloria saw the picture that had convinced her that Clyde Bonaventure, a black gangster who ran illegal nightclubs teeming with prostitutes, was her father.

The large black and white photograph from the nineteenth century showed three exuberant dance hall women vamping at the camera. The woman in the center looked like Gloria's twin sister, but older, her hair a shade darker, more brown than Gloria's blond hair, though hard to tell in a black and white photo. Gloria thought her own skin a little lighter. But the woman's face, the fullness of her lips in mid-laugh, the high cheekbones that widened her face, the nose that turned up, and, most of all, her sparkling eyes, all looked exactly like Gloria.

For a long time, Gloria gazed at the picture. Her father's grandmother, Gloria's great-grandmother. Born into slavery but apparently passing for white because all three women in the photograph looked white.

Like Gloria, for sixteen years.

Smaller pictures of her father's brothers and sisters with their children, hung on all four walls. Aunts, uncles, cousins, but her great-grandmother held her in thrall.

All her life she'd wanted to know where she came from. Now she had a family, a real family.

"Could I have this picture?" she said, pointing to the picture with her great-grandmother.

Carlton thought for moment, then nodded, "Okay."

"Thank you," and she took the picture off the wall.

-5-

Nui Binh Base Camp

Jesse Grugel, the Headhunter platoon sergeant, an E-6 staff sergeant, made Hayes nervous as they ate meatloaf, cheesy powdered potatoes and peas in the mess hall. It had been eight days since he'd returned to the company. He'd flown every day, gone out twice on night counter-mortar missions and was more tired than he'd ever been in his life.

"Sheeit, I never finished tenth grade. How'd you know that shit about them fuckin' Nazis?" Grugel said.

"Learned it in school," Hayes lied. He'd learned most of it from his Uncle Sepp, a Finn who'd fought for the Wehrmacht in World War II, something Hayes didn't like to talk about. He didn't fully trust his uncle who was usually drunk when he talked about the war.

"Well, you musta been right cuz Mr. Moss, he talked to the CO and there ain't gonna be nothin' done to Mitchell."

Grugel lit a Winston. Hayes almost asked for one. But if he resumed smoking, he'd just have to quit again. Why had Grugel decided to eat with him? Usually, the sergeant ate with the other NCOs.

"Jesus, we almost fuckin' crashed takin' off this mornin'. Bounced on the runway three, four times before gittin' in the air. Did it again this afternoon," the sergeant said. "That Mr.

Moss, he ain't a very good a pilot, and he's the fuckin' actin' commander. Sheeit."

"It's the helicopter," Hayes said. "Charlie model gunships are harder to fly than slicks. Most of our slicks are fourteen hundred horsepower but the gunships are only eleven hundred. We overload 'em too. I flew with Moss when he was a slick pilot. He's okay. Now he's a CW2. He might be acting commander of the platoon but he's still getting used to flying gunships."

"Didn't know that." Grugel took a long drag on his cigarette. They'd both finished eating.

"Was there something you wanted to talk about, sergeant?" Hayes asked.

Grugel shifted in his seat. "Naw, tryin' to git a handle on ya. Y'all are kinda famous since that ground attack."

Hayes looked away, embarrassed. "Just did my job. And there were three other guys besides me, Slobbo… I mean Sergeant Slobojan, Rivera and Rufus Roy. And Roy got hurt bad. Rivera too."

What about that warrant officer?" Grugel asked.

"He got killed right away. Never fired a shot."

"They're makin' him out to be a hero, but I heard he mighta been drunk."

Hayes shrugged, didn't say anything. Drunk or sober, he'd died.

"There's some think you mighta been smokin' reefer," Grugel continued.

Would he ever shake his reputation as a pothead? "Godammit, they can think what they want. Look, I got busted for smokin' pot. I don't do that shit anymore."

"Hey, don't git all salty on me. Jess sayin' what I heard."

More silence. Calmer now, Hayes wanted to leave but didn't want to further sour his relationship with Grugel.

"Never hearda anybody goin' back to the States like you did," Grugel said.

"Me neither. There was this Spanish TV reporter, a woman, tryin' to sell a story to CBS News that we massacred civilians in that ground attack. So this colonel brought me there. I guess it worked 'cause they didn't buy the story." Hayes didn't want to talk about his trip because a lot more had happened than the visit to CBS. The sergeant didn't pursue it.

Grugel rose to leave, then paused. "There's one thing. Jess wanted ya to know that me'n' Mitchell's square now. I know he's yer friend."

After Grugel left, Hayes decided to ask Mitchell, who'd be going home in a couple of days, if he could buy a cheap guitar in the States and ship it to him. His guitar had disappeared. He could ask Gloria, but she had enough to deal with.

He didn't find Mitchell at the Headhunter hooches so he went to the enlisted men's club, a crude shed with a few tables and chairs, a plywood bar at one end. Beer and sodas cost a nickel a can. Hayes didn't find Mitchell or many others there. None of them had seen Mitchell. Hayes went to get a beer.

"Black Label's all we got," Sergeant First Class Stanton said taking a can out of a big ice cooler behind the bar. A big man with buzz-cut brown hair and sharply defined facial features, Stanton, a Korean War vet, exuded resentment toward the younger enlisted men.

When Hayes laid a ten-cent MPC note on the bar to pay for the beer, the sweating Stanton mopped the back of his hand across his forehead and said, "You can have two. I ain't got change. You want the second one now?"

"No, I'm looking for Mitchell. You seen him tonight?" Hayes gulped a big mouthful of the ice-cold beer.

"Mitchell? That cocksucker…" Stanton looked away, closed the lid to the cooler. After a few seconds of awkward silence he said, "Didya try his hooch? Or maybe somebody else's hooch? I know some of you guys got bottles stashed."

Hayes shook his head. "Mitchell wasn't much for drinking."

The sergeant peered at Hayes, Hayes thinking Stanton wanted to suggest that maybe Mitchell was smoking marijuana somewhere.

"And he didn't smoke either," Hayes said taking another big swallow of beer. As the sergeant continued staring at him Hayes added. "And I think I'd know."

"I guess you would."

As Hayes finished his beer, he watched Stanton hurrying to close up the club early, which set off a spate of grumbling. He went over to the big maintenance shed and after wandering around for almost ten minutes, he found Sergeant First Class Gomez, the Maintenance NCO. Gomez told him that Mitchell had left more than an hour ago. While talking to Gomez someone tapped him on the shoulder.

Hayes turned to see the first sergeant. "Ah..."

"Gus McConaughey." The first sergeant stuck out his hand. Surprised, Hayes shook it. "Been tryin' to meet you, but right now I'm looking for Sergeant Grugel. Got a new crew chief for the Headhunters. Transfer from a Cav unit."

"Ate dinner with him a little while ago, but I don't know where he went," Hayes said. "I was gonna go out on the flight line. I'm looking for Mitchell. Can't think of anyplace else to look. If I see Grugel, I'll tell him you're lookin' for him."

"I'll tag along," McConaughey said.

As they walked toward the flight line, McConaughey peppered Hayes with questions about flying. He seemed friendly enough, wanted to know how long they typically flew, if they ever had any days off, how tired flight crews got.

"I've fallen asleep in the air," Hayes admitted, hastily adding, "when we were just going from one place to another and I didn't have to do anything."

"The CO's worried about flight crew fatigue," McConaughey said.

"Yeah, it's worse for pilots 'cause they hafta—" A gunshot cracked through the evening air. Hayes and the first sergeant ducked into half crouches, both their heads turning in the direction of the shot. Hayes thought it came from farther along the line of revetments filled with the parked helicopters.

"Sounded like an M-16. Wasn't an AK," Hayes said, relaxing. The two straightened, their heads cocked, listening for a few moments.

"Does that happen very often? A random shot like that?" McConaughey asked.

"No, not often, but everybody here's got a gun, right? There's a lot of city boys who didn't grow up with guns. I heard somebody over in the MASH unit accidentally shot himself in the foot a few weeks ago," Hayes said.

Led by McConaughey, they moved along the flight line until the first sergeant slowed, then stopped. "Sounded like it came from somewhere around here."

A little disoriented because he'd approached the flight line from the opposite end of his usual route, Hayes squinted trying to see the tail number on the helicopter behind the nearest revetment. Beside the sloped steel sheets of the revetment, he spotted a smashed guitar on the ground. When he bent to pick it up, the waning orange light from the dying sunset, reflected off something shiny under the helicopter's tail boom.

"Sergeant—" Hayes started, but a flashlight snapped on before he finished. The harsh yellow light revealed the body of a soldier lying on his back, an M-16 rifle on the ground beside him, the face covered with blood so fresh that Hayes smelled the faint coppery odor. Hayes recognized him immediately.

He had found Mitchell.

-6-

"Is he dead?" McConaughey asked, though they both knew the answer. After playing the light from his flashlight over Mitchell's body, McConaughey turned a slow circle, shining the light outward, his head once again cocked as he strained to hear the slightest of sounds. One hand rested on the butt of the pistol strapped to his hip. "I don't see anyone."

Down on one knee, Hayes examined Mitchell's bloody face, his lips pulled back over his teeth in a rictus of agony. A small rivulet of blood from the corner of his mouth ran down his chin. The blood on his face came from a hole in the center of Mitchell's forehead. Mitchell's open, lifeless eyes left no doubt.

"Dead," Hayes said. He touched Mitchell's neck, but as soon as his fingers felt flesh, he jerked his hand away like he'd touched a hot stove. "He's still warm."

Hayes continued staring, the reality sinking in. "Why Mitchell? Why'd you do it? You were going home."

He remembered the confrontation between Mitchell and Grugel, serious enough that a week later, Mitchell still talked about it. "Jesus, Mitchell, was it that bad?"

He got a grip on himself, noticed more blood that had soaked the front of Mitchell's jungle fatigue shirt. From the way he lay, blood from the head wound should have run directly onto the ground.

"Lemme see the flashlight a sec."

McConaughey handed Hayes the six-inch penlight. He shined it on Mitchell's chest. "Looks like he was shot in the chest too. How could he shoot himself in the chest and in the head too?"

"We only heard one shot." McConaughey said.

While Hayes held the light, McConaughey crouched and unbuttoned the front of Mitchell's shirt. He pulled up the torn, bloody T-shirt.

"Doesn't look like a bullet wound. Maybe a knife?"

Hayes shone the light on the ground around the body looking for a knife. "I don't see anything else except that guitar. I think it's mine."

McConaughey looked over at him. After a long moment, he said, "Go get the CO and the flight surgeon. I can't remember the doc's name. Haven't met him yet. Do you know where they're quartered?"

"The CO has a little trailer. Doc Goetz bunks in the back of the medical hooch. I'll find them. If they're not in their quarters, they're probably in the Officers Club."

"Bring them out here and see if you can dig up a better light. Don't tell anyone else about this yet," McConaughey ordered.

Hayes found both the CO and Doc Goetz in the Officers Club. Surrounded by what looked like every officer in the 99th, Major Blair, the CO, had a drink in his hand, as did everyone else. Hayes stood at the doorway for a moment listening to a happy buzz of conversation. Taking a breath, he shouldered his way through the group. Blair turned to face him, irritated. Hayes stopped, then remembering military courtesy, saluted. Blair returned the salute. Of medium height and build, the CO projected command presence with erect posture, an economical and decisive manner of speech, and imposing gray eyes that seemed to miss nothing.

"Sir, we have a situation out on the flight line. First Sergeant McConaughey sent me to get you and Doctor Goetz," Hayes said.

Blair eyed Hayes for a beat, then scanned the crowd to lock quickly on Doc Goetz who stood near the back holding a can of Coke. He turned back to Hayes. "What kind of situation, specialist?"

Hayes hesitated, remembering McConaughey's orders about not telling anyone else. Already, the room had grown quieter. Hayes bent and spoke quietly into the CO's ear. "Sir, it's Mitchell… ah, Spec Five Mitchell. He's dead. Looks like he was shot."

"What, is there an attack?" the CO said.

"No sir. It's not an attack. It's… I'm not sure what it is."

"Tell me what happened."

By now, several officers were leaning closer trying to listen.

"Sir, the first sergeant told me not to tell anyone else. He said to bring you and the doctor out there."

The CO looked around the room again. For the first time, Hayes noticed that he wore bright shiny gold oak leaves on his collar, the insignia for the rank of lieutenant colonel. Then he realized that the officers had gathered to celebrate the CO's promotion from major to lieutenant colonel.

"Doctor Goetz, with me. The rest of you carry on," Blair ordered. Hayes led them to the flight line while filling them in on the way.

"I'll go back to Maintenance and get a bigger light," Hayes said when they arrived at Mitchell's body.

When he returned with two big camp lights, Hayes found the doctor bent over Mitchell's upper torso, now stripped of clothing. McConaughey took one of the lights, which had a bulb and reflector almost the size of an automobile headlight. He raised it over the body.

"Looks like he was stabbed in the chest," Goetz said. He reached to position the brightest part of the light onto Mitchell's head and carefully turned the head to one side. "This is a gunshot, probably from the M-16. Big exit wound in the back of his head. I think he was standing when he was shot. Both the wounds are fatal, though he might have survived for a few minutes after the chest wound. I'm guessing that happened first, then the gunshot. From the blood on his face, he was still alive when he was shot."

The CO took the other big light from Hayes and started looking for a knife just as Hayes had.

"I don't see how he could have done it himself. He'd have to hold the rifle parallel to the ground. Hard to do, especially after suffering a major stab wound. People shoot themselves with a shotgun or a rifle, usually do it lying down or sitting. They put the barrel in their mouth and bullet comes out the top of their head. Not the back," Goetz said.

No one said anything until the CO finished circling the revetment with the big light. "Specialist Hayes, you only heard one shot?"

"Yes sir, it was a single shot. The first sergeant and I both heard it."

McConaughey nodded. "That's right. We were together when we heard it."

Hayes took the big light from McConaughey to illuminate the helicopter. Right away, he saw flecks of blood on the tail boom and a bullet hole. All four of them stared until Blair spoke to Hayes again. "Specialist, I want you to go get the military police. Their hooch is next to brigade headquarters."

"I know where it is, sir," Hayes said.

"Good. Tell them we have an unusual death here." Scratching his chin, Blair looked down at Mitchell's body, then at the first sergeant and the doctor before turning back to Hayes. "Ask them to send someone out here. The commanding officer is a first lieutenant. Tell whoever you find that I strongly suggest that the lieutenant himself come here."

As Hayes started away, he heard the CO ordering the first sergeant to get someone in Supply to check the serial number on the M-16 and make sure it was Mitchell's. Hayes stopped, turned around.

"Sir, you should know that smashed guitar over there is mine. I've been looking for it ever since I came back."

The CO considered him and nodded. "Okay, but we need to leave it until MPs take a look. Now, go get the MPs."

It took almost fifteen minutes before Hayes found the MP lieutenant and brought him to the revetment.

"You're dismissed, Specialist," the CO said. "Go back to your hooch. We'll come and get you if we need you again."

"Should I keep quiet about this, sir?" Hayes asked. He was sure some men must have seen the lights and the activity out on the flight line.

"For now."

Back at his hooch, Hayes got ready to take a shower. When he opened his unlocked locker to get his towel, he didn't see his M-16 rifle. In the afternoon, after finishing the maintenance on his helicopter, he'd put the rifle in his locker along with his flak vest and flight helmet, both still in the locker, along with a bandolier of loaded M-16 magazines.

"Hey, did someone take my rifle?" Hayes shouted over the Rolling Stones album playing on Kannegiesser's stereo.

"What would I want with your fuckin' rifle, Hayes?" Delaney said wandering out of the corner he shared with Kannegiesser. A parachute draped over the rafters, and pieces of scrap plywood nailed together walled off their space. "Didja ever find Mitchell? He ain't been here."

Crossing to another makeshift room on other side of the hooch, Hayes stuck his head through a poncho liner to see Leroy Flowers, who shared the space with Mitchell. Flowers looked up from his bunk where he lay reading one of his Bibles.

"Haven't seen your rifle, Hayes," Flowers said. "And I haven't seen Mitchell since this morning. Maybe he's working late. You know he went to Maintenance, right?"

Nodding, Hayes said nothing, an unsettling feeling welling up in his guts. He hurried to get dressed, then trotted back to the revetment.

He found almost a dozen men, most of them officers who'd overheard him talking to the CO.

Hayes strode up to Blair, who stopped talking to the MP lieutenant. "Sir, I think that M-16 beside Mitchell might be mine. I just noticed that my rifle's missing. And I know I put it in my locker this afternoon after we got back."

"Do you know the serial number?" Blair asked.

"No, sir."

The MP lieutenant looked him hard in the eye.

"What are you trying to say, Specialist Hayes?" Blair asked.

"Sir, I told you that's my guitar, and if that turns out to be my rifle, well, I think maybe someone's trying to frame me."

"Specialist Hayes, you were right beside me when the shot was fired, so that puts you in the clear," First Sergeant McConnaughey said.

"I know," Hayes said, "but what if we hadn't come out here together? What would everyone think?"

-7-

Detroit, Michigan

Outside, the wind howled through the trees rattling the bedroom window. It had been more than week since she'd returned from New York, and Detroit's weather had grown bitterly cold. Between wind gusts Gloria listened to the fuel-oil furnace laboring to heat Mrs. Lincoln's drafty old house. Several times during the past week, Mrs. Lincoln said she should hire someone to put on the winter storm windows, something her late son Roscoe usually did. But she didn't know whom to call.

Gloria spread an old woolen blanket from the closet over her bed. The extra blanket helped but she still felt cold. She thought about her dead father Clyde Bonaventure and felt tears cold on her cheeks. After witnessing his murder, she'd tried not to think about him. After all, she'd barely known him. Why should she care about a criminal who ran illegal nightclubs? She remembered her first encounter with her father and his friend, Logan Carlton, both of them drunk. And she'd seen two young women, probably prostitutes, leaving the house. But her father had helped her with the record company. So maybe he cared about her. Maybe he even loved her a little.

After awhile, she wiped her cheeks with the bedsheet, burrowed deeper under the covers and tried to sleep. She shivered through another half hour before getting up again to put on socks, a sweatshirt and sweatpants. That did the trick. She fell asleep.

The next morning

"Would you like to come to church with me, dear?" Mrs. Lincoln plopped four sausages beside a stack of pancakes onto Gloria's plate. Yawning, she heard Mrs. Lincoln cracking eggs, then the sizzle as they hit the hot sausage grease.

"Sunny-side up?"

"Okay… please." Since Gloria had let slip that her doctor wanted her to gain a little weight, Mrs. Lincoln had made feeding Gloria her mission in life.

"Roscoe and I always ate a big breakfast on Sundays before we went to church," the older woman said.

"I think I'm Catholic, so I probably can't go to your church," Gloria replied.

"What do you mean, you think you're Catholic? Either you are, or you aren't." With her apron, Mrs. Lincoln bent to pull a tray of biscuits out of the oven, their fragrance mixing with the sausage bouquet. Deftly, she plucked two biscuits from the tray and dropped them on Gloria's plate beside the sausages.

"My stepmother, she was Catholic, went to Mass every Sunday, sometimes other days too. I took the classes but never got confirmed. My stepfather wouldn't allow it." Thinking of her stepfather triggered a cough. She forked a mass of buttery, syrup-drenched pancake into her mouth. Chewing and mumbling at the same time, she said, "I don't know what that means. I went to confession last Christmas. Probably shouldn't have..." *Did God allow Catholics to worship Him in a Baptist church?* "Um, I used to sing in the choir. Well, the children's choir."

"Oh, we have a famous choir. Our pastor, Reverend Franklin, has a fine voice. He's Aretha Franklin's father, and she used to sing in our church. Reverend Franklin has this gospel caravan. Goes around to churches all over the country. Roscoe saw Aretha and her older sister Erma. Sam Cooke too. You should come with me to hear the choir."

That sealed it. She'd mix with Baptists for some good music.

Mrs. Lincoln let Gloria drive to church. "I'm going to use the safety belts. Dr. Sadowski said even a little bump could hurt the baby." Gloria carefully fastened the seatbelt around her swollen belly.

"Sometimes, I put the belt on if I'm going on the freeway," Mrs. Lincoln said. Gloria almost repeated what the doctor had told her about most people getting into accidents close to their homes. Mrs. Lincoln eyed the seatbelt but didn't put it on.

They arrived at the church, a big brick building that looked relatively new. Mrs. Lincoln led them to empty seats in a pew two rows from the front. Gloria looked around, couldn't see any other white people. Then she caught herself, remembering her black father. Waiting for the service to start, she studied people, comparing skin tones, hair and facial features. She'd always thought her slightly dark skin resulted from all the time she spent in the summer sun, that her tan lingered through winter. She spotted a couple of people with skin like hers. A few had dark blond hair. Some faces looked Caucasian though she asked herself what constituted Caucasian features. Well, she'd always thought her lips looked very full. She didn't see anyone like her with the combination of light amber skin, blond hair and a face without obvious black features.

The service started with a hymn Gloria hadn't heard before so it took her most of the first verse to catch the melody. Everyone sang louder than in the Catholic Church. She joined right in. Singing always felt good. By the end of the hymn she'd noticed some people singing harmony, particularly someone with a glorious voice on the other side of Mrs. Lincoln. During the next hymn, one she knew, Gloria began singing harmony too. But on the second verse, the other singer switched to a different lower-pitched harmony. Three-part harmony! She loved the way their voices meshed and saw an orange glow building around her. At the end of the hymn, she leaned forward, peering past Mrs. Lincoln to see the other singer, a young woman who looked back at Gloria. Reddish brown hair in an afro like Jimi Hendrix had, only larger, framed a sepia face with clear glistening skin, bright brown eyes, and lips painted a vivid pink, emphasizing her open-mouthed surprise as she saw Gloria.

She's beautiful.

During the next two hymns, their singing evolved into a harmonic playfulness with each trying to outdo the other. By then, members of the choir and others around them in the congregation had noticed. So had Reverend Franklin, who beamed in their direction. Some whoops rippled across the room as the last hymn faded and the congregation settled into silence.

"This morning Miss Susanna Quinn will grace us with *Touch the Hem of His Garment,* another of her fine solos," announced Reverend Franklin. "And she will accompany herself on piano."

"Excuse me, please." The woman who had been singing all the harmonies with Gloria squeezed past on her way to the piano. After all the fun of their harmonizing, Gloria thought the soloist's voice a little flat with none of the soulful styling that so many of Gloria's favorite black singers exhibited. She sang the words, played the music on the piano, but didn't seem to feel the song.

"When you sing a song, you gotta own that song," Roscoe had told Gloria during their recording sessions in the garage. But Gloria remembered that when she sang in the children's choir, she'd often been told to "tone it down," or to "stop tryin' to sound like Elvis." So maybe someone told Susanna Quinn to tone it down. When she filed back into the pew, Susanna Quinn looked disappointed.

Reverend Franklin finally started his sermon. Gloria heard him say "The chariot will swing low" and "A prophet is God's ambassador, and a preacher is a prophet," in a booming voice, but she fell asleep until a kicking in her belly nudged her toward consciousness. Reverend Franklin's thunderous voice heading for the sermon's climax finished the job. Eyes closed, she listened. The congregation punctuated Franklin's preaching with handclaps, shouts of "Oh yeah" and "Well,

well." Joyous laughter greeted some phrases, or "oh, no" when he mentioned the devil. Mrs. Lincoln repeatedly bellowed "Amen".

After the service, Mrs. Lincoln went off to talk to friends while Gloria lingered, one hand on her belly, thinking she needed get serious about preparing for the birth. As she made her way down the aisle, Susanna Quinn approached, offering her hand.

"You can really sing but I haven't seen you here before. I'm Susanna Quinn. Please don't call me Suzie Q or Oh Susanna." She laughed, her eyes sparkling.

Gloria took her hand, but froze when she recognized the young man in a brown leather jacket accompanying Susanna. A few months earlier, he'd been a fiery speaker at an antiwar rally where she'd played her guitar and sang. He'd grown angry with her for playing too long and finally tried to stop her. Others had to intervene and pull him away from her. She gulped, trying to speak.

"This is my boyfriend Antoine," Susanna said.

"You're Sunshine," said Antoine. He turned to Susanna. "I told you about her."

"You're Sunshine? I've heard you on the radio. Roscoe played some of the tapes for me. Your record's terrific," she said. "I was so sorry about Roscoe. We were good friends..."

"I - I, um… My name's Gloria, Gloria Doran… um, Sunshine's, um… for when I perform."

"Are you okay?" asked Susanna.

"Yeah." Gloria started to relax. "That was fun singing those hymns, wasn't it?"

"It surely was. Better than my solo. The choir director just asked me to do it this morning. Apparently the soloist scheduled for today caught the flu. I never had a chance to practice. Don't have a piano at my place."

"I thought your piano was good."

"Thanks. I was concentrating on playing instead of the singing. I don't like that song very much, but a few weeks ago I accompanied somebody else who did it, so I already knew it. I'm tryin' break into the music business. I've had a couple of backup gigs."

Antoine edged a little closer to Gloria. "You're not what I thought you were when we first met. See, I was gettin' the crowd worked up and thought you were just tryin' to sell your record."

"I didn't even know I had a record."

"I shouldn't have tried to stop you," he said, shaking his head. "The organizers, they got all pissed off at me. See, when you split, the crowd started leavin' too. I shoulda let you sing, seein' as they liked you. I never got a chance to talk about black nationalism. They were mostly white college kids anyway and they didn't wanna hear no black man—"

"They liked what you said about the war. All that stuff calling the soldiers pigs. I didn't like it 'cause my boyfriend's over there."

"He coulda gone to Canada."

"Antoine, shut up. This is not the place," Susanna said, tugging at his arm. The three of them stood silent for a moment.

"Okay. I apologize. Truly, I'm sorry," Antoine said. Susanna loosened her grip on his arm, as he looked Gloria in the eye. "I was wrong then and wrong now. Susanna says I'm a hothead."

He looked down momentarily and seemed to choose his words carefully. "Day after that rally the cops came lookin' for me. I think they talked to some of the others who were there too. They were lookin' for you. Something about some cops that got murdered in the riot."

"Yeah, I saw it happen... awful. I don't want to think about it."

"Okay. Like I said, you aren't what I thought. You're fulla surprises. You have a record on the radio, and the last place I'd expect to see a white girl like you is singin' gospel in a black church." Gloria almost told them about her father before he continued. "You don't look the same. You're a little..." His words died.

"Fat? Were you gonna say I'm fat?" Gloria said trying to sound offended. She enjoyed putting him on the defensive.

"I didn't say that." He raised his hands as if Wyatt Earp had pointed a gun at him.

"Antoine!" Susanna grabbed his arm again.

"I'm pregnant," Gloria said. No point in trying to hide it. Wearing a loose sweater and spacious black slacks, she pulled the sweater tight over her belly. "Not fat. The doctor even says I need to gain more weight."

As both Susanna and Antoine gaped, Mrs. Lincoln appeared.

"Are you ready to go, Gloria?"

"Wait," Susanna said. She quickly pulled a pencil and a piece of paper from her purse. "Here's my number. If you ever need a backup singer, give me a call."

Mrs. Lincoln let Gloria drive home. Gloria turned on the radio, immediately wishing she hadn't. They heard the end of a news story about three American pilots, who had been held prisoner, then released by the North Vietnamese. The announcer talked about the heavy American and South Vietnamese casualties in the fight to take Hue back from the Communists. Gloria switched the radio off.

"Wait, I want to hear the weather," Mrs. Lincoln said.

"Oh, okay. I don't like hearing about soldiers getting killed in the war." When Gloria stopped for a red light, Mrs. Lincoln bent forward, twisting her head to look up at the sky through the windshield."

"Looks like snow," she said as Gloria clicked the radio back on. The announcer had moved on to local news. Two people had been hacked to death at a restaurant on the western edge of Detroit near Dearborn. Then the weather came on, confirming Mrs. Lincoln's forecast of snow. A storm might dump six inches of snow on Detroit beginning late in the evening. Gloria shivered, thinking about her cold bedroom.

"Well, it usually gets a little warmer when it snows. Hope so. I was cold last night. Weren't you?" Mrs. Lincoln grumbled.

"A little bit," Gloria said, yawning. No wonder she'd fallen asleep in church.

A black Lincoln idled on the street in front of Mrs. Lincoln's house. As Gloria and Mrs. Lincoln approached the front door, State Senator Logan Carlton got out of the Lincoln.

"Thought you might be at church," Carlton said at the front door. "I need to speak to Miss Doran."

"Well, you better come in, Senator. It's cold out here," Mrs. Lincoln said. "I'll warn you that my house is a little drafty. Haven't been able to put on the storm windows. Don't know who to call."

Mrs. Lincoln hung Carlton's overcoat in the hall closet. He wore a three-piece dark, gray suit with a bright yellow tie.

"I promised to help you with your driver's license. So we need to go over to the DMV. I've made some arrangements," he said to Gloria.

"You have? I can get my license?"

"Does she have time to eat lunch? The doctor says she needs to gain some weight so missing lunch is not a good idea," Mrs. Lincoln said.

"I'm okay—" Gloria started.

"We have time. We just need to get there at two o'clock," Carlton said glancing at his watch.

"Wait a minute. The DMV's not open on Sundays," Mrs. Lincoln said.

The senator chuckled. "It is for me."

Mrs. Lincoln made sandwiches and chicken soup. When they finished eating, Carlton said, "I see what you mean about the cold. Let me call someone."

Over Mrs. Lincoln's token protests, he called a man named Howard and asked him if he could put on some storm windows.

"Yeah, you'll be paid cash, but by me, not the people in the house. And it needs to be done right away. While you're at it, scrape the snow and ice off the driveway and front walk. If it snows, come back and clear away that snow too. In fact, do it for the rest of the winter."

"I can pay for it. I just didn't know who to call," Mrs. Lincoln said after Carlton hung up. He sat regarding her and then smiled.

"I'm a state senator. I know a lot of good men looking for work and my supporters want to help them and you as well. Let's just leave it at that." He tapped his watch with a finger. "We have to go."

When Carlton rapped on the door of the dark DMV office, a light flashed on inside. A tall thin black man with big tortoise-shell spectacles hurried to let them in.

"Mr. Carlton? I'm Gordon Chavis." As soon as Gloria and Carlton passed through the door, he locked it again. He scanned the parking lot nervously, led them quickly toward the back. While Gloria kept up with Chavis, Carlton took his time.

"No need to rush," Carlton said.

"I don't want anyone to see us in here. The office is supposed to be closed."

"It ain't a felony to work on a Sunday even if you work for the government. I do it all the time," Carlton said.

"This is very irregular. My boss would not condone this." He looked back at the front window.

"What, you putting in a little extra time? He'd be delighted."

Chavis looked at Gloria, then pointed to a red line on the floor.

"Stand with your toes on that line and look at the camera," he said as he got behind a camera beside a counter. "Maybe you should take your coat off."

Gloria took her coat off and handed it to Carlton. She heard the camera click.

"Let's try again. Look at the camera this time."

She looked at the camera. When she started to smile the camera clicked again.

"That should do," Chavis said. "Now let's see. I already have your birth date. What's your height and weight?"

"I'm five foot, four and a half, and ah... hundred and twelve pounds when I'm not pregnant."

He looked at her midsection. "Address?"

She gave him Mrs. Lincoln's address.

"Is this legal?" she asked.

"Perfectly legal," Carlton said.

"Well, technically, she should take the written and driving tests. She hasn't gone through drivers' ed in school," Chavis said.

"She drives just fine. I saw her drive today," said Carlton.

"I'll take the written test if you like," Gloria said.

"No, no. We don't want to be here any longer than necessary. This is very irregular. We're all done now." Chavis said, looking nervously toward the front door again.

"What about a temporary license?" Carlton asked.

"That's gonna take longer. You never said anything about that," Chavis protested.

"Just do it," Carlton ordered.

Fifteen minutes later, Gloria had her temporary license folded in her purse and the promise that her permanent license would come in the mail.

"Now, what kind of car would you like?" Carlton asked as they sat in the DMV parking lot watching Chavis lock the front door.

"Car?"

"Yeah, a car. You heard me. Your father wanted to buy you a car. He bought cars for most of his nieces and nephews. You're his daughter. Hell, he'd probably have gotten you a Cadillac."

Surprised, Gloria didn't answer.

"We could start shopping for one right now. Some dealers are open on Sundays."

"You know, I liked the Rambler station wagon that Jimmy let me drive. It belonged to his uncle. It's gone now. But it wasn't too big. Still had lots of room, never gave me any trouble," she said. "I think I'd rather have a used car than a brand new one. They cost so much. But whatever I end up with, I want it to have safety belts."

"A Rambler, huh. Governor Romney would approve. He used to run American Motors. I'll look for a Rambler station wagon with seat belts."

-8-

As they drove back to Mrs. Lincoln's house Gloria said to Carlton, "Thank you for your help. I'm… um, I'm grateful."

He slowed to a stop in the slush by the curb on Grand River Avenue. For a long time he sat staring out the window fidgeting with his hands on the wheel. Gloria grew nervous thinking the senator must want something from her.

"I'm looking into a private school for you. There's money in your father's estate to pay for it. But it might be best to wait till after you have the baby."

Warm air hissing from the car's heater, the dank smell of melted snow from their shoes reminded Gloria of unhappy winter school days in overheated classrooms when teachers grew frustrated because she wouldn't speak.

"I um… I don't want to go back to school."

"Why not?"

She shrugged. "It's too late for that."

"No it's not."

"I hated school, never did well. Besides, when Jimmy comes home—"

He cut her off. "You should be a cheerleader. Pom poms, sis boom bah. Instead, you're pregnant by some soldier you might never see again. You have to get an education."

Did he think Jimmy was going to die? She wanted to respond, couldn't find the words. Carlton took a deep breath, tapped his fingers a few times on the steering wheel and glanced at her.

"You caught me by surprise when you came to the house the other day. I hope you don't think I'm living there. I'm working with that damn grad student, Judy. She don't like me, probly 'cause I'm a politician, or maybe 'cause I'm black."

He turned to face her. "You never had a chance to really know your father, or me. We'd been drinking that first time you met us."

And messing with a couple of whores. And he wants to tell me what to do?

Carlton pushed the front seat back. "I met Clyde durin' the war. We both signed up for this colored outfit in the Army Air Force. You probly ain't never heard of it, but lotsa black folks have. We didn't know each other at first 'cause Clyde, he flew fighters, and me, I was a navigator on a bomber. Our bomber unit never made it to Europe. But eventually, me and Clyde got to be good friends."

Gloria already knew most of this but she hadn't heard what came next.

"We were in one of the first fights for civil rights. See, after the war, when Clyde got back to the States, the fuckin'… sorry… the Air Force didn't want niggers in the officers club."

"Saying nigger's worse than saying fuck," Gloria said.

His eyes opened wide, then he snickered, "You know, you are absolutely right." He scratched his neck. "We put up with a lot durin' and after the war. White officers gettin' promoted but we didn't. They set up separate, colored officers clubs. White boys called them Uncle Tom's cabin. We mostly just swallowed all that shi… crap, but at the end of the war at Freeman Field in Indiana, we made a stand. We went into the whites-only officers club, a whole bunch of us. Direct violation of orders.

"And Clyde? He was the biggest pain in the ass of us all, 'cause he'd been a hero, shootin' down four Nazis. One more and he woulda been an ace. Most of those white boys hadn't seen any combat. He embarrassed them so they went after him. Clyde got court-martialed. He chose to leave the military, though they didn't give him much choice. Me and mosta the others backed off. Chickened out."

Carlton looked down at the floor.

"You probly heard lotsa things about your father, and most of it's probly true. The women at his clubs didn't teach Sunday school. Clyde never paid no mind to city ordinances or liquor license rules. If you're black in Detroit and play the numbers, or bet on baseball or football, you dealt with one of Clyde's boys. You need a loan, and your credit's in the crapper, you went to Clyde. Hell, the banks don't wanna make loans to nig… people like us.

"The law saw Clyde as an outlaw, though they never caught him. But in my book, he's right up there with Martin Luther King." Carlton stopped and rubbed his chin, grinning. "Well, not that high, but he had a lot more guts than me when it came to standin' up for what's right. And I'm a state senator."

Carlton reached to turn up the heat in the car and shifted to another subject. "Where'd you go to church today?"

Gloria couldn't remember the church's name. "Um, it was a Baptist church. The minister was Aretha Franklin's father."

"New Bethel, Reverend Franklin. Not sure what to make of him. Does some good things though I hear tell he's quite friendly with some of the young women in the congregation, if you know what I mean."

"I know what you mean."

Shaking his head as he smiled, Carlton drummed the dashboard with his fingers. Gloria thought he was afraid to say what he really wanted to say.

"That first time we met you, me and Clyde were lit up. Been drinkin' for a coupla hours. I hope you don't judge us by that. You should judge Clyde by his good works. Hard to find a black pastor in town who hasn't received donations from Clyde. And when folks went south for the struggle, you know, the freedom riders, Clyde supported families here. Did the same thing for some men in prison, or men who went to Vietnam. Howard, the man who's puttin' on your storm windows? He got out of prison coupla of weeks ago. He's just one of many I put to work with Clyde's money. Clyde's been the principal financial supporter for my election campaigns."

He took his eyes from her to look out the front window. She felt his apprehension. "Since that first time we met you, we learned a lot about you… 'bout what your stepfather did to you…"

Gloria felt herself flush. Her fingers dug into the leather upholstery.

"It's okay—" he started.

"It's not okay. I was raped, and that's not okay!" Her loud high-pitched voice surprised her. She'd never before used the word "rape" in the few times she'd talked about what happened to her. But Mrs. Lincoln called it rape. So did another woman she'd confided in. Usually she couldn't talk about it without tears, but now she only felt anger.

Carlton drew back but he recovered and quickened the pace of his words. "I know what happened wasn't okay. What I meant was that it's okay that Clyde and I learned about it 'cause…" He swallowed, leaned closer. "Because we wanted to help. Clyde changed after he found out about you. Just before he got shot, he was gettin' ready to go to the U.S. attorney and confess to shooting those cops, and a lot of other stuff. He was gonna come clean. He wanted to do the right thing. He was afraid you were ashamed he was your father. Kept tellin' me he'd never been there for you. It tore him up."

Seeing her distress, he stopped. Then he reached over and very lightly patted her shoulder.

Gloria felt light-headed. Her stomach reeled; a sour taste of chicken soup filled her mouth. A bead of perspiration ran between her breasts. She did not like that Carlton knew what her stepfather had done to her. She didn't want anyone to know. But since she'd run away from home, she'd begun to understand that she couldn't keep her secrets bottled up forever. Mrs. Lincoln knew. Gloria had told another woman who'd briefly been her landlady. She'd told Jimmy more about it than anyone because she could talk to Jimmy. Every time she told someone, the burden lightened a little.

But she said to Carlton, "I don't like to talk about it."

He nodded and touched her shoulder again. "Just know that you're not alone. Your father wanted to help, and now, I do too," Carlton said.

She wondered about his sincerity and why he was talking to her. She said nothing. As the silence lengthened, Carlton changed direction again.

"Have you spoken to the Detroit police about what happened at the motel when Clyde shot those policemen?"

She shook her head.

"Things have changed," Carlton said. "There was gonna be a federal grand jury looking into it. I don't think that's gonna happen now. But I think the Detroit police still want to talk to you."

"What should I say?"

He shrugged. "Tell them the truth."

"You mean, I tell them that I saw my father shoot three policemen?"

"If you have to, yes. But my advice would be that you answer each question truthfully, but don't volunteer anything more."

Now, she grinned. "I'm good at not talking. Been doing that most of my life."

"Do you have a lawyer? Frances told me you wanted to get one."

"No, I don't have a lawyer."

But an unexpected thought burst into Gloria's brain like one of those lightbulbs in the comics. She remembered a hippie friend, Lenny Papineau, from her time on the streets who had talked about his big-shot lawyer father.

"Have you ever heard of a lawyer by the name of Papineau?" she asked.

"Papineau? Cutler and Papineau is one of the biggest law firms in Detroit. I've heard of them, but that's all. Oh yeah, I think Cutler died last year so maybe Papineau's the main guy now. Do you know him?"

She shook her head.

Carlton straightened up behind the steering wheel and pulled the shifter into drive, keeping his foot on the brake. The Lincoln shuddered.

"You know, I see some of your father in you. You charge straight ahead. You're smart and quick, like a fighter pilot. More I learn about you, the more you seem like women from past centuries who had to grow up fast. You ever heard of Sally Hemmings?"

"No. Who's she?"

"She was Thomas Jefferson's mistress, starting when she was about your age, maybe younger. She was a slave, three-quarters white, but still a slave. Jefferson fathered several children with her. Those kids woulda been seven-eighths white but they were all still slaves. Jefferson, one of the greatest Americans in history, owned hundreds of slaves. He only freed a few while he was alive, and a few more in his will. He never freed Sally Hemmings."

Carlton's voice had taken a bitter tone, making Gloria afraid to respond, but she did anyway. "Aren't things different now? We don't have slavery."

"Yeah, but it's the same fuckin' country. Sorry. Hasn't changed as much as white folks think. Did you know there were once slaves in Detroit? Wasn't just a southern thing. I found this old Ph.D. dissertation at U of M that mentioned it. Finding out your father's black had to be hard. I'd be careful who you tell about it. Doesn't matter if you've been raised white and or how white you look. You'd still be a nigger to a lotta white people. Didn't matter how white Sally Hemmings and her kids were. They were still slaves."

This time she didn't complain about his language and felt a tiny shard of fear prick her heart.

"I was workin' with that grad student, Judy, on a paper 'bout Sally Hemmings. I want to get my master's degree, maybe a doctorate too. Judy didn't like the paper. Said the accounts I dug up from Jefferson's slave descendants, were unverifiable. Shit, they ain't any less verifiable than a lot of shi… crap comin' outta Jefferson's white descendants."

The car lurched forward a few feet when his foot slipped off the brake. He jammed his foot back onto the brake pedal. Then he moved the seat up.

"One more thing before we go. Just before Clyde got shot, two of the Gargano crime family died along with that little Detroit police detective. You know who the Garganos are, right? And you knew that little detective, right?"

"No, not really. He talked to me for a few minutes once but that's all," she said.

"Clyde told me he thought your stepfather killed the Garganos, that he was makin' a play to take over the organization. One of the Garganos is still out there. Clyde told me he mighta been workin' with your stepfather. Technically, he's not a Gargano. He's married to old man Gargano's daughter. Also, a couple of black thugs who sometimes worked for the Garganos dropped outta sight. Cops are callin' it a Mafia war."

"They're dead," Gloria said.

Carlton looked at her for a long moment, his mouth working without making any sound until he asked, "What do you mean? Who's dead?"

"All three of them are dead. Actually, there were four, not three."

Carlton shifted the car back into park, making it jerk again.

"How do you know that? Did you…"

He stared at her. She squirmed around in the seat, knowing she should have kept her mouth shut. The men had caught her and turned her over to her stepfather. She knew Jimmy had killed them trying to rescue her. "I don't want to talk about it. I just know they're dead."

He thought about it for a long time, then nodded and finally smiled. "Practicin' for the cops."

He put the car in gear. They drove in silence to Mrs. Lincoln's house. After walking her to the front door, he checked on the storm windows before he left.

Gloria helped Mrs. Lincoln heat up leftover meatloaf for dinner. After they'd eaten, she called information in Ann Arbor and got a telephone number for Lenny Papineau, her hippie friend who was student at University of Michigan. They spoke for only a minute because Gloria knew Mrs. Lincoln worried about the telephone bill. Ten minutes later, Lenny called back and said he'd made an appointment for her at his father's law office. Then he apologized because the earliest time he could get was more than two weeks away.

"He and my mom are gonna be in Florida for a couple of weeks," Lenny said.

Tired, Gloria and Mrs. Lincoln both retired early. Gloria lay in bed, her stomach full of meatloaf, collard greens, sweet potatoes, cornbread and apple pie with ice cream. She saw the frost had melted off her window. Outside the howling wind swirled snow around a streetlight causing an eerie flicker in her bedroom. She listened to the furnace laboring, then got out of bed, though not because of cold. The house felt warm.

She got down on her knees on the hardwood floor, rested her elbows on the bed and prayed. She prayed for Jimmy, for the baby inside her, for Mrs. Lincoln, for her father's soul, for his friend Logan Carlton, for Susanna Quinn, Antoine too, and for Lenny Papineau.

She thanked God for a good day.

-9-

Outside on the street

"Yet mae… kee sai p'bark pom," Jettrin Juntasa said.

He silently mouthed the English words, "motherfucker" and "shit in my mouth" as he sat in his big Chrysler Imperial, angry, tired, cold and sick. Angry for losing his temper, tired from running around all day, cold from the godforsaken Detroit winter and sick after overeating at a miserable Swedish restaurant called a 'smorgasbord.' He'd never heard the word before. Couldn't find his dictionary to look it up.

His stomach rumbled up tiny gas burbles flavored by meatballs, pickled herring, barbecued ribs, mashed potatoes and gravy while the single enormous belch that could relieve his discomfort hid deep in the recesses of his guts.

A bad day for eating.

It began early that morning when Juntasa sat down at his own restaurant with a breakfast bowl of jook, a thick rice porridge containing meatballs garnished with sliced ginger, cilantro, soy sauce and black pepper, topped with an egg. After bringing the food, the restaurant manager informed him that he planned to call the police about his finger. Flanked by the pretty waitress and a young Vietnamese cook, the idiot manager confronted Juntasa while clutching a large butcher knife in his undamaged right fist.

He said, "This is America. You no can do this. Not here, not in America." Then, out of lifelong habit, he bowed trying to temple his hands despite the bandage on one and the knife in the other.

Juntasa hurled his bowl of steaming hot rice gruel into the manager's face. He jumped up, upended the table into the three, then snatched the knife as it slipped from the manager's grasp. He stabbed the manager in the eye, slashed the cook's neck and face. The waitress bolted. By the time Juntasa got to the back door, he could not see where she'd gone. He returned to the two bloody men writhing on the floor, where for several minutes, he stabbed and hacked until they stopped moving.

When he heard distant sirens, he escaped in the Imperial, spending most of the day in a fog trying to figure out what to do. He stole clothing from a YMCA locker room, where he changed out of his bloody clothing. After the terrible smorgasbord experience, he drove to the house where the girl lived. Should he just grab her? He hadn't completed arrangements to transport her to Southeast Asia. His Yakuza contacts could smuggle her to Asia from San Francisco or Los Angeles, but he had to get her to the West Coast.

He thumbed open the locking blade knife, closed it, flicked it open and shut over and over again until he could whip it open one-handed in a fraction of a second. He felt like a child with a fat red balloon, who, when ordered to give it up, popped the balloon instead. He should just kill the girl, go home and get warm.

But finally, the enormous belch thundered free, easing his stomach and settling his mind. He decided to give it a little more time.

-10-

Rui Binh Base Camp

When Leroy Flowers came into the mess hall, Hayes saw a flash of the deep pink morning twilight on the eastern horizon through the open door.

"I heard Frankie Lymon died," Flowers said after he got a tray of pancakes and ham and sat down across from Hayes who had already finished eating. "You know Frankie Lymon?"

Hayes had to think. "Yeah, yeah, Frankie Lymon and the Teenagers. I remember them. *Why Do Fools Fall in Love? Goody Goody*. You say he died?" Hayes couldn't remember another time when Flowers had started a conversation about something other than the Bible.

"Heroin overdose. I thought he was a good Christian. My sister said he used to sing gospel."

After breakfast, Hayes and Flowers headed for the flight line. In the seven weeks since he'd returned to the 99th, he and Flowers had been flying together most days. Despite the constant Bible talk, Hayes had grown to like Flowers. The two of them had nothing in common, save that each had few other friends.

The whole Headhunter platoon seemed on edge. Instead of the good-natured banter, Hayes heard constant bitching about the food, the water running out in the showers, the blackouts when the generator ran out of fuel or broke down, and scorpions in the bunkers. Hayes caught men looking at him, then turning away. Conversations sometimes stopped when he approached. Did they think he had something to do with Mitchell's death? Meanwhile, he considered everybody a murder suspect because somebody damn sure had murdered Mitchell.

As the two lugged the machine guns along the revetments toward their gunship, they came up on Delaney and Kannegiesser smoking a joint.

"Kinda early, isn't it?" Hayes said.

"Fuck you, Hayes," Delaney said before sucking in a long noisy lungful of smoke. He passed the joint to Kannegiesser, then blew the smoke into Hayes' face. Kannegiesser looked away as he inhaled.

"A man is not defiled by what enters his mouth, but by what comes out of it," Flowers said. He started to take his little Bible out of his breast pocket. "That's Matthew—"

"Fuck you too, Flowers."

Delaney's hostility stung, but Hayes blamed himself. Maybe he'd turned into one of those self-righteous reformed alcoholics acutely aware of other people's drinking. Ever since his Article Fifteen for smoking marijuana, he'd decided to wait until he got home before he smoked it again. He'd concluded that it was foolish to smoke pot in a combat unit.

"Those two are high all the time," Flowers said. "They should get high on Jesus or they'll end up like Frankie Lymon."

"I just hope they don't fuck up and kill somebody else," Hayes said.

They spent the morning on a two-ship fire team supporting a 25th Infantry Division platoon. Delaney and Kannegiesser were on the other ship. The gunships ended up killing a dozen North Vietnamese regulars in the open mostly with their rockets, a good morning's work, but Hayes thoughts turned to Gloria.

She'd witnessed the deaths of both her father and stepfather. And she would have a baby soon. He had no experience with pregnant women. What could he do? Well, he could write to her.

They landed in Cu Chi to refuel and re-arm. Nesterenko, the aircraft commander, said he had to run over to Operations. While Flowers cleaned dirt out of one of the mini-guns, Hayes bummed a piece of paper from the co-pilot, Donaldson, to scratch out a quick letter to Gloria.

Dearest Gloria,

Only have a few minutes to tell you I love you. To love and be loved are the two greatest things in my life. I feel blessed to have found you. I remember your fingers dancing over the fretboard of your guitar the night we met at Clyde Bonaventure's. I fell in love with you. The love songs you sang only seemed meant for me. I cannot bear to be without you. My last thoughts before falling asleep each night are of your kisses, your caresses, the softness of your skin, the sweet smell of your hair and the warmth of your body next to me. We're locked in love. When I close my eyes, I dream we are together again. And when I awake, I despair. So in this short letter, I send my love to you. I can't be there with you, but my love is with you, and always will be.

Happy Leap Day! (It's 29 February here)

Jimmy

Hayes folded the letter, thinking he should have spent more time on it. Too damn sentimental. He had serious doubts and almost threw it away. Finally, he hurried to the nearby Operations bunker encountering Nesterenko on the way.

"Be right back. Gotta mail a letter," he called as he raced by, full of love for Gloria.

Almost immediately, he regretted mailing the letter and its mawkish tone.

-11-

March, Detroit, Michigan

With his tolerance for Detroit's winter at an end and his anxiety about the intense police investigation into what had been dubbed "the chopstick murders" growing, Jettrin Juntasa fled Detroit. He drove to Las Vegas for a few days of recreation, before continuing on to Los Angeles. There, he arranged to have the marvelous Chrysler Imperial shipped to Thailand as a gift to the king. Then he flew back to Thailand himself to attend to his business and to talk to the Yakuza.

The Yakuza in Asia owed Juntasa favors. His father's business, which he now headed, had long been a reliable source for many prostitutes for the Yakuza's Japanese brothels. Juntasa called in some of the favors and the Yakuza expanded their help in transporting the girl. Juntasa would only have to get her from Detroit to Chicago where the Yakuza had recently opened a few brothels and hostess clubs in that city's small Chinatown. Juntasa further cemented his relationship with the Yakuza by proposing a joint heroin venture.

Five weeks after the restaurant murders, Juntasa returned to Detroit and once again waited down the street from the girl's house fortified with a bacon and egg sandwich and a thermos of hot tea. When she left, he followed her to a medical office building and went inside. After she removed her coat in the lobby while waiting for an elevator, her size shocked him. She wasn't worth a fraction of what he'd paid. He got on the elevator with her, then followed at a distance until she entered an office. He continued down the hall before doubling back to study the sign on the office door.

Emily Sadowski, M.D.
Obstetrics and Gynecology

He understood "and," but little else. Forty-five minutes later at the main Detroit Public Library he finally deduced that the girl must be pregnant.

And Doran had promised a virgin.

Enraged, he'd flipped over the little library stand, sending the massive six-inch-thick dictionary crashing to the floor. He ran outside, jumped into his rented Ford, roared down Cass Avenue until he encountered yet another insidious Detroit winter phenomenon — black ice, though he had not yet learned the term. The Ford skidded off Cass and hit a tree, the impact crumpling the bumper and fender into the front wheel, rendering the car undrivable.

Abandoning the vehicle, he lumbered along Cass back toward the library until he found a telephone booth and called a taxi. Livid, he managed to calm down while waiting for the taxi.

"Take me airport," he told the taxi driver.

-12-

March, Nui Binh Base Camp

On a Sunday morning a little over a week after the confrontation with Delaney, Hayes had just finished a second helping of bacon, pancakes and scrambled eggs when the first sergeant appeared at the mess hall entrance.

"Company formation. Everybody outside. Form up in front of the Orderly Room. That includes cooks," he bellowed. Then he slid aside the curtain separating the enlisted and officers sections. "All officers fall in as well."

Assembling the entire company had never happened since Hayes had been in the 99th. He shuffled into place with everyone else.

The first sergeant called, "Tench-hut!" Slowly, the men in the company came to attention. Even before everyone had straightened up, Lieutenant Colonel Blair barked, "At ease, stand easy."

As everyone relaxed, Hayes thought Blair's eyes lingered on him as he scanned the formation before beginning to speak.

"Last night I received a report from the 370th Military Police Detachment. They have determined that Specialist Fifth Class William Mitchell took his own life." His normal penetrating gaze absent, Blair looked like he had swallowed something unpleasant. Once more Blair looked around, and Hayes felt the CO's eyes on him. Faint murmurs rolled through the formation. A hot shimmer flashed through Hayes. He looked away, spotted the flight surgeon Doc Goetz shaking his head.

"On the evening of Seventeen February, First Sergeant McConaughey and Specialist Hayes were on the flight line together when they heard a gunshot. They investigated and found Specialist Mitchell a few minutes after they heard the shot. He was already dead, and there was nothing they could do."

Blair straightened ever so slightly. His voice took on a steely tenor. "We are currently engaged in a battle that may be a turning point in this war. While this company has done all that it has been asked to do, I believe we can still do more. We have been fortunate. Many of our comrades, Americans and South Vietnamese, have been lost. Our job is to kill the enemy so he cannot take our lives or the lives of our allies. I expect everyone here to do his job to the absolute best of his ability. Anything less is unacceptable."

Blair stood at parade rest, his head slowly turning like a gun turret until, for the third time, he'd covered the entire formation. "That is all. First Sergeant McConaughey, dismiss the company."

As the formation broke up, Hayes started toward the flight line, but almost bumped into the first sergeant. "To the Orderly Room, Specialist Hayes. The CO wants to see us."

Blair, accompanied by Doc Goetz, arrived at the Orderly Room at the same time as Hayes and the first sergeant.

Opening the door, they saw Cartwright, settling into the chair behind a desk in one corner.

"Why don't you go get some breakfast," McConaughey said to Cartwright.

"I already ate breakfast," Cartwright answered. Then the first sergeant said, "Well, go get another one." Cartwright rose and headed for the door.

After Cartwright left, Blair surveyed the room. "I have voiced my concerns with the MPs' conclusion but that's all I can do. I do not want any of you to share your opinions with the rest of the company. There has already been far too much speculation"

"It's ridiculous," Doc Goetz said. "Mitchell might have shot himself. He could have stabbed himself. But he could not have done both."

The CO held up a hand to stop the doctor and turned to Hayes.

"Specialist Hayes, I'm inclined to believe what you said the night of this... Mitchell's death. Someone went to some trouble to make it look like you were involved. If you hadn't been with First Sergeant McConaughey, you might have been arrested. The MPs even considered the possibility that you and the first sergeant acted together."

Hayes glanced sideways at the first sergeant to catch the look of shock on his face.

Now he knows how I feel.

"Relax, both of you. That idea didn't last long." The CO turned back to Hayes. "Specialist Hayes, can you think of anyone who might have had reason to kill Mitchell and try to pin it on you?"

Hayes broke into a sweat. "Sir, Sergeant Grugel and Mitchell got into an argument the day I got back in company. I got between them."

"Was it an argument, or did they have a fight?"

"No, sir. No one threw any punches. I was able to... Delaney and I were able to keep them apart."

"What was the argument about?

"Sir, Mitchell was upset about being ordered to fire on women and children. Grugel said he'd disobeyed a direct order and threatened him with a court-martial."

"I remember. I spoke to Mr. Nesterenko and Mr. Moss about it. They also had a heated disagreement." Blair scratched his chin. "Mr. Moss said one of the crew claimed you didn't have to obey an order if you thought it was wrong. Is that what Mitchell said?"

"No, sir. He just said he wouldn't shoot women and kids, and there was nothing anyone could do to make him because he was gonna go home soon. It was me that said you didn't necessarily have to obey an order if it was... I don't know... if it was something obviously wrong, like shooting civilians. See, after World War II, some of the Germans said they were just obeying orders, but we executed them for it."

Hayes stopped talking as the CO studied him. Had he gone too far? They all heard the whine of a helicopter engine starting. Blair looked at his watch. "You can't just obey the orders you agree with. We have to do things in war nobody likes."

"Yes, sir, but Mitchell saw the civilians. I don't think whoever gave that order saw them. He didn't wanna kill civilians. I don't either."

"Nobody wants to kill civilians, specialist, but sometimes it can't be avoided."

Hayes almost said sometimes it could be avoided, and that was what Mitchell and Grugel had been arguing about. But all he said was, "Yes sir," before he looked away.

Blair said, "We have to get going."

The phone rang but no one moved to answer it. Normally, the company clerk answered the phone. It kept ringing. Finally, the first sergeant picked it up.

"Yeah, he's here. What? Oh shit." He handed the phone to Blair. "There's been an accident on the flight line."

Blair grabbed the phone, listened for a few seconds and said, "I'm on my way."

"What happened?" Hayes asked McConaughey as the CO hurried out the door.

"Somebody got hit by a rotor."

"Who?" Hayes asked.

"Sergeant Grugel."

-13-

Detroit, Michigan

Despite winter storms and perpetually gray skies, despite constant worry about Jimmy, Gloria saw her life getting better. Most of the time she felt safe. Mrs. Lincoln had become more than her landlady, and Gloria had made other friends like Susanna Quinn and even her doctor, Emily Sadowski. With her nausea and morning sickness over, she'd embraced her pregnancy. If State Senator Carlton seemed to view her condition as unfortunate, Gloria didn't. At least she *looked* like an adult woman. She thought of Mrs. Lincoln's home as her home too. When Gloria carried on conversations with her baby, whom she called "Sunny," Mrs. Lincoln often joined in. Like the mother Gloria never really had.

So on a rare sunny Monday morning with Detroit blanketed in sparkling freshly fallen snow, Gloria guided her red and white 1966 Rambler Cross Country station wagon downtown.

"I hope you can drive a manual, that's all I could find," Carlton had told her when he brought the car.

"It's perfect," and she'd kissed his cheek.

Lenny Papineau's father's law firm occupied two floors high up in the 45-story Penobscot Building, Michigan's tallest. Early for the appointment, with the weather pleasant, Gloria took a stroll around the building. Named after an Indian tribe from Maine — she didn't know why — she delighted in the Indian motifs and art deco flourishes. After saluting the "Big Chief" motif, she pushed through the Griswold Street brass-framed, revolving door.

When she stepped out of the elevator at the 41st floor, a secretary took her coat before escorting Gloria back to a spacious corner office where a handsome silver-haired man about fifty stood gazing at a magnificent view of the ice-choked Detroit River and the Canadian city of Windsor on the far bank.

"What a beautiful day," he said, turning to face her. "I'm very pleased to make your acquaintance, Miss Doran. My name is Parker I. Papineau. Most people call me Pip."

He shook her hand, then ushered her to a chair in front of a dark polished wooden desk with a green felt mat and a Wayne State University beer mug filled with pens and pencils. As tall as Jimmy, but heavier though not fat, Gloria thought his styled hair long for a man his age. His smile revealed a chipped tooth that toughened him. He laid a yellow legal pad on the desk as he sat. She smelled no tobacco, saw no ashtray on the desk.

"Leonard told me that you think you need legal assistance. Tell me about your problem. You may not need a lawyer, and we sometimes refer minor problems to a less expensive option like a paralegal. We also do some pro bono work." Catching her puzzled look, he said, "That means it's free. But, of course, we normally expect fair compensation for any legal work we do."

Two hours later, Gloria not only had a lawyer, she had several, all sitting around a big table in a conference room adjacent to Papineau's office. Nervous, she'd forgotten all their names right after their introductions. One lawyer, an austere, thin criminal law specialist who reeked of cigarette smoke and had fingers stained a brownish yellow, would handle any issues concerning the police. He didn't say much but seemed confident. Two more would deal with the record company; one, a gregarious tubby man in his forties, seemed senior to the other, a very young and very tall red-headed woman. She didn't smile or say anything except, "Pleased to meetcha." Finally, Papineau had introduced an older man, a probate and tax specialist.

"You're Matt Doran's daughter? Do you have any brothers or sisters?" he asked. "I knew Matt. Nice fellow. Used to talk to him at bar meetings, but he never said anything about his family."

"Not daughter, stepdaughter," Gloria said, doubting he actually liked her stepfather. How could anyone like him? "I don't have any brothers or sisters. At least, I don't think so. I was adopted when I was a baby. My stepmother's also dead."

"Yes, I heard about her accident. Tragic." Pausing, his smile fading, he said, "Did you know who your stepfather worked for?"

Gloria nodded.

"That's a major complication. The police, the government, will be very interested in his financials."

She nodded again, clasped her hands on the table, sucked in a breath of air, not liking the conversation revolving around her stepfather. Why had she worried so much about questions about her father?

"I must warn you. We might learn some unpleasant things about your stepfather—"

"I don't know why you said he was a nice fellow, because he wasn't nice at all. He raped me," she said. For a moment the room seemed to swirl and blur. She picked up the glass of water with an unsteady hand, spilling a little before she gulped it all down. Then disjointed thoughts tumbled out of her mouth like they had a mind of their own.

"He started when I was little. He hit Gina a lot. Me too. I ran away from home. And… and got pregnant. I found my real father. But he's dead. I… I…"

She stopped. Maybe she'd upset them enough so they'd stop asking about him. Sure enough, the old probate lawyer's mouth had dropped open. His eyes shifted away. The others looked uncomfortable too, except for Papineau.

He looked around the table, motioned with his head toward the door. They all filed out. Papineau moved to another chair so he sat adjacent and across the corner of the long table from her. His eyes went to her empty glass. "Can I get you more water? Maybe coffee, or a soft drink?"

She shook her head, stammered, "N-no, I'm okay." A lie that fooled neither of them.

Papineau waited for a long time, his calmness soothing her. "I've had my staff doing research. That's why Randy wanted to talk about your stepfather. Sometimes he's… maybe too direct." He stopped, turned to the yellow pad of paper in front of him.

"Was Clyde Bonaventure your biological father?"

She nodded, surprised. "How did you know?"

"An educated guess. I found out from a police contact that you were present when he was… shot. And you look a little like him, too." He clicked his ballpoint pen. "I met Clyde at some veterans events. We were acquaintances, not close friends, but there was some mutual respect. I was a sergeant in the 45th Infantry that liberated Dachau. He was a fighter pilot, a very good one. We talked about our… I guess, mutual experience,"

'Dachau? Um, what's that? I think I've heard the name before."

"It was one of those Nazi concentration camps. Awful place, horrible…" He stared at the wall behind her for a moment, then laid both his hands on top of hers. "I think you were wise to come here today. I am sure we can help you. Actually, I believe we can help a great deal."

"Is it going to cost a lot of money?" Gloria asked.

"Well, yes, it might. But it would cost you a lot more without legal help. Whatever his character, our research indicates that your stepfather was a very wealthy man, and you appear to be the sole heir. Some of that wealth may be subject to confiscation by the government, but they'll have to fight for it now. And I don't like to lose fights."

"How much money do you think my stepfather had?" she asked. She liked talking about money.

"I'd guess in the range of five to ten million dollars," Papineau said.

"Oh, there's more, at least twice that much," Gloria said. "I know a lot more about his money than you might think."

Papineau arched one of his silver eyebrows. "That could be very useful."

After she returned from the restroom, Papineau continued. "We've taken a look at the contract you brought in this morning and made some estimates from the record chart history."

"Is the record company trying to cheat me?"

"No, and your record's quite successful. It is still on the charts. You've already made tens of thousands of dollars. And so has Mr. Hayes and Mrs. Lincoln. And you'll probably make more. For a first effort by a new artist you are doing very well. But you should be thinking about what happens next."

"What do you mean?"

"The contract binds you to this record company for at least five more record albums. As long as the records sell, you'll be fine. But if they don't, you might be hit with paying back expenses, which could be substantial. You just have to be aware that you could end up paying for touring expenses and costs associated with recording, distributing and marketing your records. Also, the record company can drop you at any time for any reason. This isn't unusual, and you are in a far better position than most new artists. Frankly, it is a better contract than we might have been able to negotiate for you."

She thought about it for a moment. "What about the rights to the songs?" When he didn't answer, she said, "Jimmy told me that the songs we wrote have value. If other people use them, then they should have to pay us."

"Oh yes. You should retain the rights to your songs. I'll make sure Stan and Marcia check on that," he said, making a note on his pad.

He looked at her. "There is one big problem. You're a minor, only sixteen years old. You certainly don't look it, especially in your condition. I don't think Leonard knows how young you are. He thought you were a college student. Is there a responsible adult that you trust to make decisions or handle money for you?"

"I want to make my own decisions and handle my own money. I'm better with numbers and math than any adults I know."

"You might be," he said, "but children are considered legally incompetent to enter into contracts or handle their own financial affairs. And the law says you are a child until you turn eighteen. Do you have a legal guardian?"

"What? No. And I don't want one."

"Do you live by yourself?"

"No, I'm staying with Frances Lincoln. I pay rent, but we're… um, close."

"Could she make decisions and sign documents for you?"

Gloria scratched her cheek and chin, thinking. "She's been very nice to me, but she doesn't know much about money. I trust her, though."

"Is there anyone else?"

"I guess Logan Carlton. He's a state senator," she said. "But I don't know…"

"Your father's friend. We've met." He clicked his ballpoint pen several times. "Mrs. Lincoln's already involved, so she might be of use. We can explore ways around this. Let's not worry about it today.

"I'm curious about someone else. Who is James Hayes? Is he a musical collaborator? Marcia thinks he might have been in a band from the Lansing area."

She leaned back, smiling. "Jimmy's my boyfriend, and he plays guitar. We wrote all the original songs together and recorded them with Mrs. Lincoln's son, Roscoe. He was murdered. Jimmy's in the Army, in Vietnam… Um, he's nineteen, at least I think he is. Does that make him a responsible adult who could sign stuff for me? I don't know when his birthday is. I guess he could be twenty by now. But I trust him. I trust him more than anyone." She moved both her hands to her abdomen. "This is his baby. I love him, and he loves me," She caught Papineau's eyes. "What else do you need to know?"

"Nothing more right now," he said with another flurry of clicks from the ballpoint. "No, there is one more thing." He waved the pen and cleared his throat. "I have some questions about my son Leonard. My wife and I are worried about him. Actually, that's a big reason I agreed to see you, though I really do want to help now that I've learned more about you. But we found some newspaper stories, made a few calls. There seems to have been a lot of… ah, trouble surrounding you, including the deaths of your father, stepfather, your stepmother, Roscoe Lincoln, the murder of that police detective who was looking for you. And there was an incident in a lawyer's office in this building just a few floors below. According to the Free Press, you were there."

She squirmed, but then looked straight into his eyes. "That Free Press story was… um, right on. Those lawyers tried to cheat me and Mrs. Lincoln. And my stepfather showed up with a couple of thugs to get me. No one actually got hurt by that LSD."

His eyes widened before he finally smiled. "Okay, you'll have to tell me more about it sometime. But what about Leonard? He did get hurt, badly hurt. Someone threw him down some stairs. He missed an entire semester of school. Did it have anything to do with you? He hasn't told us very much, and neither have the police."

Gloria hung her head for a long time. He started to get up, which made her murmur, "Wait." He sat down again. She strained to keep her voice calm. "I'm so sorry about Lenny. He was just about my only friend after I ran away. It's a really long story, but my stepfather hired somebody to find me. He's the one who probably hurt your son. The police think he also killed Mrs. Lincoln's son, Roscoe. He tried to kill Jimmy. Anyway, he is dead now."

"How do you know he's dead?" Papineau asked. "Did the police tell you that?"

"Yes, an Army policeman told me."

"What's this man's name?"

She strained to remember. "Percy Dupree. I don't know how much Detroit police know about some of this because he was killed in Vietnam."

Papineau wrote the name down. They sat silently, Papineau fiddling with his pen, his eyes moving back and forth between the pen and Gloria, making her uneasy. She couldn't stand the silence.

"Everybody thinks my stepfather was this respectable lawyer. But he tried to kill Jimmy and me. He hired the man who hurt your son. He beat up my stepmother so bad she had to go to the hospital half a dozen times. Sometimes I wonder if she really did die in that truck accident."

She looked at Papineau's pen, and he put it down. "Gina knew what he was doing to me. He raped me. He took me to other men who liked doing those things with... with children. He whipped me with a bamboo cane so hard it made me bleed. My doctor says I'm probably not the only one he's hurt. Maybe that's why he made all those trips to Thailand. He was a terrible, terrible person. I'm glad he's dead."

"Why didn't you and your stepmother go to the police?" Papineau asked.

Nothing seemed to unsettle him. Still, she threw up her hands and her voice climbed. "The police never did anything. They'd come to the house or the hospital when he beat up Gina. But they never did anything. When Jimmy and me saw the police kill that woman and her son at the motel during the riot, the only thing the police cared about was who shot the policemen. If it hadn't been for the… um, the person who shot the policemen, those police would have killed the woman from the hotel's front desk." Gloria shifted around in her chair. "All those people who died in the riot. How many were killed by the police?"

"The police aren't all bad."

"I don't know about that. I don't know which ones to trust. I guess that little detective, Mr. Checchi was okay, but he's dead."

Papineau didn't say anything for a long moment. "Do you trust me?"

Nodding slowly, she said, "I think so, yes. Yes I do."

And she did.

-14-

Nui Binh Base Camp

Hayes ran hard from the Orderly Room to the flight line, passing Blair, the CO, on the way. He found one of the 99th's medics on his knees applying field dressings to Grugel's face. The sergeant lay on the tarmac at the rear of a gunship. Pieces of a shattered tail rotor lay scattered on the ground. Hayes saw Grugel's chicken plate, flight helmet and leather gloves piled on the seat of the gunship. The chicken plate was an armored vest consisting of a ceramic plate encased in ballistic nylon and plastic that flight crews could wear. He remembered the sergeant didn't like putting on the bulky gear any sooner than he had to. Some gunners and crew chiefs, including Hayes, didn't always wear the awkward chicken plates. Hayes usually sat on his.

"What happened?" Hayes asked Lieutenant Carson, the Headhunter's commander.

"Oh Christ… ah… After we went through the checklist, Moss said to start the ship. I didn't want to… Nobody else was crankin' but he said we had to get in the air." His voice high-pitched, desperate, his face drained of color, Carson continued. "Ops said we needed to get a fire team up ASAP. Moss ran off to look for you so I started it. I thought Grugel was on the ship. But he musta gotten off."

Hayes looked back at Grugel's gear again. He didn't think Grugel would get on the ship without putting on the gear. He tried to remember if he'd ever seen a helicopter start up with only one pilot on board.

An out-of-breath Doc Goetz crouched beside the medic. They all heard a rasping groan. The medic said, "I think he's conscious."

A mass of criss-crossed, blood-soaked field dressings covered most of Grugel's face. Blood ran from the stubs of fingers on his right hand. Hayes shuddered, involuntarily flexing his fingers.

"Put him on a stretcher and get him to the MASH," the doctor ordered. "Hurry up."

The MASH, a portable surgical hospital, stood a couple of hundred meters away. Carson and Warrant Officer Donaldson loaded Grugel onto a stretcher. Hayes fell in beside the stretcher with Doc Goetz on the other side. Grugel continued making bubbly moans muffled by the dressings. Hayes clasped Grugel's undamaged left hand in an effort to comfort him.

"Good," the doctor said nodding at Hayes. "Can't give him anymore morphine."

Grugel made the wet groaning noises all the way to the hospital. At the hospital, when they started cutting off the field dressings, Grugel moaned louder. Hayes continued holding his hand. Most of Grugel's bottom lip hung in a flap over his chin, his upper lip gone exposing the jagged remains of teeth and bone. When a medic turned Grugel's head sideways, a large piece of tongue fell onto the table and slid off the table onto the floor. Another medic mopped away tooth and bone fragments and loose chunks of bloody flesh from his mouth. Hayes' stomach convulsed but he swallowed hard, clenched his teeth and pushed back hard against the rising horror.

Someone pulled off another dressing. One of Grugel's eyeballs had been smashed sideways and driven so deeply into his head that Hayes didn't know it was there until someone sponged off blood with a big wad of gauze. The rotor had scythed away a chunk of the sergeant's skull, including one eyebrow. For a moment, the flattened distorted eyeball seemed to peer at Hayes from a bed of glistening bloody pink flesh before blood gushed over it again.

Taking deep breaths, Hayes turned his head away, closed his eyes for a second, concentrated on suppressing his urge to vomit. When he got a hold himself, he put his mouth next to Grugel's ear, avoiding the sight of Grugel's devastated face, and feeling like a coward, he whispered, "It's Hayes. You're gonna be okay, Grugel. Just hang on."

A blatant lie, and even Grugel, if he had any awareness at all, must have known. But the sergeant distinctly squeezed Hayes' hand. Surprised, Hayes squeezed back. Then Grugel let out a high, gurgling, stuttering groan that might have been an effort to communicate. But without a tongue and lips, Grugel couldn't talk.

"Squeeze once for yes, twice for no," Hayes said into his ear. Grugel squeezed once.

"Did you walk into the rotor by mistake?" Hayes asked in a low voice. He felt two distinct squeezes.

"How did you… were you pushed?"

One weak squeeze.

"Who? Do you know who pushed you?"

Another single, weak squeeze. Then a hand pulled at Hayes' shoulder. He'd shut out all the chatter from the medical people. They'd let him comfort Grugel, but now they wanted him to leave.

"We hafta get him to surgery." Hayes recognized Doc Goetz's voice. The doctor pulled him away, led him to a bench.

For several minutes, Hayes sat with his head in his hands, looking where the inflated rubberized canvas wall of the hospital met the floor.

His mind lurched back to the image of Grugel's smashed face. When he took his hands away from his head, they shook. Suddenly cold, he remembered the hospital had air-conditioning. He stuffed his hands into his armpits. Grugel's bloody staring eyeball flashed into his brain again. Sour stomach fluids boiled up. Doubling over and focusing on the hospital's inflated walls, Hayes seized back control of his body.

He moaned. How could Grugel possibly live? The sergeant had a wife and a kid, but he didn't know much more about Grugel. They'd never shared anything personal. He hadn't even liked Grugel, thought Grugel might have murdered Mitchell. Now he believed someone had tried to murder Grugel. Who could he tell? Neither the CO nor the first sergeant seemed inclined to do anything. Would anyone believe him?

A soldier tapped him on the shoulder. He handed Hayes an olive drab towel.

"You got blood all over your cheek and neck," the soldier said. Hayes took the towel and wiped his face and neck. As Hayes handed back the towel, he spotted Grugel's flesh, the piece of tongue, on the floor. He threw up.

"Ah shit. You shoulda gone outside for that," the soldier said. "Well, you can just clean up your mess."

Hayes glanced at the vomit on the floor before tottering toward the door. "Fuck you. Clean it up yourself."

Too late, Hayes spotted the single black bars on the soldier's collar, insignia of a first lieutenant.

Back at the flight line, Moss hurried up to him. "Where the hell you been? We gotta get going. CO wants us out there ASAP."

"I went to the hospital with Grugel," Hayes grimaced, trying to push the horrific images of Grugel out of his head. He forced his attention to the rattled Moss, his green flight suit partially unzipped and damp in front, a Smith and Wesson .38 Special dangling in a shoulder holster.

Hayes realized that someone must have reshuffled the crews putting another crew chief on his ship. He looked at the smashed tail rotor. "We need a new tail rotor, and a gunner, too. We're not going anywhere till we take care of that."

"Aw shit," Moss said rubbing both his hands across his chest. He seemed to gather himself. "Lieutenant Carson's grounded pending an accident investigation, but we got a brand new gunship driver who's gonna be the peter pilot.

Came in last night. He'll be out here soon as he gets all his gear."

Hayes said, "If you get somebody from Maintenance to put on a new tail rotor, I'll see if I can scare up a gunner. I never put on a tail rotor before, but I don't think it's hard. Won't take long. If Maintenance can't do it, get a manual and I'll do it. But we're gonna have to test flight it."

"Okay, good." Moss took a couple of steps toward the big Maintenance shed then turned back, "How's Grugel? Is he gonna make it?"

Hayes shrugged. "Alive, but it looks bad."

He had an idea, not a very good idea, for a gunner. As he hurried around the corner of the Maintenance shed, he almost bowled over Sergeant First Class Stanton, who was bent over a trash barrel brushing off his jungle fatigue shirt .

"Goddammit, watch your step," Stanton said. Eyes blazing, the muscular sergeant wadded his shirt into a tight ball. "Where the hell you goin' anyway?"

"I have to find a gunner," Hayes replied. He took a step toward the Orderly Room.

"Hold on. I'm talkin' to you," Stanton said.

Hayes stopped. "We need a replacement for Sergeant Grugel. You heard about the accident, right?"

"Yeah, I heard. Just talked to Top. I'm takin' over for Grugel as platoon sergeant. I was gonna head over to the hospital to talk to him but I… spilled some oil on myself."

"You can't talk to him. They're doing surgery. I don't think he's…" Hayes shook his head. He didn't want to say that he thought Grugel would die. "Look, we don't have any extra gunners in the platoon. Casey Barr went home yesterday. Could you do it?"

"No, no. I ain't flyin' in gunships. Top made me platoon sergeant, but I told him I ain't gonna fly like Grugel did."

"So, what are we gonna do?" Hayes asked.

One of the oldest NCOs in the company, Hayes always thought it strange that Stanton seemed to have no fixed assignment. Sometimes he supervised crews of Vietnamese laborers building bunkers, and most nights he doled out beer and sodas at the Enlisted Men's Club. Sullen and quick to anger, he had few friends even among the other NCOs.

Brown hair cut so short that he appeared bald had briefly earned him the nickname "Cue Ball" but it hadn't stuck. He was as tall as Hayes with much bigger shoulders and an even bigger belly, with upper arms that looked as big around as Hayes' thighs. Because he probably weighed close to two hundred and fifty pounds, any gunship carrying him would have to carry less ammunition if he flew on a gunship.

"Maybe we could borrow somebody from one of the other flight platoons," Hayes suggested.

That brought a quick scowl before the sergeant nodded. "I'll talk to Molson and Brown at lunch. See if they can spare anyone."

"We can't wait for lunch. We need a gunner right now."

"Well, you'll just have to wait, specialist. Ain't your concern."

Frustrated, Hayes muttered "Okay" and headed for the Orderly Room.

"Hayes, Mister Moss is lookin' for you on the flight line," First Sergeant McConaughey said when he pushed through the door.

"I just saw him. We can't go up till we replace the tail rotor and get a gunner to take Grugel's place. I ran into Sergeant Stanton and he's gonna talk to Molson and Brown at lunch to see if they got anyone. I don't think we can wait that long."

"So, you already know Stanton's the new platoon sergeant? He said he won't fly," McConaughey said.

Hayes didn't say anything. The CO, or even the first sergeant could probably order Stanton to fly. Hayes spotted George Cartwright, the company clerk, at his corner desk. "You still want to take a shot as a Headhunter gunner?"

"Damn straight," Cartwright said.

"You sure? How many times have you flown on slicks?" Hayes asked.

"Five or six."

"How about it, First Sergeant?"

McConaughey thought for a moment, "Okay, but make sure you bring him back in one piece. I'll talk to Stanton."

Cartwright started to get up, then reached to open a desk drawer. "Got a letter for you. Didn't see you last night."

Hayes grabbed the letter, an oversized red envelope from Gloria. He stuffed it into the side leg pocket of his jungle fatigue pants. The two headed toward the flight line almost at a trot. Halfway there, Hayes and Cartwright encountered Doc Goetz trudging toward the 99th's medical hooch. Head down and looking despondent, the doctor nevertheless veered to intercept them.

"I need to speak to Specialist Hayes alone," the doctor said and waited until Cartwright moved away. "Specialist Hayes, are you alright? I am considering grounding you."

"No, no. I'm okay. Grounding me would create problems," Hayes said.

"Specialist, I have the authority to ground anyone for any medical condition that could have a negative impact on flight safety. And that includes mental conditions," Goetz said.

"You think I'm nuts?"

The doctor shook his head. "I think you're very stressed. You upset a lieutenant back at the hospital. Swore at him, I believe."

Hayes looked down at the ground. He'd been hoping his mistake would blow over. "Yeah, I shouldn't have done that. Didn't see he was a lieutenant till it was too late. How much trouble am I in?"

The doctor shook his head. "Actually, I chewed him out when I found out what happened. He's only been incountry a few days. Told him he'd better get used to dealing with troops suffering from combat stress if he's gonna work in a hospital. I might have done the same thing in your shoes, but then, I'm a captain."

"Thanks Doc. But I'm okay. I'll be better off flying than sittin' on my ass thinkin' about Grugel. How's he doing?"

Goetz shook his head. "He died." The doctor looked at Hayes for a long moment, then reached out to squeeze Hayes' shoulder. "Come see me if you have to, even if it's just to talk. I'm a doctor first. Forget I'm a captain."

At the helicopter, two mechanics from Maintenance had finished putting on the tail rotor.

"Mr. Connelly's already taken it up and tested it," a mechanic said, handing Hayes the gunship's log book.

Hayes spent several minutes showing Cartwright some of the differences between slicks and gunships while the impatient Moss watched, scowling. Gunship gunners operated an M60 machine gun suspended from the ceiling by a thick bungee cord. Instead of a lap belt, the gunner had a monkey harness that went around his shoulders so the gunner could stand. That allowed more freedom of movement, more firing angles. When another pilot came out of the Operations Bunker, Moss trotted across the tarmac to meet him. Hayes tore open the red envelope from Gloria.

"What's the date today?" He asked Cartwright.

"Tenth of March, why?"

"Nothin' important."

The red envelope contained a birthday card, filled with expressions of Gloria's love. She wanted to know the date of his birthday and apologized if she'd missed it.

How in the hell did she know?

Jimmy Hayes, who had been born James Hayha in a displaced persons camp in Germany on March 10, 1948, and who later changed his name, stared at the very first birthday card he had ever received, hiding his tears.

-15-

Detroit

Jimmy's love letter arrived during an ice storm that ravaged Detroit. The rain that froze on cars, roads, sidewalks, bushes, tree branches and power lines, and the bone-chilling dampness, sunk Gloria into a funk. Almost eight months pregnant now, she tired more easily and slept less comfortably. But her spirits edged up an hour before sundown. The sky cleared to reveal sparkling silvery ice coating even the tiniest branches of every tree and bush. Two boys on ice skates with hockey sticks streaked down the street in front of Mrs. Lincoln's house.

The next morning, Gloria awoke to a cold house with no electricity. Later, she heard that a tree limb, overburdened with ice, had fallen on a power line. With the stove out of commission, she and Mrs. Lincoln donned their winter coats to huddle in front of the fireplace eating cornflakes while they listened to chainsaws and the rumble of the Detroit Edison trucks on the street outside.

"I don't like this, but spring won't be long now," Mrs. Lincoln said.

By late morning, they had electricity again. Gloria ventured out the front door to collect the mail for the first time in two days. The wind had driven rain and sleet through the mailbox slot soaking the letters inside, including a letter from

Jimmy in a strange brown envelope. Writing on the outside of the envelope indicated the letter had been delayed. When she tore the envelope open, the letter inside came out in soggy pieces. She carefully spread the pieces on two dinner plates and left them to dry on the floor beside the heating register in her bedroom.

Shortly after noon, someone knocked on the front door.

"You are *so* lucky to have electricity," Susanna Quinn said when Gloria, her guitar slung over her shoulder, invited her in.

From the kitchen, Mrs. Lincoln said, "I'm making soup from the remains of a pork roast so you're welcome to stay for lunch."

"My power's been out since yesterday," Susanna grumbled. "I almost froze to death last night."

"We got ours back a little while ago," Mrs. Lincoln said. "Be at least an hour before the soup's ready."

"You play piano too?" Susanna asked when she saw Gloria sit on the piano bench.

"Yeah. I had lessons when I was little. Always liked guitar better. Guess I like strings 'cause I messed around with a violin too. But I don't have one anymore."

"Well the piano's really a stringed instrument. The strings are being hit by… I don't know, little pieces of wood… hammers," Susanna said.

"Yeah, I guess I knew that. I was just gonna tune my guitar. The cold screws it up."

Susanna nudged Gloria over and sat down at the piano. They played around with chords until Gloria started singing and playing the Beatles' *In My Life* on her guitar. Susanna played piano and sang harmony.

"I love that song," Susanna said.

"I sang that song the night I met Jimmy."

"It's a lovely song. I don't think I've ever heard it before," Mrs. Lincoln called from the kitchen.

"It's a Beatles song, one of their best. I wish I could write songs like that," Gloria said.

Susanna smiled. "Oh don't sell yourself short. I've listened to your record. Those original songs, they're good. Did all three of you write them together? How'd you do it?"

"Huh, me and Jimmy wrote the songs. Mostly Jimmy. Roscoe… um, he made us play them better. Then they got better still after he worked on them in the studio. I don't know what he did, but they sounded different, and better. We couldn't have done it without Roscoe." Glancing at the kitchen, Gloria moved to the couch leaning her guitar against the piano, wishing she hadn't played the Beatles song. It intimidated her. The words made her worry about Jimmy and brought back bleak thoughts of the past, of her stepmother Gina and her stepfather.

Gina, never touched me, never hugged me or kissed me, and my stepfather… She pushed the thoughts away with a shudder.

"What's the matter?" Susanna asked.

"Nothing, I... um… that song made me remember things I'd rather forget."

Susanna looked at her, opened her mouth to speak, but stopped when Mrs. Lincoln walked into the room from the kitchen. "Another fifteen minutes, maybe twenty, and the soup'll be done. It's more like a stew than soup."

"Tell me about writing the songs," Susanna said.

"Um, well, Jimmy would come up with some chords that sounded good together. He's good at that."

"Well, aren't you good at it too?" Mrs. Lincoln said.

"Why do you think that?"

"I hear you when you're just starting to play but you aren't playing a song. It always sounds good to me."

"I don't know." Gloria played her guitar every day, sometimes for hours, and she usually started by playing random chords. If she couldn't decide what to play, she just experimented. Sometimes that's all she did.

"Huh, maybe you're right," she said finally. "Anyway, it was Jimmy who started with the chords. Then it was usually me who found the melodies 'cause I can do that part better than him. But Jimmy wrote the words. I can't do that. I'm no good with words.

"But Jimmy would ask me what I was thinking about. He gets into my head like nobody else." She smiled remembering good times making music with Jimmy and Roscoe. But Roscoe had died, which reminded her of her father who'd also died. Then she started thinking about Jimmy and the war. She suddenly had the urge to tell Susanna about her black father. But she held back.

"You'll get the hang of writing words." Mrs. Lincoln sighed. "I know my Roscoe didn't write music. He never thought he was good enough. I should have never let him say that."

Nobody said anything for a little while. Gloria tried hard to think positive thoughts.

I had a black father, and I have a man who loves me. We're going to have a baby. We'll be a family.

The next morning

Susanna spent the night, the two of them talking long into the night and sleeping in Gloria's bed. After they woke up, they all ate oatmeal. Susanna called a neighbor and learned her power had come back on. She left, telling them she had to go to classes. Mrs. Lincoln went back to bed feeling "out of sorts." She said she might be coming down with a cold, or maybe the flu. For lunch, Gloria heated a can of chicken noodle soup and made grilled cheese sandwiches.

"I'm not very hungry," Mrs. Lincoln said when she got out of bed to eat lunch. She finished a bowl of soup but only ate part of a sandwich before heading back to her bedroom with a mug of tea.

In her bedroom, Gloria found the fragments of Jimmy's letter had dried so she started putting them together like working on a jig saw puzzle. It didn't take her long before it started to make sense. When she finally read it through from start to finish, she discovered a letter like Jimmy had never written before.

Usually his letters were mundane accounts of life in his base camp, his friends and places he happened to visit. He'd ask whether songs he heard on Armed Forces Radio were hits in Detroit. He rarely mentioned the baby, which bothered her some, and he never talked about battles or the war. He always ended by saying how much he missed her and loved her. But this letter was only about how much he loved her, a love letter.

At first, it lifted her melancholy. The letter read like Jimmy whispering in her ear. Then she began to worry. She knew he'd written it in a hurry on lined paper with a ragged, torn edge like a page ripped from a spiral notebook. And he'd mailed it in a manilla envelope crossing out an Army return address. Jimmy must have written it in the middle of busy day.

Why did you do that, Jimmy?

She thought about the war. She tried to ignore any mention of the war on TV news and in newspapers. But she couldn't help herself. The other night some officer on TV said that in order to save it, they had destroyed an entire town. She'd heard that more than five hundred American soldiers had died in one week, a record. Five hundred boys dead. Five hundred families receiving terrible news. The war had gotten much worse since Jimmy had first gone to Vietnam.

"Is he afraid he won't be able to tell me in person?" she whispered at the letter.

And then fear tightened around her like a vice. She didn't want to think about the past. Now the present terrified her. She took her guitar out of its case and started playing, shaky at first, but she concentrated on the words in the letter, trying to get into Jimmy's head the way he got into hers.

"I believe in love," she whispered. Reading his letter again, she decided to try and turn the words into a song.

Susanna and Mrs. Lincoln said she could do it. And she wanted to believe them.

-16-

March 23, 1968, Pontiac Press, page 11

Four Bodies Found in U.P. River

From the Associated Press

The U.S. Coast Guard, Chippewa County Sheriff and Ontario Provincial Police are investigating the deaths of four men found in the icy waters of the St. Marys River this week between Michigan's Upper Peninsula and the Canadian Province of Ontario.

According to Lt. Norbert Causey, a U.S. Coast Guard spokesman, two high school students who were snowmobiling on Sugar Island last Wednesday afternoon spotted something floating on the shore of the ice-clogged river.

"The bodies were of two adult males, and we believe they'd been in the water for several weeks, maybe longer," Causey said. "Both were wedged against the shore by ice."

According to the Coast Guard, the ice in the Upper Peninsula river started breaking up last week, and strong southeasterly winds pushed ice flows to the shore.

Causey said Coast Guard searchers found a third body floating in the river on Thursday morning near Homestead, a tiny Sugar Island community. He said that body was also that of an adult male.

The Coast Guard turned the bodies over to the Chippewa County Coroner and notified the Chippewa County Sheriff.

"The coroner is trying to identify the men and determine the cause of death. We have no further comment at this time," said a Chippewa County Sheriff's deputy, who declined to be identified.

On Friday, the Ontario Provincial Police (OPP) announced that the body of a fourth man had been found in the water on the Canadian side of the St. Marys River. OPP officials would not disclose any details but a police source told the Associated Press that Canadian police, the Chippewa County Sheriff, and the Coast Guard have met to coordinate their investigations.

"The deaths of all four men are believed to be related, and there are indications that they did not drown," the source said.

Gloria almost missed the story. With both major Detroit newspapers shut down by a prolonged strike, Mrs. Lincoln had started picking up other newspapers whenever she went grocery shopping. Gloria didn't usually read the paper but a story about baby care had caught her eye.

After reading the story, she panicked, expecting police to knock on the door at any moment. She'd told the police the truth, that she'd been held captive in her boyfriend's uncle's cabin on Sugar Island by several men who worked for her stepfather. One of the men had taken her away so she didn't know what happened after that. But the police didn't know that Jimmy had shown up at the cabin later. After reading the story, she almost picked up the phone to call her lawyers. After thinking about it some more, she decided that the police might not want to talk to her at all. Even if they did, they wouldn't come anytime soon.

Gloria clipped the story and stuffed it in an envelope addressed to Jimmy. However, she completely miscalculated about how soon the police would come.

She'd just dropped the envelope on a small table by the front door, when the doorbell rang. Gloria opened the door to two large men, one in a black overcoat and the other wearing a dark brown suede jacket with a fur collar. The man in the overcoat displayed a police badge. Her insides clutched tight. How had the police found her so quickly?

"We're looking for Miss Gloria Doran," the man with the badge said. In his forties, his short black hair sprinkled with gray topped a face that seemed all sharp angles. But his smile eased Gloria's shock. "I'm Sergeant Overholzer and this is Detective Crain. We're from Detroit Police Homicide."

It took Gloria several seconds before she could speak. "Um, I'm Gloria Doran."

As she stood in the doorway she heard Mrs. Lincoln's bed creak upstairs, then slippered feet shuffling on the floor.

"Who is it, dear? Don't let the cold in," Mrs. Lincoln said from the top of the stairs.

"Come in." Gloria led the two men into the living room. She'd dressed in sweatpants and one of Jimmy's old sweatshirts, a faded green Michigan State University one that accommodated her bulky shape. She was sure the police could tell she was pregnant.

Mrs. Lincoln, in a pink flowery housecoat, came down the stairs, stopping at the landing halfway down. "Would you like some coffee or maybe tea?"

"You should be in bed," Gloria said, and turned to the detectives. "She has the flu and needs to rest. I can make coffee."

"Thanks, but don't bother. This shouldn't take long," Sergeant Overholzer said.

"I don't want to make anyone sick," Mrs. Lincoln said.

"Have a seat." Gloria pulled out the piano bench for herself.

"We're hoping you can clear up something that's puzzling us." Overholzer took off his overcoat, draped it over one arm of the couch before sitting beside it. Crain looked around the room and remained standing.

"We've been investigating a double murder that occurred several weeks ago. Maybe you heard about it? Two men were stabbed to death at a Thai restaurant."

"I remember that. It was on the radio," Mrs. Lincoln called from the landing. "Did you ever catch who did it?"

"We didn't catch him, but we think we know who it is. He's a Thai national. We think he's gone back to Asia, but we aren't getting much cooperation from police in Thailand."

Relieved, Gloria relaxed. "What does this have to do with me?"

"Nothing," Overholzer said. He smiled, but Gloria thought his relaxed demeanor could quickly harden. "We think the man who committed the murders is an ex-Thai air force pilot by the name of Jettrin Juntasa. He owned a little over half of the restaurant where the murders took place. The corporate documents show that your deceased stepfather, Matthew Doran, owned the other half. In fact, he owned parts of several other businesses with Juntasa."

"I've never heard of Juntasa. So if you came here looking for him, he's not here," Gloria said.

"You're welcome to look," Mrs. Lincoln said. She had quietly moved to the bottom of the stairs.

"No, that's not why we're here. As we said, we think he's gone back to Asia," Crain unzipped his suede jacket and Gloria saw a gun in a shoulder holster. "We wondered if you might know why your stepfather was Juntasa's business partner."

"Well, it doesn't surprise me. I'm sure you know my stepfather worked for bad people. The FBI asked me about some of them, but I don't remember hearing Juntasa's name," she said. She looked over at Mrs. Lincoln. "Maybe I should call my lawyers."

"No, no. I don't think you have to call anyone," Overholzer said. "We know you've had a difficult time with the Detroit police. I sympathize and the department should have, and could have, handled it better than we did."

Overholzer took out a notebook and flipped through the pages. He looked up and smiled again. "We know you didn't have anything to do with this, and we know who your stepfather worked for."

He studied the notebook for another moment. "There was a witness to these murders, a Thai woman. Her uncle was the manager of the restaurant and one of the murder victims. She was lucky to escape herself. But we didn't get much help from her until we found a translator.

"We're not sure what this Juntasa was doing in Detroit, but we don't think he came here to kill the restaurant manager and one of the cooks. We believe Juntasa is involved in organized crime in Asia, specifically, prostitution. Can you think of any reason why your stepfather would have been involved with someone from Thailand?"

Gloria placed both hands on her swollen abdomen and forced herself to think about her stepfather before answering.

"My stepfather made quite a few business trips to Asia, including Thailand, but I don't know who he met there. In addition to the Gargano family, I know he worked with other criminals. I sometimes overheard him talking on the telephone. This man, Juntasa, is not a name I recognize. But he sounds like the kind of person my stepfather might know. That could be another reason why he went to Thailand."

"Another reason? Why else did he go to Thailand?" Crain asked.

Regretting that she'd opened herself up, she hesitated. "My stepfather liked children… um, young boys and young girls, mostly boys. He was a terrible person, and I'm glad he's dead."

"I am too," Mrs. Lincoln said from the bottom of the stairs.

The two policemen looked at each other, some nonverbal communication flowing between them. Then Overholzer looked back to Gloria. "I'm sorry to hear that. We've heard lots of stories about Matthew Doran, but that one's new." He closed his notebook and put it in his pocket.

"Just to be clear Miss Doran. We don't know why Juntasa came to Detroit. It may have something to do with the... um, recent series of murders of some Detroit organized crime individuals. But we're confident Juntasa's no longer here. Still, you should be careful. Lock your doors and don't go for any long walks alone at night. If you see anything that causes you concern, please call us."

Each of the detectives handed her a card before leaving.

-17-

Nui Binh Base Camp

Two weeks after Grugel's death, Cartwright, who continued handling the company mail while flying most days with the Headhunters, gave Hayes two letters from Gloria. First, Cartwright held them up to his face, sniffing loudly. "Aw, no perfume," which triggered a few guffaws from the flight crews who were eating breakfast in the mess hall.

When he finished with the mail, he introduced a tall thin soldier by the name of Conrad Myers, the new company clerk. Myers had brown skin, short black hair, and rimless glasses that made his eyes look big. He also looked scared. Later, Hayes learned Myers' muslim parents had emigrated from Pakistan and his father owned a mail order camera business in New York. Myers' grandfather had been the son of a British soldier and Indian woman.

Cartwright told Hayes he was transferring into the Headhunters as a fulltime gunner.

"So you really are fuckin' crazy," Hayes said.

Momentary concern flashed across Cartwright's face. "The first sergeant thinks I'm crazy too, but he let me transfer. I may have to skip flyin' today and tomorrow 'cause I gotta finish training Myers. He can do the mail now, but I gotta show him how we do some of the reports and other stuff."

"Heard a couple of grunts transferred in to be gunners so it should be okay. Better let Stanton know," Hayes said. Every helicopter flew with two gunners, with the crew chief acting as one of the gunners. Always short of flight crews, most days at least one or two clerks or mechanics or someone else from the company volunteered to fill in as a gunner, almost always on one of the slicks. Even Doc Goetz had flown as a gunner a few times, and Hayes wondered how he reconciled that with his Hippocratic Oath.

Cartwright looked around the mess hall, leaned closer to Hayes. "You know, I don't believe Mitchell killed himself. He had a footlocker full of shit he was shippin' home. Had this nice new stereo he bought at the PX, ivory he got on R and R in Hong Kong, some silk for his mom, all his Playboy magazines, though a lot of the pictures were missing." They both laughed.

"I helped him pack up all that shit. He'd made plans too. Said he was gonna go to the Playboy Club and try and get a date with this gal who was the first black playmate of the month. Said he knew her in high school. Then there was that day he took off for Long Binh."

Hayes remembered that when Mitchell's *Playboy* magazine arrived in the mail, they'd all gather to look at the nude pictures. He also remembered Mitchell saying he'd gone to school with a Playboy bunny, but Hayes hadn't believed him.

"Wait a minute, he went to Long Binh?" Every day, a courier helicopter flew between Nui Binh, Cu Chi, Long Binh, and sometimes other bases, carrying replacements, officers going to meetings and other passengers. The division headquarters for the brigade that the 99th supported was in Cu Chi, and Long Binh, adjacent to Saigon, was the largest American base in Vietnam. All over South Vietnam, similar regular helicopter flights comprised an intricate transportation network.

"Yeah. He hopped on the courier coupla mornings before he died. Came back on the afternoon courier. Maintenance was pissed, and so was the first sergeant. Guess he didn't get a pass, but they let it slide."

Hayes thought for a moment. "Did he say anything to you about why he went there?"

"Nope, but the day before, somebody in Long Binh called and left a number for him to call back. That was unusual. Never had to take a message for anyone except the first sergeant or the CO since I been here."

"Who called?"

"Shit, I can't remember the name. Some sergeant. I told Mitchell, and I guess he went to Ops and used their phone to call the guy. Next morning, he took off for Long Binh."

Hayes looked at his watch. "Later alligator, gotta go."

As he hurried to the flight line, Hayes opened one of the letters from Gloria. It contained a newspaper clipping, nothing else. He slowed to read it.

"Oh, shit." He'd begun hoping the bodies might never be found. Nothing he could do, but what about Gloria? He'd never actually told her what he did, but she must have guessed. What did she think of him now?

When he got to his ship, he found Flowers sitting on the gunship's floor reading his Bible, two machine guns beside him.

"Got a new guy today. He's flyin' with Urquhart so you're stuck with me again," Flowers said through tight, pursed lips. Stanton, the platoon sergeant, had started changing around pairings of flight crews, upsetting many of the gunners and crew chiefs.

Flowers snapped his little Bible shut. "Urquhart's not a Christian and the Bible upsets him. Are you a Christian, Hayes?"

"I guess so, but I don't go to church. Maybe I'll start when I get home. My girl's been tellin' me about this Baptist church she's been going to. Aretha Franklin used to sing there."

"So, it's okay?"

Hayes saw Flowers hesitate, his Bible poised to go into his shirt pocket.

"Sure. Your Bible's cool long as you do your job."

Hayes got out the ship's logbook to see if anyone from Maintenance had looked at a warning light that Nesterenko had complained about. Hayes hadn't found anything wrong. The logbook showed somebody had switched out the light.

"Is Cartwright gonna be with us permanent?" Flowers asked.

"Yeah, he's transferring, but he's gotta train that new clerk today."

Flowers hefted one of the machine guns and carried it over to Hayes' side of the helicopter. "Urquhart don't like me. Told me to shove my Bible up my rear end yesterday."

Hayes put the logbook down. Flowers looked like a high school kid just turned down for a prom date. "Everyone's on edge 'cause of Mitchell and Grugel."

"Yeah, Mitchell was like a brother. You're okay too, Hayes. If my Bible reading bothers you, just say something."

Hayes laughed. "I might not believe some of it but you read all you want. I just hope I can believe this fuckin' logbook."

They took off with Nesterenko as aircraft commander and Donaldson the co-pilot. The only black pilot in the company, Donaldson would bump up to aircraft commander any day now and would probably no longer fly with Nesterenko. Their gunship comprised half of a two-ship fire team with Moss and Lieutenant Carson flying the other gunship.

They spent more than an hour trying to kill a sniper in a strategically placed spider hole. The sniper had pinned down an American infantry platoon. He'd already killed one grunt and wounded another when they arrived. Each of the gunships made several runs at the sniper with rockets and miniguns, but the sniper continued shooting at the American platoon. Every time a gunship rolled in, he retreated into his hole at the last minute to escape the rockets and machine gun fire.

"Goddamnit, we've hit this cocksucker with a coupla thousand dollars of ordinance, and he's still there," an exasperated Nesterenko said. "Are they gonna hafta call in the fucking fast movers?"

Fast movers were Air Force fighter-bombers.

"Maybe we could bum a grenade from the grunts and drop it down the hole," Donaldson said.

"Shit, I got a grenade. Two of 'em," Hayes said. A week earlier, they'd hauled two wounded South Vietnamese Rangers to a hospital. One of them left behind two grenades and a forty-five caliber pistol. Hayes stashed the forty-five in a duffel bag in his locker along with a thirty-eight he'd acquired from a pilot. But he'd left the grenades in the gunship. Technically, they weren't supposed to carry hand grenades in case somebody got shot after pulling the pin. But Hayes didn't think it a serious rule since the grunts riding in the slicks fairly dripped with grenades.

"What are you doing with a fucking grenade, Hayes?" Nesterenko said. "And why didn't you tell us sooner?"

After Moss made another strafing run with his miniguns, Nesterenko slipped over the spider hole, the skids kissing the ground, and Hayes pitched both grenades down the hole before they skedaddled.

And that took care of the sniper.

"Another morning at the office," Nesterenko said. "Time for a coffee break."

The lieutenant radioed to tell them that they had been ordered to Long Binh. On the way, Nesterenko complained about the warning light again. "Hayes, didn't you say Maintenance replaced the fucking light? It's going on and off again."

The warning light quit acting up as they approached Long Binh. After refueling and re-arming, the lieutenant said he had to go to a Green Beret compound for a single ship mission, and for them to stand by. Hayes started troubleshooting the problem warning light. Nesterenko, Donaldson and Flowers all tried to help. Nobody could find anything wrong, so they hopped over to the Long Binh maintenance facility and asked them to take a look. The pilots and Flowers went to get lunch, the two pilots planning to sneak Flowers into the officers mess as another warrant officer.

"Why don't come with us, Hayes? You don't have to stay with the ship. I hear they got steaks," Nesterenko said.

"Thanks, but I want to read a letter from my girl. And I have a friend here I want to look up."

After they left, Hayes sat in the gunship thinking about Mitchell, then Grugel. Whoever murdered Mitchell probably pushed Grugel into the tail rotor. Had Grugel known something? And who was the sergeant that Mitchell had gone to see in Long Binh?

But Hayes knew someone who might do something about the two murders, and he was right in Long Binh.

Hayes started reading Gloria's second letter as he hurried through the sprawling Long Binh Base Camp on his way to see Staff Sergeant Jimmy Ray Suggs. He knew that Suggs, a military policeman, sometimes investigated murders. Suggs had escorted Hayes to CBS News in New York. The two Jimmys had become friends.

Passing a two-story barracks, he paused to listen to the scintillating guitar in the reprise version of *Sergeant Pepper's Lonely Hearts Club Band* as it blared from a stereo inside the barracks. His fingers twitched with the chord changes before he shook his head and continued on. He saw soldiers throwing frisbees, playing basketball and volleyball, even saw a swimming pool. Someone said that Long Binh Base Camp could accommodate 50,000 soldiers. Some of them probably fought in the war, but Hayes thought he'd arrived in REMF—Rear Echelon MotherFuckers—heaven. Passing a mess hall, he caught the smell of meat cooking. It reminded him about Gloria's promise to cook him a crown roast when he got home.

"What the hell's a crown roast?" he'd muttered.

Her letter contained a lot about her preparations for the baby. She'd bought a crib, a host of baby items, begun painting and decorating the extra bedroom in Mrs. Lincoln's house.

He realized that in a few months he'd be living in a house with Mrs. Lincoln, Gloria and a baby. Hard to comprehend how his life would change. It scared him, but he vowed to write something about their baby in his next letter to Gloria.

The last page of the letter looked like Gloria had added it in a hurry. She'd panicked when two Detroit police detectives knocked on the door because she thought they'd come about the bodies in the newspaper article.

> *They asked me about two murders at some Thai restaurant. My awful stepfather owned it along with the killer. I told them my stepfather knew a lot of bad people. Cops said the killer was some air force pilot from Thailand named Jettrin Juntasa. They said he went back to Thailand.*

"Goddammit," Hayes muttered. The more he'd learned about the extent of her stepfather's criminal activities, the more it upset him. "I killed that sonofabitch, and he's still causing problems."

An hour after killing a sniper, immersed in the surreal world of Long Binh Base Camp, Hayes tried to reconcile the conflicting thoughts colliding in his mind. Another morning at the office in the fucking corporate war. An asshole from Thailand — supposedly an American ally in the war — killing people in Detroit. A sniper who died for his country, who hadn't sold his life cheaply, who probably had a family who cared about him. But the bodies in the newspaper clipping and Gloria's dead stepfather?

"Those bastards had it coming."

When he reached the military police compound, he strode inside and asked the first soldier he encountered, "Jimmy Ray Suggs around?"

"Nope. He went to see a Major Kucharski over at Second Field Force. Left about half an hour ago." The spec four clerk, a cigarette dangling from the corner of his mouth, hunched over a purple mimeograph sheet in his typewriter, a tiny eyedropper of purple correction fluid in one hand.

Major Kucharski? Hayes had never met him, but he knew of a Major Kucharski who worked for William Westmoreland, the commanding general for all of Vietnam. That Major Kucharski had sent Sergeant Suggs to find Hayes to bring him to New York to head off a false TV story accusing him and others in his company of killing Vietnamese civilians in the ground attack on Nui Binh at the beginning of the Tet Offensive.

Has to be the same major.

Hayes hurried back across the base camp to Second Field Force, which had several buildings. He'd stopped outside the most impressive one, when an attractive Asian woman in foreign military fatigues bustled out the door. The fatigues appeared tailored to show off her curves, but he spotted lieutenant bars on her collar. After gaping for a moment he straightened and saluted. She barely glanced at him while returning the salute as she hurried by.

Inside, Hayes encountered a young black sergeant first class, an E-7, three grades above himself. He belonged on an Army recruiting poster, his immaculate uniform draped on a muscular perfectly proportioned physique. He held an ice-cold can Coca Cola, dripping with tiny beads of water. It triggered a powerful thirst in Hayes. He hadn't seen a Coke since the USA.

But Hayes groaned inwardly, suddenly aware of his own faded, dusty jungle fatigues, soiled with grease spots, large dark sweat stains under the arms, his sleeves unrolled, baggy trousers bound to his calves with shoelaces to keep the material from flapping in the wind when he flew. That morning the water in the aircraft drop tank supplying the showers had run out so he hadn't been able to shower or shave.

"I'm looking for a Major Kucharski," he told the sergeant.

The sergeant picked up his Coke and took a long, slow drink as his eyes ran up and down Hayes. "Come back after you've shaved, and put on a clean uniform, specialist. You could use a haircut too." He stretched over the desk to look down at Hayes' boots. "Doesn't appear your boots have seen polish in some time. Why you wearin' those stateside leather boots? And what's with the shoelaces on your pants? You're outta uniform. You gotta lot of nerve tryin' to see an officer on General Westmoreland's staff lookin' like you been shovelin' garbage. What's your business, anyway?"

Hayes decided he needn't worry too much about a sergeant not in his chain of command, especially one who couldn't be much older than him. "Sorry, Sergeant. Maybe you didn't notice the war goin' on out there? I've been busy keeping you folks safe. Killed a sniper about an hour ago. Then I had to troubleshoot a problem with my gunship. Somebody has to do the dirty work. I'm a crew chief. I fly gunships and I prefer the old boots. Leather's a little more fireproof than nylon. I'm actually looking for a Staff Sergeant Suggs. An MP told me he'd gone to see Major Kucharski. My name's Hayes, Spec Four Jimmy Hayes."

He heard the scrape of a chair in the office behind the sergeant and a major opened the door. The opposite of the sergeant, the major was slightly built and short, his balding head and spectacles giving him a bookish look.

"Specialist Hayes, we finally meet. I'm Major Kucharski," he said. He frowned as he took in Hayes' appearance but raised a hand to silence the sergeant who'd opened his mouth to speak. "I see you've been on the job. You missed Sergeant Suggs. He's on his way to the Delta."

Hayes saluted and the major returned it. "Sir, I wanted to talk to Suggs about Specialist Mitchell's murder. He and my platoon sergeant, Staff Sergeant Grugel were both murdered."

The major looked at him for a moment, then motioned Hayes to follow him into the office. Kucharski closed the door before speaking, his voice low. "Mitchell's death is classified. I'm surprised you even know about it, though I suppose you'd have heard something. You said he was in your unit?"

"Yes sir. I found his body, me and the first sergeant. And then my platoon sergeant, Grugel, he was—"

"You said another murder?"

"Yes sir. Somebody pushed Sergeant Grugel into a tail rotor. Grugel was able to tell me that much before he died."

The major stood for a long time before moving around the desk to sit in the chair. He pointed to a chair on the other side of the desk and Hayes sat. "Tell me about the murders. Everything you know."

So Hayes told him and the major listened without interruption.

"Who else knows about this?"

"The first sergeant, the CO and Doc Goetz. We all know Mitchell was murdered. But I didn't tell anyone about Grugel yet. Didn't think anyone would believe me. The official line on Mitchell is bullshit. He didn't kill himself. I knew Jimmy Ray would listen to me and might be able to do something."

The major looked him in the eye. "I didn't know you were involved. I'm going to take a chance and fill you in on some of it. Can you keep your mouth shut?"

Hayes nodded.

The major ran his hand through his scanty brown hair. He had a trimmed mustache that reminded Hayes of Edward G. Robinson. That someone on Westmoreland's staff would grow a mustache surprised Hayes. Army regulations prohibiting facial hair had only recently changed to allow mustaches. Most of the pilots in the 99th were growing mustaches.

The major said, "Mitchell wrote a letter to General Westmoreland, said that an infantry unit had deliberately killed civilians. He threatened to tell his congressman." Kucharski's head jerked slightly like a nerve had misfired when he said it. "We already knew about it, but the general ordered me to investigate. I had Sergeant Suggs get a hold of Mitchell. He came here and I interviewed him right here in this room."

So Suggs was the sergeant who called Mitchell.

Hayes said, "Yeah, it happened same day that Suggs and I got back from the World. Some others from our gun platoon said the same thing about what happened in that ville and—"

"What the hell can anyone see from up in the air?" Kucharski said. "There were other more reliable reports from people on the ground. But we confirmed fifteen dead women and kids. Collateral damage. They shouldn't have been there." He stopped, looked away from Hayes, picked up a ballpoint pen and began twisting it with his fingers. "No goddam civilians were supposed to be there. It was… ah, maybe unfortunate. But sometimes these things happen in a war." A grim smile forced its way onto his face. "We're paying compensation even though they shouldn't have been there."

"It was a lot more than fifteen dead civilians from what I heard. I know the villagers were supposed to be gone, but you still see 'em—"

"If they're there, you have to assume they're enemy. Most of the time, the Viet Cong don't wear uniforms."

Hayes wondered if Kucharski had ever seen actual combat. "Yeah, but women with babies and little kids… you know they're not the enemy." He struggled to keep from raising his voice.

"If they didn't move out, then you assume it's a VC village, specialist." Major Kucharski snapped his response out but stopped, his lips tightly closed, angry. He stared at Hayes expecting to be challenged. Hayes swallowed but didn't say anything. He hadn't come to talk about civilian deaths.

Then Kucharski let out a breath. "For what it's worth, the investigation is still ongoing. People may be disciplined. None of us likes it when civilians get caught in the middle of this war."

The major stopped, and Hayes tried to shift the conversation back to Mitchell's death. "Couple of days after he came here, somebody murdered Mitchell. Why isn't anyone investigating that?"

"But there was an investigation. According to the MPs who handled it, the ones who were on the scene, there was some question about whether it was suicide instead of murder."

"Sir, there's no question. No way could Mitchell stab himself in the chest and then shoot himself in the head with an M-16. Talk to Doc Goetz, our flight surgeon if you don't believe me. Or the CO. Or the first sergeant. We all saw Mitchell's body. And whoever it was, he tried to make it look like I did it, 'cause he stole my rifle and my guitar..."

His words died when the major held up his hand, stopping him. It was then that Hayes noticed the ring on the major's finger, a heavy class ring with a big, faceted stone. He'd seen a similar ring, though with a different colored stone, on the CO's finger.

"My West Point ring, specialist," the major said with some haughty anger. His eyes came off the ring and bored into Hayes, who stared right back.

After a moment Kucharski's gaze shifted away from Hayes, and he offered an almost imperceptible nod. Hayes wasn't even sure he'd seen it. "The MPs made their report, now we need to contain this."

"So, you're gonna let a murder slide? Somebody murdered Mitchell, and you're tellin' his family that he fuckin' killed himself?"

"Lower your voice, specialist, and remember who you're talking to."

It was a commanding tone, but Hayes ignored it. "Sir, that's just not right."

"That's not for you to decide."

Hayes kept going. "I can see why you'd want to cover up the civilian deaths, but the murder of an American soldier?"

Finally recognizing that not only would he lose any argument with the major, he'd probably get in a lot of trouble. He clamped his mouth shut.

The major let out a long breath and grabbed a pack of Lucky Strike cigarettes on the desk. He shook a couple of cigarettes loose, looked across the desk and proffered the pack to Hayes. Hayes stared at cigarettes before shaking his head. They both sat in silence until the major tapped the cigarettes back into the pack. Kucharski seemed to look through Hayes, his hands locked together on the desk. Then he spoke in a low raspy voice trying to project his authority. "Specialist Hayes, don't forget that we're fighting a war here—"

"You think I don't know that. Jesus—"

"—and that's the priority. That's what matters. This war. This battle we're in. We can't afford to let the behavior of a handful of soldiers become the issue back home. More than five hundred American soldiers died in just a week. Mitchell's another casualty. If he was murdered, he's probably not the only one."

"But he *was* murdered, and he *wasn't* the only one. Whoever murdered Mitchell probably murdered Grugel. That makes two. Two Americans murdered and nobody gives a shit," Hayes said.

"Another murder..." The major stopped and drummed his fingers on the desk, before reaching for his cigarettes again. He took one out but didn't light it. "I don't know if that really changes anything."

Seething, Hayes kept his mouth shut until he finally thought of something to say. "What about Sergeant Suggs? Couldn't he still look into this?"

"I have him on something else, something more important. There's been another…" He stopped and Hayes knew that the major had said more than he'd meant to.

"Been another civilian massacre? Maybe bigger this time?"

"Goddammit, this is none of your concern. And it's also classified. For Christ sakes, we think the North Vietnamese and the VC murdered as many as ten thousand people up in Hue. And if you talk about any of this, you could find yourself in Long Binh Jail."

Hayes almost made a crack about calling his pal Walter Cronkite but with an effort kept silent.

"You're dismissed," the major said after a long tense moment. Hayes got up, then remembering his military courtesy, came to attention and saluted. The major returned the salute without standing. But then he rose to go to the door with Hayes and spoke in a voice louder than necessary.

"Specialist Hayes, I have seen orders awarding you a silver star for your actions in Nui Binh. Personally, I think what you did in New York was more valuable. Because of that, I've cut you some slack here. Don't blow it."

Hayes didn't reply but walked slowly past the immaculate sergeant. When he was out of the building he broke into a trot to burn off his fury.

-18-

April, Detroit

Gloria awoke with an aching back and queasiness in her stomach. She tried to sleep on her side as Dr. Sadowski had recommended, but much preferred sleeping on her back. She heard Mrs. Lincoln moving around in the kitchen, smelled bacon. Her mind meandered from one sad thought to another. She rolled around trying to find a more comfortable position to go back to sleep.

With a disturbing suddenness, her pregnancy had caught up and overtaken her. Cramps, bloating, nausea, constantly going to the bathroom, her ungainly bulk and difficulty sleeping. And the baby's kicking, once a source of joy, now hurt.

"You are doing remarkably well. Everything looks great. Remember, you are making a whole new person, and that's not easy. It takes a lot of energy, but it's the most satisfying thing you'll ever do," Dr. Sadowski said holding Gloria's hand. "Now, have you had some heartburn? How about belching and gas?"

"Gas? Yeah, sometimes it hurts, especially if I'm, you know, I'm holding it in."

"Try not to do that. Your baby's taking up more and more room, pushing on your digestive system." The doctor smiled.

"You are on the home stretch. It'll probably be about two more weeks."

Finally, she got out of bed. Wearing a fur-trimmed pink brocade robe that she'd purchased at a church rummage sale, she sagged into a chair at the kitchen table. Mrs. Lincoln poured a glass of orange juice and placed it in front of her.

"Oh, that robe looks lovely on you dear. Do you want some bacon? There's only one egg left, but I could make pancakes. Did you sleep well? This is late for you."

Gloria started to cry.

"What's the matter dear? Why are—"

"I'm scared. I'm gonna have a baby and I'm so scared." Her body shook from the sobs. She put her head down on her folded arms.

"Women have been having babies for centuries. You'll do fine," Mrs. Lincoln said. She squeezed Gloria's shoulder.

"Jimmy might die. I don't know how to take care of a baby. I can't even write songs without Jimmy." Gloria's uncomfortable bent-over posture triggered a wave of nausea and cramps that started deep in her abdomen so she straightened up.

And farted very loudly.

"Oh God, I can't even control my body anymore. I'm sorry."

"Best to let it out, dear. Don't hold back," Mrs. Lincoln said, smiling sympathetically. Then she laughed. "Probably those brussel sprouts from last night."

As she finished her pancakes and bacon, Gloria announced that she wanted to visit the record company.

"I'm going to sing them some of the songs I wrote. Maybe they'll have some musicians around that I can play with. Better than sitting around here. I might have to give up music when I'm taking care of a baby." She stopped to think about it.

"But I hope not."

The next day

Maxie Zimmerman, the president of Gloria's record company, greeted Gloria so enthusiastically she thought the frizzy hair on his head might be sticking out after a bolt of lightning hit him. Gloria, acutely tuned to racial appearance cues, thought Zimmerman's hair and fuller lips might indicate a distant black ancestor. She wondered if he'd noticed anything similar in her.

"You were right, we shoulda done that tour," he said. "Damn, damn, damn. Coulda doubled sales. Damn. Too late now." He eyed her bulk under her loose smock as he guided her into his office by one arm. Zimmerman seemed to wear the same blue suit every time Gloria saw him. Her attorneys said he'd worked at Motown but left on good terms with a loan to start his own company to develop white artists. "Glad to hear you're writin' songs. Killer, that's killer."

In his office she played the song she'd written based on Jimmy's love letter.

"Wow! That's great," he said. Then he guided her through the building, a converted warehouse, talking fast about his latest discovery. "Just signed this cool group, Body Count. Got a big followin' down around Toledo. Leader's a cat goes by Zoomer, kinda like the way you're Sunshine. Name's really Sam Patterson. He's a fan of yours. Likes the guitar in your album. He's monster on guitar too... Killer bar band, but they don't got any of their own material. I was thinkin' maybe start 'em by backin' other artists till we find'em some songs. If you got anythin' you could part with. Anyway, this Zoomer cat keeps sayin' he's got songs, but I dunno. I ain't heard nothin'. Zilch. Not like you. That one you just played, that's fab."

"Well, that one's for me and Jimmy when he gets back. I don't want to give it away. Just want to work on it with a band, but I'm working on some other stuff... not quite finished. Maybe I could—"

A cacophony of sound cut Gloria off when Zimmerman opened a door. The musical din subsided as a tall guitar player, presumably Zoomer, turned to glare at them, fire in his eyes. He wore a pink silk shirt open to his navel and dirty white jeans so tight they outlined his genitals. But a soft hairy abdomen and a little gray peppering his messy black hair that encircled his head like a floppy halo caused Gloria to peg him at thirty or more years old. Three long-haired bandmates, all smoking cigarettes, looked older than Gloria but younger than Zoomer. Sitting on the floor against one wall, three very young disheveled teenage girls, also smoking, tried to hide an open fifth of Southern Comfort behind them.

"This is Sunshine. She's got some killer songs. Wants to work on them with a band."

Zoomer smirked. "Shit, you don't look nothin' like your pictures on the album. Been hittin' the pork chops, huh?"

"C'mon Zoomer, she's pregnant, and she writes songs. Be nice," Zimmerman said.

Zoomer considered her for a tense moment, his eyes dancing between Zimmerman and Gloria. Then he jumped up and landed in a crouch, unleashing a furious blast of fiery guitar, his face contorted as if the tight pants squeezed too hard. He ended with a long drawn out warbling note that he manipulated with the guitar's whammy bar.

Gloria recognized that most of the guitar solo came from *Muleskinner Blues*, a song that had been a minor hit several years ago. After the reverberations died she forced a smile and said, "Pleased to meet you. You got any songs? Maybe I can help, or maybe you can help me with mine."

Zimmerman nodded. "See what you can do." He started backing out of the door but then turned to the teenage girls. "I don't want any of you drinkin' in here."

As soon as therecord exec was gone, Zoomer picked up the whiskey bottle and took a long swallow. Sneering at the door, he offered the bottle to the three girls, and then to Gloria. They all declined and he put the bottle down. Still looking at the door, he said, "There musta been a darkie somewhere in the family tree. Am I right?"

Nobody said anything, though one of the girls stifled a snorting laugh.

"You said you had songs? Can you play that thing?" Zoomer gestured at Gloria's guitar.

"Sure," she said. Not wanting anymore conversation with him, she started the song inspired by Jimmy's love letter. She played it slowly, partly because she wanted him to absorb the lyrics.

When I fall asleep
I taste your sweet kisses
Feel your caresses
The softness of your skin
And sweet smell of your hair

And this love song that I sing
Is only meant for you

When I close my eyes
I dream we're one again
Your warm skin pressed on mine
Our hearts race together
Our bodies locked in love

And this love song that I sing
Is only meant for you

When I wake from sleep
My eyes are open wide
And cannot see you near me
The tears run down my cheeks
Despair I cannot hide

And the love song that you sang
Was only meant for me

"That's beautiful," one of the girls said.

After a sneering glance directed at the girl, Zoomer surprised Gloria. He raced through the song's chords without missing a single one, adding a catchy rhythm. The crunchy, bass-heavy tone from his amplified guitar resonated in her body. In spite of herself, Gloria liked it, especially the guitar's sound. She'd failed miserably in her efforts to master Jimmy's Stratocaster and amplifier.

"Think you can handle that Billy?" Zoomer said nodding to the other guitar player. Then he turned to the drummer and the bass player. "Felix, Frankie work out a bottom. Somethin' like the way we do *Summertime Blues*."

He turned to Gloria. "It's got structure, great melody. I like the chord changes, but the lyrics are for shit. Except for that line about bodies locked in love. Locked in love, yeah. We could do somethin' with that. Rest of it isn't our bag. Too soft and folky."

Gloria colored. "Well, it's my song, not yours."

He scowled again, looked around the room, then picked up the whiskey bottle, took a small sip. The other guitarist, Billy, had unplugged his guitar from his amplifier. He softly practiced the chords in Zoomer's same cadence.

"Let's run through it," Zoomer said.

"Wait. I need to plug into an amp," Gloria held up the cord attached to her guitar.

"No, we can handle the guitar. Don't need any fuckin' folky ballad shit. We're rock and roll. You musta worked with a real rock and roll band for your album, right? Just sing, be easier if you don't hafta worry about playin'," Zoomer said.

A bolt of energy shot through Gloria. Yesterday, hard to get out of bed. Today? Ready to rock. "No, I gotta play when I sing. And it's my song." She took a couple of steps toward the other guitarist's amp. Zoomer moved to cut her off but not fast enough to stop her from plugging in.

"Why don't you play those chords just the way you did before. I'll put some more rhythm around it," she said. Then she struck a hard chord on her guitar and the new amplification startled Zoomer enough to make him jump. "There's a double humbucker pickup inside."

She'd once heard Jimmy and Roscoe arguing about a double humbucker pickup and remembered the name. She had no idea what the two of them had put into her guitar to amplify it or how it worked. All she knew was that it produced a nasally tone and sometimes feedback.

"Fuck," Zoomer muttered.

She dragged the only microphone away from Zoomer, grabbed a chair, sat down. She felt strangely amped, ready to turn cartwheels. But the baby inside her hung low in her middle like a sandbag so she thought it prudent to sit. She started adjusting the microphone wondering why she cared about impressing the obnoxious Zoomer.

"You can't even fuckin' stand up?" he sneered.

"Hey asshole, I'm two people here and at least one of us can play better than you," Gloria snapped. His eyes narrowed to slits and he opened his mouth to respond. Then Gloria blasted him with her own fiery guitar riposte, a fingerpicking explosion of sound that she'd learned listening to Merle Travis and Chet Atkins records. With her right hand, she picked out bass lines using her thumb, while her second, third and fourth fingers played rhythm and melody. Many folk, country and classical players were great fingerpickers, and with an amplified guitar, especially one with a tendency to lurch into feedback spasms, it sounded spectacular.

An hour later, they'd turned her song into a hard rocking piece as musically good as anything she, Roscoe and Jimmy had done. It had three guitar parts — the heavy anchoring chords that the bass and rhythm guitarists played following Zoomer's original quirky cadence; Gloria's aggressive chugging boogie woogie rhythm that propelled the song; and Zoomer's loud distorted lead notes skittering into the scant spaces left by the others and soaring to frenetic crescendos after each verse and at the end of the song. An obnoxious guy, but undeniably a talented player.

Gloria loved the result, and hated it too. The feverish scream of guitars overwhelmed her lyrics. She'd written a song about separated lovers. She'd tried to make it uplifting, reflecting the faith of true lovers that they'd be together again. She couldn't sing or play it without thinking about Jimmy. But Zoomer poured his angry gasoline over her smoldering melody to create a roaring inferno, kicking up a beautiful a nuclear mushroom cloud and obliterating her song just as effectively.

He didn't appreciate her efforts either.

"Fuckin' lyrics are no goddam good. Other than that, it rocks," Zoomer said. He looked at Gloria. "You might be halfway good if you got yourself a real guitar instead of that double humfucking acoustic piece of shit."

Fuming, Gloria sat frozen in her chair looking at a blank spot on the wall, trying to calm herself, thinking about loving Jimmy, about loving the child growing inside her. She believed in love. Anger felt bad. She had to get out of there. "Like I said, it's my song."

Zoomer picked up the whiskey bottle and took a long swallow.

"Time for a break," he said, leering at the three girls. "Who's up? I think it's you, Jessica. To the van!"

Putting down his guitar, he marched out of the room with the bottle and Jessica in tow. Gloria looked at the remaining three musicians.

"Zoomer says he can't function without a lot of sex," the drummer explained, rolling his eyes. "Be gone for half an hour, maybe an hour."

"Is he always such an asshole?"

The three musicians looked uncomfortable until the drummer shrugged and answered. "Yeah, sometimes, but he's a good guitar player, really good. Won't take any crap from the club managers. Makes sure we get what's ours and he's fair about the split. But I guess he don't like it when he's not the best player in the room. Damn, but you're amazing."

With great effort, Gloria rose to her feet and unplugged her guitar, feeling weak and unsettled. While she found Zoomer unpleasant, playing with his band had been a blast, the most musical fun she'd had since Jimmy left. And despite the ruination of her song, she felt like she'd learned a lot.

"Well, good luck, but I don't want to work anymore with Zoomer."

One of the two remaining teenage girls stood up. "I think I wanna go home. Could I hitch a ride with you?"

"Where do you live?" Gloria asked.

"Bowling Green."

"Where's that?" Gloria asked.

"It's south of Toledo, maybe twenty miles," the drummer said. "We played there three nights ago."

"I could drop you off at the bus station," Gloria said.

As they exited the room, Gloria asked the girl her age.

"Eighteen. I'm eighteen," she replied.

"No you're not. Tell me the truth. I'm not gonna do anything. I'm just curious," Gloria said.

"I'm fourteen, almost fifteen," the girl admitted.

"How about your two friends?"

"Um, Jessica's fifteen or sixteen. She's a year aheada me at school. I think Noel's younger. I just met her. She's from Steubenville." She hung her head. "I don't have any money for a bus."

"Can you call your parents?"

"I live with my mother. She's divorced. Probably can't miss work to come get me, if that's what you're thinkin'."

"Don't you think she might be worried about you?"

"I doubt it. She doesn't come home a lotta nights, especially weekends. She's a cocktail waitress at a hotel. Makes extra when they got conventions. Says it's paid dates. Like she doesn't think I know what she's doin'."

Gloria sighed. "I can give you money for a bus ticket. My purse is in the president's office. Why don't you go back and see if Noel wants to leave too."

The girl looked at Gloria for moment then started back down the hallway. Gloria got her purse from Zimmerman's office then went back out thinking she didn't really want to talk to the girl anymore. It reminded her of impending motherhood. But Gloria had run away from home too, and without help from people like Mrs. Lincoln she might not have survived. She took two twenty-dollar bills from from her purse hoping it was enough for bus fare.

Leaning against a wall, thinking about what she should do, she suddenly became aware that she was wet, very wet. At first she thought she'd peed her pants, but knew she hadn't.

"Oh God, it's time." She slid down the wall to the floor.

-19-

April, Long Binh Base Camp, Vietnam

"Goddam, the CO wants us back tonight." Nesterenko came out of the Operations bunker where he'd called the 99th to see if they could spend the night at Long Binh. "Fuckin' Moss is stayin' over 'cause they're goin' back to that fuckin' Green Beret base tomorrow morning."

"What are they doing over there?" Hayes asked.

"I don't know. Whatever it is, it's classified. Anyway, Ops needs us bright and early tomorrow morning," Nesterenko said. Then he brightened. "Mr. Donaldson, you'll get some IFR practice."

IFR meant instrument flight rules where pilots navigated by instruments without reference to the ground. Nesterenko began talking to Donaldson about navigating back to Nui Binh in the dark.

What could the Green Berets possibly want with a single gunship? The Green Berets, or Army Special Forces, usually operated in small teams. And slicks transported the teams, not gunships.

As Nesterenko and Donaldson headed for the helicopter, Flowers tugged at Hayes' arm to hold him back.

"I saw Delaney a little while ago," he said in a hoarse whisper. "I think he was drunk and smoking weed. Tried to pick a fight with me for talkin' about Jesus."

"Not everybody wants to hear about Jesus all the time, Flowers. I don't mind, but Delaney… he's touchy as hell lately. Remember how pissed he got when we caught him smokin' weed that morning."

Hayes stopped talking when Nesterenko abruptly turned to him.

"Well, shit, if we gotta fly back in the dark, what say we see if we can get some steaks first?" At lunch, Nesterenko, Donaldson and Flowers had found hamburgers, not steaks. However, they'd easily passed Flowers off as another pilot. Nesterenko had several extra warrant officer insignia, including a pair for Hayes. Hayes cleaned himself up as best he could, rubbing out most of the dirty stains on his jungle fatigues and undoing the laces around his calves. He even managed to shave. Nesterenko appraised him. "You'll do. Wouldn't pass inspection at flight school but you look better than Pigpen."

Steve 'Pigpen" Wilson, a notoriously sloppy warrant officer, flew in one of the 99th's slick platoons.

This time they got small steaks, but steaks nevertheless.

"Jesus, we must be the only people in here who aren't drinkin'," Nesterenko said as he looked around the crowded room.

"Wine is a mocker, strong drink a brawler and whoever is led astray by it is not wise. Proverbs," Flowers said patting the Bible in his jungle shirt pocket. The other three looked at him. "What? I've drunk beer before, just don't tell my mother about it."

"Well, one beer makes me sleepy," Nesterenko said.

"One beer makes me horny," Donaldson said. They all laughed.

"If you ever meet my wife, Marina, we'll be drinking tea or coffee," Nesterenko said.

"I think we better get outta here," Hayes said. He'd spotted Major Kucharski at the bar. "There's a major at the bar who knows I'm a Spec Four."

Hayes twisted away and hunkered lower to hide his face from Kucharski.

Nesterenko laughed. "Don't worry. He's a fuckin' major. He won't remember you from all the other spec fours he sees. Spec fours are just background clutter to him."

"No, he will. I was talkin' to him just today."

Nesterenko looked at him. "Okay, we need to split anyway. Gonna be late by the time we get back."

They made their way toward the door, Hayes trying to keep the others between him and Kucharski.

"Hey, that's Moss," Nesterenko said. Hayes looked and saw Kucharski talking to Moss. At the same moment, Kucharski's eyes found Hayes. He motioned them over.

"Mr. Hayes, I certainly didn't expect to see you here. Introduce me to your friends," Kucharski said. Nesterenko, Donaldson and especially Moss all looked surprised. Flowers took a step toward the door but Hayes grabbed his arm. No use in making things worse.

"Ah, sir, these are warrant officers Nesterenko, Donaldson and um, Flowers," he said, wondering about the punishment for impersonating an officer.

Moss, one arm leaning on the bar, tried to pretend he didn't know them. *Knows we're in trouble.*

"Nesterenko. Isn't that Ukrainian?" Kucharski asked.

"Yes sir, very good. Most people wouldn't know that."

"My name, Kucharski, is Polish but my family actually came from the Ukraine." The major paused. "I understand good officers take care of their men, but there were steaks at the enlisted mess too." He raised his hand in the same gesture he'd used earlier. "It's okay. I wanted to speak to Mr. Hayes."

Pulling Hayes away from the others, Kucharski spoke in a low voice. "What we talked about earlier? I'll order Sergeant Suggs to investigate when he gets back. I heard that he has some experience in these things." Then his face toughened. "But let me repeat that this is highly classified. Under no circumstances are you to talk to anyone about it, including officers in your own unit."

Kucharski turned around, faced the others. "Good to meet you, gentlemen. Carry on."

On the way back to the gunship, Nesterenko and Donaldson pestered Hayes for more information.

"Look, it's classified. I can't talk about it."

"Okay, okay," Nesterenko said. "You're something else, Hayes. You appeared to be quite well acquainted with that major."

They ambled four abreast in the dim light filtering out of Long Binh's buildings, hearing music from stereos and smelling marijuana. Nobody said anything about it. Hayes thought some barriers of rank had crumbled. He hoped they would keep flying together but knew when Donaldson made aircraft commander he and Nesterenko would be split up.

"Mitchell was my best friend. I miss him every day but he's with the Lord now," Flowers said, his voice catching. Donaldson patted him on the back as Flowers kept talking. "Blessed are those who mourn, for they shall be comforted. That's Matthew."

"You sure do know your Bible Flowers. My mom would approve," Donaldson said.

They untied the rotor and Hayes went through the pre-flight checklist carefully with Nesterenko. Hayes used a flashlight to check the fluid levels, then climbed up to look at the rotor. Finally, he examined the logbook. But Nesterenko, who had ultimate responsibility as aircraft commander, wanted to take off as quickly as possible.

"I don't know. All that time Long Binh Maintenance had the ship, all they did was replace the fuckin' warning light. I guess they did some wiring too. Same thing our guys did this morning," Hayes said to Nesterenko.

"Yeah, well, they signed off on it. Probably a little electrical glitch or some shit. I'm not gonna worry about it. It turns on and the ship flies fine. We gotta get goin'. I wanna get at least a couple hours sleep."

Donaldson, flying by instruments only, climbed the ship to 1,500 meters. Hayes looked at lights sparkling below, the expanse of Saigon, the blackness of the winding Saigon River and vehicles on roads. But when they left Saigon behind and sailed over jungle, the lights disappeared and he fought to stay awake.

At 2029 Hours somewhere over the Iron Triangle, Donaldson said, 'Aw, that fuckin' light again—"

"Turning off master caution," Nesterenko said.

"Shit, transmission temp's up, chip detector's on." Hayes detected a little panic in Donaldson's voice but the ship began descending smoothly. He leaned out peering down at the darkness knowing he could see below better than the pilots.

"I'm taking it," Nesterenko said and their rate of descent immediately increased. Now Hayes heard a new screeching, grinding sound, felt vibrations through his feet, heard Donaldson on the radio giving their position, ending with a panicked, "We're going down."

"Losing RPMs." Nesterenko's voice still calm but speaking fast. "Hayes, Flowers, see anything?"

"Nothing," Hayes started, "no, wait, trees!"

He heard the slowing beat of the rotor, knew they must have lost lift, the grinding screech sounded louder. The skids ripped through tree branches.

Flowers said, "Our Father, who art in heav—"

All in the same split second, the ship violently lurched, Hayes' side tilting upward. He heard a loud staccato cracking and tearing as the rotors smashed trees, his vision exploding into searing whiteness then back to black.

-20-

Detroit

Later, Gloria learned she'd endured nineteen hours of labor. Her doctor, Emily Sadowski, had left town to visit her sister. A colleague, Heinrich Schumacher, MD, a disciple of Carl Gauss, who pioneered a technique known as twilight sleep, handled the delivery. Schumacher and Gloria had never met until she arrived at the hospital. He immediately began massaging Gloria's abdomen with cold hands just as she felt the first sharp labor contraction. She screamed.

"I haff to turn your child around," the doctor said. Upset that a total stranger touched her so intimately and almost paralyzed from the pain, she locked up, unable to speak.

Long afterwards, Gloria learned that twilight sleep involved morphine to alleviate pain accompanied by a dose of scopolamine, which caused amnesia. In theory, women gave birth with little or no pain. Even if they experienced pain, they wouldn't remember it or much else about the birth.

Schumacher did not believe in allowing husbands, family members or anyone else, in the delivery room and thus banished Mrs. Lincoln to a waiting room.

"I will not haff a Negro in here," Schumacher said.

For several weeks, Dr. Sadowski and Gloria had practiced breathing techniques, and Sadowski had promised to give Gloria medication only if she asked for it. Following her initial scream, Schumacher injected Gloria without asking. After she woke up, all Gloria remembered was wanting to hold her baby.

"My baby, where's my baby?" she asked several times.

"I can't say, but the doctor will speak to you in a minute," a nurse said, wheeling Gloria into a private room. Gloria felt spacey and incredibly relaxed. Then the German doctor entered her room accompanied by a tearful Mrs. Lincoln.

"Where's my baby?" Gloria asked again.

He fidgeted, looked past her. "Miss Doran, I am sorry to inform you that your baby boy did not survive. We heard his heart beating in the womb, but he failed to take a breath. God did not want this baby to live." He stood beside the bed looking past her for a moment, then shook his head and left.

Her body felt too comfortable for what her brain had just absorbed. "No, no," she whispered.

Mrs. Lincoln pulled a chair to the side of the bed and sat down heavily. She leaned close, smears under her eyes where tears had ruined her makeup. Gloria smelled the perfume the older woman always dabbed on her neck. She smelled her rouge.

"I'm so sorry Gloria. I… I…" Mrs. Lincoln's words died and she looked away. "There's a black cloud hanging over us… You probably haven't heard, but they shot Doctor King dead. Shot him at a motel in Memphis last night. I think there's gonna be another riot."

Gloria didn't say anything. She couldn't. Her mind wouldn't hold onto any single thought, even the death of her baby. She forgot about Martin Luther King as soon as she heard it. Shaking her head and groaning, Mrs. Lincoln took Gloria's limp right hand and clasped it in both of hers. Her tears started again and her voice went into a higher register.

"I don't know why I told you about Doctor King. This lady from the Red Cross came to the house last night, just before that Mister Zimmerman called about you going into labor. Then she came to the hospital with me. After a couple of hours, I told her to go home." She choked back tears and swiped at her eyes. She picked up Gloria's hand again, rubbing and squeezing it. "Oh dear, I'm doing it again, not telling you."

"What? What is it?"

"It's your Jimmy. He's missing in action. That's what the Red Cross lady told me."

-21-

The Iron Triangle, Vietnam

Hayes didn't think he'd lost consciousness, but later figured out that he had.

"Hayes, Hayes, is that you?" The voice weak but clear.

A leafy branch pressed against his nose and mouth. His shoulders and the back of his legs hurt. He stayed still, afraid to move, afraid he might not be able to move. Except for the voice, he could hear nothing else.

"Hayes, answer me godammit. I heard you."

He recognized Nesterenko. "I'm here."

"Good. Wasn't sure it was you."

"Uh, you okay sir?" Hayes asked.

"Sir? You don't hafta… no, can't move. Can't feel below my neck and shoulders. I'm… I think I'm dying."

"You sound pretty good for dying." And he did, Hayes thought.

"No… bleeding… weakness… it's gaining. Felt my spine snap… like a big electric shock… then nothing. Not gonna argue. Just want you to promise..."

"Promise?"

"If you get outta here, tell Marina… my wife, I didn't suffer. It's true, no pain. Can't feel… Strange feeling, not feeling..."

"Okay," Hayes said. He still didn't see how Nesterenko could die. He sounded too good. "Donaldson and Flowers?"

"Dead… probably. I heard you, nobody else… Was that Flowers sayin' the Lord's Prayer?"

"Yeah."

"He believes."

"Yeah."

"I try to."

Nesterenko's voice sounded weaker, and now Hayes realized that he was hearing him through the earphones in his helmet. Still strapped into his shoulder harnass, Hayes felt the pain in his shoulders and legs getting worse. And now he thought Nesterenko might be right about dying. He wiggled his own toes to see if he could.

"Moss doesn't… he's afraid of you," Nesterenko said, the words gurgling and barely audible. As Nesterenko's voice faded, Hayes thought he had died. But the pilot made a final heroic attempt to speak. The only word Hayes discerned was "Marina."

When Hayes moved his arms, his shoulders hurt, but he unfastened the shoulder harness, grabbed the top frame of the gunship to pull himself up and out of the seat. To his surprise, he dropped out of the helicopter right through the tree branches. His helmet jerked his head sideways and something hard smacked his side before he hit the ground. He rolled onto his back panting.

Then he heard voices.

-22-

Nui Binh Base Camp

Major Jerry Shiffman returned a salute from First Lieutenant Max Keyser with a wave. "Sit down, Max, sit down. You must be tired."

"I'm okay, but I'm starvin'. Missed dinner last night, haven't had any breakfast," Keyser said. His jungle fatigues and boots dirty, beads of sweat cut lines through the dirt on his face. He'd shed his flak vest and left it on the sandbagged wall outside Shiffman's hooch, but he still wore a .45 caliber pistol in a shoulder holster and had several extra magazines in pouches clipped onto his utility belt.

"Well, you might be able to get a sandwich at the officers' mess. This shouldn't take long," Shiffman said, extending a pack of Pall Mall cigarettes to Keyser. He lit cigarettes for both of them with a single match. "I need a quick read on what you found out there. And feel free to speculate. This is not an official report. We can write that up together later."

Keyser nodded and took a long drag on his cigarette as he gathered his thoughts. "Okay, we didn't find the wreck till almost 0330 about four hours after they went in. And the closest place we could set down was several hundred meters away. So it took almost an hour to get there."

"Heavy jungle?" Shiffman asked.

"Yeah, pretty heavy and we were worried about an ambush.

"As you should have been."

"From what we could see from the air, it didn't look like there were survivors. The 99th dropped flares so we saw the wreckage pretty good from the air."

Shiffman nodded and sucked in cigarette smoke. He didn't want to ask the next question but felt he had to. "Did it look like any of them lived after the crash."

"Well yeah. One of the pilots was probably alive for a little while. Looked like he bled out. But I think they'd been dead for at least two or three hours by the time we got there. One of the gunners died instantly. No doubt about it. We could see his neck was broken."

"What about the other one?" Shiffman asked.

Keyser's face tightened. "That's the weird thing. We only found three bodies. At least, so far—"

"What the? Could one of them've been thrown clear?" Shiffman picked up a ballpoint pen and scribbled in a notebook on his desk. "I can check and make absolutely sure that there were four of them on board when they left Long Binh."

"We searched the area again when it got light. Thought he coulda been hurt and wandered off. Didn't find him, but they're still lookin'. The chopper ended up nose down, mostly on its side. That dead gunner was on the bottom of everything, and we could barely see him. We won't get his body until they pull that bird up. But we got the two pilots out."

"What about Charlie? I heard the radio chatter. Sounded like they got there first."

"Sure as hell did. All the rockets in one pod were gone, and they got a mini-gun, and an M60 machine gun. They got the pilots' personal weapons. They probably got a lot of ammo. If the high-side gunner had an M16, then they got that. They got the all the radios, including the handheld emergency one. Whatever maps they had, they got those too."

"Shit," Shiffman said. He studied Keyser for a few moments. The lieutenant expected promotion to captain soon, and Shiffman knew he hoped to get command of a company. "So tell me. What do you think happened to that gunner?"

"I think he might be a prisoner. I didn't find any blood where he would have been sitting, and I looked carefully. Like I said, he was on the high side. Not as much damage there. I would have expected anyone in that position to survive, though he coulda been hurt bad."

"Anything else?"

"Well, I don't know if this is solid enough to go in a report, but I believe there were two separate enemy units involved. It was muddy so we saw a lot of footprints. We trampled it pretty good ourselves, but a lot of the footprints were for sure not American. If I were to venture a wild-assed guess, I'd say one of the groups was Saigon area VC or NVA. Those guys are better equipped than your average VC troop. I saw at least two different non-American bootprints."

"Well that doesn't mean there were two different groups. I doubt the Saigon Charlies all have the same boots—"

"I know that. But after we got some light, I circled the area looking for that gunner again. I found sandal prints. Not many, but they were those rubber tire sandals. And they went off in a different direction than those bootprints.

"Huh, okay. We'll put that in the report. No downside to putting that in." Shiffman stubbed out his cigarette in a tin ashtray made from an old C-Ration cracker tin. "One more thing. You said you could see enough of the gunner to tell he broke his neck. Was he black, or white?"

"He was definitely black," Keyser said.

Shiffman went to his notebook and flipped back a page so he could see the names of the missing flight crew that he'd written down earlier, though he remembered them. "That means the missing gunner is the crew chief, James Hayes, a soldier I've met."

Shiffman stood. "Go see if you can find some breakfast."

When Lieutenant Keyser left, Shiffman sat again, lit another cigarette. For more than five minutes, he sat, smoking and thinking. Then he picked up the phone and began making calls.

-23-

Detroit

Barely awake, confused, a sense of dread dominating a roiling brew of emotions, Gloria opened her eyes.

"Tell me what happened?"

Gloria moved her head a little to the side to see Dr. Emily Sadowski sitting in a chair beside her bed. She wore jeans and a red leather jacket, the first time Gloria had ever seen her without her white medical coat. The doctor's lips pressed tight together, her eyes avoiding Gloria's, her fingers twisting a tissue.

"My baby… I want to see my baby."

Sadowski shook her head and inhaled. "Your baby is… gone, Gloria."

"No, no, no. Why can't I see my baby?"

"They told you that your baby was stillborn. Don't you remember?"

"I hardly remember anything." Actually, she did remember but clung to a hope it might be all a dream. It felt like a suffocating dream, a dream so terrible that every new breath brought more horror.

"Where am I?" she asked, confused.

"You're in Hutzel Hospital, in a private room and your baby died because of that stupid, stupid doctor. Schumacher and his twilight sleep garbage. He shouldn't be allowed to practice medicine. He's a quack."

Suddenly more awake, more memories burst into her sludgy awareness. "Jimmy, he's..."

"I'm going to get out of this goddam practice if I have to go back to waiting tables." Sadowski stopped and looked at Gloria. "Sorry. But what do you remember about the delivery?"

Gloria didn't want to answer, but said, "I sort of remember a lot of pushing and finally feeling the baby come out."

"You didn't have any pain?"

"No." But she also remembered Mrs. Lincoln telling her about Jimmy. She forced the thought away by concentrating on the loss of her baby. For a moment she felt relieved that she wouldn't have to care for a baby. Then an avalanche of guilt buried her.

My fault, my fault. Stupid fucking teenager getting knocked up.

She decided that if Jimmy died, it would be her fault. Anything or anyone she loved turned to shit, the proof being what had happened to her baby. She'd loved her baby with all her heart.

She closed her eyes, wishing Sadowski would leave so she could go back to sleep and not wake up. Instead, Mrs. Lincoln and Logan Carlton barged into the room. She cracked open her eyes, saw Mrs. Lincoln carrying a big platter.

"I made an omelet, just like that one you said you liked last week, and a great big cinnamon roll. They got one of them new radar ranges here so we heated it up," Mrs. Lincoln said.

Sadowski eased out of the room as Gloria mumbled, "Not hungry."

"But you haven't eaten for a long time," Mrs. Lincoln said. She carefully laid her platter down on the hospital bedside rolling tray and pushed it inches from Gloria's face. The sweet cinnamon and savory omelet fragrances washed over her. She closed her eyes again, felt tears seeping out but concentrated on her self-loathing.

"Jesus, look at all these fuckin' flowers," Carlton said.

"Logan, watch your mouth."

"Sorry. There's one from that lawyer, another from the record company, and here's mine. Jeez, look at the size of this arrangement. Who the hell is Zoomer?"

A faint scent of cigar smoke joined the cinnamon and omelet smells, and Carlton spoke softly into her ear. "It's going to be okay, Gloria. We'll help you, Frances and me. We'll start working on your future. You got a bright future, girl."

Not hungry. Not hungry. Not worthy.

They stayed for a long time while Gloria locked her eyes shut and said nothing. Finally, they gave up and left.

She opened one eye to inspect the cinnamon roll. Seeing no one in the room, she seized the roll and devoured it in a series of giant bites. Minutes later, she gobbled down the omelet, almost choking on it.

Dr. Schumacher arrived. She kept her eyes open the better to fuel her hate. Steeling herself, she said nothing as he examined her with cold hands. She answered his questions with nods, head shakes and grunts.

"You haff recovered. I will discharge you."

Half an hour later, Gloria sat in a wheelchair dressed in old, but clean hospital scrub pants and the smock she'd worn to the record company. Her guitar and a shopping bag full of supplies rested on her lap. As two nurses instructed her on post delivery care, Gloria responded with more grunts and nods while everything they said sank into the murky sludge of her mind.

Stupid teenager hopping into bed with Jimmy a few hours after I met him. I'm a filthy slut.

"Gloria! Is that you?"

Barely conscious, she opened her eyes, realizing she had dozed off as an orderly wheeled her to the hospital lobby.

"It's me, Susanna." She saw Susanna in tight jeans and a red peasant blouse hurrying across the lobby towards her.

"Susanna…"

"I'll take her now, thank you." Susanna took over the wheelchair as the orderly hurried away. "I'll take you outside. Who's picking you up?"

"Um…" Gloria made a tiny shrug.

"Where are you going? Mrs. Lincoln's house?"

Gloria groaned and Susanna stopped the wheelchair beside the exit door. She stepped around the wheelchair to look at Gloria.

"You don't look well. I can't believe they're letting you out of here."

Gloria shut eyes tight trying to block the tears.

"Just leave me," she murmured. "I'm no good."

Susanna muttered something, then pushed the chair through the door.

"I'll go get my car." She smiled. "Don't run off now."

Soon, Gloria sat in the front seat of Susanna's rusty red VW Beetle. Waiting outside, the cold air and gusty wind had revived her. But inside the car, her head lolled forward and she dozed again. Still, she was aware of the shifting gears, acceleration and braking, tires rattling over bumpy pavement, the clickety roar of the freeway and the air blasting around the noisy car. When they stopped, she forced her eyes open to see a shabby, two-story wooden house with a steep staircase outside leading up to the second floor. Susanna opened the passenger door and helped Gloria out. She could hear the roar of a nearby freeway.

"We're by Seven Mile Road and the Lodge. The freeway's less than half a block from here, but you get used to the noise," Susanna said. "Here, let me take that bag of stuff. Think you can make it up the stairs?"

Gloria began plodding up the stairs. Halfway up, she paused to rest, worried that she might start bleeding again. When she reached the top, Gloria leaned against a railing, making it creak.

"Careful, it's a little loose," Susanna said.

"Serve me right," Gloria said, looking down at the street.

Susanna opened the door, helped Gloria inside and sat her on a battered couch. Gloria looked around at the scratched hardwood floor and peeling paint. It reminded her of some of the boarding houses where she'd stayed when she'd run away from home.

"God's truth, it ain't much, but I could use some company." Susanna sat beside her, squeezed her shoulder. "Just us girls here. I threw Antoine out. We had a big fight. Got tired of all his black power bullshit. He couldn't pay any rent again this month, but he bought himself a damn shotgun."

"Shotgun?" Gloria mumbled.

They sat for a few minutes, neither saying anything.

"I know about the baby, but Mrs. Lincoln said something about your boyfriend?"

"He's missing in action. He might be…" She stopped not wanting to complete the thought, not wanting to do anything except go back to sleep.

"The father of the baby you lost? Oh my god, I'm so sorry."

Gloria barely heard her before she fell asleep again. When she awoke lying on the couch, the light coming through the windows had dimmed.

Susanna, carrying a mug of something hot, handed it to Gloria.

"It's tea," Susanna said. "Why don't you stay here tonight? We can talk or not talk. I'll get a pizza if you're hungry."

"You don't have to do anything for me, Susanna. I'm not worth it. I'm no good to anyone. I'm just a stupid teenager who got knocked up and couldn't even get that right. It'll be my fault if Jimmy doesn't make it 'cause I'm bad luck to everyone."

"C'mon, stop beating yourself up." Susanna towered over her, her hands on her hips, her big afro framing a face showing a tinge of anger. "I mean it Gloria. You got hit with a load of shit, and you get a pass for a little while, but you gotta work through it. I know you can do it. Don't you think your Jimmy's gonna want you to stay strong?"

Gloria stared past Susanna for a long moment, then wiped her wet eyes with her sleeve. "Okay," she said quietly and sipped some tea.

-24-

Vietnam

After falling a dozen times, Hayes fell again but this time when he started to get up, someone pushed him back down.

"What the fuck?" he muttered.

Spasms of pain shot through his back and left shoulder whenever he moved. His neck hurt worse, especially when he raised his head. The backs of his upper legs felt like someone had whacked them with a baseball bat. The aluminum seat frame must have slammed into his legs in the crash. He had the worst headache of his life, sometimes saw double and threw up several times. But he didn't have any broken bones, could walk, and move his arms, legs and even his head though it hurt to do so. He kept his head down. Despite the darkness, he could make out obstacles on the ground but bumped into small tree trunks. Branches lashed his face. Every jerk of a rope tied around his wrists hurt.

Resting on his hands and knees, he peered at a tree root in the mud and noticed the first traces of morning light. They'd been moving for almost three hours, according to his watch. He carefully rolled over to a sitting position, trying unsuccessfully to prevent the shockwaves of pain radiating from his neck.

"Water," he begged when he heard someone drinking through the nasally Vietnamese chatter. It sounded like an argument. He thought the group numbered as few as three but no more half a dozen individuals.

Despite the pain, he thought about escape. His captors didn't appear well-trained. They'd talked as they walked and moved too fast to take precautions. He doubted American soldiers would have followed a well-worn path like the one they were on. He'd smelled cigarette smoke. No American soldier out at night would light a cigarette and he didn't think the VC would either.

He pleaded again. "Water. I need some water."

An American canteen bumped his head, dialing up his headache.

Someone understands English.

In order to drink, he had to raise his arm and his head. It hurt like hell but he gulped down several big mouthfuls until someone snatched the canteen away. Then he vomited.

After prodding him to his feet, they walked slowly for a few minutes before stopping again. Steeling himself, Hayes raised his head.

Beyond a hatless shadowy man holding the rope stood three huts outlined by the dawn light of the eastern sky. The huts were surrounded by a lot of water. Rice paddies? No, but something else grew in the water, something with a sweet fruity fragrance. Trying to keep his head and neck locked, he carefully turned his entire body around to look behind him. Four Vietnamese in black pajama clothing squatted on a narrow dike of packed dirt separating two big ponds of water. That made five people, counting the man with the rope. Two carrying bolt-action rifles wore floppy hats. A third one wore

Hayes' flight helmet, had his M16 and had slung the bandolier of ammunition over his shoulder. The man with the M16 sneered at Hayes and hefted the rifle. The fourth individual, a woman next to Hayes, squatted on the dike, a long braid of hair hanging down her back. She held a large revolver that looked like an antique. She pointed it at Hayes' groin.

He postponed his escape plans.

Rope Man said something to the others. Then he jerked Hayes hard, making him lose his balance and cry out from the bolt of pain that shot through his body. He fell, got smacked in the ribs with a rifle but stumbled to his feet. They moved fast along the dike and up a slope until they got to one of the huts. It had a little shed.

Rope Man opened the door to the shed. It contained old, dirty farm implements. Rope Man kicked them aside, scraped away dirt and pulled up a trap door. Then he pushed Hayes down the hole.

Hayes bumped down steep uneven stairs that twisted to one side. In the darkness at the bottom, Rope Man squeezed past him, flicked on a flashlight, then grunting from the effort, slid a heavy wooden panel aside. A moment later, the flashlight illuminated an underground chamber. Rope Man pushed him inside.

The Vietnamese man chattered away as he shone the flashlight around the room. It appeared to be several dozen feet long and about twenty feet wide. A big chamber. Scavenged American pallets covered most of the floor. Some had old mattresses or straw mats on top. The place smelled musty like a long shut basement. Rope Man pointed the flashlight at a big, dented metal container with a little tap on the bottom. He picked up an old C-ration can, one of half a dozen littering the floor, and poured a little liquid into the can. He took a sip and handed the can to Hayes.

"Eau," he said, and repeated it several times. *Water*. Hayes drank all the water in the little can.

At the back of the room, Rope Man lifted a rusty metal pail, held it at his waist and with some perfectly clear vulgar movements, made Hayes understand the pail constituted a toilet.

"Pisse… merde."

"Piss, shit," Hayes said. Rope Man used French words. Hayes had learned enough French in Michigan's Upper Peninsula and from visiting his uncle's cousin in Ontario to understand him.

The flashlight lingered on a cardboard box beside the pail. It contained old newspapers and other discarded paper. Rope Man made more vulgar gestures.

Toilet paper.

Finally, he pointed the flashlight at Hayes' face, re-igniting his headache and effectively blinding him. Hayes heard Rope Man backing away and the wooden barrier scraped shut leaving Hayes in total darkness. He heard a faint rattle followed by a snap. Then nothing. He strained to hear more. He opened his eyes wider and saw nothing.

Silence.

Darkness.

A few hours later

Hayes awoke enveloped in the total darkness, panting and sweating. Lying on his side on a pallet, he shivered, his hands still tied together.

"Goddammit, get your shit together!" he yelled bringing back his headache. But the rest of his pain had lessened. He started wiggling one wrist, trying to slide it out of the loops. That hurt his neck but he kept working. The binding around his wrists didn't feel as tight as when his captors first tied him. Maybe the rope had stretched. It felt slippery. He could just touch the knots with the tips of his fingers. Blessed with long fingers, years of playing guitar had made them strong and nimble. He pulled and twisted with his hands trying to stretch the bonds more. He picked at the knot with his teeth. Eventually, his two middle fingers could finally reach the same loop on a knot. He stretched and wiggled his fingers to gain purchase. After a long time he thought he might have loosened the loop slightly, but his forearms began cramping from the effort.

He rested for a moment and had an idea. He got up and slowly moved around until he found the container of water. Examining the little faucet by feel, he turned it on and wet the bonds before turning it off again. This time, after a long, hard pull, one hand slid free.

He celebrated by pouring himself a can of water, and then a second. Savoring each swallow of cool water as it ran down his throat, along with the expected flash of pain, he noticed something else. His jungle shirt sleeve had ridden up and he saw the hands of his wristwatch, a Seiko diver's watch with a patina of something on the hands that made them glow a greenish yellow in the dark. He pushed the watch farther up his wrist so his jungle shirt would hide it. They'd already taken his belt, wallet and dog tags. He still had his boots, but they'd probably be gone soon. And they'd taken the shoelaces he tied around his lower legs. He checked his pockets and found a P-38 can opener that they'd missed when they searched him. Slightly more than an inch long, the P-38 had a small, curved blade on a hinge and was used to open cans. It worked well on C-ration cans, which had softer metal than civilian cans. But you could open the civilian cans with a P-38 with enough effort.

"It'll cut this rope."

Hayes found the rope where he'd dropped it. Pulling it through his hands, he estimated he had thirty-five or forty feet of rope. Sawing at it with the P-38, he cut off a piece long enough to loosely encircle his waist twice. His captors would surely take their rope back when they found he had gotten loose. Hopefully, they wouldn't notice the missing piece.

"This ain't Charlie's A-Team," he muttered, "and now I have a garrote."

He fell asleep again but the clunk of the door awakened him. He pulled up his shirt sleeve, glanced at his watch, 1714 Hours, late afternoon. The barrier slid open and Rope Man entered, a flashlight in his hand. The light played over Hayes' face, revived his headache. Then the flashlight found and lingered on the rope. Rope Man said something in Vietnamese that sounded like a joke as he picked up the rope. He gestured toward the door with the flashlight. Gritting his teeth, Hayes slowly got to his feet. The light moved around enough for him to see heavy wooden beams that looked like old railway ties reinforcing the room. The chamber looked very old and perhaps had originally been a big bomb shelter. The room might withstand everything except a direct hit.

Rope Man got behind Hayes, pushed him through the door and up the stairs.

At the top of the stairs, he saw the woman who earlier had carried the old revolver. Now she held a Polaroid camera. A pretty adolescent girl stood beside her. While he looked, the woman raised her blouse slightly to show him the revolver. At the side of the house, Rope Man took Hayes' arm and turned him around so the sun shone on his face. The two moved several feet to one side, then they stepped away. The woman said something to the girl.

"Please… Mer-ree-can, raise up head… head up." The young girl struggled with each syllable. Before he could comply, Rope man pushed Hayes' head up, making him cry out in pain. This set off a flurry of Vietnamese chatter.

"You sick… no, hurt?" the girl asked.

"Neck," Hayes said. He put his hands on his neck. "My neck hurts when I raise my head. My head hurts." He pointed to his neck, his shoulders and his head, groaning loudly as he touched each. After more conversation, they moved away from him. The girl took the camera from the woman and spoke in Vietnamese as she pointed at Hayes. The woman nodded. Rope Man joined them and listened to the girl as well. Then the girl crouched and snapped a picture. The three kept talking as they waited for the picture to develop.

With his head still slightly raised, he looked around and saw a few people visible in the distance. They seemed to be working in and around the big ponds.

Once again, he considered making a break. His hand slipped inside the top of his pants to finger the purloined rope. But with his injured neck and shoulder, he might not have the strength to strangle Rope Man. And the woman had the gun. Could he smash their heads with something? He saw several big stones on the ground. And he remembered the farm tools in the shed. Or he could just run for it. He could run fast. If he could make it to the bush, he might have a chance. But he couldn't outrun a bullet. Perspiration popped out on his forehead

After his captors looked at the picture, they took another. Then the woman and the girl left. Rope Man led him back toward the hut. When they reached the shed where the stairs led underground. Hayes spotted a short hoe just inside the door, the perfect weapon. Rope Man leaned into the doorway of the hut jabbering in Vietnamese. But now Hayes saw that he had the large revolver in one hand. The woman must have given it to him.

"Ahhh, damn," he said. All the tenseness left and he felt weak.

Two small children, a boy and a girl, came out of the house. The girl carried a steaming bowl and handed it to Hayes. Rope Man pointed with the gun at an old lawn chair and Hayes sat down. The bowl contained a rich soup, rice balls, meat that tasted like fish and unfamiliar vegetables. It smelled of the Vietnamese fish sauce, which most Americans, including Hayes, didn't like. They'd given him a spoon and chopsticks, which he didn't know how to use. Hungry, he stuffed the food into his mouth with the spoon. Then he drank the liquid from the bowl. The children laughed at him. The soup tasted like nothing he'd ever eaten before. But in less than a minute he finished it and handed the bowl back to the girl. She disappeared into the hut and returned with the refilled bowl. He ate that one too, though more slowly. For a moment, he felt like he might vomit again, but the sick feeling passed quickly.

He realized this must be Rope Man's family. He didn't want to kill them. He didn't think he could.

When Hayes finished eating, he handed the bowl to girl and Rope Man spotted the watch, He took the watch and also Hayes' boots. Minutes later,Hayeswas back in the dank underground dungeon where he dreamed about Nesterenko, Flowers and Donaldson.

-25-

Nui Binh Base Camp

"That's definitely him," First Sergeant McConaughey said. He sat across the desk from Lieutenant Colonel Blair and held up the Polaroid picture of Jimmy Hayes.

"The picture was in an envelope found at the Cu Chi front gate right after the workers left last night. Could have been left there by any of them," Major Shiffman said.

"Was there anything else besides the picture?" Blair asked.

"Yes. They included Hayes' military ID and a letter written in Vietnamese. They want to trade Hayes for a political prisoner that the Saigon government locked up about six months ago. If we agree, we're supposed to hang a red handkerchief on the gate, and they'll send instructions.

"Are we gonna make the exchange?" Blair asked.

"I don't think so," Shiffman said.

"Why not?" snapped Blair. "Can't we lean on the government? Or is he a high-value prisoner of some kind?"

"No, he's just a Cao Dai priest. The problem is he's dead. They executed him for no good reason far as I can tell."

"Oh, shit," McConaughey said shaking his head.

They sat in silence until Shiffman spoke again. "I'm not feelin' very good about any of this. There was some indication that two different groups of enemy soldiers got to the wreck before us. So I'm thinking Specialist Hayes might have been captured by a Cao Dai paramilitary unit and not the Vietcong. In fact, there's some indication that the VC are looking for him too."

Blair picked up the picture to examine it again, but it was McConaughey who spoke. "Couldn't we just send somebody in to rescue Hayes? I never heard of these Cao Dai bastards before. They can't amount to much."

"Cao Dai's the third largest religion in Vietnam after Buddhism and the Catholics. It's kind of a weird blend of both those religions, along with some Hindu and some uniquely Vietnamese elements. They used to have their own militia when the French were here. Not so much now, but they still have a few armed groups."

Blair held up the picture. "Any clues in the pictures about where they might have Hayes?"

"We're workin' on it. You can see water, and something's being cultivated. It is definitely not rice. There are a lot of Cao Dai people and they live in a lot of places." Shiffman said. "We're workin' as fast as we can, but it may not be fast enough."

"What do you mean?" Blair said.

"All those workers coming into Cu Chi, we figure some of them are VC sympathizers. Even those that aren't are probably in contact with the VC. The Vietcong very well might find Hayes before we do."

"Oh, shit," McConaughey said.

"I have everyone I know in the Vietnamese military workin' on this. Maybe I'll get lucky."

-26-

Detroit

"I said you needed some time and didn't feel like talking to anybody."

Susanna, wearing a green and yellow Wayne State University sweatshirt, stood over Gloria, who lay in bed so mushy-headed she couldn't remember waking up. "Mmmm, what'd you say?"

"I called Mrs. Lincoln. Said you were staying here."

Then Gloria remembered. Her baby dead, Jimmy missing, Martin Luther King murdered. She sank, dark despair dragging her down. The baby who answered her with kicks when she spoke to him. Gone. And Jimmy?

"Sorry I woke you. I gotta go to class so if you need help getting some breakfast… You should eat something."

Then Gloria remembered collapsing in the bed the night before. But she didn't know if they'd shared the bed or if Susanna had slept somewhere else, on the couch, or perhaps the floor.

"I'll get up." Sitting up, Gloria groaned. With Susanna's help, she tottered to the bathroom, found her sanitary pad saturated, some blood on her thighs. After she finished cleaning up in the bathroom, she pulled another pad from the bag of supplies from the hospital. When she returned to the bedroom, Susanna had stripped blood-stained sheets from the bed. The blood had gone all the way through to produce a stain on the mattress. Disgusted, Gloria groaned. "I'm sorry. I should have… oh, I'm so sorry."

"What's the big fucking deal?" Susanna said. "It's natural. Every woman does it."

Too weak to stay on her feet, Gloria sagged onto the end of the mattress. "My stepfather… it would set him off if he saw, you know, any blood. And he'd beat up my stepmother, Gina, for it."

Susanna looked at her and shook her head.

After Susanna helped her take a shower, Gloria ate a bowl of oatmeal and drank a glass of orange juice only to feel nauseous.

"I have to go. I can't miss this test. It's fifty percent of my grade," Susanna said. "You gonna be okay? If you need help, I guess you'll have to call Mrs. Lincoln. But you're welcome to stay here long as you want. Like I said, I could use the company." She paused to look at the three cardboard boxes piled up beside the door. "That's Antoine's shit."

Later that morning

Heavy footsteps clumping up the wooden stairs to Susanna's second story flat preceded a tapping at the door.

"Who's there?" Gloria called.

"Me, Antoine." A key turned the lock, the door swung open. "Susanna, I'm sorry and—"

Antoine gaped at Gloria. He wore a khaki shirt with ridiculous red epaulets on the shoulders, khaki pants, a shiny gold badge pinned on the front of a brimmed khaki cap. He looked like a dictator from some African country. "Sunshine… er, Gloria. What are you doing here?"

Gloria saw Antoine's eyes drift to the boxes stacked beside the door.

"Susanna said if I didn't get my stuff outta here, she'd throw it out. I figured she'd be at class now. I still have my key…"

Gloria sat wrapped in a blanket on Susanna's ratty couch, her legs drawn up under her, afraid to move lest she trigger more bleeding, cramping or nausea. But she felt like the fog in her brain had started to clear.

"You don't look like you feel good," he said. His eyes shifting back to the boxes told her he didn't really care.

"Yeah, I'm not doing so great." Why did she say that? She bit her lip.

Antoine seemed not to hear. His attention stayed on the boxes. "Hey, where's my shotgun?"

"In the bedroom," Gloria said. "I was looking look at it, thinking of buying it from you."

"Not for sale." He strode into the bedroom and came out holding the shotgun. He smiled at it. "I got elected minister of defense."

She kept thinking about the shotgun. So many bad things had happened to her. But it was heavy, awkward and the pump seemed stiff when she'd tried it.

"I don't really want a shotgun, maybe a pistol. Could you do me a big favor, Antoine, and buy one for me?" She smiled, tried hard for sincerity. "I'll give you the money and pay extra."

That startled him. "You're about the last person in the world I'd expect to want a gun. You're one of those naïve peace-and-love, flowers-in-her-hair, white hippie chicks." He showed some teeth when he said it. Maybe an attempt at a grin to hide his condescension?

"Well, you really don't know me Antoine just like you didn't know Susanna. You're wrong about most of what you think about me, and some of it would surprise the hell out of you."

Talking to Antoine seemed to clear more fog in her head.

He stood holding the shotgun, staring at her. She knew they'd never liked each other. Unafraid, she stared right back, thinking about Jimmy and about the men he'd killed. So easy to underestimate Jimmy. His soft face, slender frame and easy-going manner masked a toughness and a capacity for violence. She wanted to feel tougher and be more like Jimmy.

"I know I blew it with Susanna. You can tell her that. I guess it's too late now."

Gloria detected some calculation in his voice. He looked down at the floor, avoiding eye contact. Then he looked up. "But what I'm doin's important. I can't stand by while white people keep on oppressin' us. That's something you wouldn't understand."

She shook her head. "You call me naïve? You don't know what you're talking about, Antoine. You're the one who's naïve, you and the rest of your revolutionary friends. My boyfriend's in Vietnam. He may be dead…"

The words stuck in her throat. She shouldn't have said them but she swallowed hard and continued. "He didn't have any choice. And don't give me your shit about going to Canada. Jimmy's like most of those soldiers. They never thought about what was going on over there—"

"Well, they shoulda thought about it instead of bein' pawns of the rich white imperialists that—"

"You mean like the way you're thinking about what you're gonna do with that shotgun? Really, Antoine, what *are* you gonna do? You gonna shoot it out with the cops like those Black Panthers in Oakland?"

"Black power. It's all about black power. We're gonna start an uprising. That's what the Panthers were doin'. We're gonna make the big white power pigs give us a coupla states, maybe three or four, and a lotta money too. Reparations, a black nation. Black people are owed that for bein' slaves, and black people will rise up when they get the chance. You wouldn't understand, Sunshine, 'cuz you ain't black. You don't come from slaves. If you were black, you'd get it. Even Susanna got it. She just didn't want to do nothin' about it, at least not yet. Once we act, once we start the uprising, she'll come 'round. Black people everywhere will get with it. That's black power."

He stopped and raised his clenched fist. "Black power, motherfuckers!"

Suddenly aware of his loud voice, he lowered his fist, shrugged, his hands palms out, face contrite. "I really don't have nothin' against most white people. Just the pigs in power. Don't have nothin' against you, Sunshine."

She watched Antoine maneuver to pick up the top two boxes and thought about Jimmy again. He could have gone to

Canada to avoid the draft. Jimmy had told her he'd spent several summers with his Uncle Sepp's cousin who lived in northern Ontario. Ten years old when he learned to play guitar in the cousin's polka band.

Why hadn't he gone to Canada?

Antoine kicked open the apartment door, his arms wrapped around two stacked boxes, the shotgun dangling from two fingers of one hand. He staggered through the door and down the stairs.

When the country called, Jimmy had answered, just like her father Clyde Bonaventure, like Logan Carlton, like her lawyer Pip Papineau, like the others with Jimmy in Vietnam. She hated the war. Thought Jimmy hated it too. Thought the fucking politicians running the country had made a big mistake. But that didn't make Jimmy wrong or naïve. It hit her that not only did she love Jimmy, she admired him. He hadn't taken the easy path. If he hadn't gone, they'd just send somebody else.

The positive thoughts about Jimmy revived her and gave her strength and, best of all, hope.

Antoine returned, still carrying the shotgun, like a soldier in a foreign army. How had he avoided the draft? What had Susanna ever seen in Antoine? Antoine looked at her, his face scornful.

"See, Antoine, I think you're the one who's naïve. All that shotgun's gonna do for you is maybe get you killed."

He stopped as he started to lift the third box, unable to let what she said pass. He dropped the box to the floor with a thud. "Tell me little Miss Sunshine Hippie Chick, why do you want a fucking gun?"

She put the question aside, felt quite adult about it too, then cut right to business. "So, Antoine, if you can get me a pistol, I'd prefer a revolver, but I'll take anything. I'll pay you twenty-five dollars more than whatever it costs. Just tell me how much you think it'll cost and I'll give you the cash. And oh yeah, I'll need bullets too."

Incredulous, Antoine opened his mouth, but before he could speak she went back to his question. "I'm a little worried somebody might be after me, and I'm not gonna sit on my ass. And I hope they're as naïve as you are about me, Antoine."

Antoine grunted, "Okay," picked up the box and went down the stairs. When he came back, she gave him fifty dollars from her purse and promised more when he got the gun. Then he left.

When his heavy steps faded, Gloria started to cry.

What if Jimmy doesn't come back? Is that why I want a fucking gun?

-27-

April and May, Vietnam

In total darkness, Jimmy Hayes sat on a pallet. Awake? Asleep? He didn't know. When he opened and shut his eyes, he saw no difference. No light, only impenetrable darkness. He dreamed that he woke up only to enter another dream that repeated, trapping him in a nightmare where he couldn't wake up. Had he died? Gone to hell or purgatory? He didn't understand purgatory.

"It's between heaven and hell," Gloria once told him. Or had she just spoken to him?

"Sunshine?" He looked around, didn't see her. "Gloria, are you here?" If he saw Gloria, that meant a dream, a good dream, a dream he clung to.

He ran fingers through his beard with one hand. He scraped the pallet with the other until he felt pain.

Pain. Awake, but no Gloria.

"She's going to have our baby." He thought about it. "She must have had our baby."

All the hours that had passed while he pretended to strum every chord, mouth every word of every song he knew in elaborate imaginary shows with all his heroes — Hank Williams, Buddy Holly, Chuck Berry, Bo Diddley, Roy Orbison, the Rolling Stones, the Beatles, but Gloria always the star. He tried to count days by the arrival of food. But sometimes days seemed to pass with no food. He dreamed about counting the days, mixed the dream count with the awake count. Thinking about the passage of time depressed him.

Dangerous, very dangerous.

So he gave up counting, gave up singing, tried to give up arguing with himself about sleeping or waking up. Why did it matter? Might as well sleep all the time.

A new thought intruded.

"If I die, she'll find someone new. Someone else will raise my son or daughter." He smiled, accepting the likelihood he'd soon join his dead comrades. "Your biggest mistake was falling in love with me, Sunshine. But you'll have another chance."

"No," she said. And this time she sat in front of him wearing the same green, pink and yellow dress she'd worn the night they'd met, her green eyes bright. She held her guitar, long fingers fluttering over the frets. But he heard no music. "Come home, Jimmy."

"I can't." But he couldn't remember what had happened to him.

Her guitar gone, Gloria now wore baggy, dirty sweats. She appeared so pregnant that her bare abdomen stuck out of the bottom of the sweatshirt. Her middle began inflating like a balloon. She splayed her hands over her swelling belly as she danced and sang, discordant, her stomach growing, stretching and bouncing like a giant water balloon. "You promised you'd come home."

A headache burned. "It hurts too much."

"A promise is a promise."

He saw her naked, no longer pregnant, legs splayed apart, guitar blocking his view of her sex. He stared, tried to see around the guitar. He reached for her, his fingers entwining the guitar strings. Then his fingers fell off one by one until he slid the stumps of his hands into the strings weaving them into a knot, casting them out into long silky lengths that extended to infinity.

"You promised," she whispered.

This time when he awoke, he had no doubt.

"No, no." He could no longer talk to Gloria. He wanted to go back to sleep to dream about Gloria. Offered a begging prayer to endure the waking nightmare forever for one more fleeting glimpse of Gloria. Instead he sat on the pallet cursing, filthy, itchy, rubbing his eyes with dirty knuckles, pounding the pallet so hard with his fist that he felt a board crack.

Then he heard faint muffled pops — the distinctive sound of fully automatic gunfire — then more random gunshots.

"Oh shit." He started counting like he'd seen a lightning flash.

At fourteen, the door crashed open. Dim light shocked his eyes. Screaming men with guns pushed inside. North Vietnamese? Vietcong? A blinding flashlight beam, a fist smashing into his side, hands grabbing under his arms. A hulking soldier, a huge Vietnamese, dragged him to the door, pulled him through and up the narrow twisting stairs. On the way up, Hayes looped fingers inside the soldier's leather belt, slid to a holster. Empty.

The big soldier slammed him down, kicked his face, but Hayes felt only joy at the expanse of silvery sky doubled by its reflection in a mirror of water speckled with white flowers.

Dawn, one more time before he died.

Head spinning, a taste of blood, his mouth numb, Hayes spat, started to push himself up. His hand slipped against warm wet flesh. He saw eyes, inches away staring into eternity from the flawless face of the girl who'd helped her mother with the camera when they took his picture. Her mother stretched out next to her, both torsos shiny with the gore of machine-gun exit wounds. Killed from behind. Hayes pulled his hand away, opened his mouth to vomit. The choking spasm brought up nothing. Blood dribbled from his nose and mouth onto the girl. His empty stomach heaved again.

When the big soldier pulled him off the dead girl, Hayes lashed at him catching him in the crotch. The big man doubled over, screamed a torrent of Vietnamese. Hayes tried to grab his pistol but more hands grasped his arms tight from behind, pinned him to the ground.

Hayes felt calm, ready to die, his insides clenched tight.

If they shoot me it'll shut all this off. Maybe I can grab a weapon and kill somebody first.

Some of the soldiers loosely held their weapons as they laughed with no humor, their eyes bright, disconnected. Hayes had seen it before after combat, men cracking sick jokes, taking pictures of bodies with Polaroid cameras. Once, the Headhunters had flown low over some dead Vietcong, killed with rockets. A pilot accidently left the radio channel open and they all heard Flowers intone, 'Let death take my enemies by surprise. Let them go down alive to the realm of the dead for evil finds lodging among them." Hayes remembered the words because somebody had asked Flowers about it and he'd written them down. The words had been tacked up in the Headhunter hooch with a Polaroid picture of the bodies until Sergeant Grugel found the picture and took it down.

But as Hayes scanned the group looking for his chance, he saw too many alert soldiers to act.

And he didn't want to die. Not yet.

An argument started. A soldier who'd acquired the antique pistol wanted to shoot Rope Man. Two soldiers restraining the wailing Rope Man resisted. The soldier waved the pistol around. He pointed it at Rope Man, made wet explosive sounds as he pretended to pull the trigger. Another soldier ran up from somewhere behind Hayes. He chortled and grabbed at the big antique revolver. They bumped together, the two lurching back and forth like two drunks squabbling, the other soldiers watching and laughing. The two ended up directly behind Rope Man, who was bent over and kneeling, no longer restrained but crying and screaming. The two soldiers behind him had stopped arguing. They seemed to be trying to cock the old gun. Hayes didn't see exactly what happened, but one of them pulled the trigger making the gun fire with loud boom. The bullet passed through Rope Man's head with a spray of blood. Flecks of Rope Man's blood and brains splattered onto the pants of a soldier who'd been hurrying down the hill from the house. He had the command presence of an officer.

The officer raged at the two soldiers, slapping both before he turned to Hayes. Short, with bony hard facial features that exuded competence, he glared at Hayes, or maybe at the big soldier holding him.

Hayes felt the big soldier's grip tighten as the officer spoke rapidly. Soldiers bound Hayes hands and feet. He took in both Vietcong and North Vietnamese uniforms before a bag or a hood suddenly covered his head. They picked him up. Next, he found himself being suspended by the bindings around his hands and feet. He could no longer see, but it only took a few seconds before he understood that they had him suspended on a pole. He gritted his teeth and concentrated on Gloria.

She must have had our baby. I have to stay alive.

-28-

April and May, Detroit

"Hey, did you fall asleep?" Susanna asked as she and Gloria sat on the couch watching *I Spy* on the TV. "This is my favorite show, the only one where the black guy is just as important as the white guy. And he's smarter."

"Um, no, I um… I was praying."

"Really?" Susanna said. "Last five minutes or so, I could have sworn you were asleep."

Gloria squirmed, looked away. The recurring thought of Jimmy possibly dead sucked her toward a suffocating abyss, almost paralyzing her. So she would pray. It pulled her away from the abyss.

"What were you praying for?" Susanna glanced at the TV as a commercial ended.

"I started worrying about Jimmy after the TV news and that Vietnam story. I couldn't stop thinking what might have happened to him…"

"You shoulda said something. We coulda turned it off. In fact…" Susanna reached for the TV, turning it off. When she settled back on the sofa, she squeezed Gloria's knee. "Jimmy's gonna be okay. Just keep the faith."

"You didn't have to do that. Really, I'm better now."

"It was almost over. How do you pray if you don't mind talking about it?"

"Um… I got upset watching the news. Couldn't stop thinking Jimmy might be dead. I finally closed my eyes, thought about God, let my thoughts go free. Like when you're lying in bed or on a beach and you're thinking about something and…"

"I sometimes fall asleep like that in church," Susanna said laughing. She laughed a lot, and Gloria loved that about Susanna.

"Maybe God's telling you you're tired."

They both laughed and then Gloria said, "It's the way your head gets before you fall asleep. All your thoughts kind of collapse and mix together, then connect in new ways. That's what I try to do. Sometimes it takes a long time. Sometimes it happens right away. Then you think about whatever's bothering you in a new way. It seems better. Maybe only a little better but still better. Like tonight, I got into it right away. I ended up thinking, Jimmy's missing but that doesn't mean he's dead. All those soldiers who died in that story on TV. Everybody knows they're dead. When somebody gets killed, they tell you. So I felt better 'cause I decided Jimmy's not dead. But I had to let go of everything before I could get to thinking about it that way."

"Huh, maybe… But how's that praying? Doesn't sound like God's even involved," Susanna said.

"Maybe you're right. For me, God makes it happen. When you go to church, don't you feel like God is nearer, at least a little bit?"

Susanna thought for a moment. "Yeah, I guess so. I believe in God. I go to church to think about God. But it never seems like I actually see anything or hear anything from God. I'll probably go to hell for saying it, but I'm a little doubtful about it all."

Susanna turned on the TV and they watched the end of *I Spy*. When it was over, Gloria finally spoke again. "Ever since my stepmother died, my feelings about God have changed. I think they're stronger. Long as I can remember, my stepmother Gina took me to church every Sunday. It was a kind of a safe haven for us."

"What do you mean, Gloria?"

Gloria pursed her lips, made a decision. She'd wanted to tell Susanna what had happened to her, and this seemed like the right time to do it.

"My stepfather, he beat up Gina, and me sometimes. But he didn't just beat me, he raped me." She paused for a moment taking in the shock on Susanna's face, and marveled at how easy it was to finally tell her. "He started when I was about six or seven and it went on until I ran away."

Susanna gaped and took Gloria's hand. "Maybe what I do isn't praying. But all those years sitting in church always made me feel better. Maybe I'm crazy. But it works for me."

Susanna wrapped her arms around Gloria. "You're not crazy. You're beautiful. What you said about prayer is amazing, the way it's helped you."

After awhile, Gloria said, "You know, I learned some of this from playing guitar. See, I usually start playing without any idea of what to play. I know all these songs. I just let myself go and it's like shuffling cards. I play whatever comes into my head, bits and pieces from all over. I put random pieces together in different ways. I can see the pattern of the guitar chords, the way they fit together. It's like a trance, I shut out everything else. I even see colors when I really get into music. If you let yourself go, it's like God takes over."

Susanna said, "I've had some orgasms letting myself go like that."

And they both laughed again.

Gloria ordered a new queen-sized bed and a twenty-four-inch Zenith color TV to replace Susanna's tiny black and white one. Susanna took three classes and worked two part-time jobs, leaving Gloria alone much of the time. But instead of watching TV, Gloria played her guitar most of the time.

First day they had the new TV, they watched Martin Luther King's funeral in Atlanta. Susanna skipped two classes.

"Did I tell you that Jimmy met Walter Cronkite?" Gloria said when Cronkite came on the air at the beginning of the program.

"Walter Cronkite? Wow!"

But the funeral started before she could say more. They saw all the politicians, Robert and Edward Kennedy, and Jacqueline Kennedy too, Richard Nixon, Eugene McCarthy, George Romney and the vice president, Hubert Humphrey.

"All the white guys who wanna be president. Humphrey's probably gonna run too," Susanna said. "I guess if I have to pick one, it'll be Bobby Kennedy."

"Are there any black men who would have a chance?" Gloria asked.

Susanna shrugged. "No, at least not now. Maybe in a few years. I like Andrew Young, but Jesse Jackson seems pretty good. Maybe Carl Stokes will try first. He's already mayor of Cleveland."

When the Morehouse College Glee Club led everyone in singing *We Shall Overcome,* Gloria and Susanna sang along. They both cried at the funeral's end.

"He was my hero," Susanna said.

Gloria envied Susanna's easy-going comfort with sex, and they talked about sex a lot. A junior majoring in sociology with a minor in music, Susanna had thought about changing her major to something related to public health. She had a part time job at the county health department working with an epidemiologist who tracked sexually transmitted diseases.

"You have to get down and dirty. 'Who have you been fucking?' 'What did you do?' 'When did you first notice that sore?' 'Who else have you been fucking?' This lady I'm working for is in her fifties, and they asked me to help her because most of the people she deals with are young, a lot of them younger than me. High school kids, even junior high. You wouldn't believe what some of them are doing."

Susanna frowned for a moment, then flashed a tentative smile at Gloria. "I keep forgetting you're sixteen. Stop me if you don't want to hear about this stuff."

"It's okay. It's not like I'm a virgin," Gloria said.

"Some of it really upsets me," Susanna continued. "Like, we had a kid, thirteen years old, with gonorrhea, in his mouth.

Turns out his uncle probably infected him 'cause that's the only person the kid says he had any sexual contact with. Wasn't easy getting that much out of him. Kid's father's in Jackson State Prison. His mother's an alcoholic former prostitute. Doesn't much care about the boy. In fact, she was pissed off 'cause the uncle, who's her half-brother, is the only one in the household who's working. So he's her meal ticket. Shirley, that's my boss, isn't sure she should tell the police. If the cops do anything, and that's a big if, the best outcome, would be the kid ends up in foster care. That's shitty 'cause there's no chance in hell anyone's gonna adopt a thirteen-year-old black boy. More likely, he'll end up out on the street with a mother who's already angry at him."

"What do you mean that it's a big 'if' that the police will do anything?" Gloria asked.

"Oh, cops in Detroit think this kinda thing's normal behavior with black people. We're subhumans far as most cops are concerned."

Gloria paused to choose her words. "What about white kids? Bet it's the same thing when something like that happens. Bet the white men still get away with it. My stepfather sure as hell did."

Susanna looked at her for moment, then nodded. "You got a point, but Detroit cops treat black people a lot worse than they treat whites. You don't have firsthand experience with it, but you grow up black, you learn quick that cops are not your friends."

"My stepfather whipped me hard enough so you can still see the marks on my back."

Gloria pulled up the T-shirt she was wearing and turned so Susanna could see her back.

"Holy shit."

"Like I told you before, Gina got it worse. She went to the hospital at least half a dozen times. He broke her ribs, knocked out teeth. She got hurt bad. The nurses would call the cops but the cops never did anything about it. I think it has more to do with the fact that my stepfather was rich and the cops are men. I think that's more important than race."

"Yeah maybe, but I still think this sex stuff is different. This thirteen-year-old kid was blowing his uncle. No way did he want to do it. They should throw that bastard in jail for rape."

"Yep, definitely rape. That's exactly what my stepfather made me do. He called it training."

Susanna frowned, got up and went to the refrigerator. She took out a bottle of wine.

"I know you're not old enough, but do you wanna glass? I sure do."

"Okay," Gloria said.

Susanna unscrewed the cap on the bottle and poured the wine into two juice glasses. She settled back into the couch next to Gloria.

"I got nothing against blowjobs. Guys love it, and you can't get pregnant. I don't think I'm *that* easy. I've never done anything sexual with a guy unless I really liked him. Okay, maybe there was some kissing and a little touchy feely with some guys that I didn't know that well. But anything serious, I have to at least *think* I love him." She snickered. "It's not like most guys aren't gonna tell you anything they think'll help 'em get into your pants. They all got those hormones. But so do I. I have to admit, first time a guy stuck his hand down my pants, I didn't try very hard to stop him. At least not right away."

This time Gloria had to force herself to laugh. She'd never had a boyfriend until Jimmy. They had sex only a few hours after they met. And she'd initiated it. She'd wanted someone to love her. Now she knew that sex didn't equate with love. Had she and Jimmy gotten it backwards? Susanna learned about sex over a period of years with friends, and eventually, with lovers. Gloria missed out on that.

Susanna said her family lived in Inkster, a mostly black, working-class suburb west of Detroit and next to Dearborn, which was a big white suburb that kept black people out. Susanna's father had a job at Ford's giant River Rouge plant as a foreman and a union rep. Her mother worked part-time as a librarian.

Susanna showed Gloria her high school yearbooks with pictures of her as a cheerleader, a runner-up for prom queen, and in group photos of at least a dozen clubs.

"I wanted to race against the boys in track. I could've beat most of them in the hundred. I'm fast, in more ways than one." Her eyes twinkled as she raised her wine glass.

Susanna had a retarded older brother who worked as a busboy at a Dearborn restaurant. Her younger brother attended University of Michigan on a football scholarship.

"He wants to play pro ball, but I don't know if he's gonna make it. Darren's a good receiver, fast, good hands. Started six games last season as a sophomore. Trouble is, he's only a hundred and fifty-five pounds. So my mom's makin' sure he graduates with a good degree. He's an accounting major. Darren and Antoine got along pretty good, too. Antoine has a degree in business administration."

Susanna looked away and took a big swallow of her wine.

"Sounds like you have a nice family." Gloria didn't want to admit that she'd never gone to high school. The nuns held her back in third grade and again in seventh grade. Because she wouldn't speak, the teachers deemed Gloria a "slow learner" and "difficult."

Susanna said. "Couple of months ago, my mom found out that Antoine had moved in with me. She got all unglued. Said she thought she'd brought me up better than that. My dad didn't say much, but I could tell he didn't like it either. Darren stuck up for me, but they weren't gonna listen to him. I told my mom that Antoine and I would probably get married after I graduated, but my mom mostly stopped talking to me."

"What's she say now?" Gloria asked.

"When I told her Antoine and I broke up, she just shook her head and didn't say anything. Hard to tell what she thinks 'cause we haven't been speaking much. I could tell she's disappointed, though. Maybe she'd been looking forward to a wedding. Who knows. Before we broke up, it felt like Mom was starting to accept the arrangement. I mean, she actually called and asked how Antoine and I were doing. She and my Dad liked Antoine, but they only met him a couple of times."

They watched the Oscars with the TV sound turned down low. Susanna rose from the couch to turn the sound up.

"This TV's great. Thanks again for getting it. I love color. My parents just got one too." She went to the refrigerator and took out the wine. She held it up for Gloria, who nodded. She re-filled both their glasses. After watching almost an hour of the Oscars, Susanna again poured another glass for herself and topped off Gloria's. Relaxed and a little warm with thoughts of Jimmy flitting in and out of her consciousness, Gloria told herself that Jimmy would come back, the wine helping her believe it. Jimmy had promised to come home, and Jimmy kept promises.

Gulping her wine, Susanna gripped the glass so tightly that Gloria saw her knuckles turn white. The tenseness showed in her face.

She spoke in a voice strained and high. "Dr. King was the thing Antoine and I argued about all the time. Antoine's too damned impatient for nonviolence. He doesn't think black people will ever be equal unless they fight for it. I'd say, 'Look at everything that's changed since Dr. King, civil rights, voting rights even the war on poverty,' but Antoine kept saying it hasn't changed enough. Then after the riot he got a lot angrier. Said it was open season on black people for the cops and the National Guard."

Sipping some wine, Gloria said, "Yeah, he might be right about that." Susanna's head snapped around. Gloria told Susanna how during the riot, she and Jimmy saw Detroit police shoot a black woman and her sons, and then a black man shot the cops. "I thought I was going to have to tell a grand jury about what I saw, but now it looks like I won't have to do that."

"So was that what you were talking about that morning in the church?"

Gloria nodded.

"I knew you met Antoine at an antiwar rally. I remember he came home really pissed off. Said some white chick singer was tryin' to sell her records."

"Yes, and I wasn't too happy with him either. I didn't like some of the things he said, and I knew he didn't like me singing."

Susanna laughed without mirth. "That's Antoine. He gets all wound up. Gets angry with anyone who disagrees with him. He had a good job at National Bank of Detroit but said he got fired after he got in a fight with his boss. Won't listen to anyone when he's pissed off. At least I could get him to shut up. He's smart. Graduated from Wharton and then was gonna go for an MBA until he got caught up in all his black power shit."

Susanna drained her wine, looked at the empty glass and went to refill it. Again, she held bottle up for Gloria, but Gloria shook her head.

"Actually, Antoine's not street smart, and he wants to be rich. His father's a wealthy doctor in Philadephia. After he graduated, Antoine wouldn't take any money from him, which was okay when he was working. Anyway his family's well off." Susanna stared at a blank wall, started to smile but it died. "Most of the time, we were great together. And he was a great lover. He never asked me, but I thought we were gonna get married. Thought I could get him to settle down."

She swirled the wine around in her glass thoughtfully and then clunked it down on the coffee table too hard.

Gloria turned to her. "You still love him, don't you?"

"Yeah, but it's over." The corners of Susanna's mouth twitched as she struggled to resurrect her smile. Then tears welled in her eyes and ran down her cheeks. "He might as well be dead… oh, I didn't mean to say that."

Gloria reached out and hugged Susanna. They went to bed lying side by side, Susanna snoring but sleeping restlessly from the wine, Gloria awake, her mind racing, resisting all her efforts to calm herself with prayer. Her baby died and if Jimmy died, then Gloria might as well die too.

Sixteen years old, never been to high school, got pregnant, couldn't even get that right. But I'm good at blowjobs. What a fucking loser.

-29-

May, Vietnam

Hayes' new captors hurried through the bush in broad daylight. They carried him suspended from a pole strung through the ropes binding his wrists and ankles, his head covered with a hood. Branches whipped him, tree trunks whacked him. Soon he could no longer feel his hands or feet. Whenever they stopped, somebody usually kicked him. A blow from something hard — a rifle butt? — broke a tooth. A kick started a nosebleed.

At first, he fantasized that an American helicopter would see them. But the fantasy died, overwhelmed by the agony of the ropes, blood clogging his nose and the excruciating pain when breathed through his mouth over the broken tooth. However, rage and pain awakened a brain and body grown somnolent during his long confinement in darkness.

Finally, the captors dropped him, and a soldier pulled off the hood, sliced off the bonds on his hands and feet. They tied his hands again with a long length of rope. As feeling seared back into his numb hands and feet, it reminded him of playing outside in the subzero Michigan winter days. Warming up made your frozen feet felt like they'd caught fire.

He lay in a dense forest near a small scrubby tree with a pile of hard earth beside it, a termite mound. A soldier scraped away leaves and dirt beside the mound revealing a worn square wooden panel and slid it aside.

"Oop, oop!" said the soldier who had shot Rope Man. He slapped Hayes hard across the buttocks with the flat of a bayonet. "Oop, oop."

Hayes jumped up, swayed on his unsteady, fiery feet. Another soldier took the length of rope from Hayes' bound hands and entered the hole. The rope jerked him into the opening. He bumped headfirst down steep stony stairs landing on packed dirt at the bottom.

"Oop," said the man with the rope. When he got up, he hit his head on the low hard ceiling. Three more soldiers scrambled down the stairs, crowding into the small chamber. Lit only by light filtering down from the tunnel entrance, Hayes saw that the man who'd shot Rope Man still held the bayonet and had the antique pistol stuck awkwardly in a holster that was too small for it.

Pulled by the rope, Hayes stumbled into a dark passage. He tried to duck-walk, but even bending in half his head scraped the hard earthen ceiling. The sudden total darkness ignited a claustrophobic panic. He froze.

I'll get stuck and die in here!

The bayonet pricked at his rear several times until he felt it pierce deeper into his flesh. It shocked him out of the panic. He lunged forward sprawling on his belly. He began crawling on his forearms and knees, lunging ahead and pulling his legs up one knee at a time through the dirt. He moved this way while negotiating several turns.

The sounds from the soldier in front ceased, and Hayes felt the rope on his wrists pulling to the left. The man had entered another opening that led down more stony earthen stairs, deeper into the earth. This time Hayes managed to go feet first.

Partway down, his feet tangled in the rope, and he bumped down the last few feet on his butt. The soldier leading him snapped on a flashlight revealing an oblong chamber with wood-framed openings for three more tunnels. The walls and floor felt like extremely hard-packed earth rather than rock. The passage of people had worn the wood framing the tunnel openings shiny. Here, he could stand only slightly bent with his head brushing the ceiling. Through his shredded pants, he caught sight of his knees slippery with dirt and blood. He'd lost his socks. But as the flashlight beam jittered around, Hayes memorized the chamber's layout.

Hayes decided the Vietcong must want him alive for a reason, undoubtedly nothing good. Now he regretted spending so long underground without trying to escape.

After more chatter, the soldier with the rope pulled Hayes into one of the tunnels. They must have travelled for more than an hour, sometimes going up, sometimes down, entering new passages, some of them so small he had to crawl fully prone. The first time they encountered a tunnel that small, two other soldiers joined the soldier with the rope and partially dragged Hayes. And the soldier who'd shot Rope Man kept stabbing at his ass with the bayonet.

They finally climbed down more hard dirt stairs reinforced with wood and entered another tunnel, warmer and a little smoky. Hayes smelled cooking odors, sweat and excrement. Bare light bulbs illuminated some tunnel sections. They encountered other people. Sometimes the leader shouted into a tunnel and faint calls came back. They stopped to wait for others to pass but more often others held up for them. The air grew steadily warmer, more fetid, a rank odor of unwashed human bodies leavened with human waste. In a lighted section, they stopped at an alcove with a small hole in the ground, a toilet. He saw three men use it. The leader pointed to it and looked at Hayes. Hayes shook his head, but he made a motion indicating he wanted to drink. The man offered Hayes a canteen but snatched it away almost as soon as he started to drink.

Hayes knew he smelled bad because he heard, "Mui hoi" from passing Vietnamese who grabbed their noses. They must be telling him he stunk. Many of the soldiers struck him or spit on him.

"Con cho American!" a woman snarled as she prepared to squeeze past. She spit in his face, kneed him hard on his thigh narrowly missing his crotch. Not the first woman they'd seen, but the most unusual. She wore an oversized gray athletic sweatsuit. Hayes had never seen a Vietnamese dressed like that. He'd never seen anyone wearing sweats in Vietnam's hot, humid climate. Moreover, she'd tied the drawstrings of the sweatshirt's hood tight so he could only see her face. Escorted by a Vietcong soldier, she travelled in the same direction as Hayes' group. But Hayes' group stopped to let them pass.

For a moment she pushed against him, her face only inches away. That was when she spit and kneed him. Her eyes burned with hatred. But she looked oddly familiar. Once past, she paused to talk to the soldier with the rope. Both looked back as Hayes wiped the spittle off his face. But Hayes grinned at her, setting off an angry retort in Vietnamese. Then she and her escort hurried on ahead.

A few minutes later, they emerged into a very large chamber containing many people. Plywood sheets peppered with propaganda posters and papers with gaudy Vietnamese characters lined the walls. Half a dozen light bulbs kept the darkness at bay. The chamber had an irregular shape and had been formed by widening out several converging tunnels. Hayes saw about thirty people, but he couldn't see the entire room. They pushed past soldiers and around an obtuse bend to a bigger part of the chamber crowded with more people.

Here, the ceiling sloped higher, and a big portrait of Ho Chi Minh illuminated with its own light hung on the wall. Under the picture on a low dais, three Vietnamese soldiers, one of them a woman, all of them high ranking by the look of their uniforms, sat at a table covered with a faded red cloth. All three looked older, well-groomed and relatively clean. Hayes' handlers pushed him to a spot immediately in front of the table. Surprised, he saw the woman who had spit on him. Though directly beside him, she edged away.

"I am Bich. I will translate. For you, and for them." She pointed at the three officers.

She pronounced her name "Bih." Hayes knew that it meant jade because the girl who had helped take his picture with the Polaroid camera had the same name. For a moment sadness about the death of Rope Man and his family welled up until he forced his attention back to Bich.

"What is this?" Hayes asked her.

"Your trial," she said.

"My trial? For what?"

Before she could answer one of the three high-ranking officers slapped the table and began speaking loudly.

"He wants you untied," Bich said. Hayes raised his hands and Rope Man's killer hacked at the binding rope, luckily not cutting Hayes hands.

When the two men and the woman at the table stood up, the big chamber grew silent. Then two of the officers sat down, while the man at the center man began speaking loudly.

"He says that the court accuses you of killing six Viet people… maybe more, at a village called Tra Lam. You threw them out of a helicopter."

"No, I didn't," Hayes said to Bich, but she remained focused on the officer who was still speaking.

"Many saw you do this, and they will speak now."

A middle-aged woman in shabby black trousers and a dirt-stained white blouse in the front row began speaking. Bich and Hayes both strained to hear her voice.

"She says her husband is a farmer. Americans take him and a boy away in a helicopter. Boy was thirteen. They covered their eyes with a… a blindfold. Then they came back close to ground and pushed the boy out."

Hayes had heard about this trick before though he'd never witnessed it. You took a couple of prisoners up in a helicopter to extract information. You blindfolded them and gradually descended until the helicopter hovered a few feet above the ground. In the noisy, windy helicopter, the blindfolded men still thought they were high in the air. Likely, they'd never been in a helicopter before. You pushed out the one least likely to know anything, making sure the other man knew what had happened. The remaining man, assuming that his friend had plummeted to his death, usually talked. Even the one who harmlessly hit the ground in terror often spilled his guts.

"They take husband up. The Americans wanted us say we were VC. They want us sign paper. We say we grow rice."

Hayes thought she lied and the village was probably a VC village. But when he looked at the peasant woman, Hayes saw the sorrow in her eyes. The woman's voice grew louder with more pleading. Bich stopped translating for a few moments. Then her eyes narrowed and she continued.

"My husband, he die first. He fall down long way and land near me."

The woman started wailing, causing a major disruption. After a modicum of calm returned, the female officer stood up and spoke.

Bich said, "She ask the village woman to look you… at you," Bich said.

A soldier took her by one arm and they squeezed down the row until she looked around Bich at Hayes. Wiping tears and still sobbing, she stared at him for almost half a minute before mumbling a few words, which Bich repeated loudly, but in Vietnamese. He had little doubt that she'd identified him. The barrel of the antique pistol pressed into his neck. Bich ducked away. Several others stepped or leaned to the side.

I'm going to be killed.

Then the moment passed.

"What happened?" Hayes asked Bich. Before she could answer, and perhaps she didn't want to, the peasant woman squeezed past Bich and poked her finger slowly toward him. She touched the Headhunter patch stitched on the front pocket of his filthy jungle fatigue shirt. Despite the dirt and dim light, the crude caricature of a headhunter with the bushy hair and bone through his nose, holding a minigun in one hand and a rocket in the other, was still visible.

Bich said, "She says picture show Gook... bad name Americans call Viet people. It shows how Americans hate all Vietnamese."

Which made no sense at all. Hayes didn't think the headhunter on the patch resembled a Vietnamese. If anything, the cannibal appeared to be black, which had caused some tension within the Headhunter platoon. He recalled that Mitchell and Flowers never wore the Headhunter patch. Wearing it was not mandatory.

As she pointed to Hayes' patch, the village woman spoke rapidly.

"She saw same picture on the helicopter, but she did not see your face." Bich paused, couldn't seem to find the right words. "You wore a big hat on your head and..." Bich stopped to ask the woman a question in Vietnamese. "Sunglasses. She saw her own face in your sunglasses."

Hayes never wore sunglasses. He didn't have any. He sometimes wore a pair of clear safety goggles that he'd gotten from Maintenance to shield his eyes from the wind. Still, he thought she'd told the truth, or tried to. She must have seen another Headhunter gunship and he knew which gunship she'd probably seen. And both Delaney and Kannegiesser wore sunglasses.

About a dozen more Vietnamese spoke. Not all of them were from the village. The VC had gone to a great deal of trouble to bring them down into the tunnels. Most told the same story with variations. One of them had only seen two people pushed out of the helicopter, and another claimed to have seen ten. Two others agreed with the first woman and said six. They described a traumatic and chaotic day at the village, and it didn't surprise Hayes that they all remembered it differently.

It did surprise him when two soldier observers who had hidden outside Long Binh Base Camp recounted how a helicopter with the same picture on its nose landed at Long Binh, then took off after sundown. Hayes doubted they were strictly telling the truth. Long Binh was a very large base camp with many aircraft, including helicopters, taking off and landing all the time. Hard to believe they'd seen his helicopter well enough in the dark to identify it.

But it all made him think about the crash of his helicopter. Had the enemy somehow, shot the gunship down? Or sabotaged it? He'd thought the crash occurred because of a mechanical problem but now he wondered about enemy involvement.

The parade of Vietcong soldiers and peasants continued, including some from other villages. According to Bich's translations, they recounted numerous instances when helicopters with the Headhunter markings killed innocent civilians. The Headhunters only seemed to kill civilians, never any North Vietnamese or Vietcong soldiers. Bich herself also spoke at some length and did not translate what she said for Hayes. When he asked her what she'd said, she hesitated.

"I told them how much Americans pay when they kill civilians. Americans paid for killing those six villagers. In the months of March and April they paid for sixty-three Vietnamese killed by helicopters with that same picture."

"How do you know that?"

She didn't answer him, and the officer in the center of the table said something to Hayes.

"He asks if you want to speak," Bich said.

There were lots of things Hayes wanted to say and to ask the witnesses. Had the government moved the villagers away? Why had they come back? He had heard that the Vietcong collected their own taxes, took food, drafted young men to fight and killed village leaders sympathetic to the Saigon government. He wanted to tell them that he hadn't done what they accused him of. He wanted to tell them how the soldiers who seized him had slaughtered Rope Man and his family. Would anyone believe him?

He felt the tense silence in the chamber, all eyes staring at him. He'd always thought Americans fought to protect South

Vietnam from an oppressive Communist regime in North Vietnam. He'd never deliberately killed civilians. And unlike Mitchell, he'd never seen anyone in his company, or any other soldiers deliberately kill civilians. He had seen civilians killed by mistake. Or so he'd thought. He believed he fought on the right side and that Americans were the good guys. But now he had doubts. The villagers certainly didn't think well of the Headhunters. Nothing he said could change that. Finally, he remembered what a drill sergeant in basic training had told them.

"My name is Jimmy Hayes. My rank is specialist fourth class. My serial number is U.S. five four nine seven four six seven oh." He said it loudly. Then, with his eyes looking at the officers on the dais, he added, "I am a soldier and did not do what everyone here said I did. I have only killed enemy soldiers."

Bich's mouth popped open, but she appeared to translate what he'd said. Then the other male officer on the dais, who had not spoken, rose from his chair and stood in front of Hayes. Despite standing on the dais, he still had to look up at Hayes. Hayes pegged him as a Vietcong officer and the other two as North Vietnamese. The Vietcong officer reached for the rank insignia on Hayes' collar and spoke rapidly in Vietnamese. He ripped the little black plastic insignia off and held it up.

Bich said, "He says this proves you lie. This shows that you are a pilot officer."

"No, I'm not a pilot, I'm a crew chief," Hayes said. Then he remembered that the night they'd crashed, he and Flowers had worn warrant officer insignia to eat steaks at the Officers Club. He'd forgotten and had never taken them off. The VC officer continued speaking.

Bich kept translating, "He says that you lie. You are a dishonorable soldier. You commit war crimes against our people."

"No, no. I didn't do what those villagers said." Hayes stopped. Trying to shift the blame to somebody else wouldn't help him. "I've killed many enemy soldiers in this war. If I killed any civilians, it was an accident. The Vietcong soldiers who captured me today, they killed civilians. And it was no accident." Hayes pointed at the soldier who was still leveling the antique pistol at him. "I saw this man kill a farmer in the village. He and the other soldiers killed children…"

He stopped speaking because Bich had stopped listening and wasn't translating what he said. Instead, she strained to hear the VC officer who'd continued to rattle off angry words. The chamber grew chaotic as others started shouting. Finally, the senior officer pounded his fist on the table several times. "Yen tinh! Yen tinh!"

The room grew quiet and the senior officer gave a brief speech. As he spoke, he looked around the room. But when he finished, his eyes fixed on Hayes. Grunts of approval rippled around the chamber.

"What'd he say?"

"You are to be executed," Bich said, her eyes wide. Then her mouth curled into a grim smile. "Good."

No surprise but Hayes' heart pounded, and his body suddenly felt slick with cold sweat. His legs trembled and he almost sat down on the ground. Taking deep breaths, he swayed but remained upright.

"When?" The word came out in a high croak. He desperately wanted a drink of water. He wanted to eat. Most of all, he wanted to sleep and shut off this nightmare.

Bich grinned. "Maybe you did not do this. But Americans did it. You are American so you will pay."

-30-

After his trial and death sentence, his head fuzzy, Hayes' captors led him away. Someone gave him a canteen of warm water that tasted foul, like creek water. Thirsty, he drained the canteen. Then the same soldiers prodded him through a series of tunnel passages. There seemed to be no urgency, and they went slower. Finally, he recognized they'd come to the underground junction chamber with the three other tunnel entrances. He noticed that the accompanying soldiers had dwindled to two guards, the man leading him by the rope tied to his wrists, and the soldier with the antique pistol.

As they rested, Hayes studied the chamber they were in by the dim light of the flashlight. When they moved again, they took a different tunnel. This meant Hayes now knew where three of the four entrances in the chamber went. Most important, he knew which one led to the surface.

Warmer, lit with light bulbs and big enough to allow him to walk bent over, the new tunnel reeked of Vietnamese fish oil and other food. A stink of human sweat and feces underlay the food odors. Still, his mouth watered and his stomach churned. He hadn't eaten anything for two or three days. They passed a small chamber where an old woman sharpened punji sticks with a knife. Surrounded by bundles of punji sticks and wood shavings, she grinned at Hayes, revealing a missing top front tooth. He grinned back. In the next room they passed, two men with tools in their hands hunched over an unexploded American bomb. Neither paid attention to Hayes.

Are they nuts? If they make a mistake, the explosion could take out the whole tunnel complex.

Several dozen feet farther down the tunnel, the soldier leading Hayes by the rope stopped and pushed him into a curved alcove about eight feet deep. Hayes sat down with his back against the farthest dirt wall.

The soldier with the pistol and bayonet followed him in. He sat beside the entrance, as the other soldier, who apparently ranked higher, said a few words to him, then left. The remaining soldier pulled out the antique pistol, pointed it at Hayes.

"Boom-boom!"

Hayes almost tried to jump him. But he'd have to get up, spring across the space and somehow overpower the man. He'd never make it in time.

The more senior soldier returned with two big bowls of soup. When he started to hand a bowl to Hayes, the soldier with the pistol argued with him. Tired, the leader gave both bowls to the man with the gun, shrugged at Hayes, then left again.

Grinning at Hayes, the soldier began eating the soup. He kept the pistol on his lap as he ate with chopsticks and a spoon, twirling noodles in the spoon before devouring them. He noisily slurped and groaned with pleasure. When he finished the first bowl, he turned to the second continuing to torment Hayes. He'd hold a chunk of fish under Hayes' nose, then snatch it away to eat with exaggerated gusto. But he always kept the cocked revolver in one hand or within easy reach. Still, Hayes almost sprang at him.

The trip through the tunnels and his trial had taken a long day, making it late afternoon, or, more likely, evening now. Like Hayes, the soldier had eaten nothing all day.

Yeah, he's hungry.

The attack on the ville to capture Hayes occurred at dawn so the attacking unit had probably spent most of the night preparing and getting into position.

So he's tired too. And with a full belly, he'll get sleepy.

The leader who'd led Hayes by the rope through the tunnels returned. The two soldiers talked. The leader tried to give his pistol to his comrade, but he wouldn't take it. Instead, he brandished the antique pistol, pointing it at Hayes and saying "boom, boom." Finally, the leader shrugged, said something while pointing to his watch. Then he left.

They just split up the guard duty.

A few minutes later, Hayes made a big production out of yawning. He curled up against the far dirt wall, his back to the remaining guard. He pretended to sleep, although the emotional turmoil of his impending execution, the pain in his mouth, the slashes and bruises from the beatings made sleep impossible. But he'd seen the guard yawn several times even before he'd finished eating.

He had to act before the more competent soldier returned. Curled up in a fetal position, his bound wrists close to his mouth, he began sawing the rope against the broken edge of his tooth, moving only his hands. He embraced the terrible pain. The shock of it energized every nerve in his body. His eyes teared in agony. Pain wouldn't kill him, but he'd die if he didn't escape. Slowly, one by one, the rope fibers tore. At the same time, the remainder of the tooth loosened and began wiggling. He tasted blood, felt it running over his lip to drip into the dirt. He kept sawing away. Finally the rope parted, freeing his hands.

For a few moments he lay still, waiting for the pain to subside, but it only diminished slightly. In the dim light he examined the remaining rope. Too short. Slowly, he slid a hand down into his pants and found the garrote. He'd carried the piece of rope around his waist or in his underwear for weeks. Soft, greasy, dirty, but enough rope to wrap one end around his left hand, make a large double loop and wrap the other end around his right hand. Then he slowly rolled over.

The guard sat with his back against the wall, his head lolled forward, the big pistol on his lap.

He's asleep!

In slow motion, Hayes raised to his knees, then bent forward balancing on his elbows to pull his knees up. As he leaned forward again, the slumbering soldier's eyes popped open, but not before Hayes dropped both loops over the man's head and pulled them tight. If the Vietcong soldier had reached for the pistol on his lap, he could have shot Hayes. Instead, the pistol slid off his lap while both the man's hands shot up to his chin where one of the loops had snagged. He got two fingers under the loop just as it slipped off his chin onto his neck trapping the fingers. With his other hand, he scraped at his neck trying gain purchase under the rope loops. He wrenched at the rope with the two trapped fingers.

That's okay, you're tightening the other loop.

Hayes, facing the soldier, looked into his bulging eyes and used all his strength to hold the garrote tight. For several seconds the man fought hard against the choking rope, kneeing at Hayes while his free hand finally scrabbled for the gun. Hayes nudged it out of reach with his knee.

The soldier's struggling stopped so quickly Hayes thought him faking. He kept the pressure up until fatigue overtook his arms. Utterly spent, Hayes sagged forward listening to his own panting, the guard's limp body sprawled against him with the two fingers still trapped in the garrote around his neck. Hayes felt for a pulse on the man's neck. Finding none, he lowered him to the ground, still looking at the bulging eyes in the darkened face.

He thought about taking the man's boots, but they'd never fit. He strung the garrote rope through the belt loops of his dirty pants. He'd lost so much weight that he'd constantly been pulling up his pants.

He examined the old pistol, a single action requiring you to cock the hammer before pulling the trigger. It held six rounds, one already fired. So he only had five shots, if all the bullets fired. The cartridges, like the revolver, looked very old.

No one had passed the entrance to the little room, and the food smells had diminished. Looking both ways and seeing no one, Hayes crept down the tunnel in the direction he'd come from. He passed the room with the bomb but saw nobody in it. In the next room, the punji stick woman lay on a mat. At first Hayes thought she slept, but then saw her eyes were open and fixed on him. Gray streaked her hair and deep wrinkles surrounded her eyes. He pointed the pistol at her. A shot would surely alert everyone. He raised his other hand and put a finger to his lips.

"Shhhhhh."

She didn't move and continued looking at him. For a long moment they stared at each other, then he moved quickly away. He scrambled down the tunnel until he reached the chamber with the other three tunnel openings. Just as he entered, the lights winked off. But his eyes were already on the entrance that led to the surface. This time the sudden total darkness didn't panic him.

"They know I'm loose now," he said and squeezed through the opening.

He knew he had to move faster and the tunnel didn't seem as small this time. He tried duck-walking for a few steps but decided he could move faster on his hands and knees with the pistol stuffed in a pocket. He churned through the tunnel, reaching the crude stairs that led up to the last chamber before the surface. Behind him, he heard scraping noises.

They're catching up.

He scrambled up the stairs and pushed open the trap door. As he hoisted himself out, he heard someone coming down the stairs from the outside. Hayes pulled out the revolver, froze rigid, stopped breathing. The footsteps stopped, then started again. He crouched, extending the cocked gun in front of him. Just enough light filtered in from the surface for Hayes to see a slight shadowy change as someone reached the bottom of the stairs.

He shot. The thunderous boom hurt his ears but the split-second flash of orange flame lit up the chamber like a bolt of lightning. Sure that he'd hit the intruder, he started for the stairs to the surface, then stopped. He found the soldier on the ground, still alive, gasping, groaning and shuddering wet breaths of air. Hayes felt around with one hand that got sticky with blood before he found a pistol in its holster and an extra magazine of bullets clipped to the belt. The soldier began screaming as Hayes dragged him to the trap door that Hayes had just climbed out of. He opened it and tried to push the wounded soldier down. The man got stuck in the opening and Hayes left him there.

That might slow them down.

A pistol in each hand he scrambled up the stairs to the surface. Then he realized that the soldier he'd shot might not have been alone. He put the new pistol and its magazine in his pockets. When he reached the surface, he found the entrance open. Hayes eased his head outside with one arm holding the big antique revolver. Breathing in a deep lungfuls of fresh air, he looked around, saw no one, but he could see little in the dark. He had to take a chance. He pulled himself out of the tunnel and started running. Smashing through bushes, tripping on the uneven ground and bouncing off small trees, he finally smacked a big rock hard with one foot and fell.

He'd made too much noise. His shoeless, sockless feet hurt. He thought about climbing a big tree but could barely see the trees in the dark. He stumbled into some thick bushes. Instead of trying to pick his way around them, he lay down and crawled into them. When the bushes grew too thick for crawling, he stopped and lay still. Tired, hungry, thirsty and with myriad painful cuts and bruises, he decided to wait until daylight.

-31-

Nui Binh Base Camp

Sergeant First Class Emilio Gomez, the senior Maintenance NCO, surprised First Sergeant Gus McConaughey in the Orderly Room. McConaughey had never seen Gomez in the Orderly Room.

"Need to talk you, Top. In private," Gomez said glancing at the company clerk. Gomez, a short stocky man with black hair and a magnificent thick mustache, usually had a twinkle in his brown eyes, but not this day.

The first sergeant nodded. "Can I get you some coffee? You look bushed, Emilio."

"Yes. Black. And I am bushed. Was up all night and just got back from Long Binh."

McConaughey looked at the clerk. "Specialist, go to the mess hall for some coffee for Sergeant Gomez, and get me a refill while you're at it." Turning back to Gomez, he asked, "Did you eat? They got meat loaf, and mac and cheese. I got some hot sauce here too."

"Estupendo! I missed lunch," Gomez said.

"Bring a big plate of everything, some of those brownies if there's any left, and the coffee," McConaughey ordered the clerk. "Then I guess you might as well knock off for the day."

Gomez sat down and scraped his chair closer to the first sergeant's desk. He spoke in a low voice. "I haven't told this to anyone yet. I wasn't sure who to tell."

"Okay, but you don't have to whisper, Emilio."

Gomez nodded, but kept his voice soft. "Ever since that crash last month that killed those three, I've been tryin' to figure out what happened."

"Wasn't it a transmission failure?" McConaughey said.

"It was, but why'd the transmission fail?"

"Shit, don't they just break sometimes? The end of a pistol barrel blew up on me once. Lucky I wasn't killed."

"Probably bad ammo," Gomez said, shrugging. "But you're right. Shit happens."

"Well, maybe the transmission took a round."

"Don't think so. Nobody said anything on the radio about receiving fire and they weren't flying low. Maybe they got a warning light but from what I know about Nesterenko, he wouldn't ignore a warning light."

"Well, didn't they have some trouble with a warning light?" McConaughey asked.

"Yeah, and I thought we fixed that, and Long Binh fixed it again… so yeah, I guess he coulda… But let me get on with it." Gomez paused and ran his hand through his short hair. "After they pulled that wrecked bird out, I asked them to leave the transmission so I could take a look at it. Couldn't get over there right away, too busy. But this morning, me and Spec Five Sorenson — he's my best mechanic — took the courier to Long Binh. We took what was left of the transmission apart, and you'll never guess what we found."

The first sergeant opened his mouth to say something, but Gomez continued before he got words out.

"We found sand in the filter."

"Sand? Are you trying to say the crash was caused by sand in the transmission? How'd it get there?" McConaughey paused. "I guess helicopters kick up a hell of a lot of dust."

"Top, the transmission is sealed, and this wasn't dust. It was sand. It didn't get in there by accident. Somebody had to have dumped it in. I'm not even sure it was sand. Could have been carborundum or aluminum oxide."

"What the hell is—"

"Those are abrasives. They look like sand but they're man-made. Sandpaper doesn't have sand. That's carborundum or aluminum oxide particles. The stuff I found almost looked too uniform to be real sand."

The screen door banged when the clerk kicked it open. He entered with a tray loaded with food, a second smaller plate with three brownies and two cups of coffee. He put it all down on the desk. Conrad Myers wasn't much of a clerk, but McConaughey recognized he had world-class waiter skills.

"There you go, Sarge," Myers said before leaving.

McConaughey opened a desk drawer and took out a little bottle of Tabasco. Gomez sprinkled the sauce over everything except the brownies before he started eating.

"So you think that helicopter mighta been sabotaged?"

"No doubt about it," Gomez said, shaking more Tabasco onto his meat loaf. "No other explanation."

"There's already been an accident report, which came to the conclusion that the crash resulted from a transmission failure."

"And they were right. The transmission failed and the fuckin' investigators speculated it coulda been for any number of reasons, the most likely being ground fire. Nobody really believes that. But they're givin' those guys medals and they won't officially put it down to a maintenance fuckup, which is what they think really happened." Gomez sighed and shoveled big forkfuls of mac and cheese into his mouth before gesturing with his fork. "Look we're in a war. If they'd crashed stateside, the investigation mighta been more thorough. They mighta caught it. Hell, I'm kickin' myself for not going down there sooner."

McConaughey drank more coffee. "How long would it take for a handful of sand to bring down a helicopter? Would they get any warning?"

Gomez shrugged. "I don't know. I never saw anything like this before."

The phone rang. McConaughey looked at it, considered ignoring the call, then picked it up.

"First Sergeant McConaughey."

"Givin' you a heads up First Sergeant. The CO's on his way to the Orderly Room along with that Major Shiffman."

McConaughey recognized the voice of one of the clerks in Operations.

"Okay, thanks," McConaughey said and hung up the phone. He looked at Gomez. "The CO's on his way here. You wanna stick around and tell him your story?"

Gomez shrugged and gulped coffee to wash down the last brownie. One hand rubbing his belly, he looked at McConaughey. "You tell him. I wanna get my boys goin' and then hit the sack."

McConaughey drummed his fingers on the desk. "Okay, maybe that's best. CO's got a major from Brigade with him so he must have something else to talk about."

As Gomez trudged out the door, he met the two officers in front of the Orderly Room and waved a salute.

"Sergeant Gomez, I'm sorry we did not get you any Dos Equis for Cinco de Mayo," Lieutenant Colonel Blair said lightly.

"'S'alright sir, I managed to get by with that Filipino San Miguel horse piss they call beer."

The two officers filed into the Orderly Room to Blair's office, a corner that had been partitioned off with plywood. McConaughey dragged his chair into the office.

"Major Shiffman has bad news, Top. We've just learned that the VC are saying they are going to execute Specialist Hayes. He might even be dead already."

"Shit! How do we know this?" the First Sergeant asked.

Blair nodded at Shiffman.

"We've been informed by a member of the media, Josefina Madrid. She's a freelancer, mostly does stories for European TV. She's also a lefty who has Communist sources. We've had trouble with her before," Shiffman said.

"I'll say we've had trouble with that fucking cunt," Blair muttered. "I'd like to fire a rocket up her ass."

Shiffman winced but nodded his head. "I'm sure she's right. And she claims she's not happy about it despite the fact Hayes was responsible for killing her chance to peddle a story to Walter Cronkite about your ground attack."

McConaughey slammed his fist on the CO's desk startling the two officers. "Goddamnit. Hayes has been gone seven weeks, and I get the idea nobody's trying very hard to get him back. Thought you said he was being held by some Cao Dai religious fanatics. How the fuck did the VC get him?"

"Take it easy, Top," Blair snapped in a tone usually reserved for issuing orders.

Shiffman raised the palm of his hand in front of Blair whose face flushed with irritation. "I think the First Sergeant has a point. I feel the same way."

"Why?" Blair asked.

"I've been convinced from day one that the Cao Dai captured Hayes. A South Vietnamese colonel told me a few days ago, there were still negotiations going on between the Cao Dai and the South Vietnamese government. We've tried to pressure the government but they haven't responded."

"We're fighting for those bastards and they won't help us get an American prisoner back?" McConaughey snarled.

"They stonewalled the Cao Dai too. Anyway, I thought I knew where they were holding Hayes. It's a little village with three tiny villes. It's less than six kilometers from where that helicopter crashed. Most of the people in the village are Cao Dai. They farm lotus plants there. It's a Vietnamese cuisine delicacy and Tra Lam's been a prosperous village."

"Why didn't we send the cavalry in?" McConaughey asked.

"We sent in a Lurp team on a reconnaissance mission. They were there two days and parts of three nights. They came up empty," Shiffman said. "And the ARVNs went in three separate times and searched it. Nothing."

"Huh. So maybe you were wrong and he wasn't there," Blair said, his face drawn.

"Oh, he was there alright. Early this morning, the VC, or maybe the North Vietnamese, we're not sure, hit that village. They killed more than a dozen people, including several children. A few of the people escaped to the woods and saw them take away an American prisoner. They also saw them execute some of the villagers."

Shiffman looked at them and spoke in a soft voice. "I went out there myself. I talked to a couple of the survivors. I saw the underground room where they kept Hayes."

"Jesus H. Christ," McConaughey said. "Do you know where they took him?"

"No, we don't." Shiffman stayed silent, seeming to be deep in thought. He took out a cigarette, offering the pack to them. McConaughey took one and Blair declined. Shiffman tapped the cigarettes onto the desk and took out his lighter before continuing.

"I believe this is a propaganda move by the VC and North Vietnamese. Madrid says she thinks they held a trial accusing Hayes of murdering six Vietnamese by throwing them out of a helicopter on Two April. That's the same day of the crash. Furthermore, they are accusing the Headhunters of killing a specific number of civilians during the months of March and April. The number matches one that was on a report about incidents where we pay compensation to families of deceased civilians. I learned that there's also an ongoing investigation into an action where some Vietnamese were killed apparently by dropping them out of a helicopter on the date mentioned in the communiqué."

"I'm aware of it," Blair said. "A couple of Green Beret officers and one of our pilots might be disciplined. But Hayes had nothing to do with it."

"Sounds like they have spy somewhere," McConaughey said.

"They have spies everywhere," Shiffman said, holding the unlit cigarette. "I have to go, but I wanted to let you know. I liked Hayes, and I've been doing everything I can to get him back."

The two 99th men watched him leave and continued to sit without speaking. Blair looked at his watch. "You got something else to say, Top? Then say it."

"I didn't like the way he was talking about Hayes in the past tense," McConaughey said. But he made no effort to leave Blair's office in the Orderly Room. "Sorry, but I'm about to make your day worse."

Then McConaughey proceeded to tell Blair what Gomez had told him.

-32-

Cu Chi District, the next day

Early in the morning, when the first sliver of sun turned darkness into deep shadows, Hayes spotted the silhouettes of two Vietcong soldiers. They looked like a giant alien, two-headed creature taking big slow steps. They stopped, two heads swiveling left, then right, with two AK 47 assault rifles seemingly attached to the heads. The lead soldier raised an arm and motioned behind him. At first, Hayes saw and heard nothing, but lying completely still, afraid to move so much as an eyelid, he rehearsed picking up the big revolver that lay in front of his face, cocking it, shooting each man in turn. Then he heard soft scratchy swishing noises, saw a pant leg push through the brambly bushes beside him. He held his breath, watching the man join his companions, then he watched all three creep out of view.

He breathed long and slow, letting his pounding heart calm. His nose clogged with dried blood, the cool air passing through his mouth brought flashes of pain from the broken tooth. Had he slept? Yes, but now all the painful places in his body awoke. In his clothes, damp from dew, he felt cold, nauseous. When he shifted to grasp the pistol, cramps exploded across his abdomen. For a long time he lay still trying to ignore the cramps and nausea. Soon, the sun drove away the gloom, warmed him. The air smelled fresh. Birds sang, insects buzzed. He felt slightly better.

With no shoes or socks, the stones and roots in the tunnels had taken their toll on his feet. His sprint from the tunnel entrance caused more damage. How far could he walk? Which way should he go?

Then the cramps grew too intense to ignore, he crawled out of the bushes, pulled down his pants, leaned his back against a tree and relieved himself. Then he threw up. Stumbling a few feet away, he sat down against another tree and started examining his feet. He found cuts covered with dirt on the bottoms of both. Most appeared superficial. But the toenail of the big toe on his right foot had split. A deep cut cleaved the pad under the base of the toe. The entire toe looked swollen, encrusted with a bloody mass of scab and broken skin.

Thirsty, and with the cramps already returning, he knew he had to find water. Vietnam had lots of water, but the sun had already burned away the dew. At first glance, the terrain appeared flat. On closer examination he detected subtle elevation changes. Water flowed downhill. He started limping in the direction of down.

Sometime around midday, Hayes found a creek. After he'd drunk his fill, he soaked his feet then tried to clean himself. He vomited most of the water he'd drunk. He drank again, more slowly. His dysentery had grown worse. Before he'd come to the creek, he'd been stopping every few minutes though he had little left to expel. He decided to follow the creek. Creeks would lead to streams, which would lead to rivers, which could lead to people. Would the Vietnamese help him? Fingering the Headhunter patch on his shirt, he couldn't find purchase to tear it off. Fuck it. There couldn't be that many people who knew about Headhunter gunships.

He moved away from the creek looking for more bushes he could crawl into. A wave of dizziness struck and he sat down heavily. The dizziness lifted but returned when he got up. He stood still until he felt could start moving again.

I'm okay if I go slow.

He thought about Gloria, the way she'd giggled and kissed his cheek when he caressed her pregnant belly the last time they'd lain together. He loved her so much. They'd had so little time together. He sunk into a fantasy with Gloria until it felt like a dream, then pulled himself out. Took one step. Two steps. Then three. And four. Rest, and let Gloria slide back into his mind. Drift into the dream with Gloria. Snap out of it.

One step, two steps, three steps, four. Don't rush. Look left. Look right.

He picked his way parallel to the creek, taking his time, taking care, stopping to dream whenever he felt dizzy or when the dysentery struck. He'd hunted deer in Michigan with a bow and arrow. He knew how to move silently in the woods. He tried to shut off thoughts about his painful feet, about the nausea and cramps. He focused on spotting people before they saw him. He carried the antique revolver in one hand, his finger curled around the trigger guard.

And then he saw the American patrol before they saw him. More accurately, he heard the snap of a twig and the crackle of a boot on dry leaves.

Hayes sank to his knees. A shadowy American soldier blinked into sight through the trees about thirty yards away. The shape of his helmet made him undeniably American.

"Help," Hayes cried. He waved a hand, the one without the gun. "I'm American."

Muzzle flashes and bullets whizzing past. He sprawled forward, lay flat.

"Oh shit," he said and passed out.

-33-

Detroit

On her last day at Susanna's flat, Gloria went to see State Senator Logan Carlton. He had called and said he wanted to speak to her about something important. Gloria felt rundown. The weeks of constant worry about Jimmy had taken a toll. Almost June now, and she'd heard nothing. She thought it had slowed her recovery from the birth.

Wearily, she knocked on the front door of her father's house where the senator had asked to meet her. He opened the door immediately.

"I saw you pull up," he said.

"So, you tracked me down." She offered a wan smile.

He shrugged. "Frances told me where you were."

She stood by the front door, the silence stretching out. "You wanted to talk to me?"

She walked uninvited all the way into the living room. It looked exactly the same as the last time she'd visited but smelled a little musty.

Maybe he hasn't moved in.

"Yes, but first, I had a visit a little while ago from a strange man dressed up like a fuckin' Indian… whoops, sorry 'bout that."

"It's okay." She sat down on the red leather couch.

"Anyway, he came to my senate office, and asked about you. Said he was looking for Matt Doran's daughter 'cause he owed her money from some business deal he had with Matt. He was wearin' buckskin clothes, you know, heavy suede. I swear he looked like Tonto. Soon as he opened his mouth, I could tell he wasn't no Indian. I think he mighta been from China."

She grimaced, scratched her cheek. "Do you remember a while back two people were murdered at a Thai restaurant? It happened the same day you helped me get my driver's license."

"I remember goin' to get your license. But unless it's politics, I don't pay much attention to the news."

"A few weeks after that, a couple of police detectives paid me a visit. They said my stepfather was part-owner of that Thai restaurant. The other owner was some criminal from Thailand. They said he's the one who killed those people. I told the detectives I didn't know anything about it.

"So you could end up owning that restaurant?" Carlton said with a little laugh. She thought he didn't take anything she said seriously.

"We should tell the police about that guy," she said.

"The Detroit police? Fat fu... fat chance." He frowned shaking his head.

She knew the senator did not like the Detroit police. She tried to remember everything the detectives said. They'd told her the man had gone back to Asia. She doubted that anyone who'd had business dealings with her stepfather would want to give her any money.

"I can call those detectives. I think I have their cards back at Mrs. Lincoln's. You'll talk to them, right?"

His frown deepened, but he nodded.

"Was there something else you wanted to talk about?" she asked.

The pain that came over his face was unmistakable. "Yeah, I wanted to talk to you about school."

The phone rang. It hung on the wall in the kitchen so Carlton got up to answer it. "Hello." He moved the phone away from his ear as he listened. Gloria heard somebody speaking loudly but couldn't make out the words. "Yeah, yeah, calm down. She's here." He held the phone out toward Gloria. "Susanna, for you."

"How did she know…" Gloria muttered as she got up, took the phone

"It's Antoine." Susanna's voice skidded on the edge of hysteria. "He's in jail. He's been there three days. Cops caught him breaking into a pawn shop, or maybe it's a gun store. I don't know. He got beat up in jail this morning. Some deputy called me and suggested I might want to bail him out 'cause he'll probably get beat up again, or worse since he's such a pretty boy—"

"How much is the bail?" Gloria interrupted.

"Bail?" the senator asked. He reached for the phone, but Gloria turned her back on him to keep the phone away.

"Okay, okay, take it easy and start over," she said.

"Who needs bail?" The senator asked. Gloria waved a hand at him while she listened to Susanna.

Was Antoine trying to steal a gun for me?

"It's Susanna's boyfriend, Antoine. He got arrested and then he was beat up while he was in jail. I'm going to have to help."

It all took several hours. Gloria called Pip Papineau's office and asked for help arranging bail and if he would represent Antoine. She had enough money in her bank account for the cash required for bail. But she needed an adult to sign for the bail bond, which would be forfeited if Antoine didn't show up in court. She finally persuaded the reluctant senator to sign.

"I don't like it. If this gets out, it won't help my reelection chances," he grumbled. But he signed.

When Susanna went to meet one of Papineau's lawyers and pick up Antoine, Gloria drove back to Susanna's little apartment and gathered the few belongings she had there. Gloria knew the three of them could not share the tiny apartment. She'd also deduced that Susanna had decided to give Antoine another chance.

Susanna must have detected Gloria's skepticism about the relationship when they met on the street outside the apartment. "He'll be sleepin' on the couch but I need to try and keep him away from those black power idiots."

She said it loud enough for Antoine to hear. He sat in her VW, his face turned away.

Late in the afternoon, tense, tired and feeling a little sick, Gloria eased the Rambler into the driveway making sure to avoid blocking Mrs. Lincoln's Oldsmobile. But Logan Carlton pulled in behind her, blocking both cars. As she started to get out she noticed a car parked half a block up the street with a man sitting in it who seemed to be looking at her. Pretending to search for something in the car, she stole several long looks but couldn't see him well. Quickly, she followed Carlton up to Mrs. Lincoln's front door.

"That man in the car back there, I think he's watching me," Gloria said. Carlton turned back and peered up the street. "He's sitting in that dark car parked on the other side of the street."

"Just some guy in a car," Carlton said. "You seen him before?"

"It's too far to see his face." She stared at the car again. As they watched, the car made a U-turn and sped away.

"Well, there he goes. Looks like a Ford. Got them big round tail lights," Carlton said.

Puzzled, Gloria filed the information away. She didn't recognize different cars very well. "Lately, I feel like somebody's been after me, or following me… I don't know. Maybe it's my imagination."

The senator didn't seem to hear her. "I don't think you shoulda been hangin' around with a woman whose boyfriend just got arrested. Shows poor judgment. But maybe I should expect that. You're only sixteen."

Gloria said nothing.

Maybe losing the baby was for the best. I don't know how to be a grown-up.

Mrs. Lincoln opened the front door and stepped onto the porch.

"Gloria! I thought I heard somebody out here. Come in, child. You too Logan. Are you hungry?"

Gloria's fatigue vanished as she helped Mrs. Lincoln prepare a big salad and a pot of spaghetti with only a few meatballs. Carlton ate most of the meatballs. Gloria noticed that Mrs. Lincoln did not make any garlic bread that normally accompanied her spaghetti. However, she found a slice of bread when Carlton asked her if she had any rolls. Gloria also picked up that while she'd stayed with Susanna, Carlton and Mrs. Lincoln had grown quite familiar with each other. Saying he had to drive to Lansing for a breakfast meeting the next morning, the senator left as soon as he finished eating.

"I'm tryin' to lose some weight," Mrs. Lincoln explained after he left, "so you're gonna have to suffer with me if you've come back to stay."

"I'm back if you'll have me, and I wouldn't mind losing a few pounds myself," Gloria said, determined to regain her pre-pregnancy form. Susanna, despite a fondness for pizza and wine, watched her weight carefully and had instilled some of the same consciousness in Gloria.

They both rose from their chairs and hugged each other. "Welcome home. I've missed you, child."

That night, Gloria's despair about Jimmy succumbed to her prayers, so she slept.

The next morning, Susanna telephoned Gloria.

"Can you come over? Me 'n Antoine need to talk to you."

"Okay," she said, and Susanna hung up abruptly. The request felt like an order, but Gloria wanted to talk to them too.

Driving to Susanna's, Gloria decided that Antoine must have told Susanna that Gloria had asked him to get a gun.

How could I have been so stupid?

She tried to remember how long she'd worried about someone stalking her. After she lost her baby, fear slowly took hold of her like a disease. All the way on the drive to Susanna's, she kept glancing in the rearview mirror to see if anyone was following. A few times she thought a car lingered behind her too long, but it always turned off. When she got to Susanna's, she stayed in the car. She looked around but didn't see anyone suspicious. She grew more apprehensive as she climbed up to the apartment. When Susanna opened the apartment door, Gloria saw a blanket and a pillow on the couch. The three of them sat around the small kitchen table, looking tense and unhappy.

"Thanks for bailing me out of that jail," Antoine said. He had a big stitched-up cut on his bulging upper lip. Shiny black, bloody scabs mostly obscured a large cut over one eye. The black-and-blue swollen flesh had closed the eye completely.

"You could have called your father," Susanna said, making Antoine look at her. "You oughta call him now. You need to tell your family about this."

Sighing, Antoine avoided looking at either of them until he took a deep breath and started talking.

"These two pawnshop guys stole my money and then told the cops I broke in. Fuckin' white trash crackers, and the fuckin' Detroit cops…"

"Antoine," Susanna said, "just tell her what happened."

So he did, slowly, with an embarrassed reluctance. Susanna sat with her arms crossed like a teacher monitoring an exam. Antoine said he'd gone to the pawnshop and agreed on a price for a thirty-eight special revolver with a box of shells.

Gloria noticed that he did not say what price he agreed to.

"I looked at the gun. It was okay, but I said I'd have to come back later with the money. The man told me to come back early the next morning." Antoine looked at Susanna like he wanted her to speak.

Susanna said nothing.

"I shoulda known better. They told me to come at six-thirty in the morning but they don't even open till nine. Anyway, when I get there, the guy takes the money and goes into the back to get the gun. I heard some glass break, figured he'd knocked something over. Then a few minutes later, these two Detroit cops busted through the front door with their guns out and arrested me.

"Turns out this second white guy, he was older and he lived upstairs, was the pawnshop owner. He tells the cops he heard someone breaking in so he called them. Cops fuckin' believed him and they arrested me."

"We both thought you needed to hear this. I believe Antoine," Susanna said, though she didn't sound like she did.

Gloria decided to come clean.

"You were buying that gun for me, right, Antoine?" Antoine looked at her with his one good eye as Gloria turned to Susanna. "First day I was here, Antoine came by to get his stuff. I asked him to buy me a gun and I gave him the money for it. This whole thing's my fault."

Susanna, her eyes suddenly teary-eyed, nodded. "Ah, okay, Antoine told me that, but… I'm glad you did too." She clasped Antoine's hand in both of hers. "I believed you, Antoine. Really I did."

She turned to Gloria. "Why did you want a gun?"

Gloria didn't know what to say. She remembered thinking about what Jimmy would do. He'd killed her stepfather and he'd killed those men at his uncle's cabin on Sugar Island. Jimmy killed people to take care of her. But now she had to take care of herself.

"Are you okay?" Susanna asked.

"No… um… my boyfriend..." It took Gloria a few moments to force her attention back to Susanna and Antoine. "For awhile now, I've felt like someone's after me. Some Detroit detectives came to see me and said my stepfather was part-owner of a restaurant where two people got murdered. The other owner was this man from Thailand. The detectives said he killed those two people. They said he went back to Thailand, but I think he might still be around here."

Gloria looked at Antoine. "That day you came for your things, I wasn't feeling so hot.

"I'll say you—"

She waved a hand at him. "I was afraid and seeing that shotgun you left at Susanna's made me want to get a gun. I think my head was still messed up 'cause of drugs they gave me at the hospital. I had a lot of other things to worry about. I shoulda never asked you to do it."

She sighed. "You know, I once tried to shoot my stepfather." She looked at Susanna. "I told you about him.

After I ran away, he tried to kill me and I went right back at him. I felt awful afterwards. Made me as bad as him."

Susanna stared at her, incredulous. "Your stepfather really tried to kill you?"

"Yeah, he tracked me down and sent these thugs with guns to bring me back. One of them took a shot at me. I went home in the middle of the night and stole a pistol from my stepfather's desk. Then he came home. He was a long ways off when I shot at him so I missed, thank God. But I burned down our house too… I lost my temper. I went crazy."

"You burned down your house?" Susanna said. "You never said anything about this before."

Gloria tensed. "No, and I probably shouldn't have said anything now. My life's a mess. I've been trying to fix it."

Susanna glanced at Antoine. "Can I tell Antoine what you told me about your stepfather whipping you? Just the whipping."

She shrugged, then nodded.

"Gloria told me he whipped her. You can still see the marks on her back. And he used to beat them up, especially her stepmother. He put her in the hospital."

"More than once," Gloria added.

"I'm sorry," Antoine said. "I remember you saying I didn't really know you."

Gloria fidgeted with her hair, and Antoine seemed focused on his own problems. "When I said you didn't know me, I meant something else. You said that I was a rich white girl, and that I didn't know what it was like to be black."

"I'm sorry. I know you understand us better than I—"

"You need to get off that black power kick, Antoine," Susanna said.

Gloria shook her head. "No, that's not it. None of us really understands what it's like to be in somebody else's shoes, especially when they're another race, but... um..."

They both looked at her, waiting for more. Gloria swallowed, wondering if she was doing the right thing.

She picked up Susanna's hand, then Antoine's, put them side by side on the table with her own hand. "Susanna, you have the darkest skin. Antoine here is a lot lighter.

Antoine said, "Yeah, well lots of black people have lighter skin. There's lot of variance even in Africa. And then there's miscegenation. That's when the slave owners and—"

"Yeah, I know about that," Gloria said. "But look at my skin. It's only a little lighter than yours, Antoine."

"Same thing must be true for whites, right? And whites got that tannin' thing goin' on." Antoine chuckled.

"And there's that miscen... misinnation..." Gloria struggled with the word.

"Miscegenation."

"Yeah, yeah, it's white people and black people fucking, not just slaves, anybody," Gloria said. "Their kids are half black and half white. And then if one of those kids grows up and sleeps with a white person, their kids are one-quarter black."

Antoine nodded, Susanna looked amused.

"Tell me, at what point is somebody considered white, and not black? When they're only a quarter black? When they're one-eighth black? One-sixteenth?"

"Why does it matter—" Susanna started.

But Antoine said, "Well, there used to be a law, probably still is down South, says if you have one drop of black blood, you are black," Antoine said.

"What are you trying to say, Gloria?" Susanna asked.

"What I'm trying to say is a few months ago, I found out who my real father was, and he was black. He had very light skin, lighter than Antoine's, almost the same shade as mine. But he was black. Everybody knew him as a black man. What I'm getting at, is…" She paused for a moment. "Does that make me black?"

"I don't believe—" Antoine started.

Gloria cut him off, her voice rising. "I'm the same rich girl, grew up in Grosse Pointe where my stepfather beat on me and my stepmother, and raped me, but that's okay 'cause we don't talk about that stuff. But if I tell people my father was a black, how long's it gonna be before somebody calls me a nigger? I really hate that word. Somebody told me I shouldn't tell anyone about my father. But you know what my boyfriend said when I told him I was half black? He said 'You're still a hundred percent beautiful.'"

Susanna reached across the table to take Gloria's hand. "You say 'was' when you talk about your father. Is he dead?"

"Yeah, he's dead. My father was Clyde Bonaventure and my stepfather killed him. Right in front of me. I don't know exactly why." She sniffed, looked down at the table. "At first, I thought it was about me, but now I think it had to do with that Mafia war that was in the news a few months ago. My stepfather's dead. My stepmother's dead. My father's dead.

My Jimmy's missing, and he might be dead too. But I don't think so 'cause he's the strongest person I know."

She looked hard at Antoine.

"Antoine, you're wrong about black power. That hippie peace and love stuff? I believe every word. When I was singing *All You Need is Love* at that rally, I meant every word. It made me feel good. It made people who heard me singing feel good too. When you spoke, you made them angry. When I tried to shoot my stepfather, I felt terrible. Susanna and I, we cried watching Martin Luther King's funeral on TV. He preached justice and love. Maybe he wasn't successful enough for you, but he made life better for black people. They killed him for it, but they didn't kill his ideas. You know, they killed Jesus for saying the same things, but he's still goin' strong, two thousand fucking years later."

"Right on," Susanna said.

But Gloria suddenly felt uneasy and a little embarrassed. She wasn't sure why, though Antoine always seemed to upset her. But he hadn't really done anything this time.

"Sorry, didn't mean to get so worked up but I shoulda never asked you to get that gun, Antoine. I must have been out of my mind."

Susanna's ancient candlestick phone let loose with a high-pitched jangly ring that startled all three of them. Susanna got up to answer it.

"Hello… yeah, she's here," and she handed the phone to Gloria.

"Hello."

"Logan Carlton here. I just heard from my contact in the Capitol that Specialist Fourth Class James Hayes has been found. He's in a hospital but he's gonna be okay."

-34-

Chu Chi Base Camp

On his third day at the 12th Evacuation Hospital in Cu Chi, Jimmy Hayes went to MARS.

"Mars? Why would I wanna call Mars?" Hayes grumbled to Staff Sergeant McLaren, a battle-ax of a nurse who seemed to be the main person taking care of him. He felt better having gone from 'I wanna die', and later, 'I feel shitty, lemme sleep', to thinking that he wouldn't mind another sponge bath like the one he'd received when he first arrived at the hospital from a younger, prettier nurse named Kitty. But he hadn't seen Kitty since.

"Glad you're feeling well enough to complain," McLaren said. "MARS stands for Military Auxiliary Radio System." McLaren picked up the empty breakfast tray. Hayes had eaten everything in sight. "It's a way to call the USA. Goes through shortwave radio and connects to the telephone system at home. You need to know the telephone number, and you only get five minutes. Has to be a collect call. But I can get you to the front of the line."

"Oh yeah, I could talk to my girlfriend. I know the number where she's staying. She must have had… Yeah, I'd really like that."

So a little after 1030 Hours Hayes, using crutches, clumped to the front of a line of a dozen soldiers waiting to make calls.

Mrs. Lincoln answered the phone. She accepted the charges without hesitation, surprising Hayes.

"Is Gloria there?" In Michigan, it was after 11:30 the previous night. A few seconds later, Gloria said, "Jimmy, I have to tell—"

"Sunshine, I love you."

Long pause. Even through bursts of radio static he could hear the shakiness in her voice.

"Me too, I love you Jimmy, but… our baby…our little baby boy, he didn't… he's…he's in heaven Jimmy."

He heard the sadness through the static howling in his ear. Couldn't speak right away. Later, he wouldn't remember the rest of the call, just a spec four saying, "Time's up," as he pried the phone phone away.

He spent thirteen days in Cu Chi some of it in the hospital, a couple of visits to a dentist, but mostly he answered a lot of questions from skeptical officers. Major Shiffman seemed to be the only intelligent intelligence officer, and Hayes spent more time talking to him than all of the others.

"What you say indicates we have a well-placed spy," Shiffman said.

"I know I'd seen that VC translator before, but I can't remember where," Hayes said. "Maybe she worked as a hooch maid or something like that."

Hayes had to talk to an American born Japanese captain named Nagano, a psychiatrist whom he learned from other hospital patients had the nickname, "Chinkerbell." Slight, graceful and very young looking he pressed Hayes about the long periods of solitary confinement in total darkness and about his other combat experiences.

"Yeah, I had bad dreams in that fucking dungeon. Didn't know whether I was awake or asleep, whether it was real or a dream. But I haven't had any of those since I got out. I'm okay now," Hayes said.

When he got back to Nui Binh, Hayes did nothing but rest and eat for most of two days. He wrote letters to Gloria. He had to deal with the loss of their baby. He didn't know what to say other than to tell her he loved her. He wanted to know more about how their baby died, but was afraid to ask lest he upset her. Late at night, wrapped in his poncho liner, he cried.

He met two new crew chiefs assigned to the Headhunters. They'd both trained on the new advanced Cobra gunships. Almost since he'd come to Vietnam, Hayes had heard that the 99th would start receiving Cobras to replace their Charlie model gunships.

A streamlined helicopter with rockets, a minigun and a 40-millimeter cannon in its nose, the Cobra didn't differ that much from other Huey helicopters mechanically. But Cobras only carried two pilots, no door gunners, which meant Cobra crew chiefs didn't fly.

"I don't wanna get killed fightin' in this fuckin' mess," one of the new men said. His companion seemed to agree. Hayes thought they might have been sent to the 99th by mistake.

His first night back, none of the 99th's helicopters returned until well after dark. None of the Headhunters returned at all. The gunships spent the night with a First Cav unit near Bien Hoa in preparation for an early morning operation.

His second day back, Hayes finally talked to the platoon sergeant, Sergeant First Class Stanton.

"You're supposed to be fuckin' dead," Stanton said, taking off his sunglasses to glare at Hayes.

The remark puzzled Hayes because Stanton had no sense of humor. Hayes shrugged. "Sorry to disappoint you, Sarge, but I'm still here. Haven't been cleared to fly yet. Doc Goetz has to sign off. Guess I better go see him."

"Doc Goetz ain't here no more. Got transferred."

"We got a new doc?"

"Yeah, and he's a nigger, too."

Stanton pulled a handkerchief out of his pocket and blew his nose. He spent an inordinate amount of time dabbing and wiping at his nose while avoiding eye contact with Hayes. "Lemme know when you're back on flight status. Go see the doc soon as you can."

Stuffing his handkerchief into a pocket but still not looking at Hayes he said, "I'm lookin' for two new crew chiefs that came in for us."

Hayes pointed at the hooch he'd just left. "They're in there. They're Cobra crew chiefs. I don't think they're expecting to fly."

"I'll straighten their asses out on that. They're in the fuckin' Army, not on vacation." He spit, then headed toward the hooch.

Hayes ambled over to the medical hooch to meet the new flight surgeon, a chubby affable young black doctor named Morrison.

"Specialist Hayes, I got a call from a Captain Nagano at 12th Evac about you. He doesn't think you should go back on flight status," Morrison said.

Hayes looked at the doctor. "Doc, there's lots of guys out there been in the shit more'n me. There's nothin' wrong with me. What's the big deal?"

"Nothing. I agree with you. If you have problems after you go home, that's not my concern. Never thought much of shrinks anyway, specially one called Chinkerbell. I already cleared you to fly."

A few hours later, the company clerk found him sitting on his bunk writing a letter to Gloria. "The CO and the first sergeant, they wanna see you in the Orderly Room."

When Hayes got to Lieutenant Colonel Blair's small office, he came to attention and saluted, which the CO returned with a wave.

"Sit down, Specialist. This might take awhile." Already there, the first sergeant sat in front of the CO's desk. Hayes nervously lowered himself into an empty chair.

"Doc Morrison's cleared you to fly though the first sergeant and I are worried. Do you want to continue flying as a crew chief? Nobody would think any less of you if you want to stop. We've usually been able to accommodate enlisted men who want to get off flight status. Technically, it's voluntary."

After several seconds, Hayes decided to tell the truth. "Sir, I'm not anxious to get back in the air, but I'll do it if I have to. I had a lot of time to think when I was a prisoner, maybe too much time. And I was sort of put on trial—"

"The first sergeant and I have read the reports," Blair interrupted.

"Okay. Sir, it was all bullshit, but after listening to those villagers, I don't think they were making everything up. Somebody dropped some of those villagers out of a Headhunter gunship. We kill a lot of civilians. What are we supposed to be doing here? I know we're supposed to be fighting against Communism but—"

"We try as hard as we can to avoid killing civilians," Blair interrupted again.

"I know, sir, and it didn't really bother me until I heard those villagers talk about it. I doubt most of those them give a crap about Communism. I don't like the VC any more than you do. I strangled one of the bastards..." His voice trailed off.

"I didn't mean to snap," Blair said. "As I said, I read the reports and as far as I'm concerned, you deserve another medal. You probably won't get one because there weren't any witnesses. At least, not American witnesses."

Blair yawned and stretched, pushing his chair back from the desk, Hayes didn't care about medals. He just wanted to get home in one piece like he'd promised Gloria.

"S'cuze me," Blair said, yawning again. "I think the first sergeant and I have a solution. You won't have to fly, at least not as much. But first, tell me about the crash."

Hayes told them as much as he could remember about the helicopter crash. Blair frequently interrupted him with questions and made him go over parts of the story several times.

"You were there with the aircraft the entire time it was on the ground in Long Binh?" Blair asked. It was the third time he'd asked about the repairs in Long Binh. Hayes had already told him about how he and Flowers snuck into the Officers Club so they could get steaks.

"Not exactly, sir. I was there when they worked on it. The others, they went to lunch at the Officers Club because they thought there'd be steaks. Right after they left, the Long Binh mechanics finished so I went to see somebody else I knew in Long Binh. I was gone about forty-five minutes, maybe an hour."

"What about earlier in Nui Binh, were you there when they worked on it?"

"No sir. I wasn't sure what they did that morning in Nui Binh, only that it was fixed."

"Who told you it was fixed?" McConaughey asked.

Hayes had to think. "Spec Five Sorenson. He's good, and when he says something's fixed, you can depend on it being fixed right."

First Sergeant McConaughey spoke. "Sir, I think Specialist Hayes needs to know what Sergeant Gomez said."

Blair nodded.

"Sorenson and Sergeant Gomez went to Long Binh and examined that wreckage. They believe someone put sand in the transmission. In other words, somebody sabotaged your helicopter."

Stunned, Hayes couldn't speak for several seconds. "Somebody killed those three guys… and I shoulda died with them. Who'd do something like that?"

"We're asking ourselves the same thing," McConaughey said.

Hayes told them about Sergeant Grugel, specifically how Grugel, before he died, answered some questions by squeezing Hayes' hand. This time, Blair reacted angrily.

"You should have come forward with this information, Specialist," Blair said, his voice raised.

But Hayes got angry, too. "Sir, I didn't think anyone'd believe me, and even if they did, nobody was gonna do anything. It happened right after we had that formation where you talked about Mitchell. That whole thing was a crock of shit. Mitchell was murdered, and we know it."

Blair opened his mouth to speak but stopped. He glanced at his watch.

Hayes sat silently twisting his cap in his hands, thinking he'd gone too far. Then he spoke again, calmer this time. "I did tell somebody, at least part of it. The person I saw in Long Binh was that Major Kucharski, you know, the officer on General Westmoreland's staff. Cartwright and I figured out that Mitchell had talked to somebody in Long Binh because he was really upset about the Headhunters killing civilians."

"You went to see a major on Westmoreland's staff? That's a pretty ballsy thing for a Spec Four to do," McConaughey said.

"He was the major who arranged that trip I made to talk to Walter Cronkite and CBS in New York. That worked out pretty damn good for the Army," Hayes said. "Besides, I didn't set out to see him. I was looking for this friend of mine, Jimmy Ray Suggs. He's an MP staff sergeant with CID, and he's investigated murders before. I tracked him down to Major Kucharski's office, but the major had him working on something else. I ended up talking to the major kinda by mistake. Then later, that night at the Officers Club, we all ran into Major Kucharski again. I thought me and Flowers were gonna get in trouble, but the major didn't care. He told me he'd changed his mind and was gonna let Jimmy Ray look into what was going on here. Must not have happened or you'd have heard about it."

For a long time, the three of them sat without saying a word until Blair looked at his watch again.

"Here's what we're going to do, Specialist Hayes. I'm promoting you to Sergeant E-5. You will take over as platoon sergeant of the Headhunters."

"What! Sir, I'm not the right man for the job. I'm a draftee and I have no plans to stay in the Army. I'm counting the days till I can be a civilian again."

Blair chuckled. "That shouldn't be a problem, though you might consider a military career. I could help you get on track to becoming an officer. You have potential. But back to the immediate problem, we need a new Headhunter platoon sergeant. Top thinks you're the right man for it.

"Consider everything we've talked about today to be confidential. Somebody, almost certainly somebody in this company, has murdered five people." Blair looked first at Sergeant McConaughey and then at Hayes, holding each in his gaze. "Right now, this war is still the priority. We can't let this affect our combat performance. So you will keep quiet about it. But I want the two of you to make every effort to find out who this murdering bastard is. And be careful. He's already killed five men."

-35-

June, Detroit

The good news about Jimmy triggered a frenzy of musical activity for Gloria. In the big garage behind Mrs. Lincoln's house, she played her guitar until her fingers hurt. She'd lost most of the calluses on her fingers. After three weeks of practicing, her fingers ached all the time.

The needle in her love-hate relationship with Jimmy's electric guitar veered further into the hate spectrum. His Fender Stratocaster and amplifier constituted a complex instrument full of unfamiliar variables that Gloria couldn't seem to master. She could turn up the volume, but not much else. She could not create the kinds of tones she'd heard from Jimmy or that she heard on the radio.

Worse, her acoustic guitar had started giving her problems whenever she plugged it into the amplifier. The night she'd met Jimmy, he and Mrs. Lincoln's son Roscoe had installed a pickup inside her guitar so she could play it through an amplifier. She loved her Epiphone FT 120 Excellente and had actually grown fond of the tinny, amplified tone it produced despite the problems with feedback. Now bursts of static corrupted the sound, and sometimes the amplification cut out.

Perhaps the biggest shock came when she discovered she couldn't sing. At least she couldn't sing the way she expected to sing. Her vocal skills had withered as much as her formerly facile fingers. Her voice cracked, she sometimes missed notes, she strained to hit any note accurately. Her brain crackled with new musical ideas, but she struggled to express them. The harder she worked, the more her fingers hurt and the more frustrated she got.

"Dammit, dammit, dammit! This is awful, just awful," she snarled when a flare of static spoiled a riff that had taken entirely too long to perfect. She wanted to smash the guitar.

Susanna, who had come over to sing harmonies and play around with a Wurlitzer electric piano, winced, and glanced at Antoine. He'd been wandering around the garage inspecting all the musical gear. He wiped dust off Roscoe's Gibson Les Paul electric guitar. "Man, this stuff looks expensive. Where'd it all come from?"

Gloria scowled at him. Antoine couldn't play any instruments or sing. He just hung around, irritating her. Everything irritated her. And she felt tired. She'd stayed up late the night before watching the TV news about Robert F. Kennedy's assassination.

"Roscoe knew music people all over Detroit so this stuff probably didn't come from one place," Susanna said.

"What difference does it make?" Gloria asked. She wished Antoine would leave.

Antoine faced Gloria and flashed one of his insincere smiles. While his damaged face had mostly healed, he now looked like a thug.

"Thought there might be a music shop or some place where you could find help," he said, crouching to study the label on the organ that had been put on by the music store where it had been purchased. "There's gotta be a lot of smart people around here who know about guitars and amplifiers. I mean, Motown and all that stuff? It's a local business. I could try and find somebody. I got nothing else to do, and I owe you."

"You don't owe—" A loud blast of static drowned her out. Still holding her guitar, Gloria had pushed back her chair toward the amplifier and the movement triggered the static.

"Shit!" She glared at the amplifier for a long time. Slowly her body relaxed. She forced a smile at Antoine as she carefully laid the guitar down. "That's a good idea, Antoine."

"I'm gonna look at these labels, then I'll head out," he said.

"I'll come with you," Susanna said. "Your face is still gonna scare people."

Dr. Sadowski had taken Antoine's stitches out and the bruises had faded from purple to brown and yellow .

"If it's okay, I'll come too. I need a break. My fingers are killing me," Gloria said. "But let's take two cars. I'll probably want to come back and practice some more."

Later, Gloria and Susanna sat beside each other in a booth at a Big Boy restaurant where they'd stopped for lunch. Antoine sat across from them. At the second music store they'd visited, Gloria bought a Gibson J-45 guitar with a hardshell case for Jimmy. She'd paid almost $200 after carefully examining guitars in two music shops.

"I don't know how I'm going to get it to him," she said.

Antoine thought for a long moment. "I know a place that could pack up that guitar and send it to Vietnam. Bank I worked at had a customer that sent specialized electronics all over the world. We used to handle some of the shipping for them. Want me to take the guitar and have them send it to your boyfriend?"

"That'd be great, Antoine."

"You have to pay with cash, though, and they're not cheap," he said.

Gloria nodded. "How much would it cost?"

Antoine shrugged. "I don't know. I never sent anything to that part of the world. Fifty bucks? Might even be more. They insist on doing the packaging 'cause they want to make sure it gets there undamaged."

Gloria reached for her purse and gave Antoine seventy-five dollars.

"Boy, you sure don't hesitate to spend money," Susanna said.

"Hmmpf, it's not like I'm blowing money on Cadillacs and whiskey like some of those singers. And we're eating at a Big Boy, not the London Chop House," she said. Gloria had ordered the Big Boy double patty-hamburger and so had Antoine. But Susanna asked for a green salad.

"Somebody's got to eat healthy," she said.

Gloria uncrossed and re-crossed her legs, then leaned forward to look past Antoine out at Jefferson Avenue. "Listen, how'd you like to see where I used to live in Grosse Pointe? I just thought of something I've been meaning to do. I don't want to go out there alone."

"I should go take care of shipping that guitar," Antoine said.

"Right. But why don't you take my car and I'll go with Gloria, if you'll give me a ride home." Susanna looked at Gloria.

"Sure," Gloria said.

"What do you want to do in Grosse Pointe?" Susanna asked.

"Something I need to find that's worth a lot of money. A tackle box full of keys. I'll tell you later."

When their food arrived, Antoine had the waitress put his food in a bag so he could eat it in the car. Then he left with the guitar and the address for Jimmy that Gloria gave him.

"Are you sure you can afford all this?" Susanna said after he was gone. "Antoine needs to call his father. I'm sure he can afford to pay for Antoine's lawyer. Antoine knows he has to call, but he's avoiding it."

Gloria waved a hand while trying to swallow a big bite of her hamburger. She drank some Coke to wash it down then stabbed several French fries onto her fork. Waving the fork at Susanna, she said, "I'm starving. Hardly ate any dinner last night and skipped breakfast this morning."

"Slow down before you choke." Susanna laughed and took a dainty bite from her salad. "See? Tastes just as good when you eat slowly, and it lasts longer."

Wedging her loaded fork against the edge of her plate, Gloria pried off all but one French fry. "About the money, first, the record company paid me for that record. Maybe it wasn't a big hit, but it still made more money for me than some people make in a year. The president of the record company thinks it would have been a hit if we'd toured. And my father and my stepparents died. That's two fortunes that I'm probably inheriting. I always knew my stepfather was rich and that he was a huge crook. No surprise the government wants to confiscate a lot of the money. But there's still gonna be lots left."

"Huh. How much are you going to… Never mind. It's none of my business."

"I don't mind. Just don't blab it around. It should be millions. And my father, Clyde Bonaventure, he was wealthy, too, probably a millionaire. He never got married. But he had brothers and sisters, who have kids. Some of them may be looking at his money. He changed his will when he found out about me so now I'm supposed to be the sole heir. But I don't think all my new aunts and uncles and cousins should be cut out."

"Maybe you should be talking to them," Susanna said.

"Yeah, maybe, but here I am talking to you. I've never even met any of them." She took the last bite to finish the burger and eyed her remaining French fries." You want to get hot fudge sundaes?"

Susanna shook her head. "Nah, but you go ahead. I'll just watch. It's fun to see someone fall off the diet wagon."

Gloria stared at her French fries, then pushed the plate away. "Maybe you're right. I ate too fast. I'm a little queasy anyway, almost like being pregnant again."

"I didn't mean to—"

"It's okay. Haven't been eating much lately, and I'm tired all the time," Gloria said. She rubbed her stomach and kept looking at the French fries. "You know, there's a lot of my stepfather's money out there that nobody knows about. My stepfather was a lawyer and an accountant. He helped a lot of crooks hide their money. They'd start these businesses where they could pretend to earn it legally. Sometimes he got paid by cutting himself in for part of the business, but most of them just paid him cash, 'cause that's what they had. He stashed it in bank accounts and safety deposit boxes overseas. He bought a lot of gold and silver. I don't think the government knows about most of that."

"Do you think you have to tell them?"

"I don't know. Probably. Maybe I'll ask my lawyers. But if I end up talking to the cops, they might start asking me about other things. I've had so much trouble with the police. What I want to do is see if I can find the tackle box where my stepfather kept his bank books and safety deposit box keys."

"Okay, but are you gonna skip that sundae, 'cause I could change my mind about getting one," Susanna said.

"No sundae. I have climbed back onto the wagon."

-36-

At the same time

On a hunch, Jettrin Juntasa followed the rusty VW out of the Big Boy parking lot. He followed it all the way to a pawn shop on Gratiot Avenue.

It puzzled him that Gloria Doran seemed to be around more Africans than whites. In his experience with American soldiers, whites and blacks didn't mix together very well. He'd tried to learn more about her from a local African politician he'd seen visiting her, but the man had quickly grown suspicious.

Juntasa's focus had now shifted from taking the girl back to Thailand to finding out what had happened to the money from his heroin venture with Matt Doran. The $10,000 he'd paid for the girl paled in comparison to the heroin money. He'd finally begun to grasp that heroin produced more profit with less work, and most especially, with less trouble, than whores. This new understanding had been driven home by the number of fingers he'd chopped off in the weeks he been back in Thailand. He thought about how much money the heroin venture must have generated and about how clever Doran could be about hiding money. The girl might know. What had Matt Doran said? "She knows too much about my business."

This particular young African man, who'd obviously been in a fight recently, looked like someone Juntasa could talk to. And he had been sitting in the restaurant with the girl and a young African woman.

A few minutes after the African entered the pawn shop, Juntasa also went inside.

Holding up a guitar, the African was saying, "C'mon man, it's brand new, never even been played." He pointed to the bruises and fresh scars on his face. "I got doctor bills to pay." A chubby white man behind the counter shook his head and looked at him, impassive. The two argued for several more minutes while Juntasa examined some switchblade knives, a small semiautomatic pistol with pearl grips and an obsidian chess set. When the African man left the store, counting the money he'd received for the guitar, Juntasa followed him outside.

"You want to make more money?" Juntasa asked as they reached a small rusty car. He held up a twenty-dollar bill and gestured with his head toward his dark blue Ford Falcon. "We talk."

Inside the Falcon Juntasa handed over the twenty-dollar bill and spoke slowly. "What is your name? Do you know Gloria Doran?"

The African nodded. "I'm Antoine, and yeah, I know her."

"She rich girl?"

Antoine shrugged. "Yeah."

"I do business with her father, Matt Doran. He owed me money."

Antoine stared and Juntasa thought he looked a little nervous. Good.

"That's her stepfather, not father. But you know he's dead, right?"

"Dead, yes. I know. You want more money?"

Antoine looked around the parking lot, seemed to gain confidence and nodded. "Always need money."

"Matt Doran owes money so now she owes money."

Antoine shrugged and said, "I heard she's inheriting his money but she's only sixteen. She won't get it right away."

"In-heri-ting?" Juntasa said trying to process what he'd heard. He didn't know the word.

"That means she gets his money but it has to go through a court first. Probably take months."

"Ah," Juntasa said.

Antoine glanced at the twenty-dollar bill that he hadn't put away and said, "I think she might have some other money."

"Other money? Where?"

"That'll cost you more."

Juntasa smiled, took out his wallet and gave Antoine another twenty.

"More than that," Antoine said, his eyes on the wallet. "I can see you got it."

Juntasa cursed inwardly. The African was smarter than he looked. Nevertheless, he pulled four more twenties out of the wallet and handed them over. "Now you tell."

"I heard her mention a tackle box that's worth a lot of money."

"Tackle box? What is tackle box?

"It's a box fishermen use to keep their hooks and stuff," Antoine said. And when he saw the continued puzzlement on Juntasa's face, he gestured with his hands, "It's a metal box about this big. They're different sizes, but probably bigger than a shoe box."

Juntasa nodded. "Where she keep box?"

Antoine grinned. "I think they're gonna go get it this afternoon. It's at the house in Grosse Pointe where she used to live."

Juntasa smiled. He knew the house. He'd been there before. "What is in tackle box?"

Antoine seemed to think about asking for more money, but after glancing at Juntasa he said, "I think she said something about bank books and keys, and that it was that it was worth a lot of money. That's all I know. I can try to find out more, but if I do, I want split of the money."

Juntasa made a show of thinking then said, "Maybe." He took out his wallet and rooted through it. Finally he pulled out a business card and handed it to Antoine, who examined it.

"You're Jason Lee, and you're a realtor?" he asked.

Juntasa nodded. He'd had the cards printed when he first came to Detroit to look for the girl. He told people that he was searching for her because she was owed money from the sale of her foreclosed home. The telephone number on the card was for an answering service.

Antoine folded the twenties around the card and, grinning, got out of the Ford. Juntasa had no intention of sharing any money with him and doubted the African would call the answering service.

But if he did, it was still paid up.

-37-

Nui Binh

The morning after the meeting with Lieutenant Colonel Blair, First Sergeant McConaughey led Jimmy Hayes from the mess hall to his small hooch located behind the Orderly Room.

The first sergeant had a bunk, a wooden footlocker and tall metal locker. An old Styrofoam cooler sat in one corner. McConaughey pulled a box fan off a folding metal chair and placed it on the concrete floor.

"Sit down," he said as he sat on his bunk. Hayes spotted a five-by-seven color photograph of a pretty Asian woman thumb-tacked to a framing two-by-four beside the bunk. McConaughey's wife, he assumed. The hooch smelled faintly of incense. Some men burned incense to mask the odor of marijuana but Hayes realized that the first sergeant must like the smell. No surprise. McConaughey called Asia, not America, home.

"Let me make clear that you becoming platoon sergeant is an order. I expect you to carry it out to the best of your ability. You should move into the NCO hooch with the two slick platoon sergeants today."

"Sure, okay."

"What did you do in civilian life?"

"I was in a rock and roll band."

"You're kidding. You can make a living doing that?"

"Sure. Ever heard of the Beatles? I made enough to eat. Just before I came over here, my girlfriend, another guy and me made a record that's sold some."

"You're a sergeant, E-5 now," McConaughey said. "Same pay grade as a spec five except you have sergeant stripes. So when you tell your men what to do, they have to do it. That's the Army, and they're all in the Army."

Hayes didn't like it but thought it unwise to say so. "Why is Sergeant Stanton no longer platoon sergeant? Doesn't he know how to do this better than me? He's a sergeant first class. Is he leaving?"

A sour look overtook McConaughey's face like he'd smelled something bad. "If I had my way, he'd be leaving. He hasn't been doing the job, and the CO thinks it's starting to affect combat efficiency.

"The biggest problem is morale. You've got Headhunter crew asking to transfer to slick platoons, and nobody wants to go to the Headhunters. Several men don't want to fly. The platoon might be developing a serious drug problem. You know Specialist Delaney?"

"Yeah, but we're not the best of friends," Hayes said. "He's a crew chief. Been in the platoon longer than me. Must be getting close to the end of his tour."

"He's been under the influence of drugs and couldn't fly twice in the last ten days. The CO gave him an Article Fifteen the first time and then court-martialed him. He's a private now. Doc Morrison took him off flight status. I'm sending him to Maintenance, but he probably won't be much use to them."

"Too bad. I thought he was a good crew chief," Hayes said shaking his head.

"You got busted for smoking marijuana. I hope you understand the problem better than me. We need these guys back to doing their jobs. I'm hoping they'll listen to you. They respect you, or at least they should. You won't be asking them to do anything that you haven't done. That wasn't the case with Stanton."

McConaughey looked at the picture of his wife for a moment.

"You want some coffee from the mess hall? Or I've got some Cokes."

"I'll take a Coke," Hayes said. McConaughey took out two cans out of Styrofoam cooler and snapped holes in them with a church key.

"Stanton was a machine gunner in Korea with the 7th Cavalry Regiment. I found out that unit was involved in a massacre of civilians at No Gun Ri. I don't know if he was there or not, but I suspect he was. I was in Korea too, but our paths never crossed till now. I'm trying to find out more about him."

Hayes wondered where McConaughey was getting his information. "A machine gunner? And he didn't want to fly as a gunner here?"

"Yes and no. He wouldn't fly on gunships but he did fly gunner on the courier several times. He disappeared for a day or two on more than one occasion. Said he went into Saigon. The CO won't do anything or talk about it. There must be somebody higher up taking care of Stanton. Lately, it's gotten worse. Pilots are complaining. Maintenance is complaining. Morale's a problem. The CO wants him out as platoon sergeant."

Hayes thought about it as he took a long drink of his Coke, savoring the icy sweetness. For almost two months he'd had nothing to drink but water, sometimes bad water.

"You know who else thought you had leadership potential?" McConaughey said, and Hayes looked up at him. "Sergeant Grugel. He thought you were a natural leader. After he cooled off, he liked the way you stuck up for Mitchell."

Hayes nodded, resolving to give the platoon sergeant job his best shot. "Yeah, I hope I can do half as well as him. When do I start?"

McConaughey reached into his pocket and came out with a set of the little black rank insignia that everyone wore on the collars of their jungle fatigue shirts, tiny sergeant's stripes. "Right now. I'll give you a copy of the promotion orders when the clerk finishes them."

The first sergeant helped Hayes fasten the insignia onto his collar and then Hayes started to get up.

"Hold on, we're not done yet," McConaughey said. "I want to talk about these murders."

Hayes sat back down. "Why did Sergeant Gomez go check on that wreck? Did he think I did something wrong?"

"No. The official accident report concluded the crash was due to transmission failure and left it at that. What it didn't say was that most people thought it was a maintenance fuckup. Gomez wanted to look at the wreckage because of the implication that somebody at the 99th might have made a mistake. I guess, as the senior maintenance NCO, he took it personally. What he found was something worse than a maintenance problem."

"If it was a maintenance problem, somebody in Long Binh probably screwed up. We flew a lot that morning, and the ship was fine. The Long Binh mechanics were the last ones to work on it before we crashed," Hayes said. "I helped their two maintenance guys. One of them was a staff sergeant who seemed to know what he was doing. They replaced the warning light that the 99th put in, and they changed out some of the wiring that looked old. At the time we were all thinking that it was probably the wiring."

"Then you left?"

"Yeah."

"So, what about after you got back? What did you do? Were you still with the helicopter?"

Hayes shrugged. "Yeah, we were all there. Didn't do much. I wrote a letter, and I think the pilots were reading, or maybe sleeping. Flowers read his Bible and took a nap. We were waiting around for the other Headhunter ship, you know, the lieutenant and Moss. We were supposed to be a fire team that day, but our ship got hung up with that light. And now I know the other ship was with some Green Berets at that village—"

McConaughey interrupted, "And the two pilots were CW2 Moss, who's now a WO1, and Lieutenant Carson who's on very shaky ground. The CO's trying to save his career. The two crew were Specialists Kannegiesser and Delaney, who has a drug problem. Kannegiesser, by the way, is one of your men who doesn't want to fly."

The first sergeant stopped, lit a cigarette. Hayes was pretty sure that McConaughey was thinking along the same lines as him. The murderer might be one of the four crew on the other gunship. They were all at the 99th when Mitchell was murdered. They were all on the flight line when somebody pushed Grugel into the tail rotor. And they were all in Long Binh the same day somebody sabotaged Hayes' helicopter.

"Probably not Carson. He was piloting the gunship when somebody pushed Grugel into the tail rotor," Hayes said. "When we went to dinner at the officers club looking for those steaks, nobody stayed with our helicopter. Nobody was with the ship for about an hour."

"So somebody could have gotten to the helicopter then?" McConaughey asked.

"Yeah, and it was dark part of the time."

"And you said you saw Moss at the officers club?"

"Yeah, he was talking to that Major Kucharski. The only time I saw Delaney and Kannegiesser was that morning at Nui Binh." Hayes stopped and snapped his fingers. "No, wait. Flowers told me he saw Delaney in the afternoon, and he thought he mighta been drunk or stoned or both."

They both sat silently thinking.

"I don't know why anyone would commit those murders," McConaughey said. "What do you think?"

"Well, I think it has something to do with Mitchell raising hell about killing civilians. He wrote a letter to General

Westmoreland. Major Kucharski told me that. The major said they already knew what had happened at the village. He wanted to talk to Mitchell because Mitchell was threatening to tell his congressman. So, the major had Jimmy Ray Suggs from CID in Long Binh call Mitchell and set up a meeting. You see, Major Kucharski already knew Jimmy Ray."

"Who's this Jimmy Ray again?"

"Jimmy Ray Suggs. He's this military police staff sergeant who brought me to see Walter Cronkite about that ground attack we had here. That Spanish TV reporter was going to say we killed a whole bunch of civilians in that ground attack. That happened just before you got here. It was Major Kucharski ordered Jimmy Ray to take me to CBS, and it was Jimmy Ray who called Mitchell to get him to see Major Kucharski. So the major talks to Mitchell and I'm guessing that Mitchell wouldn't agree to keep his mouth shut."

McConaughey took out his cigarettes and shook one out of the pack. Hayes watched as he lit it, inhaled and blew out a lot of smoke.

"So then somebody killed him."

Hayes leaned back out of the smoke. "The major knows a lot more about it than he told me. But he seemed surprised when I told him about Grugel."

"Yeah, but Kucharski wasn't anywhere around here when Mitchell or Grugel died. It's somebody in the company," McConaughey said, stubbing out the cigarette. "Probably somebody on that ship."

They both sat thinking. Then McConaughey said, "You'd better be careful. Get yourself a forty-five. Anybody says anything, just tell 'em ever since you were a prisoner, you're a little nervous."

Hayes looked at him. "Huh, I am nervous. I've been sleeping with a pistol under my bunk since I got back here. I picked up a couple of guns when I escaped those tunnels. One of them's a nice Commy nine-millimeter. I need to get some ammunition for it, though I have two full clips. Other pistol's some kind of antique. I don't know what it is, but it packs a hell of a wallop." He didn't tell the first sergeant about the forty-five and the thirty-eight that he also had.

"See Sergeant Gomez. Armament can probably get you nine-mil ammo. Gomez will know what to get for your piece. He's good with guns."

"Okay," Hayes said.

"I'm gonna find Sergeant Stanton now and tell him he's done as platoon sergeant. Ordinarily, I'd have the two of you make the transition together, but not this time. One of his many problems is that he doesn't like today's young soldiers. Being relieved by you isn't going to sit well with him. So just start doing the job."

The both rose and McConaughey offered his hand.

"Good luck," he said. "Come see me when you have questions. And remember that the other platoon sergeants will help too. They didn't care for Stanton either."

"Okay, but let me know when I screw up," Hayes said.

"Oh yeah, that's my main job around here."

-38-

Grosse Pointe Shores, Michigan

"Actually, we're in Grosse Pointe Shores, not Grosse Pointe," Gloria told Susanna as she steered the Rambler up the long winding driveway to the ruins of her former home. "This is the first time I've been here since I burned it down."

Stopping in front of the garage, she tried to ignore the anxiety building up inside. "Guess I didn't do a very good job on the garage." The late afternoon sun peeking between a tree and the garage hit her in the eyes. She squinted at the ominous structure, the only part of her former home still standing. "Don't know why it didn't burn. I poured enough gas on the cars inside, extra on my stepfather's Corvette."

"That's the garage? It's bigger than our house in Inkster," Susanna said.

"Yeah, there were three cars in there, but there's probably room for half a dozen. My stepfather, he'd smack Gina if she parked too close to his precious Corvette." Gloria shivered, then pulled an envelope from the Rambler's glove box. She tore it open and took out a key. "It's a key to the padlock on the garage door. My lawyers gave it to me in case there's something in the garage I want to keep. Haven't made up my mind yet, but I'll probably sell the place."

"You're kidding. It's really nice out here. Maybe you should build another house. It's like you have your own private park." Susanna got out of the car and Gloria followed. "You can just see some water through the trees. Is that the Detroit River?"

"No, it's Lake St. Clair. By Grosse Pointe standards, our house wasn't that big, but there's a lot of property, and you can't see any of the neighbors. My stepfather didn't want anybody to see us."

Gloria walked slowly toward the exposed concrete basement where the house had stood. Somebody had hauled away the rubble, leaving only the damaged garage, a big stack of salvaged bricks and a ten-foot-deep concrete basement.

The sun flickered through leaves dancing in the cool breezes blowing in from the lake but sweat slicked Gloria's armpits and torso. She felt weak and a little light-headed.

Susanna said, "Do you mind if I look around? This place is really cool."

Gloria continued staring at the bare basement where muddy puddles strewn with leaves and dirt covered most of the concrete floor. Finally, she said, "Yeah, sure, go ahead. I'll be in the garage." But she didn't move from the edge of the basement, encircled by a flimsy slat fence. The fire's burnt smokey smell made her queasy.

She remembered her anger the night she set the fire. Angry with her stepfather who'd raped her and beaten Gina. Angry with the thugs he'd hired. They'd shot at Gloria, missing by mere inches. Angry with the Detroit police who'd been looking for her. Angry at everyone and everything that night, full of fury until it turned to shame. That night, she'd learned an important lesson. She learned that loving Jimmy, loving the baby inside her, and indeed, loving anyone or anything, brought her peace while anger and hate corroded her soul.

So why did she suddenly feel so sad? And not just a little sad. She suddenly started crying. She wailed so loudly that Susanna, who'd wandered a good distance away, heard her.

"What's the matter?" Susanna called, running back to her. Dizzy, Gloria sagged forward against the fence, only a few feet from the edge of the basement hole. Susanna grabbed her around the waist and pulled her back.

"I - I don't know. I remember this time he beat up Gina. I can see it… the blood on her face. I was at the top of the stairs. He - he saw me and I ran away and hid under my bed."

"You're okay now, Gloria. Let's get out of here," Susanna tried to pull her toward the car.

But Gloria sat down hard on the ground, still sobbing. She whacked her head trying to get rid of the picture in her mind. "He made me suck his… he'd hold my head down. If I did it wrong he'd slap me." She held her head with both hands. "Oh God, I can't stop seeing it. I thought I was over this. I can see it so clear. I don't want to see it. I don't want to remember."

Susanna sat down beside her and put her arms around her. Gloria began rocking back and forth, holding her head, rubbing her eyes, crying too hard now to speak. When she hit herself on the side of her head again, Susanna grabbed her arms and pinned them to her sides. Gloria cried for several minutes until she regained some control. When Susanna loosened her grip, Gloria held out the padlock key still in her trembling fingers. Susanna took the key.

Gloria whispered. "Go in the garage. The metal cabinet in the corner to the right. See if you can find a big green metal tackle box. Go get it. Then we can go."

A few minutes later Susanna came out with the tackle box.

"I don't think I can drive," Gloria said, climbing into the passenger seat of her car. She let Susanna fasten her seatbelt. After adjusting the driver's seat, Susanna leaned across Gloria to crank the passenger-side window down.

"You okay now?" Susanna asked.

Gloria whispered, "Yes." Then Susanna turned the car around and started down the driveway. Gloria shut her eyes but didn't sleep. Minutes later as they sped down Jefferson Boulevard back toward Detroit, Gloria groaned, "Pull over. Hurry."

As soon as the car stopped she unsnapped the seatbelt, tumbled out the passenger door and threw up on the side of the road. When Susanna ran around the car to her, Gloria continued to vomit. When she finished, she jammed her fists her eyes. Susanna grabbed her in a bear hug again.

"I can't stop seeing it. I know it's not real, but..." She struggled to free herself from Susanna's grip.

A police car, lights flashing, pulled in behind them. It felt like a dream to Gloria as Susanna spoke to the police but Gloria heard no words. Lights on a bus stuttered through the trees, followed by a roar as it spewed black smoke. The sickly smell of diesel fumes made her vomit again.

A gray-haired policeman asked, "What's going on here? Have you been drinking?" Gloria tried to answer no but couldn't force out any words.

"No, she's sick," Susanna said.

Gloria lay down on the curb and promptly fell asleep.

Later that evening

"How do you feel, Gloria?" Emily Sadowski asked.

"Not so hot. Where am I?"

"You're in private room in Bon Secours Hospital. It's almost midnight." Sadowski glanced at the room's open door. She spoke softly. "The police drove you here. You got sick and passed out on Jefferson Boulevard. Frances Lincoln, Logan Carlton, Susanna Quinn, one of your lawyers, I didn't catch his name, are all out there."

"I guess I'm a royal pain for everyone."

"You are going to be okay, Gloria. You should feel good that you have so many friends that care about you."

"What's wrong with me?" Gloria asked. She rubbed her watery eyes with the bed sheet. "Am I going crazy?"

"No, but you're going through a difficult time. You lost your baby, and I know you really loved your baby. You thought your boyfriend might be dead. But most of all, you were a victim of that awful stepfather. My guess is that it all caught up with you when you went back to your old home. I believe that you've suffered a breakdown. I don't like the term, but some people might call it a nervous breakdown. It's more like an emotional breakdown "

"Is it going to happen again?" Gloria asked.

"Maybe. But if it does, hopefully it won't be as bad because you'll know what's happening," Sadowski said. After a moment, she added, "And you have friends to help you."

"Yeah, I guess."

Sadowski took a deep breath. "Isn't that what friendship's all about? Friends help each other. And Gloria, you're sixteen years old. Most people think that still makes you a child. Even those policemen. They've seen too many kids in trouble with drugs—"

"I don't take drugs and I'm not a child," Gloria snarled. "I'm - I'm..." She couldn't finish.

"I don't think you're a child," Sadowksi said. "But you're not fully grown up either. Maybe if you could see me see me more often. I haven't seen you for weeks, a couple of months. I can help you make the transition to adulthood. You've had challenges no sixteen-year-old should have."

"More comfy chairs and talking about myself? Yeah, okay. I'll try and work it into my busy schedule," Gloria said, "and I'm sure you'll send me a bill."

Sadowski frowned. "I want to be a friend and help too. I left my practice because of what happened to you. I have time on my hands. You've done so well considering everything that's happened. You really have. But sometimes there will be setbacks and learning to deal with them comes with being an adult."

Sadowski looked at the door again, shook her head, turned back to Gloria. "You have friends, but I don't think we all agree on what's best for you. You should rest, get your strength back. You need to be strong. Growing up's not easy."

-39-

Nui Binh Base Camp

Dirty, tired, hungry and pissed off, the Headhunters did not return to Nui Binh until late afternoon. They'd spent two days supporting South Vietnamese Rangers and two rainy nights sleeping either in the gunships or in makeshift tents formed by snapping ponchos together.

After Hayes told them he'd replaced Stanton as platoon sergeant, none of his vague fears materialized. Instead, everyone appeared relieved they no longer had to deal with Stanton. Hayes spent more than an hour talking to them and taking notes about a litany of complaints. The only difficult problem concerned Sanderson, a crew chief who'd been denied an R and R to Hawaii to meet his wife.

"Stanton said there's no more allotments, but all the married pilots get to go," Sanderson grumbled.

"You could go to Bangkok, Sanderson. You'll get laid and pick up some tricks to try out on the old lady when you get home," said a gunner to a roar of laughter.

Hayes thought he could solve most of the problems and would talk to the first sergeant about Sanderson. He left the mess hall intending to go to Operations to do the next day's flight schedule, but Kannegiesser intercepted him.

"That morning you caught Delaney and me smoking dope, well, I am really sorry. I wasn't cool with what Delaney said." Kannegiesser spoke in his deep voice, sounding like a recording.

His eyes quickly shifted away when Hayes pressed him. "Smokin' dope before you go up is stupid. You oughta know that. It could get you killed. But tell me what happened with Delaney."

Kannegiesser offered a shrug and looked around. "He started smoking and drinking more, a lot more. We used to light it up after we got in and we'd finished with the maintenance. Shit, you know how it was. You used to smoke with us sometimes."

"Not gonna deny it," Hayes said, "but, my position's different now. I stopped that shit after I got busted. Is that what happened to Delaney? Did he just get caught? Getting' busted all the way down to Private E-1, that's pretty heavy."

Kannegiesser nodded. "Yeah, he got caught, and Stanton was after him. But he was messed up. He fell asleep when we were going through the checklist. He went on sick call, and we had to get somebody else. Then a couple of days later the same thing happened. And he never went to see the medics, either. He was..." Kannegiesser hesitated, looked around avoiding eye contact with Hayes.

"What?"

"Ah, nothing." Kannegiesser shifted uncomfortably and then pulled a pack of cigarettes from his shirt pocket. With two fingers, he started pulling a cigarette out of the pack when bright stuttering flashes of light from behind Hayes startled Kannegiesser and he almost dropped the cigarette. Thunder rippled above making them both duck their heads.

"Shit, it's gonna rain," Hayes said.

"I have to go see about Delaney." Kannegiesser started walking away. Hayes caught up with Kannegiesser since they were headed in the same direction as the Operations bunker. Kannegiesser quickened his step and said, "I don't need any help."

"I'm going to Ops anyway. Besides, I want to talk to Delaney. We used to be friends."

Kannegiesser kept walking faster, either worried about the rain or trying to get away from Hayes. But the taller Hayes had no trouble keeping up despite lingering soreness in his feet. As they passed Operations, Kannegiesser slowed. Lightning flashed again illuminating the distressed look on Kannegiesser's face. He stopped when the thunder boomed again.

"Shit, I can't stop you," Kannegiesser said. "You're gonna see how fucked up Delaney is. I don't want him to get in more trouble."

Kannegiesser headed for an old bunker behind the big Maintenance shed. During mortar or rocket attacks, Maintenance workers sometimes ran out the back door to shelter in the bunker, but most of them sheltered in the two bigger, more substantial bunkers on either side of the shed's big open front entrance. Hayes had heard that sometimes soldiers had liaisons with hooch maids in the rear bunker. Kannegiesser walked around to the far side of the bunker where Hayes saw a form sprawled on an old lawn chair. Delaney.

The first few heavy drops of rain hit Hayes' face and shoulders. Not moving, Delaney seemed oblivious to the rain. Kannegiesser crouched over him.

"Delaney, wake up."

Hayes bent down, putting his face inches from Delaney's. He couldn't see any movement. He put his ear next to Delaney's nose and wasn't sure he detected any breathing. He slapped Delaney's cheeks, and that elicited a low groan.

"Jesus, I thought for second he was dead," Hayes said. "Let's get him outta the rain." Hayes looped a hand under one of Delaney's arms. "Help me drag him inside the bunker."

The rain grew rapidly as they dragged Delaney around the bunker to the entrance. Just as they got there, lightning sparked so brightly that for an instant Hayes saw the entire flight line bathed in harsh white light brighter than daylight. A booming crash followed a miniscule fraction of a second later, rattling the Maintenance shed and unleashing a deluge of rain. By the time they pulled Delaney the last few feet into the bunker, the rain had drenched Hayes and Kannegiesser as thoroughly as if they'd fallen in a river. The rain pounding the metal roof of the Maintenance shed sounded like a freight train rushing by.

"What's he been doing? You don't get like this smoking pot," Hayes said.

"Opium. He's been smoking opium." Kannegiesser bent over Delaney almost like a mother soothing a sick child. As long as Hayes had been in the 99th, Kannegiesser and Delaney had flown together. "He started spending all night out here. I'd bring him food, but he hardly ate. Usually, he stayed in the bunker, but it's funky in here. He wasn't this bad last time I saw him. At least I could talk to him. I was tryin' to get him to stop smoking that shit but he told me to fuck off."

"Jesus Christ, when did he start smoking opium?"

"After he went to that Green Beret camp. At first it was just a little."

The rain hammering the Maintenance shed roof began to abate but now Kannegiesser spoke in a whisper. Hayes asked, "Was he the one pushing people out of the helicopter?"

Kannegiesser tried to evade the question by bending closer to Delaney and whispering, "Wake up, Delaney, wake the fuck up."

"Goddammit, answer me," Hayes said as he shook Kannegiesser by the shoulder. "Did you and Delaney throw those villagers out of the helicopter?"

Kannegiesser jerked himself out of Hayes' grip. "Let go of me. I didn't do nothing. Wasn't even there. Delaney told me he only threw one of them out, the first one. But just seeing it fucked him up. He's not as hardcore as he acts. He was never the same after that day, and he won't talk about it."

"What? You weren't there? Where the hell were you?" Hayes tried to think back to that day they'd gone to Long Binh. He knew for sure that Kannegiesser and Delaney flew with Moss and Lieutenant Carson. "If you weren't there, who the hell was flying gunner?"

"I flew gunner till we got to Long Binh. After we landed, you know, while you were getting that light fixed, Moss and the lieutenant went to meet somebody. Me and Delaney smoked a pipe and then drank some beer at an EM club.

Delaney told me he saw Flowers. When the two officers came back, they said we needed to go to this Green Beret camp to pick up some guys. Except, they didn't want me along. They had another gunner."

"So where were you?"

"I went off post. The lieutenant signed a pass. Moss told me about this bar that was, like, a five-minute Lambretta ride away. Said the bar girls were really pretty and clean. And he was right. I got laid, okay?"

Shaking his head, Hayes let it hang for a couple of beats before deciding that Kannegiesser had told the truth, though maybe not all of it. "They were gettin' rid of you."

"Yeah, maybe… probably." Kannegiesser finally tried to light his cigarette, but it was soaked. He flipped it into the corner of the bunker. "Remember that day when Mitchell and Grugel almost got in a fight about opening up on that village? Me and Delaney argued about that. Moss wanted to kill everybody down there. Delaney was all for it too. I didn't agree, and Delaney called me a pussy. It wasn't no big deal far as me and Delaney were concerned. We've been flying together so long. But after that, Delaney started talkin' shit about you. That stuff you said about the Nazis really pissed him off. In his book, you're either all in or you're out when it comes to the war. He says all them fuckin' war protestors ought to be shot."

Hayes felt around Delaney's neck until he found a spot next to his windpipe where he detected Delaney's weak pulse. He put his face close to Delaney's nose and mouth and this time he felt the soft breaths against his cheek.

"He's breathing and his heart's beating. Real weak."

"Is he going to be okay?" Kannegiesser asked.

"I hope so, but we better get a medic. Let's get him into Maintenance first."

"We do that and he'll get in more trouble. Let me stay here with him."

Hayes considered it for a moment. "No, it's too serious for that. Besides, he's already busted down to E-1. He can't be busted any lower."

"They might put him in Long Binh Jail," Kannegiesser said.

"Yeah, they might. And it'll be a lot harder for him to get opium in there."

They dragged Delaney into Maintenance where a cluster of men soon surrounded them. Sergeant First Class Gomez hurried up and, looking at his men, snapped, "Get back to work." Then he asked Hayes, "What's going on?"

"It's Delaney. He's in a bad way. We can't wake him up. I think he mighta smoked too much opium," Hayes said. "Can you send somebody to get Doc Morrison?"

"Opium?" Gomez's eyes opened wider. Then he looked around. Most of the onlookers hadn't left. "Stratton, go find Doc Morrison, or one of the medics. Tell him we got an emergency. The rest of you, get the fuck back to work. I ain't gonna say it again."

Twenty minutes later, Doc Morrison told one of his medics and Kannegiesser to put Delaney on a stretcher and run him over to the MASH hospital.

"Well, he's breathing," the doctor said. "I suspect there's more than opium involved here." He turned to Kannegiesser. "Was he drinking too?"

"I don't know. I've been gone for two days, but maybe."

After they left, Hayes went back outside with a flashlight borrowed from Gomez. The rain had settled into a steady, heavy downpour, but Hayes couldn't get any wetter. With the flashlight, he examined the ground around Delaney's lawn chair. He found a small ivory pipe in the mud. When he entered the bunker, the dank smell brought back a vivid memory of the underground chamber where he'd been held. He shivered, looked around and saw an Army cot in the corner. It had several tears in the canvas, but still appeared functional. He got down on his hands and knees and looked under it. Other than a couple of used condoms, he didn't find anything. When he played the flashlight beam around, he spotted an old, flattened air mattress rolled up and wadded into a corner of the bunker. He unrolled the mattress and a small plastic sandwich baggie fell out. He held it in the light and saw brown powder inside. He went back into the Maintenance.

"I found this in the bunker," Hayes said to Gomez, holding up the baggy. The powder looked like dirty brown sugar.

"What is it?" Gomez asked.

"I don't know. Kannegiesser said Delaney was smoking opium, but I don't know if this is opium."

"I've never seen any before," Gomez said.

"Me neither, but I thought it was like dark vegetable matter, sticky. I must have seen a picture somewhere. This is more like powder."

"You better give it to Top."

"I will, but first I gotta stop by Ops," Hayes said.

At the big Operations bunker, Hayes received congratulations on his promotion to platoon sergeant. The captain in charge of Ops helped him do the schedule for the platoon, but it wasn't difficult. He accommodated most requests he'd received at dinner. As he started writing names on the white board, Lieutenant Carson, the Headhunters' commander, ambled into the bunker. He didn't say anything until Hayes stopped at the space for the gunner on the gunship to be piloted by the lieutenant and Moss.

"Put in Kannegiesser. I don't see him up there anywhere else," Carson said. Hayes tried to think fast. Moss and Carson had gotten Kannegiesser out of the way so they could put their own man on the gunship the day they threw people off the helicopter to their deaths. Why?

A clean-cut, handsome man sporting one of the more successful mustaches among the 99th's pilots, Carson looked every bit the picture of a dashing helicopter pilot. But the West Pointer's career had begun skidding downward. When he'd arrived, Carson seemed to fall under the spell of Moss. A CW2 on his second tour, Moss, as aircraft commander, was clearly in charge of the aircraft when they flew. But it often seemed like Carson deferred to Moss like an older brother. Maybe Carson's West Point pedigree masked indecisiveness and immaturity.

"Are you going to stand there all fucking night, Sergeant?"

Hayes said, "Sorry, sir, Kannegiesser doesn't want to fly anymore."

"Tough shit," Carson said.

"I can do it," Hayes said.

"No, make it Kannegiesser. That's an order, sergeant."

"Yes sir," Hayes said and wrote Kannegiesser's name in the last empty slot.

Finished at Operations, Hayes left in a hurry to look for the first sergeant. Rain fell steadily keeping his clothing waterlogged. He took detours to avoid puddles and tip-toed along discarded rotor blades that sunk into larger puddles when he trod on them. The darkened EM Club loomed ahead and he saw no lights on in most of the hooches, including both Headhunter hooches. Hayes wanted to go to bed, but when he rounded a corner of the EM Club he saw a light still on in the Orderly Room.

"Jesus Hayes, you look like you drowned," Cartwright said as Hayes entered the Orderly Room. Cartwright had shaved and wore clean jungle fatigues, though they already had sweat stains under his arms.

"Yeah, I might as well be a grunt out in the goddam bush," Hayes said. The former clerk stood behind the current company clerk, who was hunched over some papers on his desk. Hayes could not remember his name. The clerk had shed his jungle fatigue shirt because of the humidity and it was draped over the back of his chair. Hayes smelled sweaty wet clothing, some of it his own.

"I was just showing Conrad here how to do R and R orders. I got this idea about how Sanderson might get to take his Hawaii R and R." Yawning, Cartwright turned to the clerk, "You got it, Conrad? Think you could type up Sanderson's R and R if you have to do it in a hurry?"

"Yeah, I told you before I can do R and R orders. But I can't do them until I get the okay from the first sergeant, and he's gotta talk to the CO. I don't see how you're gonna be able pull that off when there's no allotment."

"Not your problem, Conrad. Me and Hayes'll take care of that nefarious deed. I gotta talk to Hayes about it now. You better skedaddle so you're not involved. I'll shut this place down when we're done."

Conrad looked dubious, but he left.

Hayes looked through the screen of the Orderly Room's back door at first sergeant's darkened hooch. He'd have to give him the baggie in the morning.

"First Sergeant's probably asleep," Cartwright said. "Early to bed, early to rise."

"Yeah, I'm tired too," Hayes said, "but tell me what you have in mind for Sanderson."

"Okay. I found out that there's sometimes empty seats on R and R flights, even flights to Hawaii. If you show up with R and R orders, and there's an empty seat, you get to go. Seems guys get killed or wounded or stuck in a firefight out in the boonies. Sad. This spec five clerk in Long Binh who works in the unit that handles R and R flights told me about it."

"So, are you saying that there might be empty seats on a Hawaii R and R flight, and all we have to do is send Sanderson down there with orders?"

"Wish it were that fucking simple but too many people want to go to Hawaii. My spec five buddy says that there's this lieutenant in his office who decides who fills any empty seats, and he's getting rich doing it."

"You mean he takes bribes?"

"That's about the size of it. I heard of a few guys forkin' over as much as five hundred bucks, though a hundred or two is more the going rate. I think we could raise the cash if we took up a collection. But I can see some other problems."

"Like what?"

"Sanderson's wife would have to buy a ticket to Hawaii on short notice, probably makin' it expensive and risky. This whole thing could fall through. Sanderson's not exactly rich. Even if we could raise the money, I'm not sure how we'd get it to her.

"And finally, I don't know how to get the first sergeant and the CO to go along with it."

Hayes stood in middle of the Orderly Room looking down at the floor for a long time, thinking. "Okay, we might be able to pull this off.

"First, forget a collection. I'll put up the money to bribe the lieutenant and pay for the wife's ticket."

"Jesus Christ, Hayes, did you rob a bank? I know you got some back pay coming but still…"

"Rock and roll. My girl and I, and my late friend Roscoe, we made a record, and it made some money. After I got captured, the record company sent me my share of the royalties in a money order. It's sittin' in my locker. And I might get the first sergeant to go along with this. The last hurdle is the CO. I don't know how that'll go. But we oughta take our best shot."

"This falls through, it could cost you a lot," Cartwright said.

"Yeah, it could. And a rocket could hit the Orderly Room right now and turn us both into hamburger."

Hayes remembered that before he got drafted, before he met Gloria, he'd been sleeping in his car, sneaking into dormitory cafeterias to eat and spending most of any money he made with his band on new musical toys. And before that, he and his uncle depended on the fish they caught, the rabbits they killed and the deer they hunted illegally to make it through the winter. In his entire life, he'd never had as much money as he had now, and if he lost it all, he wouldn't miss it.

"Something else I wanted to tell you," Cartwright said, sitting down on the chair that the clerk had vacated. "When you were gone, I helped Conrad with the mail when I could. I mean, he didn't know people, and he's kinda shy."

"What are you getting at, I'm tired," Hayes said.

"What I'm getting at, is that Warrant Officer Moss, formerly CW2 Moss, might have a girlfriend with the same last name as that major who's on Westmoreland's staff. His name's Kucharski, right?"

"Yeah, that's his name."

"Well, Moss gets letters from a Gail Kucharski in Indianapolis, Indiana."

"How do you know she's related to the major?"

"I don't, but I don't know she isn't related either. Hell of a coincidence if she isn't though."

Hayes thought about it and nodded. "Let's get out of here and get some sleep."

-40-

Grosse Pointe

An uptick in the hospital activity woke Gloria early. Wary from her previous hospital experience, she'd resisted efforts by the resident in charge to take any medication. She felt surprisingly good considering what had happened.

The first hint of trouble came when Susanna Quinn stuck her head into Gloria's room. She sat in the chair beside the bed, bent low and whispered, "I'm not supposed to be here but I wanted to give you a heads-up."

"A heads-up on what?" Gloria asked.

"That Senator Carlton's on the warpath. His lawyer and your lawyer were arguing about you. Then the senator told Dr. Sadowski that she's fired and can no longer see you. Carlton said he's gonna get a real psychiatrist. Sounds like he wants to go to court to become your legal guardian. He wants to make you go to school."

"They can't do that."

"I don't know, Gloria. We were all in the waiting room. Mrs. Lincoln was there too, but she didn't say anything. Carlton didn't notice me 'cause I was in the corner sleeping, then pretending to sleep after I woke up. When he noticed me, he told me to beat it. Said I better not try to see you. Even threatened to have security escort me out. He was throwing his weight around as a state senator."

Gloria groaned. "I thought he was my friend. He helped me get my drivers license and got me a car. But a couple of weeks ago, one of my lawyers said they didn't like some of the things he was doing regarding my father's estate. He took out some money for his reelection campaign. And his lawyer's legal fees are high. Damn, and I told them not to worry about it." Gloria squeezed Susanna's arm. "So you came up here anyway. Thanks."

Susanna smiled. "I'm glad you're feeling better. But brace yourself for more bad news. Last night, maybe an hour or two after the cops brought you in, they told me that they saw a man in a buckskin jacket in your car. When I went out and checked, I couldn't find that tackle box. It's gone."

"Oh no."

"And Carlton had your car towed away."

"Oh shit, but why?"

"Maybe because he didn't have the keys, and he didn't know I had them. He's acting like he's already your guardian."

They both heard footsteps in the hall.

"Quick, hide in the bathroom," Gloria said.

Susanna had just scooted into the bathroom when a security guard entered the room followed by a nun with rimless spectacles dressed in a white habit.

"Don't you dare wake her up," warned the nun, grabbing at the man's arm.

"She's already awake," the security guard said before turning to Gloria. "Senator Carlton asked me to check on you. Has anyone been up here?"

"No," Gloria said trying to sound sleepy.

"Okay. Sorry to disturb you." He backed out of the room.

After the nun left, Susanna came out of the bathroom. She patted Gloria's shoulder and kissed her cheek. "I better split."

"Thanks, Susanna. You're a true friend.

The hospital discharged Gloria after breakfast. Mrs. Lincoln, and especially Logan Carlton, stuck to her like magnets. They waited outside her room as she changed into the clothing she'd worn when she was brought to the hospital. Carlton drove her to Mrs. Lincoln's home with Gloria wedged between him and Mrs. Lincoln. The three ate a tense silent lunch. Afterwards, Gloria sat in the kitchen just outside the living room strumming her guitar. She saw Mrs. Lincoln and Logan Carlton sitting on opposite ends of the couch about as far apart as possible.

"For Chrissakes, would you stop playing that damn guitar?" Carlton said.

Gloria flashed her teeth in a patently fake smile. "No need to shout, I can hear you. I gotta work on building up my calluses." She launched into an elaborate finger-picking run."

"I'll take the goddam thing away and you won't get it back anytime soon."

"Logan…" Mrs. Lincoln started.

"Go ahead, try," Gloria said. "I'll break it over your fat fucking head."

She stopped playing and gripped the guitar's neck with both hands.

"Watch your language young lady—"

"At least I don't take the Lord's name in vain," Gloria snapped. "That's the third commandment. I know you've violated the seventh and maybe number eight—"

"Stop it, both of you." What Mrs. Lincoln's voice lacked in volume it made up with a tone with which mothers have cowed children for centuries.

Carlton clamped his mouth shut, glared at Gloria. He squeezed both hands in and out of fists. Gloria took several slow, deep breaths while counting to ten in her head, determined to act like an adult.

"We just want to do what's best for you, dear," Mrs. Lincoln said. "You scared us yesterday."

"Sorry," Gloria said, "but I feel much better now that Dr. Sadowski explained what happened."

Carlton looked at her and said, "I'm petitioning the court to have Mrs. Lincoln become your legal guardian but I will make the major decisions.

"What? *You* are going to make decisions? You hardly know me," Gloria said.

"I think you need an adult to help you make decisions," Mrs. Lincoln said.

Carlton nodded. "We have several concerns. I checked your school records and learned that you have never even been to high school. So at least until you are eighteen, you will go to school. I'm hoping to get you into an accelerated program. If you work hard, you might even graduate in the next two years. We have no doubts about your intelligence."

Shaking her head and gritting her teeth, Gloria spoke so softly that she barely heard herself. "No, I don't think so."

"We'll just put your music on hold for a little while," Carlton said. "You can go back to it."

Gloria couldn't let that go. "But Jimmy and I have already recorded enough songs for another record album. When he comes home, we can tour." She locked eyes with Mrs. Lincoln. "Roscoe's part of those songs so you'll make money too. That first record did okay but the second one, when we can play shows, should do a lot better. And Jimmy and I can write more songs."

Carlton shook his head again. "That's another big concern we have, this James Hayes, the soldier who got you pregnant. I was in the Army Air Force, and I know how these things happen. I'm not blaming you. You were only fifteen and he took advantage of you. Frankly, he could be prosecuted for statutory rape. You shouldn't fool yourself that he really cares anything about you. He's probably relieved the baby died. I found out from my Washington contact that he got in trouble with drugs in Vietnam. And before the Army, he was one of those long-haired, pot-smoking hippies. Even the name of his band, Universal Joint, refers to drugs. He's not the kind of person we want you to be around."

Gloria's hand gripped her guitar so hard it hurt. Late at night when she lay in bed, she sometimes worried that Jimmy might no longer want her. Too many things had happened to him. And to her.

Looking at the senator and Mrs. Lincoln, she felt outnumbered and unprepared. So, she fell silent.

"Were you and Susanna on drugs yesterday, Gloria?" Mrs. Lincoln asked. "I thought Susanna was a good influence for you, but now I'm not so sure. That boyfriend of hers seems a very unsavory character, trying to steal a gun like that."

Mrs. Lincoln probably didn't know that her son Roscoe had often smoked pot. Gloria had seen him and Jimmy share joints, and once she'd tried marijuana with them. And she and Susanna drank wine together.

She said nothing.

"Those two policemen are sure you were on drugs," Carlton said. "They've had to deal with a lot of marijuana and LSD overdoses. Do you know that some young people end up in mental hospitals after taking that stuff? People have even jumped out of windows and died. You wouldn't think things like that would happen in Grosse Pointe, but there it is. Damn shame, if you ask me. I'm going to see about introducing a bill to increase the penalties for peddling drugs, especially to teenagers."

"Tell her about the psychiatrist, Logan," Mrs. Lincoln said.

"Oh, yeah. I'm getting you a new doctor. He's the best adolescent psychiatrist in town. Expensive, but he's treated a lot of young people hooked on drugs. That Polack woman—"

"Logan, you shouldn't call her that," Mrs. Lincoln said.

"Yeah, yeah, okay, Polish woman. Anyway, she's not a psychiatrist. I don't think she knows anything about it. Hell, she's only been a doctor a couple of years. So I've dismissed her."

The haranguing went on for almost an hour. Gloria said little, content to leave the impression that she'd accepted her fate. But she began to form her own plan.

"I'm going upstairs to take a nap," Gloria announced when the one-sided conversation lagged. As she trudged up the stairs she heard Carlton confide to Mrs. Lincoln, "That went better than I expected."

In her room, she sat on the bed, took off her shoes and lay down, thinking she was too upset to sleep. But trying to make out the words as Mrs. Lincoln and Carlton spoke downstairs, she dozed off.

She awoke sweating, but quickly dashed off a letter to Jimmy to tell him what had happened and about her plan. She used paper torn from a grocery bag lining her wastebasket and crammed the letter into an envelope where she been keeping guitar picks. She didn't need a stamp as letters to soldiers in Vietnam went postage-free.

After getting dressed, she tucked the letter under the waistband of her jeans and pulled her blouse over it before heading downstairs.

"I'm going for a walk," she told Mrs. Lincoln who was in the kitchen starting to prepare dinner. The older woman looked at Gloria and then the hamburger she'd just taken out of the refrigerator. She put the hamburger back.

"I'll come with you. Carlton had to go to Lansing."

"Suit yourself." Gloria knew the older woman rarely went for walks and saw that she had on the silvery gray leather pumps that she called her "French shoes." She usually only wore them to church and grumbled that they hurt her feet.

"Carlton and I want to help you. I know you don't think so, but we are genuinely worried about your future. Some day you'll thank us."

Gloria shrugged but didn't reply. Nor did she communicate beyond grunts and sighs whenever Mrs. Lincoln tried to start a conversation while they strolled through the neighborhood. But Gloria's stubbornness finally crumbled. Instead of wearing out Mrs. Lincoln, Gloria had grown tired, and felt a headache coming on.

She stopped, and for the first time since they'd left the house, made direct eye contact with Mrs. Lincoln. "You know, I wish I *had* gone to high school. When I looked at Susanna's yearbooks and saw all the stuff she did, all the fun she had, I'm really sorry I missed out on that."

"Well, it's not too late for you."

"Yeah, it is. I've been pregnant and had a baby. I lived on the streets on my own for months. I have a serious relationship with a man. And Jimmy's a man who cares about me. He loved our baby as much as I did. I can't see myself going to school and doing the things Susanna did. I already know what I want to do with my life. I'm already doing it."

Mrs. Lincoln grunted.

"I'm not against learning more. Maybe you could get me a tutor instead of that stupid psychiatrist. There are things I need to learn."

"Really? What do you want to learn?"

"More about money and finance for one thing. You know how good I am at math, but I don't know much about money. And I'm inheriting money. I'm making money with my music. Even when my lawyers explain financial things to me, it's hard to understand. Like, they told me Logan Carlton's taking money out my father's estate for his re-election campaign..." She stopped. "I guess we have a lot to talk about."

Mrs. Lincoln didn't reply right away, but finally she nodded. "I want to do what's right for you and I truly believe Logan does too."

Gloria didn't want to let that go, but she felt tired. Mrs. Lincoln's feet probably hurt. She pulled the letter to Jimmy out of her jeans and pointed up the street. "I'm gonna run over to that mailbox, and then we can go home."

Gloria trotted to the mailbox and pushed her letter through the slot. Half a block away, Mrs. Lincoln waited under one of the streetlights that had just turned on. Gloria ambled back, feeling better that she and Mrs. Lincoln had started speaking.

She sensed a car gliding along the street behind her, heard the thunk from an automatic transmission forced into park as the car jerked to a stop slightly in front of her. Where had she seen those round taillights before? The driver-side door flew open. A big man in a buckskin jacket ran around the front of the car. Gloria quick-stepped to the side, avoiding his outstretched arms. She screamed. Then she rushed toward Mrs. Lincoln. Still screaming, she saw Mrs. Lincoln begin lumbering toward her. Gloria passed the front of the stopped car as a hand grabbed her blouse and yanked her off her feet ripping a seam up to her armpit. She landed on her rear end hitting both the grassy swale and the concrete sidewalk. Pain flashed up her spine. She rolled sideways onto the grass. A hand grabbed the back of her jeans while another clamped on her neck. Panic-stricken, using both of her hands, she hauled the hand off her neck and up to her mouth. She bit two fingers so hard the bones grated against her teeth. The man shrieked, ripping his hand out of her mouth, her teeth tearing flesh from his fingers. She rose to her knees. But a blow to the side of her head knocked her down again. Rolling onto her side she clawed at the buckskin-covered arm that still held the back of her jeans. Then she saw him draw back his bloody hand to hit her. She kicked wildly hitting his leg and knocking him off balance so that the fist meant for her face glanced off her shoulder.

Then Mrs. Lincoln arrived.

Though Mrs. Lincoln didn't move fast, she barreled into Gloria's assailant with the irresistible force of a slow-moving train. The collision pushed him away from Gloria. As Gloria scrambled to her feet, the buckskin man pummeled the older woman's face and body. The attack drove Mrs. Lincoln to her hands and knees. Blood dripped from her face. Gloria screamed again. She charged the man from behind, hitting him with her fists. He turned back to Gloria and grabbed her shoulders. She punched him hard in his stomach. He let go, but suddenly she saw a knife in his hand. Gloria staggered backwards, the knife narrowly missing her outstretched hands. He spun around again to slash and stab at Mrs. Lincoln, his arm moving up and down like a cook chopping cabbage.

"No! no!" Gloria kicked him hard. She'd aimed for his crotch but connected with the back of his thigh. With both of her hands, she grabbed the arm with the knife. The man crashed into her, his face coming so close she smelled a sickly rotten odor from his breath. She kneed him, and this time connected with her target. He gasped, pushing her with one hand while the other slashed at her with the knife. It ripped through her blouse and sliced down her side.

The front door of the nearest house banged open. "Hey you. Stop! I'm calling the police."

Gloria saw the man turn toward the house so she charged at him again. He shoved her to the ground. Then he kicked her head hard enough that she saw stars. Another door opened, and now two voices shouted. She heard footsteps slapping the sidewalk and a car door slamming before tires squealed on the pavement.

She crawled to Mrs. Lincoln, saw her shattered glasses hanging crookedly on her blood-smeared face. But the blood soaking the front the woman's dress frightened Gloria more.

"Are you…?" Mrs. Lincoln couldn't finish and Gloria saw the pain in her eyes, saw blood on her teeth, more blood running out of the corner of her mouth.

"We called the police and there's ambulance coming," said one of the neighbors. A stocky black man, he pulled Gloria away from Mrs. Lincoln. "Here, let me help her. I used to be in the Army."

The Army. This must be what it's like for Jimmy.

Her head spinning, she lay down on the grass.

-41-

Nui Binh Base Camp

Hayes and Cartwright slogged through mud in heavy rain to their respective hooches too tired to talk. Hayes felt less confident about Sanderson getting his Hawaii R and R than he'd let on. But he would try. Better to fail making the effort than guarantee failure with no effort.

At his new spot in the NCO hooch, Hayes stripped off his wet clothing in the dark, letting it drop to the concrete floor before wrapping himself in his poncho liner. He listened to the steady drumbeat of rain on the roof while thinking about Sanderson, then Delaney, and finally the war. He'd been sucked into a fight between the murderous communist North Vietnamese fanatics and the corrupt cabal of thieves running South Vietnam. Officers and politicians using the war to advance their careers with lies while his friends died. It all made him sick. In the hospital he'd learned about Lyndon Johnson's decision not to run for another term as president. The news angered him.

I wish I could walk away from this shit. If the fucking Vietnamese want to fight a fucking a war, it's none of our fucking business.

For a moment Hank Williams' *Mind Your Own Business* floated through his mind. The very first song he'd learned to play on guitar, taught to him by his Uncle Sepp's cousin, Jarmo.

Hayes slept, but it seemed like only a few minutes had passed before he heard a long, mournful, "Nooooooooo!"

The scream came from outside some distance away. Pulling on boxer shorts and his wet boots, he ran for the door.

Outside, he saw a flashlight flickering on the screening of one of the Headhunter hooches. Inside, he discovered Kannegiesser sitting on his bunk bent over with his head in his hands, Cartwright with a flashlight beside him.

"Delaney died," Kannegiesser said, his voice stricken. "Oh shit, he's dead." He groaned and fell silent. Cartwright snapped the switch to turn on the overhead lights revealing Kannegiesser's tear-stained face. The light set off a cacophony of complaints.

"Hey, turn off the fuckin' lights!"

"Shut the fuck up!"

"Godammit, it's the middle of the night!"

"Hey, we just found out Delaney's dead," Hayes shouted back, which shut everyone up. Hayes told Cartwright that Delaney must have suffered a drug overdose.

"He was smoking opium. I don't know exactly what happened, but Kannegiesser and I found him passed out in the rain. He was alive, but we couldn't wake him up. They got him over to the MASH unit, but I guess he didn't make it."

Kannegiesser sat on his bed, unmoving, head bowed as if in prayer. Hayes turned off the lights; the hooch slowly settled down again. Doc Morrison had given Kannegiesser a couple of pills and told him to take them, but he hadn't. Hayes found a canteen of water and watched Kannegiesser swallow the pills.

Back in his bunk, his mind racing, Hayes couldn't sleep. He almost got up to bring the pipe and the baggie that he'd found to the first sergeant. But the thought of going out in the rain and mud again to wake up McConaughey nixed that idea. Nobody could do anything in the middle of the night.

Then a new thought exploded. Had someone murdered Delaney? Could Kannegiesser have killed Mitchell, pushed Grugel into the tail rotor and sabotaged the aircraft causing the crash that killed his three crewmates? Then if Delaney, closer to Kannegiesser than anyone else, had grown suspicious, Kannegiesser might have murdered him. Kannegiesser had the opportunity to cause all of those deaths. He could have lied about going off post at Long Binh.

But no, Hayes decided that Kannegiesser, a very simple guy, lacked the cold-blooded cunning it would take to fake the sorrow he'd just witnessed. He knew Kannegiesser had enlisted after dropping out of high school. His parents, brothers and sisters back home regularly sent letters and packages of home-baked treats, which he shared with everyone. They'd sent him many record albums that Kannegiesser played on a stereo he bought secondhand from another soldier who'd rotated home. He'd gone to Bangkok on R and R and would be going home in another month.

If Kannegiesser had died with Delaney surviving, Hayes could easily see Delaney as the murderer. Touchy, quick to react against any perceived slight and a little mysterious, Delaney pushed back against authority. Hayes had always thought Delaney harbored a secret. Kannegiesser might have been Delaney's only real friend in the platoon.

But the men still cared about Delaney's death. The entire 99th Assault Helicopter Company consisted of men who might not have been friends in civilian life, but they'd sacrifice their lives for each other in war.

Except for at least one murderer.

Eventually, Hayes slipped into sleep and had a nightmare. When he woke up, he couldn't couldn't remember the nightmare but still felt the fear. He heard the whine of the helicopter turbines on the flight line and knew he'd overslept.

Pulling on fresh jungle fatigues, he ran for the flight line hoping to catch his platoon before liftoff. He ducked into the Operations Bunker to tell them that he would fly instead of Kannegiesser. Glancing at the whiteboard, he discovered someone had removed both Kannegiesser and Lieutenant Carson from the flight schedule.

"The CO called in the middle of the night and grounded them both," said a spec five who worked in Operations. "The lieutenant was really pissed but we've got a coupla spare pilots right now so replacing him wasn't a problem. You'll never guess who volunteered to fill in for Kannegiesser. That fuckin' Stanton. Bastard avoids flyin' guns like the plague, but he was always bumpin' people off the courier whenever he wanted to go somewhere. Whaddya thinka that, Sarge?"

"Jesus, um..." Hayes stammered and stared at the whiteboard. He nodded to the spec five. "I guess it works."

He hurried outside in time to see the company's helicopters — gunships and slicks — lazily climbing into a formation. He watched them until they disappeared behind a bank of leaden gray clouds.

Hayes entered the mess hall feeling like he hadn't made a very auspicious start as platoon sergeant. After he got coffee and loaded his tray with scrambled eggs and pancakes, he spotted the first sergeant and went over to his table. McConaughey had finished eating but had a full steaming cup of coffee in front of him.

"Can I join you, Top?"

Yawning, McConaughey gestured to a chair. "The CO grounded Kannegiesser and Lieutenant Carson last night. I didn't figure it was worth wakin' you over."

"Yeah, I was just at Ops. Would you believe Sergeant Stanton volunteered as the gunner?"

Surprised, McConaughey choked off another yawn. "Jesus, I can't figure him out. I got a buddy who works in the Pentagon. He found out Stanton was assigned to the Green Berets a coupla years ago. I'm guessing he washed out of the program, or maybe it was some kinda TDY assignment."

TDY stood for temporary duty and before Hayes could say anything, McConaughey continued. "Stanton's had a lot of short assignments, but there's nothing in his records to show he was ever actually a Green Beret. He's also been in Asia several times before, including places in Southeast Asia other than Vietnam."

"Where else is there?" Hayes asked.

"Thailand, maybe Laos. I don't know. It's not in the files so it's probably classified."

Hayes wanted to ask McConaughey more about Stanton but let it go. He had other things to talk about. "Last night, after Kannegiesser and Doc Morrison took Delaney to the MASH, I found this pipe outside, and this baggie rolled up in an old air mattress inside the bunker."

He laid the pipe and baggie on the table then after gulping a mouthful of eggs, he said, "I don't know what this is but I don't think it's opium and I know it's not marijuana."

"Looks like heroin." The first sergeant held the baggie up to the light and shook it. "When I was stationed in Germany, I got sent to Turkey on a little task force. There was a heroin problem developing in Europe, including at some American bases. The heroin was coming from Turkey. The heroin that Turkish police showed us looked like this, though not quite the same color."

Hayes took the bag back to look at it more closely. "Heroin? I wonder if they looked for needle marks on Delaney at the hospital. Where would he get a needle?"

"You can smoke heroin." McConaughey picked up the pipe. "I'll bet that's what happened. Delaney smoked some heroin but it was so strong it killed him."

McConaughey pushed back his chair and crossed his legs. "Do you know anything about heroin use in the company?"

"No, and before last night, I never heard of opium either."

"How about Kannegiesser? You think he's using drugs?"

Hayes considered it. "Marijuana for sure, but I doubt if he's into anything else. Kannegiesser knew Delaney was smoking opium. He was tryin' to take care of Delaney, get him to stop. At least, that's what he told me. I asked him where

Delaney got the opium and he said Delaney wouldn't tell him. I believe him about that, but he might not be telling me everything."

McConaughey put the baggie and the pipe in his pocket. "I'll give these to the CO. He might want to talk to you about it."

"Sure. I'll tell him what I know." Then he quickly finished his pancakes before speaking. "I need your help with something else, Top. I got an idea how Sanderson might get his Hawaii R and R. Cartwright—"

Shaking his head vigorously, McConaughey interrupted. "There's no more allotments for Hawaii."

"Well, there might be another way," Hayes said. Carefully, he outlined a sanitized version of the scheme he and Cartwright had cooked up.

When he finished McConaughey took a long slow sip of coffee. "It's too simple," he said. "You're not telling me everything. Is Sanderson's wife willing to fly to Hawaii on the chance that there's gonna be an empty seat for her hubby on that R and R flight? And if there's an empty seat, how do you know Sanderson will get it?"

"I was gonna pay for the wife's ticket."

McConaughey shook his head again. "There's gotta be more to it than what you've said."

Hayes knew he had to tell McConaughey more. "Well yeah, there's this lieutenant..." Hayes stopped and gulped down coffee for courage. "There's this lieutenant who decides who gets on the airplane when anything opens up. And, um, apparently he can be persuaded."

"Ah," McConaughey said, displaying teeth in an expansive smile.

"I'll need to cash a money order, about twenty-three hundred and something."

"Twenty-three hundred dollars? The Army's not going to give you cash for that money order. You'll have to put it in a bank account. But there might be a way around that," McConaughey said as Hayes sipped at his coffee. "Some of our Filipino allies are deeply entrenched in the local black market, mostly selling goods that, er, fall off trucks. They also are very clever about exchanging MPCs, piasters and dollars, and they end up with a fair amount of American currency. After all, that's they're goal. They can't send home piasters of MPCs."

Hayes was stunned. "So, you're gonna help me with Sanderson?"

"Hell, yes. I like the way you're thinking. I'm pretty sure I can get the CO to sign the orders too. He didn't like what happened to Sanderson. Long as it doesn't interfere with our combat mission, I think he'll go along. And he's smart enough not to ask questions."

In the next hour and a half, Hayes followed McConaughey to the Filipino compound where they met several Filipino officers and sergeants. McConaughey and the Filipinos mostly spoke Tagalog so Hayes didn't know for sure what happened. But when they were done, Hayes had cashed his money order for the entire amount, minus one hundred and fifty dollars. Even that, technically, would pay for materials for the 99th's new basketball court. McConaughey said that the materials more than likely had already fallen off a truck.

"Look at it as a service charge. If you like, we can call it the Jimmy Hayes Basketball Court," McConaughey said.

"Long as you don't have to add 'memorial' to that."

Hayes actually had to endorse the money order over to McConaughey's wife in the Philippines. She, in turn, would distribute the money to the families of the Filipino officers and sergeants. Hayes learned that McConaughey had had a working relationship with the Filipinos in Nui Binh since the day he arrived. And he also found out more about the first sergeant's Korean-Japanese wife.

"Her mother was a comfort woman in World War Two. You ever heard of them?"

"No," Hayes answered.

"Her mother was Korean and forced into prostitution by the Japanese. They sent her to the Philippines. Her father was some unknown Japanese soldier."

Hayes didn't know what to say.

"Cindy's a good business woman and she's built up this hotel, restaurant and bar. It started with the military, but now it's mainly tourists and doing really well. We make three times as much from the business as my pay as first sergeant. I've got my twenty years in and I'm not gonna re-enlist again. We have a business, and I'm gonna work on it full-time. To hell with the Army and this goddamn war."

Back at the Orderly Room, they found a new crisis.

"Sergeant Stanton disappeared," Conrad, the company clerk, said. "Ops called about five minutes ago looking for

Sergeant Hayes. They said the Headhunters touched down in Long Binh to refuel, and Stanton just up and left."

"Jesus H. Christ on a fucking crutch!" McConaughey roared. "First time he flies gunner and he pulls another disappearing act. That's it. I'll have his ass court-martialed."

Hayes knew that the CO would have the final say about any court-martial and Stanton always seemed to get away with everything. But now more than ever, he understood why the CO had pushed him out of the platoon sergeant's job. Stanton's unreliability interfered with combat operations, which crossed the CO's red line.

"Ops said they need a gunner for a mission. If we can get somebody on the courier, they'll pick him up in Cu Chi, but the courier's about to leave."

"I'll do it," Hayes said.

"Call Ops and have them hold the courier. Hayes is on his way," McConaughey said to the clerk. He nodded to Hayes. "Scat!"

-42-

Detroit

Frances Lincoln almost bled to death before an ambulance, siren wailing, rushed her to Henry Ford Hospital's emergency room. Still dazed and also bleeding, Gloria arrived at the same hospital ten minutes later driven by one of the neighbors. A nurse sat her on a gurney in a corner of the ER and gave her a wad of gauze to press against the long cut on her side. Then she drew a curtain for privacy.

As her head cleared Gloria overheard two men speculating about how long it would take "the fuckin' chest cutter" to get there for "another tap city nigger."

Fully alert now, Gloria heard one of them say, "Shit, it don't matter. She's gonna bleed out." Suddenly, she knew they were talking about Mrs. Lincoln.

Gloria slipped off the gurney, pushed through the curtain past the young men, both of them white, and hurried out of the emergency room. In the hall, she spotted a phone in a tiny office and dialed her lawyer. She got the answering service, but the woman who answered already knew Gloria from her hospitalization the day before.

"I'll get a hold of someone right away," the woman said. "Are you okay?"

"I got slashed, but Mrs. Lincoln's hurt bad. They think she's too poor to pay…"

A doctor, or at least a young man with a stethoscope slung over his neck, and one of the men she'd overhead burst into the office. Both of them gaped at Gloria. Her tattered bloody blouse hung from one shoulder. Blood from the slash wound smeared her torso and soaked her bra, which barely covered one breast. The knife had slashed through the bra strap.

"Miss, you need to get back in there so we can work on that cut. You're bleeding all over my desk," the doctor said. He had kinky hair, light, almost white skin but black facial features.

Trying to cover herself with the hand holding the gauze, Gloria hung up the phone with the other. "I just called my lawyers. You better take good care of Mrs. Lincoln out there, or I swear I'll sue you for every fucking penny you have or will ever make."

The doctor gulped and, with a wave of his hand, dismissed the other man. "We're giving her blood and she's stable for now. We're waiting for a trauma surgeon."

Half an hour later, after a nurse had closed the wound on Gloria's side with fourteen stitches and helped her into a loose Detroit Lions football jersey, her attorney Pip Papineau appeared. Dressed in a crisp gray suit and red tie, and lugging a heavy briefcase, he looked ready for court.

Smiling, he said, "I was at a bar meeting. Maybe I should schedule meetings with you at hospitals. How are you feeling?"

"I'll be okay," Gloria said, "but Mrs. Lincoln's in a bad way. She needs a surgeon."

"And she's got one. I called a doctor. He's a former client."

"Is he a surgeon?"

"Brad? No he's a gas passer... sorry, that's an anesthesiologist, but he knows a lot of surgeons. He called a thoracic surgeon who's on his way. Might be here already. Brad says he's the best in town. And Brad's getting ready now. I alerted the resident on my way in. They've started prepping Mrs. Lincoln. It's a good thing you called."

Gloria wiped her eyes. "Oh, thank God."

Papineau smiled. "She's in good hands. There's nothing more we can do now." He sat down in the chair beside the gurney and waited until Gloria finished composing herself. "Tell me what happened."

Gloria started to shrug but winced from the pain. "Mrs. Lincoln and I went for a walk and I was attacked. She tried to help."

She was unable to finish because a man in a worn tweed sport jacket and jeans pushed aside the curtain. Gloria jumped when she saw the pistol in a shoulder holster but relaxed when she recognized him.

"I'm Detective Crain, Detroit homicide. I don't know if you remember but my partner and I—"

"I remember."

"I'm Pip Papineau, Miss Doran's attorney." Papineau extended his hand.

"Attorney? Why does she need an attorney?" Crain warily took Papineau's hand. "My partner, Sergeant Overholzer... we were on a stakeout when we caught this on the radio."

Fumbling inside his jacket, he took out an envelope with several photographs. "Did you get a good look at the man who assaulted you? Would you recognize him if you saw him again?"

"I know who he was," Gloria said.

Crain's lips tightened. He handed her the pictures. "See if he's in here."

She shuffled through the pictures and immediately put one on top. "That's him. That's the man who attacked us."

"You're sure?"

"Yep, it's that man you told me about, that man from Thailand, Juntasa. He looks different. Like his hair is longer and he's bigger than… um, I guess I thought he'd be small because he's Oriental. But no, he's bigger than you, more than six feet tall."

"You're absolutely sure that it was the man in this picture?"

"Yes. Don't you believe me?"

"It's just that we're sure he left the country."

She almost shrugged again but stopped herself in time. "Well, he must have come back."

With some prodding by the detective, she gave an account of the attack. Crain took notes. Papineau listened.

"You think the car was a Ford because it had big round taillights? You're sure they were round and not square?"

"Yeah, they were definitely round."

"How big was the car?" Crain asked.

"I guess it was regular size..." She stopped and reached under the bottom of the football jersey so she could lightly scratch her skin near the stitched cut, careful not to touch it. "Um, you know it was about the same size as my car, or maybe even slightly smaller. I have a Rambler station wagon. It wasn't as big as Mrs. Lincoln's Oldsmobile or Senator Carlton's Lincoln. And I'm pretty sure I'd seen it before."

"You did? Where?"

She told Crain about the day she and Logan Carlton had seen the car on Mrs. Lincoln's street. "He said it was a Ford because of the taillights, and I remember it was dark colored, either black or Navy blue. Now I'm sure it's dark blue."

After another half an hour of gentle questioning by the detective and Papineau, the detective, preparing to leave, said he or his partner might call her again. Papineau walked out with the detective, but returned a few minutes later.

"Detective Crain's skeptical about some of your story. I don't think he's convinced the assailant was this man Juntasa. He thinks you probably picked out the picture because you'd seen it before. But he's putting out an alert on a dark blue Ford Falcon. I think we better look into hiring some security for you."

"He's wrong. I never saw that picture before," Gloria said.

"It was on TV."

"Oh."

Papineau slumped into the chair beside the gurney. "You know, if I'm going to help, you need to tell me about these things when they happen. I wish you'd told me you'd seen that car earlier, and about talking to those detectives."

"Sorry, it didn't seem important at the time, and Mr. Carlton didn't think it was anything."

Papineau's eyes narrowed at the mention of Carlton. He spent a long time looking at her, making her uncomfortable, the frustration evident on his face. Then he opened his briefcase and shuffled through some papers. He had something to say that he didn't want to say, but he finally said it. "It's possible that Logan Carlton could become your guardian. He's using his political influence and the best alternative option, Mrs. Lincoln, is out of the picture now."

"Shit!"

Papineau's eyebrows arched at her profanity, but as he opened his mouth to speak, he grinned. The grin infuriated her.

"It's not funny, dammit. Why do I need a fucking *ahhhhduullllt* guardian?" 'Adult' rolled off her tongue in a low voice as smooth as maple syrup spreading across a pancake. "Adults have fucked up the whole world, especially fucking politicians like Logan Carlton. I'm sixteen, but I haven't started any fucking wars. Guess I need to go to fucking high school to learn how to do that." She stopped and took a few deep breaths trying to get a grip on her emotions. It didn't work. "Logan Carlton doesn't want me around Jimmy? Fuck him! Jimmy gets me, and he's the only one who does. I need him, and I think he needs me. We love each other. How many of his friends are dead in that fucking war? He won't talk about it. He was a prisoner, and I was starting to think he might be dead." She pounded the gurney with her fist making her side hurt. "God, he's just gotta make it through another month."

"I wasn't trying to make light—"

Ignoring Papineau she kept on talking. "Why can't I live my own life? I just want to play my music. I want to write songs like the hippies and the Beatles, songs about peace and love. I'm not hurting anybody. People are trying to hurt me. Logan Carlton, my guardian? He's totally fucking flipped out. He just wants my money for his fucking reelection. I'll give it to him if he'll just leave me alone."

Gloria stopped talking for a moment and wrested back a little control. "I love Mrs. Lincoln, but I don't know... She lost her son, Roscoe. I can't take his place. All I can do is be her friend and she can be mine. We have our little squabbles but we get along pretty good. If she…" She couldn't finish and looked away not wanting to catch Papineau's eyes and feeling embarrassed that she was not acting more mature.

Finally, she did look at him. "I'm grateful for everything you've done, but I don't need a guardian. I've survived without one since I left home last summer. Some ways, I did better than I did with the adults in my life before I left. I can take care of myself better than Mr. Carlton can. And I will, no matter what."

Papineau took his glasses off and wiped them with this handkerchief. Avoiding her eyes, he gripped the handle of his briefcase and seemed to be ready to leave. "I didn't mean to set you off. I was going to say that guardianship, if it happens, is only going to last for two years, till you're eighteen —"

"Two years? That's one-eighth of my whole life."

He nodded. "Yes, I guess it is. I can see how it looks like a long time to you." Taking his time, he closed up his briefcase and stood. "I've been practicing law twenty-eight years and you are the most difficult, most remarkable client I've ever had. I am inclined to agree that you don't need a guardian. You are not a typical sixteen-year-old. But what I think doesn't matter. It's what a judge thinks. And the judge in this case is a black man who appears sympathetic to Carlton. I'll fight for you and keep fighting no matter how it turns out. We'll win in the long run, but the immediate future does not look good."

Before he could leave, Gloria asked him, "What about money? I'm supposed to be rich, but when will I actually get any of the money I inherited? Carlton took my car away. Bail for Antoine cleaned out most of my bank account. Right now, I don't even have bus fare to get home… wherever that is now."

Papineau stood halfway up, reached in his back pocket and took out his wallet before sitting down again. He handed her two twenty-dollar bills, and yawned. "If Carlton is appointed your legal guardian, he'll gain control over your finances until you're eighteen. Like I said, that's only for a couple of years." He looked at the remaining bills in his wallet. "Do you need more?"

"Yeah, I could use a few thousand dollars."

He looked genuinely puzzled. "For what?"

"Oh, I dunno. I might want to buy Cadillacs for myself and a couple of friends. Maybe some whiskey and drugs so we can have a party before Carlton shuts down my life."

His face tightened. "I know you aren't serious, but I can assure you that even if Carlton becomes your guardian, he won't have free reign with your money. I suspect when I tell the court he took money for his reelection campaign, he'll have to put it back. And if he gives us any trouble, I'll tell the newspapers that he's stealing money from you. I may not be able to stop him from becoming your guardian, but we'll still have considerable leverage."

Gloria really did want several thousand dollars but knew that Papineau, in effect, controlled the inheritance from her stepfather. She had to ask him for money and that meant telling him why she wanted it. And he now represented her in negotiations with the record company. If Carlton became her guardian, there would be two men between her and her money. She mostly trusted Papineau, but not with all of her secrets. Not with her plan.

When she didn't say anything, he picked up his briefcase. "Could I maybe drop you off somewhere?"

She shook her head. "No, I'll stay here until Mrs. Lincoln's surgery is over."

"Of course."

"One more thing," she said.

"What?"

"Logan Carlton fired my doctor, Emily Sadowski. I was rude to her the last time we spoke. I want her to continue as my doctor and I want to help her if I can. She's done a lot for me."

"I think I can help with that," he said.

Gloria spent the rest of the night waiting to hear about Mrs. Lincoln. She wandered around the hospital and discovered the cafeteria unlocked and empty. So she went inside and started singing *The Star Spangled Banner*. She wanted to practice singing and felt like she needed a challenge to get her mind off all her problems.

After the national anthem, she sang prayers for Mrs. Lincoln, *Amazing Grace* and *How Great Thou Art*. But the hymns made her think of funerals so she switched to popular songs she'd heard on the radio — *Lady Madonna, Do You Know the Way to San Jose?* and *Mrs. Robinson*. Singing lifted her so she forgot about the slash on her side. Lost in her musical reverie, the clatter of pots and pans brought her back to reality. When she stopped singing, several early morning kitchen workers started clapping. Gloria smiled and made a little bow.

Shortly before ten in the morning, the anesthesiologist walked into the lounge where Gloria dozed in a chair. "Are you Gloria Doran? I'm Bradley Porterhouse. First off, Frances Lincoln has come through the surgery in great shape. It was touch and go at first, but everything looks good now. I believe she'll be okay. Complete recovery will take a long time, however. No visitors for at least a couple of days. I'm sorry, but Gary Brewer, the surgeon, had to run off to another hospital."

Porterhouse studied Gloria for several seconds. "You look familiar. Have I met you before?"

"I don't think so, unless... maybe you saw me sing?"

He snapped his fingers a couple of times as he stared at her. "That's it, Sunshine. That's who you are. You're Sunshine.

My daughter has your album. Wow! I wish I had it with me so you could autograph it."

A few minutes later, she felt good enough to call Pip Papineau from a pay phone in the lobby to update him about Mrs. Lincoln and to thank him. Then she spotted Logan Carlton in the midst of an animated unpleasant conversation with an elderly lady at the information desk. Gloria slunk away from the pay phone and ducked into a women's restroom. She waited a couple of minutes and then came out. She didn't see Carlton anywhere in the lobby.

Hurrying outside, she couldn't believe what she saw: Logan Carlton's Lincoln Continental idling at the curb.

"Well, you took my car so I'll take yours," she said, climbing into the driver's seat. She drove a couple of blocks, then pulled over to adjust the seat and mirrors and tune the radio to Keener 13 — WKNR — before continuing. As she drove up Grand River Avenue toward Mrs. Lincoln's house, she heard the disc jockey announce that, "Once again, last night's most requested song was Zoomer and Body Count with *Locked in Love*." Narrowly missing a car pulling out of a parking place, she slammed on the brakes to stop at the side of the road.

The song sounded almost exactly the same as when she'd played it with Zoomer and his band in the practice room. It had the same basic arrangement and fiery guitar solos. Screaming guitars mostly drowned out Zoomer's singing except when he repeated, "locked in love."

Furious, she sat thinking about how she could get even with the loathsome Zoomer. Logically, she should call Papineau. But it soon occurred to her she could help herself.

So she sat in the car, allowing pride in her accomplishment to push away her anger. The song she'd written all by herself was the most requested song on Detroit's biggest rock and roll radio station. That meant a lot of people had probably bought the record. And maybe not just in Detroit.

And it really rocks!

Half an hour after she parked, she shifted into drive and headed for the record company. There, she found Maxie Zimmerman, the president, dressed in his rumpled blue suit.

"No, I didn't give my song to Zoomer. He stole it. And if you don't pay me for it, I'm gonna sue," she told him. A few minutes later Gloria walked out of his office with nearly three thousand dollars, all the cash Zimmerman could muster.

She drove to Mrs. Lincoln's house to pick up her guitar and called Susanna.

"I'm going away, Susanna. I don't want anyone else to get hurt on account of me."

"Where are you going?" Susanna asked.

"I'm going to the beach. I'm gonna buy myself a French bikini and lie in the sun till Jimmy comes home."

She hung up before Susanna could ask any more questions and drove to the airport. There, she paid cash for a one-way ticket to Honolulu. After buying the ticket, she gave the astonished clerk a hundred dollars to record her name as Zsa Zsa Patterson instead of the name on her driver's license.

She left Logan Carlton's Lincoln idling in a 'no parking' zone.

-43-

Cu Chi, Vietnam

Hayes caught up with the Headhunters in Cu Chi. And so did the wayward Sergeant Stanton. After the courier flight landed, Hayes ran across dirt recently sprayed with dust abatement oil. It smelled like tar and stuck to his boots. He saw Stanton talking to Moss by one of the six Headhunter gunships parked beside the main runway.

"Sergeant Stanton, you are relieved. I'll fly gunner for the rest of the day. You can go back to Nui Binh." Panting, Hayes bent over and tried to brush away flecks of tarry dirt stuck to his trouser legs. When he straightened up he saw his face reflected in Stanton's mirrored aviator sunglasses.

"Well if it isn't Boy Wonder, fresh from the Commy underground, ready to save our delicate asses," Stanton said.

Hayes ignored the insult. "Sergeant, if you hurry, you can still catch the courier back to Nui Binh."

"What if I don't want to go back?" Stanton stood with his hands on his hips, a sneer on his face.

Hayes stood his ground. "I could care less where you go, but Top wants to see you. He's upset. Anyway, you aren't flying with the Headhunters. Not now, not ever."

"That so? Well, sonny, you can just hightail it back to Nui Binh. Last time I checked, I outranked you."

"Last time I checked, I was platoon sergeant. Apparently, the previous one was incompetent."

Stanton colored but didn't say anything right away. He looked around, his lower lip trembling. Several other pilots had joined Moss. Hayes heard a snicker. After looking at the pilots, Stanton took off the sunglasses and and pocketed them. His eyes burned with suppressed rage. He spoke in a low bestial growl. "You ain't nothin' but a pussy Hayes, so fuckin' lucky, and you ain't no goddam hero. You don't know shit about this war. If it's got fuckin' slant eyes, you kill it. We ain't gonna win till we exterminate all the fuckin' gook vermin. Too many pussies like you ain't got the balls to do what needs doin'."

With a hacking throat-clearing cough, Stanton spat on the ground in front of Hayes, then turned and left.

"What an asshole," somebody said.

Hayes shrugged, tried to relax. Sweat beads had popped out on his forehead and his insides fluttered. Something about the confrontation seemed important, but Hayes couldn't pull it out of the jumbled thoughts in his head.

"Offhand, I'd say he doesn't like you," Moss said.

"Yeah, he's pissed 'cause I replaced the incompetent bastard." Hayes got his flustered nerves under control. "What happened with Stanton? I thought he bailed on you guys."

"I was just asking him that. He disappeared when we were refueling in Long Binh. We came here without him. Good thing you showed up. We're flyin' cover for an ARVN insert."

"How'd Stanton get here from Long Binh?"

"No idea, but several other aircraft came here from Long Binh about the same time. He probably hitched a ride on one of them."

Hayes looked back toward the courier, trying to see if Stanton got on it, trying to figure out what he'd missed in the encounter.

-44-

Detroit

Shortly after she sat down near the departure gate, Gloria heard an announcement that her flight had been delayed and wouldn't leave for another five hours. The flight, scheduled to stop in San Francisco before going to Honolulu, had to wait for Honolulu-bound passengers from New York. A Delta representative explained that Delta had taken an aircraft out of service due to a mechanical problem. The airline put some New York passengers going to Honolulu on a plane to Detroit so they could catch the Hawaii-bound plane leaving Detroit.

"So we're holding this flight, and it will now be full. Don't worry, everybody's gonna get to paradise," the man said.

Gloria only had her guitar and the clothes she wore — jeans, the Detroit Lions jersey and sneakers. Her bra had been ruined in the attack, so she considered taking a taxi to shop for one, and maybe more clothes. But that would cost her more money. If she bought clothes she'd probably have to buy a bag or suitcase. Based on her previous experience with running away, she knew she would go through her money more quickly than she'd like. Besides, after several braless hours, she felt more comfortable without one. A bra would irritate her injured side. Susanna said a lot of her friends were going braless and Susanna often didn't bother with one herself.

"My girls like to be free," Susanna would say, laughing. Gloria already missed Susanna and her laughter.

Gloria tried unsuccessfully to sprawl over several chairs and sleep. She wanted to take out her guitar and play, but that would draw attention.

Restless and hungry, she went to a nearby restaurant and bar where she splurged on an overpriced cheeseburger. A cocktail waitress asked her if she wanted any beer or wine. She ordered a Coke instead, musing that while Logan Carlton considered her a child, she didn't look like one.

Her thoughts turned to Mrs. Lincoln. She'd almost died trying to help Gloria. She'd let Gloria live in her home, helped her with her pregnancy, taught her a lot about cooking and keeping house. And she'd begun to accept Jimmy as part of Gloria's life. When he went missing, and when Gloria lost her baby, Mrs. Lincoln tried to comfort Gloria in the hospital. When Mrs. Lincoln got out of the hospital, who would help her? She'd probably need a lot of help. Suddenly, running away didn't seem like such a good idea.

She was there for me. What kind of friend am I?

She couldn't finish the cheeseburger, and felt a headache coming on.

After paying the bill, she walked outside the terminal for fresh air. But the air reeked of exhaust fumes, and with the honking horns from buses, vans and taxis, her headache worsened. Vehicles maneuvered for positions at the curb or to get back out onto the road. Two policemen directed traffic around a big tow truck preparing to haul away a car. As Gloria approached, she saw with horror the dark blue car with big round taillights. Frightened, she bolted back into the terminal and ran straight to a women's restroom.

She sat in a stall for a long time trying to think through the implications of the car. Had Juntasa followed her to the airport? Or, had he come to the airport for the same reason she'd come, to get out of Detroit? Or did the blue car belong to someone else?

Gloria returned to the gate moving slowly, studying everyone and everything around her, trying to spot Juntasa before he saw her. She kept looking back to see if anyone followed her. In a corner beside her departure gate with a good view of the entire area, she settled into an empty chair.

What am I going to do?

She'd planned to hide out in Honolulu until Jimmy got out of Vietnam. In the letter she'd mailed before the attack, she'd told him about going to Hawaii, that she would wait for him there. As soon as he came, they could sort everything out together. She thought that she'd evaded everyone, including Juntasa. But would she be safe in a strange city where she had no friends?

Except for a brief nap in the hospital waiting room, Gloria had missed a night's sleep. So despite trying to remain vigilant, she fell asleep and when she awoke, it was forty-five minutes until her flight's departure. Upset passengers pressed around the counter at the departure gate. After looking around for Juntasa, Gloria approached the counter. A young Asian woman argued with the airline representative who'd made the announcement earlier.

"I bought a ticket in New York all the way to Honolulu. You can't just take it away."

"I'm sorry ma'm, but we can. There aren't enough seats for everyone so we've had to bump a few people. We'll get you to Honolulu tomorrow and get you a hotel tonight. It'll be less than a day late."

"But I'll miss my father's tsuya."

"I'm sorry, but there's nothing I can do."

The young woman was pushed aside by another disgruntled passenger. Gloria followed the Asian woman to the edge of the crowd.

"I can help you," Gloria said. "You can have my ticket if you like."

"What? Are you sure?"

"Yeah. I've decided not to go." Gloria proffered the ticket. The woman looked young, though older than Gloria. Wearing a suit, she'd dressed entirely in black down to her earrings – complimented by a gray blouse.

"Um, what is a tsuya?" Gloria asked.

"It's like a wake. You see, my father died" She bowed her head for a moment, then reached into her purse. She took out a string of dark brown beads and held them in both her hands. "He's… ah, he was Buddhist. I'm not Buddhist. Well, maybe a little. This is my mala. They're prayer beads." She shook her head, looked down for a moment. "I need to be there. Why are you giving up your ticket?"

"It's a long story, but you can have it. And you don't have to pay me for it."

The woman put the beads into one hand and took the ticket to examine it.

"Your name's Zsa Zsa Patterson? Well, Zsa Zsa, I insist on paying you for the ticket. I can afford it. Let's go to the counter and do this right."

"Ah, no. I don't want to do that. See, I was running away but I changed my mind. I'd just as soon have some people think I've gone to Honolulu. Besides, that man at the counter might think somebody else should get the ticket."

The woman looked back at the counter, then nodded. "Yes, you're right. I guess it'll be okay. They've never checked my I.D. before when I go back home." She put the ticket in her purse along with the beads. She took out a checkbook. "But I insist on paying you, Zsa Zsa." She quickly scribbled out a check and handed it to Gloria.

"Okay, thanks." Gloria saw that the check was for the amount of the ticket and was made out to Zsa Zsa Patterson. She wouldn't cash it, and probably couldn't. But she folded it and put it in her purse. The first boarding announcement echoed through the terminal.

"I really appreciate this," said the woman. "Let's stay in touch. You can reach me at the Sloan Kettering Cancer Center. I'm a doctor there."

Gloria almost said that she didn't look old enough to be a doctor. Instead, she said, "I'm sorry about your father."

"Thank you again. And let me offer my sympathy and support for whatever trouble made you decide to run away."

"Thanks," Gloria said, and, with a crooked smile added, "I'm trying to grow up."

-45-

Nui Binh

When the Headhunters and Jimmy got back to Nui Binh, Hayes ate dinner with Cartwright and Sanderson. Initially doubtful about the Hawaiian R and R scheme, Sanderson had embraced the plan. After dinner, Hayes went to Operations and worked out the flight schedule for the next day. He chatted with two new gunners transferring from the slick platoons, then took a quick shower in the lukewarm water flowing from the scavenged aircraft drop tank. Back at his hooch, he found a fat letter from Gloria on his bunk. Ripping open the envelope, he immediately sensed trouble.

Instead of her usual precise fountain-pen script on cream-colored stationery, she'd scribbled her words with a ballpoint pen on both sides of a scrap of coarse, brown paper. And the content disturbed him more than the messy presentation. Police had taken her to a hospital. Logan Carlton and Mrs. Lincoln wanted to force her to go to school and stop her from playing music.

"They're going to lock me up in a place for crazy teenagers who take drugs." And worst of all, she wrote, "THEY AREN'T GOING LET US BE TOGETHER WHEN YOU COME HOME!!!!!" She'd pressed so hard on the angry block letters that her pen had poked holes in the paper.

The letter got worse. Gloria said that a murderer from Thailand, a former air force colonel named Jettrin Juntasa, "is after me." After re-reading the letter several times, Hayes still couldn't make sense of it. Why would an air force colonel from Thailand pursue Gloria? And Hayes didn't understand why the police had taken Gloria to a hospital. Had she been hurt and didn't want to tell him?

The business about Mrs. Lincoln and Logan Carlton breaking them up and stopping her music made him realize that he faced a whole new set of problems when he got home. He'd always had a shaky relationship with Mrs. Lincoln, but from Gloria's previous letters, he'd thought she and Gloria had grown close.

In the last, and most startling paragraph, she wrote, "I'm going to run away again, to Honolulu where nobody will look for me, and I'll write to you when I get there. I'll wait there until you come home."

Reading through the letter several times, he felt a growing responsibility. After everything she'd endured, his capture had made things worse for her. And he suspected that she shared his burden over the men he'd killed on his short trip back to America. Why else had she sent him that newspaper clipping? Finally, he folded up the paper and stuffed it in a pocket. Nothing he could do for someone on the other side of the world. He couldn't even write to her. So he decided to work on his own problems. He'd go see Moss.

Moss and Hayes had a history. First time Hayes saw combat he'd flown on a slick piloted by Moss. The Vietcong ambushed the 99th's flight of helicopters as they touched down in an LZ — landing zone — just as the grunts hopped off. The crew chief on their helicopter died. That night, Hayes and Moss had gotten drunk together though Moss had a head start and got far drunker. A few days later, Moss went home, his one-year tour in Vietnam over. After several months passed, Moss came back on a second tour to fly gunships. And Hayes, partly as a result of his performance during the ambush, also ended up flying on gunships.

Hayes found Moss in boxer shorts and a T-shirt lying on his bed reading a Mike Hammer paperback with a blonde displaying a lot of cleavage on the cover. He wore headphones hooked up to a reel-to-reel Teac tape deck and a can of Schlitz sweated on a footlocker beside the bed. Hayes smelled incense in the air and wondered if Moss had been smoking marijuana. He'd heard rumors that some of the pilots smoked pot.

When he saw Hayes in the doorway, Moss pulled off the headphones. "Hayes. If you're looking for somebody in charge, it ain't me. And Lieutenant Carson's gone."

"Wanted to talk to you."

Moss turned off the tape deck and lowered the paperback. "'Bout what?"

Hayes leaned against the doorway waiting for Moss to invite him in. The officers lived in long hooches divided up into small rooms, two men per room. But with Carson gone, Moss had no roommate. "I want to talk about the day you and some Green Berets went to that village outside of Long Binh and threw those villagers out of the helicopter."

"That's classified," Moss said, placing the paperback face down on the bed, trying to sound calm. Skittering eyes betrayed his unease.

"Fuck that. I damn near got executed by the VC 'cause they thought I did it. I know you and Carson were the pilots, and I know Delaney was crew chief. I also know you and Carson got Kannegiesser outta the way so you could put somebody else in as gunner. I want to know who the fuck that was. Delaney's dead, Carson's gone, and Kannegiesser says he doesn't know."

Moss avoided Hayes' gaze. He picked up the can of Schlitz from his footlocker and drained it. "Shit, that's even more classified." He concentrated on placing the empty can exactly into the wet ring it had left on the footlocker. Finally, he looked up. "You might as well come in. Grab us a couple more beers. They're in that cooler."

Hayes pulled two cans out of a Styrofoam cooler, punched holes in both with a church key he found nearby and handed a beer to Moss. Thirsty, he gulped several mouthfuls of the icy beer. "Thanks."

Moss raised his beer fractionally. "Congratulations on your promotion to platoon sergeant. I told Carson it was a big improvement over Stanton."

"Where'd you get the ice?" Hayes asked.

"Mess hall. They got another freezer, a big one. You can probably get some if you ask nice. We got a big new generator while you were gone so now the power hardly ever goes off. Gettin' civilized around here."

Moss looked at his beer without drinking. After a second swig of beer, Hayes sat on the other bunk, closer to Moss.

"Look, I can't tell you who the gunner was. I'm already in enough trouble gettin' busted to WO1. Best you leave this whole fuckin' thing alone."

"I got busted from Spec Four to PFC and was back to Spec Four in matter of days. Now I'm a sergeant. I wouldn't worry too much. You're a good pilot. You'll be back to CW2 soon enough."

Irritated, Moss said, "Not if I can't keep my mouth shut."

Moss sat up straighter so he could prop his back against the plywood wall that had a big poster of Jimi Hendrix tacked to it.

"I like your poster," Hayes said gesturing with his beer. How could he pry the information out of Moss? He veered to a new vector. "How'd you meet Gail Kucharski? She Major Kucharski's sister? Maybe a cousin? Is she pretty?"

Moss's eyes widened, and he almost dropped his beer. "Jesus Christ, Hayes, who told you about her?"

Hayes didn't answer, hoping the rattled Moss might name the gunner.

But Moss relaxed and smiled. "Yeah, well, she's better lookin' than her brother. Impressive hooters and a thing for pilots. She's also a lot nicer than her goddam brother."

Deflated, Hayes felt outmaneuvered. But Moss surprised him.

"I feel like I owe you, Hayes. You been through more shit than anyone in this fuckin' company, some of it with me. That day McLean was killed and we got drunk out on the flight line? You put me to bed. I went home and never did thank you."

"Yeah, I remember you were pretty torn up over McLean."

"Yeah, me and McLean were close." Moss gulped more beer. "You know somethin', Hayes? Back in the World, us soldiers ain't too fucking popular right now. Anyway, I reported to Wolters to train newbie pilots. Jesus, that was the last fucking thing I wanted to do. I just wanted to come back here and kill the fucking VC bastards."

Moss drained his beer, and Hayes drank about half of his. Then Hayes got two more beers for them.

"Hayes, you gotta back off on this shit."

"What do you mean?"

"I like you, Hayes. Can't figure you out. Why are you so upset about a few villagers getting wasted? It's not like you're any kind of pussy. Stanton's got you all wrong."

Hayes drank the rest of the beer. "The VC put me on trial. I listened to some of those villagers, and, yeah, it was a VC village, but I don't think the villagers were lying. What happened there wasn't combat. Wasn't an accident. Sounded more like murder."

Moss shrugged. "Yeah, well, that's what we get paid for. Murder the bastards. They all hate us anyway. We won't win the war by being nice."

Hayes decided to give up on getting anything from Moss and stood up to leave.

"You really oughta back off on this, Hayes, before you get hurt."

"Why do you say that?"

Is he threatening me?

"Kucharski may not look like much, but he's dangerous. He'll fuck up your life."

"What's he done to yours?"

Moss slowly shook his head and took a long drink of beer. "Hope you don't owe that Kucharski anything, 'cause he'll collect."

Hayes shook his head. "If anything, he owes me."

They were silent for a moment.

"Shit, I met him through his sister by chance. Sold my fucking soul to come back to this hellhole. Then I get busted for doin' his fuckin' dirty work." Moss finished off his beer. "Hayes, if you wanna know who the fuckin' gunner was, why don't you ask his royal fucking highness, Lieutenant Colonel Kucharski."

"He's a lieutenant colonel now?"

"Yeah, probably make full bird way too soon."

Then Moss caved in the empty can in his hand as Hayes chugged the rest of his beer, knowing he would get no more out of Moss. "I might just ask him."

-46-

Detroit

After selling her ticket, Gloria returned to her corner seat, watched the passengers board and the plane depart. She couldn't decide what to do next but felt safe in that corner. Muzzy with fatigue, she decided to walk out of the airport. She imagined the murderous Thai colonel lurking everywhere. He could watch the taxis, or search for her in the airport. Outside, she thought she could more easily see him following if she looked back every few steps. Once away from the airport, she'd find a phone and call a taxi.

Gathering her courage, she pushed through the door and started up the sidewalk. When the sidewalk ended she continued along the side of the road making good progress and getting away from the crowded terminals. Now she would be able to spot Juntasa even easier.

Her legs ached and as the sun sank, the dazzle of cars, now with their lights on, made it harder to see. She traversed another section where she plodded along the busy road's asphalt shoulder, bathed in harsh light from streetlamps. Soon she reached darkness again. After crossing several roads and making bad guesses at intersections, the airport didn't seem much farther away. She stumbled down a steep grassy embankment to get on another road that appeared more promising. When she darted across it, two cars almost hit her.

But she continued along the narrow shoulder, bumping against a guardrail with every step. On a long curve, horns blared as cars suddenly came upon her. Most whizzed past only a few feet away, blasts of wind pushing her against the guardrail. At the end of the curve, the road split with one lane going left and the other right. At the split, she ran across one of the lanes. This time a car barely avoided her by slamming on its brakes and skidding to a stop.

"You trying to get yourself killed?" the driver shouted through an open window. He glared at her for a few moments, then sped off when the cars behind him honked their horns. Meanwhile, Gloria climbed over the guardrail and hurried into a dark wooded area. Shaken and exhausted, she sat down with her back against a small tree to regroup. The big cut on her side throbbed and her head lolled forward. She started to doze off but managed to snap herself alert.

"What's the matter with me? Am I having another breakdown?"

One arm rested on her guitar case and the other one hung limp protecting her damaged side. Walking out of the airport had been a mistake. She didn't know how to correct it. A few minutes later she saw the flashing lights of a police car slowly gliding around the long curve.

"Oh no!" She scrambled to her feet, picked up her guitar and purse, and waded deeper into the brush to hide. She'd only taken a few steps when the police cruiser's spotlight flashed on. Weaving through the brush, she looked back over her shoulder just as the spotlight found her. Blinded by the light, she tripped and sprawled into some brambles.

At least I'll be safe from Juntasa. But what about Logan Carlton?

Reaching into her purse, she pulled the driver's license out of her wallet and dropped it into the bushes.

I won't tell them who I am.

A policeman seized her arm. "I got her." His partner tripped on her guitar case and cursed. Gloria instinctively bent to pick it up. The first policeman jerked her back. He shouted. "Other hand, behind your back."

He didn't wait for her to comply but wrenched her arm back, snapping on handcuffs

"Ow! That hurts."

"Shut up."

The policeman who'd tripped on the guitar case picked it up along with her purse. He shone a flashlight on her face. "Take it easy, Jason, she's kinda cute."

Each grabbing an arm, they half carried her back to the cruiser, with 'Romulus Police Department' in bold letters on the door.

Gloria didn't answer their questions; nor did she reply to any of the other questions when they took her to the police station. She reverted to her childhood coping mechanism. She withdrew into herself and did not speak. No longer handcuffed, she sat with her eyes closed, head bowed, sliding into a fantasy where Jimmy had come home. She let herself go slack and relax the way she did in prayer.

When Jimmy comes home, everything will be okay.

"I think she's on drugs," the policeman named Jason said.

Her eyes fluttered open, her quasi-dreamlike state shifted into a marginally higher level of awareness. Under stares of the two officers, and a sergeant who had joined them, she remained silent.

"Are we gonna charge her with something?" one of the officers asked the sergeant. "How about felony jaywalking?" He laughed at his own joke, but no one else did. Then he reached over and raised Gloria's chin with one finger that smelled of cigarettes. "C'mon, cutie pie, tell us your name. Talk to us and we'll let you go."

Just then a fourth man knocked on the door and entered the small room. Short, very young, dressed in shabby civilian clothing, he spoke in a weak, high-pitched voice. "Sergeant Simmons, I found this in her purse. It's a check made out to Zsa Zsa Patterson. Maybe that's who she is. Or maybe she's the person that signed the check. But I don't think so 'cause it's a Japanese name."

The sergeant took the check and examined it. "Okay, Peanut. Didya find anythin' else?"

The little man hesitated for a moment. No. No I.D., no drugs or anything like that. She's got a nice guitar."

"So, Zsa Zsa, that your name? Are you Zsa Zsa Patterson?" the sergeant asked. He waited almost half a minute before sighing. "Okay, I'll put her in a holding cell for the night. Maybe she'll talk in the morning. I think you might be right about the drugs." He turned to the two patrolmen. "You guys get back out there and protect the citizens."

The cop who had been saying she was cute smirked. "Sure you don't want some help friskin' her, Sarge?"

"Get back to work," the sergeant snapped.

The two officers left her alone in the small room with the sergeant. He said, "Lemme know now if you gotta go to the can. There's a toilet in the cell but you ain't got no privacy when you use it."

Gloria said nothing.

"Okay, now I'm gonna frisk you. It's gotta be done."

The two policemen who'd brought her in had already searched her but she didn't say anything. The sergeant lifted her Detroit Lions shirt to look at the top of her jeans. "No belt, good. I'm gonna need your shoes. Well, maybe just the laces."

He ran both hands up and down each of her legs. He went all the way up to her crotch where it seemed to Gloria he left his hand much longer than necessary. At the same time, his other hand moved slowly over her rear end. She couldn't stop herself from gasping. When she grabbed his hand and tried to pull it away, he clamped both of her wrists into one of his fists. A big man, his grip hurt.

"Take it easy, honey. Don't make it harder on yourself. It ain't gonna hurt none. Sometimes you just gotta go along to get along." His free hand moved up her undamaged side under her shirt and cold fingers felt around her back, which brought his face closer. She smelled fetid hamburger, onions and tobacco on his warm breath. As she turned her face and tried to back away, his hand snaked back to her front and slid first over one bare breast and then the other. "Ohhh, my God, honey. You are such a sweet thing." He fondled her breasts, making no pretense at any kind of search. His breathing morphed into panting. His fingers brushed over the bandage on her side but he seemed not to notice.

Gloria struggled against his grip on her wrists but he pulled her hands down toward his own crotch. "Hadda gal in here once… hid a knife between her tits… I gotta check you out." She tried to get away but he pulled her closer. His lips brushed her cheek, and she smelled his sour breath again. "C'mon, sweetheart. Let's be friends. You don't have to go in that jail cell if you—"

Gloria kneed him between the legs as hard as she could. With a screeching groan that sounded like a hacksaw going through tin, the sergeant let go with both his hands, grabbing his genitals as he collapsed to his knees. Gloria snatched the Zsa Zsa Patterson check and bolted out of the interview room heading for the front entrance. She took in an older woman with a telephone in her hand and the small man, Peanut, walking toward the front door carrying a little shopping bag.

"Unnnh… stop her, stop her. She attacked me!" the sergeant roared from behind her.

But Gloria had already brushed past Peanut and pushed through the front door. She streaked into the parking lot running along a row of parked cars. At the end of the long single-story police building she saw a street where a big black car, it's parking lights on, idled beside the entrance into the police compound.

Can't go there.

She ducked between a car and a big pickup truck.

Maybe I can hide under the truck.

Crouching close to the ground she heard the sergeant come through the front door.

"—got me square in the nuts. Goddam, it hurts."

"You gonna shoot her, Sarge?"

"No Peanut, I ain't gonna shoot her. Goddam, my fuckin' balls."

Frozen, afraid to move, Gloria heard a car door open very close, not the one beside her, but the one next to it.

"Peanut, where the fuck are you going?" The sergeant's voice had come closer.

"Going home, Sergeant Simmons. I'm already half an hour over. You want I should stay? You have to pay me."

"Shit. Okay, godammit, but run inside first and tell Martha to call everybody back. I'll organize a search. That little bitch won't get far."

Hearing two sets of footsteps going away, Gloria rose for a quick look. Slightly bent over with one hand between his legs, and the other resting on his holster, the sergeant teetered toward the other end of the parking lot, which was bounded by a concrete block wall. Peanut went into the station through the front door. Quickly, Gloria duck-walked around the back of the truck to get between the next two vehicles. She found a dirty car with ugly horizontal tailfins It was big and speckled with rust. The front door hung open. She pushed the driver's seatback forward, squeezed herself into the back on the floor and pulled back the seatback.

Used bags from McDonald's, napkins, plastic cups, ballpoint pens and a three-ring binder littered the floor but she found enough room. Getting as low as possible, she'd no sooner settled when someone, presumably Peanut, got into the driver's seat. He shut the door. She heard the muffled voice of the sergeant outside just as the car started.

"Sure you don't wanna stick around Peanut? When I catch her, I'm gonna strip-search her. You might wanna see that. Might change your perspective." The sergeant laughed.

"Sarge, I'll stay if I can get paid. Otherwise, I'm goin' home."

"Awright, beat it, you useless fuck."

The car thunked into gear and backed out of the parking space. The radio turned on. Gloria heard a woman disc jockey from the Windsor, Canada, rock and roll station introducing the Rolling Stones. *Jumpin' Jack Flash* began blasting through the car. Gloria stayed motionless. Peanut never got onto a freeway or went very fast. Every time they stopped, a wave of panic hit Gloria. She thought Peanut had somehow sensed her presence. Finally, he made a slow sharp turn, crunched onto gravel and jerked to a stop. She heard the transmission clunk, then the rasp of the parking brake. Peanut got out and slammed the door shut. She heard a click when he locked the car.

For several minutes, Gloria stayed on the car floor trying to decide what to do. She'd made one bad decision after another, been molested, the police wanted her, and she'd lost her guitar and all her money.

Maybe Logan Carlton's right. I can't take care myself. She wanted to cry but forced herself not to. Carefully, then quickly because the dome light popped on, she unlocked the front door and got out. She looked around trying to decide what to do.

Down the street and around the corner of the first cross street, she saw a big dark car parked. It looked too nice for the neighborhood, but she quickly turned her attention to the small rundown house where Peanut lived. The shake-shingle siding had dark gaps where pieces had fallen off. Painted white a long time ago, now the house appeared a dingy gray in the dim light. The yard, like the other yards she could see, was choked with weeds and garbage.

She snuck up to Peanut's lone front window. What she saw sent an angry jolt of energy through her.

Peanut, his back to the window, was hunched over a coffee table counting money. Her money, almost $3,000 of her money. Now she remembered that when Peanut brought the Zsa Zsa Patterson check to the sergeant, the sergeant had asked him if he'd found anything else. Peanut mentioned only her guitar, nothing else. He had stolen her money.

I have to get it back.

Gloria studied the front entrance to the house and then walked back to the car. She pulled the car door open, then slammed it shut and ran to the front door of the house. She pressed herself against the wall next to the low wooden stoop.

Peanut flung open the door. He looked around, zeroing in on his car, but neglected to look behind the door where Gloria hid. Leaving the door open, he stepped to his car, cocked his head and surveyed the street. Gloria quietly climbed onto the low stoop and entered the house. She locked the front door behind her, then ran through the house to the back door, which she found already locked. Coming back to the front room, she scooped up the money from the coffee table and wadded it into the front pockets of her jeans.

"Who the fuck are you?" A man with crutches stood in the doorway of a room that opened off the living room. He wore white underwear briefs, but nothing else. He looked a little older than Peanut with a handsome, lightly bearded face and a muscular upper body. But one of his legs ended above the knee, the stump trembling below his underwear. He hopped forward and swiped a crutch at Gloria. She jumped back easily avoiding it. The man almost toppled over trying to re-balance himself. He got control and took another hop toward her.

"I'm Gloria," she said. "I came to get the money back that Peanut stole from me."

"He stole money from you?"

"Yeah, about $3,000."

"How the fuck did he—"

They both heard Peanut pounding on the front door crying out, "Lemme in, godammit. Open the door. Are you there, Benny? Open the fuckin' door."

The bearded man lowered himself onto the arm of the battered couch, steadying himself with one hand while loosely holding his two crutches with the other. When one of the crutches started to fall away, he tried to snatch it back and lost his balance. He slid onto the couch, muttering, "Godammit." But he managed to gain control of both his crutches. "Let him in. He won't hurt you, and it doesn't look like I can. Fuck!"

Wary that he might try and hit her with a crutch, Gloria hesitated. "Okay, I was gonna leave anyway. Sorry for barging in, but I needed to get my money back."

"Wait a minute. I wanna get to the bottom of this. We don't steal. I can't believe Peanut would do this." When Gloria didn't move, the man struggled to his feet and stumped with his crutches to the front door. "Shit, I'll let him in."

When he opened the door, Peanut stormed past him but stopped when he saw Gloria. "How did you…" His eyes went to the coffee table.

"I already took the money back," she said.

"Aw man." He sat down heavily on the couch. "I knew it was too good to be true."

While they spoke, the man with the crutches disappeared into the bedroom. He came out wearing a red silk robe with yellow dragons. Gloria thought it beautiful. He hopped over and sat beside Peanut on the couch, putting an arm around him.

"What the fuck did you do now, Peanut? I told you we'd get through this."

Peanut said, "She got arrested outside the airport. Fuck if I know why. Anyway, when I went through her stuff, like Simmons told me to, I found a whole buncha cash. I, um, I figured we needed it."

"Goddam, Peanut, I'm gonna get paid by the fuckin' VA. You know that."

"Yeah, but when's that gonna be? The rent's overdue and we don't have it. Then there's 'lectricity and the gas company.

Fuckin' Ma Bell already turned off the phone. And I'm tired of eatin' oatmeal."

"I gave you money for McDonald's."

"Gettin' tired of that, too."

Peanut looked at Gloria. "How did you get here? What did you do to Sergeant Simmons?"

Gloria took a few steps to one side so she could lean against the wall. She looked at the two of them, puzzled by the relationship. Not family because they didn't look anything alike. "I hid in the back of your car. When I looked in the front window and saw you counting the money, I decided to take it back. It's my money and I need it. I earned it."

Benny asked, "What do you do?"

"I'm a musician."

But Peanut still wanted an answer to his question. "What about the sergeant? Not that I feel sorry for the bastard."

Gloria said, "I kneed him in the, you know, between the legs. He was getting too personal…" Her voice trailed off.

"Yeah, everybody knows he does that with women prisoners," Peanut said. "'Specially if they're good-lookin' like you. Did he use the line about the woman who hid a knife between her boobs?"

"Yes." Gloria flushed and her knees buckled a little before she steadied herself, her fatigue returning with a vengeance. She looked away from Peanut and found herself staring at Benny's stump. It was red like it may have happened recently. "What happened to your leg?"

Benny shrugged but his nonchalance seemed poorly faked. "I stepped on a land mine. They tell me I'm lucky to be alive, but I'm not sure I agree."

"You were a soldier?"

He nodded. "Yeah. I'm a kickass Gyrene…'cept my ass-kicking days are over."

"Gyrene? What's that?"

"Marines. I was in the Marine Corps."

"Oh, my boyfriend's in Vietnam, in the Army."

"Oh yeah? Where?"

She thought for a moment. "I don't know where, but he's in the 99th Assault Helicopter Company. He was a gunner and now he's a crew chief on a gunship. And he was a prisoner for more than a month."

"What do you mean, a prisoner?"

"His helicopter got shot down and he got captured. Then he escaped. He hasn't told me much about it."

Benny looked at her and slowly nodded. "So, he's in combat. That's tough. When's he comin' home?"

"Soon, July." She looked around the small living room, taking it in for the first time. Aside from the couch and a coffee table, she didn't see much furniture. Everything seemed to shimmer in the dim light. Her legs ached, the cut on her abdomen throbbed, her mouth felt dry. "Ah, how much is your rent?"

"Eighty-five a month," Peanut said. "It ain't worth even that. Fuckin' furnace barely works in the winter."

"My disability from the VA should start any day, and I still got a little of the money I saved when I was in 'Nam."

"Yeah, well it's either the rent or we sell the car." Peanut took a deep breath and let it out in a long sigh.

Gloria reached into her jeans and took out a hundred-dollar bill. Almost all the money she'd gotten at the record company had been in hundred-dollar bills. Taking a few steps, she dropped it on the coffee table. "Here, that'll cover the rent. I sort of owe you for the ride. I didn't want to stay in that jail cell." She looked at Peanut. "What's your job at the police station? That sergeant doesn't seem to like you."

"Job? I ain't gotta job and I don't get paid nothin'." Peanut looked at her with soft sad eyes that looked too big for his face. "I'm on probation. Have to do twenty-five hours of community service a week. If I work more than twenty-five hours, or more than six hours on any day, they're supposed to pay me, but Simmons makes sure that never happens. He hates my guts. Everybody does."

Shaking his head, Benny looked at him. "C'mon, Peanut, you know that ain't true."

"Yeah, it is. Nobody likes a fairy, or a queer, or a faggot, or whatever you want to call me."

"You told me Martha treated you okay."

Peanut nodded. "Yeah, sometimes she does. That don't mean she likes me. It's more like she's fascinated with me. She told me I ought go to hairdressing school. She said her hairdresser's a homo."

"What are you on probation for?" Gloria asked.

Peanut flushed and looked away. Finally, Benny said, "He got caught in the restroom at a city park. Damn cops arrested more than twenty homosexuals and a judge threw the book at them. The cops were leadin' them on, right Peanut?"

"I don't wanna talk about it."

"See, this undercover cop was—"

"Stop it, Benny. Just stop talkin' about it. Nothin's gonna change." Peanut stomped out of the room. "I'm goin' to bed."

That was when Gloria figured out the relationship. They were both homosexuals, and living together. She had never met or known a homosexual couple, or at least she didn't think she had. "Wait a minute. Do you guys wanna make some money?"

Peanut paused at the bedroom door and Benny leaned toward her. "We don't want your charity." With a finger, he slid the hundred-dollar bill in her direction.

"Benny," Peanut whined.

Gloria swayed on her aching legs, the hundred-dollar bill swam in her vision. She sat on the coffee table, bent over trying to clear her head. Then she straightened and twisted to face Benny. "Charity? No. I need a place to crash. You need money. I can't even stand up. I can't go back out there tonight. Please don't turn me in. I'm afraid what that sergeant's gonna do to me. Let me sleep on the couch, or the floor, or out in the car. The money's my rent, just let me get some rest."

Benny stared at her for a long moment and smiled for the first time. "Okay, take the couch. I ain't turnin' away a soldier's girl. We can figure out the money in the morning. Maybe make it a loan." He grabbed his crutches and stumped into the bedroom. Gloria barely heard his muffled voice. She sagged onto the couch, thinking she should take off her shoes.

It felt so good to be off her feet. Before she could reach for her shoes, her eyes closed and she fell asleep.

-47-

Rui Binh

The ease with which the scheme for Sanderson's Hawaiian R and R came together amazed Hayes.

The CO agreed to sign the orders without hesitation.

"Didn't ask any questions but he knows we ain't playin' by the rules," the first sergeant said.

Cartwright helped Hayes mail $500 cash to Sanderson's wife. "You can't just stick it in an envelope and mail it. We'll send it registered mail and insure it."

After waiting more than a week for a space to open up on a Hawaii R and R flight, Cartwright's contact, who'd been promised twenty bucks if Sanderson got the R and R, called.

Early the next morning, Hayes hitched a ride to Long Binh on the C and C — command and control — helicopter. Lieutenant Colonel Blair flying the C and C ship, led the entire 99th Assault Helicopter Company – two platoons of slicks and the Headhunter gun platoon — in a tight formation into Long Binh for a big multi-unit combat assault. Hayes, who had never seen it from the vantage point of the C and C ship, had always marveled at the skill and concentration required of the pilots.

When they landed, the C and C crew chief handed Hayes his helmet. "CO wants to talk to you."

Hayes put on the helmet and said, "Sir, Sergeant Hayes here."

"Just wanted to wish you luck, Sergeant Hayes." Blair's voice crackled in his ears.

"Thank you, sir," Hayes said but the CO kept talking.

"Call on me if you need my help. I'll be at 12th Group HQ for the next hour, maybe longer. Specialist Sanderson was my C and C crew chief when I first got to the 99th. I want him to get his R and R."

That explains why he signed those orders.

Next, Hayes proceeded with his mission to bribe the lieutenant. Cartwright had briefed him on where to find the bent lieutenant. A sloppy, overweight man with a crewcut, he sat eating a C-ration chocolate cookie and drinking a Coke for breakfast, or maybe an after-breakfast snack. He didn't have an office, but a corner of a small administrative hooch. Tall file cabinets blocked the little alcove from view. Hayes ambled to the corner and dropped two hundred-dollar bills on the desk in front of the lieutenant.

The lieutenant looked at the money for a moment, then pushed his chair back so he could look around the otherwise empty hooch. "Hawaii R and R?"

Hayes nodded. "Yep."

"When?"

"Tomorrow."

"Cuttin' it a little close. Orders?"

Hayes placed a copy of Sanderson's orders on the desk. The lieutenant studied them, glanced at Hayes' nametag. He fumbled around in his desk before taking out a long, typewritten list of names. He carefully printed Sanderson's name, rank and serial number on the bottom.

"We're set. Make sure he's on time with his orders."

"Will do," Hayes said.

With several hours to kill in Long Binh, Hayes decided to visit Lieutenant Colonel Kucharski. He didn't think he'd catch him, but his luck held. Outside the colonel's office, he found the same sergeant first class who had jacked him up over his dirty uniform. This time Sergeant First Class Bell eyed him warily.

"Specialist Hayes. You come to see the colonel? He didn't tell me you were stoppin' by."

"It's Sergeant Hayes now. And yes, I was hoping to see him. But I don't have an appointment."

Bell looked at his watch, studied Hayes. "You're lookin' good, especially... well, we heard aboutcha. Colonel's got a meeting with some of our allies, but it probably won't start for another twenty minutes, half an hour. Fuckin' Thais are always late. Let me see if he'll see you."

But the door to Kucharski's office opened and Kucharski came out offering a tight smile. Hayes saluted and Kucharski returned it. "Good to see you, Sergeant Hayes. I heard about your capture and escape. Come in. I have a few minutes. I want to hear your story firsthand so I can tell the general. It's the kind of thing he likes."

Inside the office, Kucharski indicated a chair and Hayes sat. Before Kucharski could say anything, Hayes seized the moment, speaking in a calm tone, striving to sound less confrontational than his words. "Sir, I came here to ask you who replaced Specialist Kannegiesser as gunner the day a Headhunter gunship went to a hamlet near here with some Green Berets and killed some villagers by tossing them out of the helicopter. I know Warrant Officer Moss and Lieutenant Carson were the pilots. Specialist Delaney was crew chief. But Moss and Carson got rid of Kannegiesser and replaced him with someone else. Someone who probably did the dirty work. Who was that?"

Kucharski sputtered, "Where'd you hear that?"

"Sir, the VC were going to execute me because they thought I did it. But I heard the whole story from some of the surviving villagers. I don't think they were lying," Hayes said. "I think I've earned the right to know."

Kucharski shrugged, seemed to relax. "No, you haven't, sergeant. You escaped. You weren't executed. We're all glad you weren't. But that's history now. Doesn't earn you anything except the rest of your life and maybe another medal."

But Hayes pressed on. "Last time I was here, we talked about the murder of Spec Five Mitchell and Sergeant Grugel. You told me you were gonna have Jimmy Ray Suggs investigate those murders. But that never happened. Now the number of murders is up to five. Maybe six. And I think—"

"What do you mean, five murders?" Kurcharski interrupted.

"Sir, the helicopter that crashed and killed Warrant Officers Nesterenko and Donaldson, and Specialist Flowers, and led to my capture, was sabotaged. Our Maintenance NCO examined the wreckage. He found sand in the transmission."

"Sabotage? That wasn't in the accident report."

"You're right sir, it wasn't. Our Maintenance NCO, Sergeant First Class Gomez asked the depot maintenance people to keep the wrecked transmission so he could take a look at it. He took the transmission apart and found the sand. Somebody probably put the sand in while we were at the Officers Club that night."

Frowning, Kurcharski scratched a hand through his short hair. "Jesus Christ," he muttered and looked Hayes in the eye. "How do I know I can believe this Sergeant Gomez? How competent is he? Maybe he's trying to deflect attention from his own maintenance errors."

"Sergeant Gomez is very competent. Maybe you should talk to him yourself," Hayes said, hastily adding, "sir."

"Well, you or your CO should have said something about this—"

"Sir, I'm saying something now. Mitchell's murder was covered up. You said so yourself. Then nothing happened after I told you about Sergeant Grugel. Now there's been at least three more. And really, it would have been four if I hadn't escaped."

Hayes stopped as the closed door opened and Bell stuck his head in. "Everyone's down in the conference room except the Thais. I have it on good authority that they're within a minute of arrival."

"I have to go," Kucharski said. He looked relieved. "I'm having lunch with a Colonel Braddock and… never mind. I should have some time before the lunch. We'll finish this."

Hayes said, "Yes sir."

After Kucharski left, the sergeant first class handed Hayes an ice-cold can of Coke. "I woulda brought this in, but I didn't wanna interrupt."

"Thanks." Thirsty, Hayes drank several large swallows while looking at the muscular Bell.

Maybe he was the gunner.

"So, Sergeant Bell, you gonna tell me who that gunner was? And don't try and say you weren't listening. I'd wager you listen in to most of the colonel's conversations."

Bell chuckled. "You're as sharp as the colonel says. But identifying that gunner is not something I'm willing to do."

He stopped talking and looked past Hayes, who turned around to see what had caught his attention.

Three noisy Thai officers came through the front door, two wearing dress uniforms, the third, a woman in tight camouflage fatigues. Hayes immediately recognized her as Bich, the Vietcong translator in the tunnels who'd laughed when she told him of his death sentence. His stomach lurched as he started to turn back to hide his face. But he couldn't stop looking at her.

Underground, she'd worn a baggy gray sweatsuit, a hood covering her hair. Now, the tailored fatigues emphasized an appealing figure. And he had probably seen her before in Long Binh. Those tight camo fatigues. No American female soldier would get away with wearing a uniform like that. Shiny, dark hair tied in a tight bun stuck out under a red beret. Nut-brown skin glistened, and scarlet lips peeled back revealing impossibly white teeth when she laughed.

Hayes wanted to kill her. His hand slipped over the Makarov pistol in his pocket. But he finally turned and asked Sergeant Bell, "Those are the Thais, right? Who's the woman?"

"Y'all like that stuff?" Bell grinned. "That's Bich, the Thai's translator. Speaks half a dozen languages. We use her too. Kind of a freelancer, but she's a first looey in the Royal Thai Air Force."

Bell looked past Hayes again, smiled and waved. "I'll introduce ya. She likes Americans, 'specially African men."

At first Hayes didn't follow Bell. Then it hit him that Bell might be, probably was, Bich's lover, or perhaps one of her lovers. Bell was a sergeant who heard the conversations of an officer on staff of the commanding general of American forces in Vietnam.

"Ah, that's okay. I already got a girl back home."

"Well, hell, me too, but that don't mean I passed up a shot at the poontangaliscious Bich." Eyebrows arching, he grinned again.

The Thais disappeared into their meeting with Colonel Kucharski at the far end of the building. Hayes' mind raced. What to do? Then the door to the meeting room suddenly reopened. Bich hurried out like she'd forgotten something. This time she spotted Hayes. Her mouth popped open. She stood frozen for a moment, panicked, then ran for the front door. Hayes pulled out his pistol and racked the slide to chamber a round. He caught her by the door and pointed the Makarov at her.

"What the fuck, Hayes!" Bell shouted.

"She's a spy. Get the colonel." But as soon as Hayes spoke, cold calculation replaced the panic on Bich's face.

"I'm not a spy," she said.

"Hey, let's talk about this," Bell said. "Put the gun down before you—"

"You better get the colonel. I'd just as soon shoot her."

"You're in a lot trouble Hayes. Now put—"

"Maybe you're the one in trouble. You tell her what the colonel says in his meetings? I gotta get you some pussy to find out who that fuckin' gunner was?"

Meanwhile, Hayes saw Bich's hand inching toward the pistol so he shoved the Makarov against her nose. "Don't think I won't shoot. Now get the goddam colonel."

Bell backed up slowly toward the meeting room. Hayes prodded Bich into Kucharski's office. He pointed to a chair. "Sit." The door had a small barrel bolt. He slid it locking them inside.

"You are wrong. I am not a spy," Bich said.

"Drop the act, Bich. You know who I am. I saw it on your face."

She pressed her shaking hands against her thighs. A bead of sweat rolled down her forehead into an eyebrow. She swiped it away. The sudden movement made Hayes tense on the Makarov.

"Don't point the gun at me. You want kill me by mistake?" She wiped more sweat from her brow, slowly this time.

"Wouldn't be a mistake," he said.

But some doubts crept in. Would anyone believe an American sergeant with a checkered record over a pretty spy, apparently trusted by senior officers? And how many of them had she slept with?

"You know, I never did what you and your VC friends said. I didn't throw anybody out of a helicopter."

Silent, she avoided looking at him. Then he remembered Gloria's letter.

"Do you know a Thai Air Force colonel by the name of Jettrin Juntasa?"

He hadn't expected it but her face showed the name registered.

"Colonel Whop Whop," she said. "He's not in the Royal Thai Air Force anymore. I heard the king asked him to leave."

"Colonel Whop Whop?"

"He was one of the first to fly helicopters in the Royal Thai Air Force. He got the name... what do you call it? Nickname? Whop Whop. It's like the noise a helicopter makes."

"Okay."

No doubt finding it easier to talk about than her being a spy, she continued, "He's a bad man, big bad man worse than his father. The whole Juntasa family, they're bad. How do you know him?" She leaned sideways to avoid the pistol. Hayes rested the barrel of the gun on his forearm, pointing it to the side, but keeping his finger curled over the trigger guard.

"Keep talking."

She spit out the next part. "He buys and sells girls. He owns whores. Bangkok, Kuala Lumpur, Penang, Singapore,

Taipei, Hong Kong. Poor families sell young girls. He makes them whores for American soldiers. His name 'Whop Whop' is also for cutting fingers." She splayed out her fingers on one hand and made a chopping motion with the other. "Whop whop. Why do you want to know about him?"

Hayes shrugged. "He murdered some people in Detroit."

"Deetroyet? What is Detroyet?

"Dee-troit," Hayes said carefully. "It's a big city in America."

"Oh." She puzzled over it for a few moments. "Why did he go to Dee-troit?"

"I don't know."

She thought some more. "I heard he sometimes sells white girls from the West to rich men. Make beaucoup baht."

"Baht?"

"Money," she said. "Maybe he goes to Dee-troit to buy girl. Do you have poor families in Dee-troit? Asian men pay much baht for white girl. More for blond girl."

Hayes didn't say anything, but Bich must have seen his distress because she smiled triumphantly. He shifted the gun back so it pointed at her head, which killed the smile.

"I think you want to shoot Colonel Whop Whop, not me."

Hayes nodded, but he said, "You'll do."

Bich and Hayes sat in Kucharski's office for another half hour before the door rattled when someone tried to open it.

"Open up, Sergeant Hayes or we'll break it down." Hayes opened the door and two military policemen followed by Lieutenant Colonel Kucharski entered.

"Put down the gun, sergeant," Kucharski ordered.

Hayes laid the gun on the colonel's desk. The MPs did not draw their weapons.

"She's a spy, colonel. She works for the VC. When the VC put me on trial, she translated for them."

"You're sure about this, sergeant?"

"Yes sir, absolutely sure."

Kucharski studied Bich for a moment, then glanced back at Hayes, and finally at the two MPs. "Take her down to the meeting."

One of the MPs asked, "Sir, do you want her cuffed?"

"No, but stay with her and watch her carefully."

When the two left with Bich, two more MPs marched into Kucharski's office.

"They'll stay here with you Sergeant Hayes. We may want to talk to you further," Kucharski said, eyeing the Makarov. One of the MPs took it and ejected the magazine and the bullet in the chamber.

For the next several hours through the open door of Kucharski's office, Hayes observed officers, including two full colonels, going in and out of the meeting room at the end of building. One of the officers was Major Shiffman who gave Hayes a quick nod. Two men in blue jeans and sports shirts, probably CIA, sauntered past. The two MPs came out with Bich, still not handcuffed. She looked at Hayes on the way past, her face devoid of expression.

What are they gonna do to me? Bust me back to Spec Four?

Finally, the meeting broke up. Kucharski and Shiffman entered the small office. Kucharski dismissed the MPs.

"You've created a mess, Sergeant Hayes, but you're free to go," Kucharski said. "Don't talk about this to anyone."

Hayes stood up and saluted. Kucharski seemed not to notice until Hayes picked up the Makarov and magazine from the desk.

"Sergeant, you shouldn't be carrying that weapon around," Kucharski said.

"Sir, at least five men have been murdered in my company, and I came close to being number six."

Kucharski looked at Hayes, sighed and said, "I'll overlook it."

Hayes saluted again, and this time Kucharski returned the salute.

Walking out of the building, Hayes asked Shiffman, "Sir, may I ask you what went on in that meeting? Am I in trouble?"

Shiffman laughed softly. "Trouble? Sergeant Hayes, it's the rest of us who're in trouble. You are golden. You found a spy. Bich admitted right away she was the translator you saw in the tunnels."

"She did?"

"Says she's working for the CIA, though that seems to be a very recent development. Those CIA bastards wouldn't let her say much. They stonewalled us. The Thai officers also said she has been passing information to them. Everything's getting kicked back to Washington. You were lucky I happened to be in Long Binh today. Before I arrived, Colonel Kucharski wanted to arrest you. Now he's acting like your number one supporter. The whole thing seems to be turning into an Army-CIA dispute that'll be settled at a higher level. But Kucharski's not gonna be around much longer so I wouldn't worry about him."

"How's that?"

"He's been working for Westmoreland, but Creighton Abrams is about to take over as commanding general. Westmoreland's getting kicked up to chief of staff. It was announced months ago, but it's just now happening. So Kucharski's going home. He's on a fast track to make full colonel. He just wants to get outta here without any blots."

They headed for the Long Binh Operations Bunker hoping to catch a ride back to Nui Binh on the afternoon courier. A half dozen soldiers surrounded the courier helicopter, which had shut down. Hayes recognized the two pilots — both from the 99th — standing to one side talking to a captain he remembered from Long Binh from Operations.

"What happened?" Hayes asked one of the pilots.

"We took some ground fire just outside the perimeter."

"It was an AK," the other pilot said. "The ship's got some holes. We're not going back tonight. One of our passengers got shot."

"Who?" Hayes asked.

"Spec Five Sanderson. Got hit in the leg. We took him to 24th Evac and then came here."

"He ain't goin' on R and R, but he'll be goin' home," said the other pilot. "If there's such a thing as a million-dollar wound, he got one."

-48-

Detroit

On a clear Saturday morning Susanna Quinn drove a sullen Antoine downtown to see Pip Papineau. Antoine had stopped talking to her about his case and had had little or no contact with the lawyers. So Susanna had arranged the meeting. While she believed in his innocence, his refusal to call his family in Philadelphia angered her. Yes, it would embarrass him but she couldn't accept allowing Gloria to pay for his legal defense when he had a family that could afford it.

His silver hair in disarray and dark bags under his eyes, Papineau greeted the two at the entrance after they knocked. "I'm sorry, but I'm about to start an emergency meeting to go over Gloria Doran's disappearance. I don't know how long it'll take. If you want to leave and reschedule, I'll understand," he said.

"I think Gloria ran away. She told me—" Susanna started.

"I can wait," Antoine interrupted. "My hearing isn't till the end of next week, right?"

Papineau said, "Well, the prosecutor's pushing a plea deal, but let's talk about it after this meeting. Okay?"

Antoine agreed. Remembering that she'd spoken to Papineau on the phone but had never met him, Susanna said. "I'm Susanna Quinn."

"Gloria's friend." Papineau looked at her scratching his chin then extended his hand. "Glad to meet you."

He led them back to the reception area outside his big corner office, gesturing to some chairs. They could hear voices murmuring inside the office and when Papineau went in he left the door almost halfway open. Susanna and Antoine settled into the chairs beside the open door. No one in the inner office could see them. Susanna thought Papineau might have left the door open on purpose.

"We ready to start?" she heard Papineau say. "I have an investigator, Steve Mendelsohn, used to work for the DA, looking into this. Very good investigator but expensive. That's why he's not here. I don't pay him to sit in meetings."

"Yeah, well, I think Detroit PD's on top of this. We've been to the scene of that double murder and talked to the Wayne County dicks, so you mighta wasted your money." Susanna remembered hearing about some murders that morning on the radio but hadn't paid any attention.

"Maybe, but Sergeant Overholzer, I'd like to hear your take on them," Papineau said.

"Sure, why not. Wayne County Sheriffs believe it was a fag crime of passion. My partner and I are inclined to agree. They called us right away 'cause it initially looked like our boy. That's why I called you."

"And I appreciate that you did," Papineau said.

"Anyway, the scene was fresh when we got there, and I gotta say, it really did remind us of Juntasa. But why would he kill a coupla fags? We've since learned that Juntasa's car, that Ford Falcon, was abandoned at the airport. Got towed well before the murders. We matched prints in it to the prints from the Thai restaurant murders. Don't know how he coulda gotten to the murder scene. It's five miles from the airport. Between us and Wayne County, we checked the taxis and rental cars. No cars reported stolen at the airport either. I think he split, went back to Asia. So now we're goin' over the airline manifests, every damn flight. Haven't come up with anybody yet that mighta been Juntasa."

"Damn, I wanna get my Lincoln back. D'ya think it could be at the airport?" This was a new voice, but right away Susanna recognized it belonged to State Senator Logan Carlton.

"I don't think so, senator," the policeman said. I doubt your car's anywhere around here. We're pretty sure Gloria Doran drove it away from the hospital. We've sent alerts statewide and to surrounding states. She ran away once before, so she's probably runnin' again. She's good at it."

"I'm not so sure about that." Susanna heard a woman's voice that sounded familiar but she couldn't place it.

"Hold on, doctor. Let's stay with the murders," Papineau said. "Any chance the two men might have killed each other?"

"No. No murder weapon found at the scene. Wayne County thinks some other fag did it. One of the victims, Albert Penty, goes by Peanut, looks like he mighta had multiple fag connections. Coupla months ago, he got caught in a Romulus park restroom soliciting to have his, um… soliciting oral sex."

"Oh, don't hold back on account of me, detective. Go ahead and say he was a disgusting faggot looking for a blowjob." The woman's voice dripped with sarcasm, and this time Susanna recognized Dr. Emily Sadowski.

The detective paused before continuing. "Sorry. I don't want to imply that just because the two victims were homosexual that we don't take this seriously. The other vic, Benjamin Connelly, was a Marine. Real war hero. Lost a leg in Vietnam. Was awarded a Navy Cross. That's the highest medal except for the Medal of Honor."

"Okay," Sadowski muttered. "Didn't mean to snap at you."

"Did you talk to Romulus PD?" Papineau asked.

"No we didn't. It's a Wayne County case, but they mighta talked to Romulus."

"Does Wayne County know about the young woman they detained that night?"

"I don't know. This is the first I've heard. What's it got to do with this?"

Nobody said anything for a moment and Susanna heard the rustle of papers before Papineau continued.

"Let me tell you what Mendelsohn learned. He talked to some people at Romulus PD, including a sergeant by the name of Simmons who mighta been the last person to see Penty alive. Penty, okay, let's call him Peanut, was on probation."

"Yeah, yeah, we know that already," the Detroit detective said.

"Okay. But that night, two Romulus patrol officers arrested a young woman walking on one of the roads just outside the airport. She almost got hit by a coupla cars, and somebody called the police. The Romulus officers brought her back to their station in handcuffs. She wasn't cooperative. No ID, there was some speculation she was on drugs."

"Lotta that kinda speculation's been on target lately. I'm introducin' a bill to…" Senator Carlton's voice died.

"Anyway, among the woman's possessions was a check made out to Zsa Zsa Patterson. And it was signed by a Yumi Fujiura. F-U-J-I-U-R-A. It's Japanese. There was no address on the check but it was written on a New York bank account. The amount was $190, which happens to be the exact cost of a ticket from Detroit to Honolulu on Delta Airlines."

"I don't see why any of this is relevant," Overholzer said.

"Bear with me. Mendelsohn got most of what I just told you from the two Romulus patrol cops. When he found out about the Patterson check, he looked for airline flights that cost that much. He talked to a Delta rep who sold a one-way ticket to Honolulu to a young woman who paid cash and who paid an extra hundred bucks to put Zsa Zsa Patterson down on the manifest. The description of the young woman the rep gave Mendelsohn and the description from the two Romulus cops, matches Gloria Doran."

"Holy shi… crap! So you're sayin' Romulus PD had Gloria Doran in custody the night of the murders?" It was the Detroit detective speaking.

"Yes, I am, and that's not all. Right after the Delta rep sold her the ticket, she was threatened by an Asian man with a knife. She said he was a great big Chinaman. He wanted to know where the woman who bought the ticket was going."

For a few ticks, Susanna heard nothing until the detective spoke. "Doesn't add up."

"What do you mean?"

"If she bought a ticket to Honolulu and paid an extra hundred bucks to use a fake name, how come she didn't go to Honolulu? How come she ended up in jail in Romulus?"

"She must of changed her mind and sold the ticket to Yumi Fujiura. There was a long flight delay."

"Could I say something now?" Susanna heard Dr. Sadowski's urgent voice.

"Okay, go ahead," Papineau said.

"Gloria Doran is sixteen years old and—"

Logan Carlton interrupted, "No shit. She badly needs adult supervision and you—"

"Shut up, you supercilious snob. Don't you dare talk over me. You've done enough damage already."

"Hold on here—"

"Let her finish, senator." Papineau said. His voice, while not raised, held a a commanding tone.

"Yeah, I wanna hear this," Overholzer added.

After a few silent moments where Susanna imagined the doctor composing herself, Sadowksi continued.

"Gloria's sixteen, and she's trying hard to grow up. She suffered serious emotional, physical and sexual abuse as a child. In the last six months, she's witnessed the murders of her biological... ah, I have to be careful here about patient confidentiality. Let's see. Okay, two men in her presence were murdered. She was present when her stepfather died but she won't talk about that. She was pregnant and carried a baby to term, then lost the baby due to what, in my opinion, was medical negligence." Her voice cracked and she paused for a few seconds. "The same time she lost her baby, the same day, in fact, she learned that her boyfriend, the father of the baby, had gone missing in action in Vietnam. Three days ago, she suffered a serious breakdown."

"A mental breakdown?" the detective asked.

"I'd call it more of an emotional breakdown. Sometimes we use the term nervous breakdown, but it's not a term I like. When people experience severe trauma they can react in a variety of ways. Doesn't necessarily occur at the time of the trauma. We're seeing an awful lot of that in soldiers returning from Vietnam. On the day of her breakdown, Gloria Doran had gone to the burned out remains of the Grosse Pointe home where she grew up. I think that triggered her breakdown. Then, the next day, she was attacked by this monster. She saw the main stabilizing adult in her life almost die."

"Yeah, we haven't been able to talk to Frances Lincoln," the detective said. "I checked this morning before coming here. Frances Lincoln is still critical but expected to recover."

Sadowski paused again, and Carlton immediately seized the initiative. "Looks like I'll have to put her in a residential drug treatment facility. Or maybe in the county foster system."

Papineau and Sadowski both spoke at the same time.

"Enough!" Papineau said.

"Gloria Doran does not use drugs!" Sadowski said. "She tried marijuana once and didn't like it. And ever since she lost her baby, she's afraid of drugs, including medication from doctors. The Henry Ford nurse who stitched up her laceration told me she refused pain medication and even resisted a topical anesthetic for the stitching."

"I fired you so you stay away from her, Sadowski. I'll get a goddam restraining order."

"You have no authority to fire me," Sadowski said.

"Can we get back to the murders?" the detective said echoing Papineau's earlier comment, but it seemed to Susanna the detective was losing patience with Carlton.

The talk stopped for a few seconds before Papineau exerted control. "Let's do that, but first, we should allow Dr. Sadowski to finish. I think she was trying make a point."

"Um, okay. Really, what I wanted to say is that given everything Gloria has been through, it's not likely she's making good decisions. She's highly intelligent, and, I would like to stress this, she's very mature for her age." There was a slight pause, as if Sadowski expected Carlton to interrupt. "I was concerned, Mr. Papineau, when you said she was almost struck by some cars. That doesn't surprise me. We really need to put more effort into finding her before she hurts herself."

Papineau sighed loudly. "Well, that's the main reason I'm having this meeting. I invited Wayne County detectives, but they declined. I'm grateful all of you came and I know Sergeant Overholzer has been up all night, as have I. Anyway, Wayne County was too busy and I updated them with what Mendelsohn learned. I'm afraid it's much worse than you think, doctor. First, I apologize, sergeant, for taking the long way around on this, but I wanted to get some of these other facts out in the open. And just because my investigator's good, I don't mean to imply that you and the Detroit police, and

Wayne County lack any competence. Mendelsohn himself admitted that he got lucky.

"I'm certain that Gloria Doran is the girl picked up by Romulus. Among her things that Romulus has is her guitar. Interesting side note on this is that Simmons told Penty to inventory her possessions."

"They let a probationer do that?" asked the detective.

"They did. It was the patrol cops who told Mendelsohn about that, and I think it's relevant for reasons I'll get to. After they talked to her, Sergeant Simmons decided to put her in a cell overnight."

"Oh my God," Sadowski groaned.

"He ordered the two Romulus officers to go back on patrol. Shortly after they left, Gloria Doran allegedly assaulted Sergeant Simmons and escaped custody."

"What! She escaped? And she assaulted a police officer?" Overholzer said.

"Yes, she kneed him in the groin and then ran out of the police station. And she grabbed that Zsa Zsa Patterson check on the way out. Romulus conducted a search for her until the chief shut it down."

"Why would he do that?" Overholzer asked.

"Seems Sergeant Simmons has a reputation for conducting, shall we say, very thorough personal searches of female prisoners."

"Oh my God. This is really bad," Sadowski said.

"Mendelsohn got this from the two patrol officers and from a woman who's the dispatcher at Romulus. The chief was concerned that this would blow up because there've been several previous complaints about Simmons. Furthermore, they didn't really have anything solid to charge Gloria Doran with in the first place."

"Well, assaulting a police officer's a felony but, yeah okay. It still doesn't connect with those murders."

"Oh, I'm coming to that. I was puzzled as to where she got the money for all this. She paid a hundred and ninety bucks cash for an airline ticket, and another hundred to keep her name off the manifest. So last night on a hunch, I called her record company and found out that she got almost $3,000 from them right after she got out of the hospital. Seems she wrote a hit song, something called *Locked in Love…*"

"I've heard that on the radio," Sadowski said. "That's her song? Because it was by somebody else, not her."

"Yes, Zoomer Patterson, and there's that name again. According to the record company president, he stole the song from her. So the record company president gave her the cash after she threatened to call me and sue.

"But let me jump right to the connection. Wayne County detectives recovered the Zsa Zsa Patterson check at the murder scene. They also found a hundred-dollar bill. Both items were under an overturned coffee table. Most of the cash that Gloria Doran picked up at the record company was in hundred-dollar bills."

"Okay, you've sold me on the girl being at the house, but how the hell did Juntasa find her there?" Overholzer said.

"I don't know for sure, but the initial call to the Romulus cops came from a guy who almost ran into a big, black, slow-moving Lincoln on a blind curve on the road by the airport.

There was blond woman in front of the Lincoln and the caller thought she was a hooker and the guy in the Lincoln was trying to pick her up. Upset him 'cause he lives in Romulus so he called the cops."

Papineau continued. "You believe Gloria Doran took the senator's Lincoln Continental from the hospital. And now we're sure she went to the airport. And we know Juntasa abandoned his car there."

"So you think that fuckin' Chinaman has my car?" the senator said. "That cocksucker."

"Okaaaaay," the detective said, stretching the word out as he thought it through. "Maybe he followed the cops to the station when they took her in, or maybe he knew they'd take her there. Yeah, I can maybe see that. But I still don't know how'd he find her at the house."

"We don't know how she got there either, but we do know she was there," Papineau said. "We also know that Peanut left the station to go home at the same time she escaped. The most logical explanation is she rode with him. So maybe Juntasa followed them. And here's another thing. Peanut inventoried her possessions when they brought her in. But nobody at the station knew she had several thousand dollars until I told them."

Silence for a short moment.

"Somebody ought to get in trouble over there. Letting a probationer do that. Jesus Christ," Overholzer said.

Susanna heard Papineau take in a deep breath before he said, "I know Gloria was there, and I believe this Juntasa killed the two homosexual men, but he did not kill her. He apparently wants her alive."

After another long pause, Susanna heard the Overholzer speak again. "That may be true, but he clearly tried to kill Frances Lincoln and he maybe tried to kill Gloria Doran too. We've learned a little about Juntasa. The waitress who survived the restaurant attack said he cuts off fingers as a method of discipline. He did that to the manager of the Thai restaurant. But when the manager threatened to go to the police, he lost his temper and killed him along with the cook. The attack on Miss Doran looks like it started as an attempted kidnapping. It was only after Gloria Doran bit him in the hand that the knife came out. This guy has a very volatile temper. The two men he killed at the restaurant had more than forty stab and slash wounds. He's a very dangerous individual."

"For now, our only logical course is to assume that Juntasa has Gloria Doran and that she's alive," Papineau concluded.

"Of course, and that doesn't change anything we're already doing. No way could he get her on an airline flight, but we've been checking. We know he's a pilot, and we're looking at private aircraft. We've come up dry on car rentals so far. Not many Asians around here so we think he'd be remembered. He could have another car. That's a possibility. Perhaps he has an accomplice we don't know about. Personally, I think he's still around here, laying low, waiting till everything cools off."

"Well, there's the senator's Lincoln Continental," said Papineau. "I think you should be looking for that Lincoln."

"Yeah," the detective said. "I'll get right on it."

Susanna heard chairs creaking. She motioned to Antoine that they should leave. The two hurried out through a door to the hallway where they waited. Half a minute later, a man in jeans, a rumpled houndstooth jacket with a revolver in a holster clipped to his belt, hurried by.

Senator Carlton appeared next. He scowled at them as he passed. Then he stopped and looked back. "Aren't you Susanna Quinn?"

Susanna nodded.

"Have you heard from Gloria?"

"No, not recently."

"If you do hear from her, you should call me." He took a card from a pocket inside his suit coat and handed it to her.

Susanna couldn't stop herself. "You used to be her friend. Why did you turn against her?"

"Against her? What do you mean? I'm trying to help her."

"Doesn't look that way to me. I think you're after her money."

"No, no…"

Susanna saw Dr. Sadowski and Papineau entering the hallway. Carlton saw them too. He turned to Susanna, his face in some distress. "Why do you think that? I promised her father that I'd take care of her. She hardly has any education. She got herself knocked up by some fuckin' soldier. She hangs around with hippies and musicians who are drug addicts. She's got way too much money for her own good. I want her to go to school so she has some kind of future."

"You have her all wrong, Senator. I lived with her for more than a month and I'm not a hippie or a drug addict. You know what she did? She taught me how to pray. All I can say is that Gloria's a beautiful person. She makes people around her better. But I guess it didn't work on you."

Carlton stared at her, his lower lip trembling. Then he turned and walked away.

When he was gone, she found Papineau staring at her just like Carlton had. He asked her, "Did you listen to the meeting?"

Susanna nodded.

"Anything you can add?"

"No… Well maybe. Gloria called me after she left the hospital. Told me she was gonna buy a bikini and lie on the beach. Never thought she meant Hawaii. She was pretty upset when she called. I didn't get to say much because she hung up."

"Okay. Well, I was hoping you might know why this Thai man was after her. Do you think she has any idea?"

Susanna thought for a long time. "I probably shouldn't say anything, but if it'll help us get her back. She wanted to go out to her old house in Grosse Pointe. She wanted to get this tackle box that had keys bank books in it. She said that it was worth a lot of money."

Susanna tried to remember everything that had happened that day. "When we went to the house it was like you said, Dr. Sadowski. It really affected her. She started to cry. Gloria asked me to go inside the garage and get the tackle box. So I did, and we put it in the car. Then later, the hospital security guards said they saw someone going through her car. And the tackle box was gone."

An awkward silence ensued. Antoine tried to put an arm around Susanna, but she edged away. Papineau glanced at them, then at the doctor and brushed back his long silver hair, his face knotted with worry.

The four of them were standing in the hallway when they heard the phone ring in Papineau's office. The lawyer scowled. "Could one of you grab that, please. Just see who it is."

"I'll get it," said Antoine, the closest person to the phone.

"Hello?" He listened for a few seconds. "Yeah he's here. No, I'm Antoine." He listened again. "Who?" More listening. "Yeah, okay.

Antoine looked Papineau. "This guy talks funny, hard to understand but I think he said for you to stand by. They're going to put on a Sergeant Jimmy Hayes from Vietnam."

-49-

24th Evacuation Hospital, Long Binh Base Camp

A sleepy Jimmy Hayes found Spec Five Sanderson lying on a cot, one leg encased in bandages and an inflated sleeve. Hayes had gotten up too early for breakfast, too early to even find a cup of coffee. He'd tried to see Sanderson the night before, but the medics told him Sanderson was in surgery.

Sanderson was with a dozen other soldiers in a staging area awaiting evacuation. Several appeared grievously wounded. The area stank of antiseptic with an underlying tinge of burnt, rotting flesh. Sanderson, sweating despite the air conditioning, greeted Hayes with a grimace.

"You don't look like somebody with a million-dollar wound. You okay? You need a shot of morphine?" Hayes asked.

"Fuck! C'mon Hayes, don't join the fuckin' crowd tryin' to turn me into a fuckin' junkie. I don't wanna end up like fuckin' Delaney." He turned his head to one side, raised up to look over the line of cots and whispered. "Fucker down there's got gangrene. Can't you smell him? At least I'm better off than him."

Hayes took in a soldier three cots away while stifling an inappropriate urge to laugh. Sanderson almost never swore, maybe the least profane soldier in the Headhunters. "Suit yourself, but you look like you're in serious pain. Nothing wrong with taking a shot when you're hurting."

Sanderson gritted his teeth. "I can handle it. I don't wanna take another shot till they put me on the fuckin' airplane. All that fuckin' bouncin' around's gonna hurt more. I'm goin' to Japan for more surgery. Fuck! Fuckin' bullet shattered two fuckin' bones in my fuckin' leg. Doc said I'm gonna walk with a fuckin' limp for the rest of my fuckin' life."

Hayes glanced at Sanderson's khaki uniform folded on the floor beside the cot. Since he'd never gone on R and R, Hayes had never thought about what you wore.

Sanderson saw him looking. "That fuckin' Sergeant Slobojan in Supply gave me the uniform. You'd be amazed the shit he can come up with. I loaned my civvies to Wirtanen in Second Platoon when he went on R and R. And he lost them. How the fuck can you lose your fuckin' clothes?" He sucked in a noisy breath, rubbing his eye with a fist, unable to stifle a groan.

Hayes wasn't sure whether the moisture he was rubbing away was from the pain or sadness. "You okay?"

"No, godammit. I won't see Diane for months now. She's probably on her way to Hawaii. Might already be there. What's gonna happen when I don't show up? She's gonna go nuts."

Hayes saw distinct wetness in Sanderson's eyes. "I'm sure the Army will take care of her."

"Hayes, you got a lotta faith in the fuckin' Army."

Hayes looked at the uniform again. "You still got your R and R orders?"

"Yeah. Under the fuckin' uniform. You can take all that shit back. Thank Slobojan for me. He's okay for a fuckin' lifer." Sanderson winced and pushed his head deeper into his pillow. "Goddam, maybe you're right. I need another shot. My fuckin' leg…" He sucked in a deep breath. "God fucking damn."

Hayes walked out of the ward until he found a Spec Five with a shoulder patch that had a red cross on it and told him about Sanderson.

"Oh yeah, figured he'd change his mind." The Spec Five talked to a doctor, and Hayes watched them inject morphine into Sanderson's arm. Soon Sanderson started to relax and get sleepy. He murmured. "Thanks Hayes. You're a good fuckin' platoon sergeant."

Carrying Sanderson's khaki uniform, Hayes set off for the R and R departure point thinking he might be able to get back the money he'd bribed the crooked lieutenant with. He'd be ecstatic to get half and wouldn't be terribly upset if he got nothing.

His plan blew up when he almost collided with Lieutenant Colonel Kucharski. He did the only thing he could. He saluted. As he returned the salute, Kucharski glanced down at Sanderson's R & R orders. Then his eyes shifted toward a bus parked in front of the hooch where Hayes had bribed the lieutenant. A dozen men, a few in khaki uniforms but most in jungle fatigues, waited to board the bus.

"Sergeant Hayes, were you planning to go on an unauthorized R and R? Is that why you're here?" He snatched Sanderson's R and R orders and the uniform. "I think you may be guilty of desertion. You pulled a gun on Sergeant Bell. You also threatened a Thai lieutenant who is a superior officer."

"What? No. These are Sanderson's orders, and uniform. He got wounded last night. I was just taking them back."

"Sergeant Bell!"

Sergeant Bell appeared as if by magic wearing a .45 pistol in a holster on his hip. Bell took Hayes by the arm taking care to keep him on the other side of his body from the pistol. He marched him to a jeep with Military Police markings where an MP sergeant sat in the driver's seat. Bell gestured to the front seat. "Get in." When Hayes was in, Bell climbed into the back seat behind him.

Acutely aware that he had the Makarov in his pocket and no handcuffs on, Hayes thought about running. But he knew he wouldn't shoot anyone. He'd never get away. Besides, this had to be a mistake.

They drove to the Long Binh Stockade, more commonly known as "Long Binh Jail," or more derisively, as "LBJ," the president's initials. Razor wire surrounded the big rectangular compound that had guard towers at each corner. It reminded Hayes of pictures he'd seen of Nazi World War II prison camps. Inside the stockade, he observed Bell talking to a captain and a sergeant. The captain looked unhappy; the sergeant impassive. When Bell left, the sergeant and the captain marched Hayes into a small room and ordered him to strip to his underwear. The sergeant told him to hold out his arms and turn around. Hayes complied. The sergeant pilled the Mararov out of the clothing on the floor.

"You can get dressed now," the captain said. Hayes started getting dressed. The captain picked up the Makarov, ejected the magazine and racked the slide. "Nice piece. Where'd you get this?"

"Took it off a Vietcong troop I killed," Hayes said.

"You infantry?" the captain asked.

Hayes shook his head. "I'm with the 99th Assault Helicopter Company in Nui Binh."

The sergeant said to the captain. "We got another guy from the 99th here. Brought in by that same Sergeant Bell. That sick guy in Max."

"Yeah, did we get paperwork on him yet?" the captain asked.

The sergeant shook his head. "Same as this guy. Awaiting transit to Leavenworth."

The captain considered this for a moment and shook his head. "I don't like it. No paperwork. Something's going on, and we don't know shit. I'm gonna talk to the CO when he gets back." He turned to Hayes. "We're putting you in Maximum Security. Orders, but it's probably best, you being white. You go into one of the tents, the Chucks'll beat you… Holy shit!"

He'd just found the money Hayes had in his wallet.

"Where'd you get all this money, sergeant?"

"A record album. Just before I shipped out, my girl and I, and another guy, made a record and it sold pretty good. That's part of my share."

"Right, and you toured with the Beatles. Or was it the Rolling Stones?"

"Well, I backed up Chuck Berry once," Hayes lied, hoping to connect with the captain's fantasy. His friend Roscoe had once played with Chuck Berry, one of Hayes' heroes.

The captain studied him.

"Even if I believed you, I still need to know where you managed to get this cash. Nobody incountry gives out this amount of American money."

Not true, he thought. Hayes almost told them to check with First Sergeant McConaughey but caught himself. He didn't want to cause trouble for the first sergeant, who'd helped him. "I got it here and there. Took me some time."

"I bet it did. Maybe we should start a black market investigation," the captain said.

"Go ahead," Hayes said. "The money's legit. I earned it and I want to make sure I get it back when I get outta here. So maybe we better count it."

The captain finally nodded and started counting. When he was finished, he had the sergeant count it again. Hayes watched. Finally, all three agreed that Hayes had $855 dollars as well as $4.60 in MPC. The captain wrote out a receipt, and both he and Hayes signed it.

"I'll keep this in our safe," he said. "Sergeant, take the prisoner to Max."

"Don't I get a phone call or something?" Hayes asked. "My unit needs to know where I am."

The captain looked at the sergeant, then back at Hayes. "We'll tell them."

Feeling confident he'd get out soon, Hayes followed the sergeant to a conex, a big metal box formerly used as a shipping container. About six feet wide and nine feet long, they had several at the 99th that they used to store helicopter parts. But he'd never heard of anyone living in one. Someone had cut small holes in each of the four sides. Inside, a canvas Army cot lined one wall with a plastic bucket in a corner.

"The bucket's your toilet if ya hafta go, but you have access to a latrine out here at meal times, which is three times a day. So best not to use it unless you really hafta 'cuz you're gonna clean it." The sergeant tossed two full canteens onto the cot. "Gets hot in here." He looked up at the sky. "Let's hope it doesn't rain. If it does, we'll bring a poncho."

"Where's that other guy from the 99th?" Hayes asked.

"You're next door to him," the sergeant said, glancing to one side. "If you're thinkin' about climbin' out, don't. You'll get shot. We got guards up in those towers. You get out for chow three times a day, and you get an exercise period, usually after dinner. You don't give us trouble, we won't give you any."

The sergeant clanked the door shut. Hayes sat on the cot, wondering how long it would be before he got out.

"Hey fuckin' new guy. Ya gotta name?" The voice emanating from the adjacent conex sounded familiar.

"Name's Hayes, Jimmy Hayes."

"Jesus, Hayes! What the fuck are you doin' here?"

"Who are you?" Hayes asked.

"It's me, Delaney."

When Hayes told Delaney that he was supposed to be dead, he didn't seem to care, even after Hayes told him how broken up Kannegiesser had been.

"Shit, he'll get over it," Delaney said.

"Delaney, I want to know who replaced Kannegiesser as gunner that day you threw all those villagers out of the gunship."

After a long pause, Delaney said, "I only pushed out one. I didn't… I can't tell you. I might get killed if I do."

"Well, everybody back in the company thinks you're already dead," Hayes said. After that, Delaney refused to respond to anything Hayes said.

When two guards came to get the maximum security prisoners for lunch, Delaney looked around the dining area and reluctantly sat down at a table across from Hayes.

He asked, "Where's your canteens?"

"Back in the conex. Why?"

"We're goin' back for hottest part of the day. You'll need all the water, you can get."

Hayes grunted, but he'd only drunk a couple of mouthfuls from one canteen. He glanced around the mess hall keeping his head down. Five other inmates, all of them black sat at two tables. Two guards, both armed with .45s, watched the prisoners. The blacks eyed Hayes, making no effort to hide their interest. One of them raised a clenched fist when their eyes met. It did not look like a friendly gesture.

"Careful. I heard two of those guys are in for murder. I don't know about the other three, but none of them likes honkies." Hayes' confidence about getting out ebbed.

"You got any money, Hayes? You can get dope here if you got money. I'll pay you back, man. Shit, there ain't nothin' else to do. Some opium would be outta sight, but all you can get is pot."

"Are you fucking crazy Delaney? Maybe you didn't die, but nobody had any trouble believing you did. Just before I came here, Sanderson told me he didn't want to end up like you. Sanderson got shot in the leg, by the way."

Delaney shrugged. "So? He'll be goin' home, right? I'm happy for him. Happy for anybody who makes it outta this shithole alive."

"You expect me to help you when you won't tell me who that gunner was? And by the way, I do have money."

"I told you Hayes, I'll get killed if I say anything about that. I'm not kidding either."

Delaney got up to use the latrine, which was a piss tube in the ground just outside the mess hall door. One of the guards followed him to the door and watched him through the open door.

"How'd you get started on opium?" Hayes asked him when he returned. He tried sound casual and friendly.

"Got some in Saigon, day after you got shot down. We were stuck in Long Binh and Stanton gave me a pass…" Delaney stopped, then started up again like it hadn't happened, sounding like a record skipping when the needle hits a scratch. "I wanted to try some opium. Later, I found out you could get opium in Nui Binh if you asked the right shitburner." He caught Hayes' eyes and shook his head. "I don't wanna talk about it."

"How about the stuff that almost killed you? Did you think that was opium? It was heroin, in case you didn't know."

Delaney swallowed. He tried to mask his surprise by mopping up the last of the thin, salty stew gravy on his tray with the remaining toast it had been served on. Classic Army shit on a shingle, poorly cooked.

"Heroin? I thought it was this special sugar opium. Man, it *was* special. Blew my mind. Best high I ever had. I passed out. When I woke up, I was in that MP hooch in Nui Binh handcuffed to a wall. I can barely remember it. Two MPs drove me from Nui Binh straight to this hellhole. Two hours, no escort either. I thought for sure we'd get ambushed."

"Where'd you get it? The shitburner?"

Delaney looked at Hayes, slowly shaking his head. "No, not him. I don't wanna say where I got it. You wouldn't believe me, just like you don't believe I'll be killed if I tell you who that gunner was."

They didn't speak for a few minutes, which gave Hayes time to think about everything Delaney had said. He thought he might know who'd given Delaney the heroin and who'd substituted as gunner. And maybe it was the same person who'd murdered five men in the Headhunters.

"I think somebody tried to kill you with that heroin. You might as well tell me about it because they're probably still trying to kill you."

Delaney didn't say anything. He just sat across from Hayes and looked down at the floor.

They refilled their glasses with ice-cold lime Koolaid from a big jug on another table. They each chugged down two full glasses. They'd seen the black inmates doing the same thing

Delaney finally spoke again. "Why the fuck are you here, Hayes? Somebody send you to get more on me? Shit, I already been busted to Private E-1."

"No," Hayes said. He'd started thinking again that he hadn't done anything wrong. Still felt sure he'd get out, eventually. "I don't really know why I'm here. I got in trouble with this Lieutenant Colonel Kucharski. Moss warned me but—"

"Alright, assholes, back to your cages. Lunchtime's over," one of the guards shouted.

They ambled back to the maximum security conexes, nobody in a hurry to get there. Delaney and Hayes, side by side, trailed by the five black inmates half a dozen meters behind. One of them, a large man with enormous shoulders, kinky, orange-brown hair caught up with them. He looked Hawaiian or Samoan, though with skin darker than the other blacks. The man bent his head between Delaney and Hayes and said softly, "Heard there's a hundred bucks with a get-outta-jail card for wastin' Private Delaney here."

Delaney stopped, and Hayes saw his face grow pale. Hayes stepped between the black man and Delaney. He smelled the marijuana on him.

"So, are you first in line?" Hayes asked.

"Naw. Ain't my style. I be a little more stylish than my friends back there."

"What are you in here for?" Hayes asked.

The man's face tightened, his eyes reduced to slits. "Murder. I shot a lieutenant. Bastard needed killin' afor he killed the whole platoon."

"Why you tellin' us this?"

This time he grinned, revealing a gold front tooth. "'Cause it's bullshit. Nobody's gettin' a hundred bucks. Nobody's gettin' outta jail. I don't wanna see nobody hurt, even a jive-ass junkie honkie." He put two fingers on Hayes' chest right on the Headhunters patch and gently pushing him away. His eyes flicked to Delaney and then back. "Seen that picture once before on a chopper that saved my fat ass. I got no quarrel with youse."

He dropped back to his friends.

Hayes got out of Long Binh Jail late in the afternoon. The same sergeant who'd brought him to the conex came to get him. Hayes lay on the cot sweating, wearing only boxer shorts that were as wet as if he'd been swimming in them. Sweat covered every square inch of his skin. Once in awhile, a very slight breeze wafted through the small conex openings. He hoped the humidity augured rain. He'd drunk most of the water in the canteens. His misery ended with the rasp of the metal conex door squealing open.

"Get dressed," the sergeant ordered. "A major and a first sergeant here to see you."

Taking his time, Hayes pulled his fatigues over his sweaty body. In the same room where he had been processed into LBJ, he found the same captain with Major Shiffman and First Sergeant McConaughey. The first sergeant looked tense, Shiffman impatient.

Hayes saluted slowly. The captain and Shiffman returned the salutes.

"How you doing, sergeant?" McConaughey asked.

"Oh, I'm just peachy," Hayes said. "Am I still a sergeant?"

"Far as I know," McConaughey said.

"Did you know Delaney's here? He isn't dead."

"What! Are you sure?"

"He was in the conex right next to me."

"I want to see him—" McConaughey started. "Wait, they put you in a conex?"

"Yeah. It's gotta be against the Geneva Convention. It's about as bad as anything the fucking VC did to me."

"We need to talk to you about the spy, Bich," Shiffman said to Hayes. Then the major turned to the captain. "What is Sergeant Hayes charged with? Why is he in here?"

"He's being held until he can be shipped back to Fort Leavenworth," the captain said. "And yes, our maximum security prisoners are housed in conexes. They get enough water. The white boys are safer there. We've had some racial problems."

"But what's he charged with?"

"I don't know. Same as that other guy he just mentioned, Private Delaney. We were told to put 'em in maximum security until arrangements were made to send them back to Fort Leavenworth."

"Who told you that?" Shiffman asked.

"Ah, um, we got it from a lieutenant colonel. Name's Kucharski."

"He gave you orders? I want to see them."

"No written orders. It was a verbal command." The captain swallowed.

"He came here with these prisoners and ordered you to put them in maximum security without any charges?"

"Ah, not exactly. That Colonel Kucharski called the CO who told us to do it. It was an E-7 sergeant by the name of Bell who actually delivered the prisoners."

"Where's your CO? I want to talk to him."

"Major Rosen went on R and R last week. Bangkok. But he's in the hospital now. Came back early. Picked up some kinda infection."

"So you're the senior officer in charge?" Shiffman asked.

"I am."

"And you've placed two men in maximum security with no known charges against them. This colonel, Kucharski who's not in your chain of command, is directing what you do here?" Shiffman stopped to think for a moment. "I'm ordering you to release Sergeant Hayes to my custody, Captain…" He squinted at the captain's nametag. "Ayres. It's another verbal order, but I'll put it in writing if you have a clerk handy."

"That's okay. I'll release him on your say so. This whole thing has been very irregular. We usually get a load of paperwork on inmates."

"What about Delaney?" Hayes asked. "I just heard there's a hundred bucks and a get-out-of-jail card for anyone who kills Delaney."

Shiffman grimaced, but McConaughey spoke: "We need to get Delaney outta here. We were told he was dead, and the

CO's already written a letter to his family. Something's going on here, and we need to get to the bottom of it."

"You were told that he was dead? Jesus Christ. We have no paperwork on him either. I'll release him too. I don't like any of this and I could tell the CO didn't like it either," Captain Ayres said. "Sergeant, go get Private Delaney."

The sergeant hurried out of the room, and Ayres walked over to the safe on top of cupboards that lined one wall. He took out the envelope with Hayes' money and tossed it to him. "You want to count it again?"

Hayes shook his head.

Ayres opened the cupboard. He took out the Makarov and handed it to Hayes.

"Sergeant, tell me why you tried to go on R and R in Sanderson's place? The CO's pretty pissed off, and so am I. What did you think you were doing?" McConaughey asked.

"I didn't do that. I went to the hospital to see Sanderson. I picked up his uniform and his orders there. That's all, then I ran into Kucharski."

"The colonel told the CO you were on your way to go on R and R in Sanderson's place. You were right outside the departure point. I never heard you talk about wanting an R and R. All you had to do was ask. Why risk getting charged with desertion?"

"Sarge, I didn't do it." Hayes glanced at the captain who was listening carefully. "I was going to see that lieutenant I told you about. He owed me some money."

McConaughey nodded, held Hayes' eyes for a moment before he turned to address the captain.

"Captain, Sergeant Hayes here is rather gifted in the art of poker. He gets into some very high stakes games. Sometimes officers don't like to acknowledge their debts to enlisted men."

The captain nodded. "Well, that explains some things, sergeant."

Just then, the sergeant banged through the door dragging Delaney. Delaney had his hands cuffed behind him and wore no shirt or boots.

"He didn't wanna come," the sergeant said, throwing Delaney's fatigue shirt and boots on the floor. "Keeps sayin' somebody's gonna kill him."

"That Colonel Kucharski—" Delaney started.

"Shut up, asshole. You're getting outta here," the MP sergeant said. "Now get dressed."

Delaney looked around and saw Hayes and the first sergeant. "Is it true? I'm gettin' out?"

"Yes. Unless you keep pissin' off the sergeant here," McConaughey said. "Do as he says and get dressed. And hurry up."

The sun had dipped low almost to the horizon as the four soldiers walked away from the stockade. They were mostly silent until they came to an enlisted men's mess hall where they stopped. Major Shiffman addressed them.

"We'll eat here. I want to keep Colonel Kucharski in the dark as long as I can." The major offered a tight smile that seemed to amuse McConaughey.

Inside, they found fried chicken and mashed potatoes. When a messhall sergeant suggested that Shiffman eat in the officers mess, the major ignored him. Then he told the others, "I need to talk to Sergeant Hayes here, alone."

He led Hayes to a table in a far back corner and after they settled in, Shiffman leaned over his tray and kept his voice low. "Sergeant, I need you to tell me everything you can about this woman, Bich. And also tell me what you know about Juntasa. I've learned that's why the CIA is so interested in her. I thought he had little to do with the war, except for providing whores for American soldiers."

"Sir, my girl in Detroit thinks this Juntasa is after her. In the last letter I got from her she told me he killed a couple of people in Detroit. The police there want him for murder. The letter's not like she usually writes. It's all mixed up. She said she was gonna to fly to Hawaii to get away. I would love to go to Hawaii, and I almost wish I'd thought about going in Sanderson's place."

"You're sure you didn't hear this first from Bich?" Shiffman said. "She was babbling on about him when we first started interrogating her. Most of us didn't who he was, but one of the CIA men knew more about him. He wouldn't tell us anything. Said it was classified. This morning a friend who's a South Vietnamese colonel told me there's a rumor going around that Juntasa is making heroin."

"I don't know anything about that. All I heard from Bich was that he was this bad guy called Colonel Whop Whop, and that he'd once been a helicopter pilot for the Thais. I first heard about him from my girlfriend, not Bich."

Hayes' fatigues felt like his personal, full-body hair shirt and he reached into his pants under the table to scratch himself, hoping Shiffman wouldn't notice. "I asked Bich about Juntasa because of what my girl said in a couple of letters. Bich said he cuts off people's fingers and sometimes procures young white women for rich Oriental men. My girl said police told her that her stepfather owned a restaurant together with Juntasa in Detroit. Anyway, this Juntasa's wanted for murder in Detroit. The detectives investigating the murders were trying to find out if my girl knew anything about her stepfather and this Juntasa. Now she thinks he's been following her."

"Why didn't they ask her stepfather?"

"Oh, sorry," Hayes said, striving for nonchalance. "He's dead."

Hayes gulped down an entire glass of cherry Koolaid, then stared at the empty glass. "Look, you can check this out with Detroit police if you don't believe me."

"I'm going to try and do that, so let's hope it checks out. Your story's a little hard to believe."

Pausing to gather his thoughts, Hayes told Shiffman about Gloria's stepfather and how he had worked for a crime family in Detroit. "She's told me that he knew a lot of other bad guys, besides the people he worked for in Detroit."

Shiffman stared at him for a long moment. "Could he have been involved in the heroin business?"

Hayes shrugged. "I don't know, but it's possible."

With the major's prodding, Hayes once again reviewed everything he could remember about Bich in the tunnels. When Shiffman had debriefed him immediately after his escape from the tunnels, they had both assumed that Bich was a Viet Cong guerrilla who happened to speak English. But now, she appeared to be a major spy.

The mess hall was largely empty when Shiffman, still skeptical, finally stopped questioning him. "I understand it a little better now, and I think you are telling the truth as you believe it. You've always played straight with me, but I can't believe it's as bad you seem to think."

"I don't really care if I get busted. I don't even care about the damn spy, or the war. Only thing I care about is Gloria..."

Shiffman nodded. "I doubt your girlfriend's in the kind of danger you seem to think. That part of your story is just too hard to believe."

Hayes, Delaney and McConaughey got bunks at a hooch for transient enlisted men. As a senior NCO, the first sergeant could have easily found better accommodations for himself but chose to stay with them. Hayes suspected he wanted to keep an eye on them both. Hayes had just returned from taking a shower when Shiffman came for him.

"I had an idea, and I think you're gonna like it. Come with me. Somebody owes me and maybe the Army owes you." Hayes quickly pulled on his soiled fatigues. After a ten-minute walk through the now darkened base camp, they came to a bunker festooned with antennae. Inside, the air conditioning made the bunker uncomfortably cold. A squat man in a swivel chair with his back to them faced a stack of radios and other electronic boxes. Two spec fours at small tables flanking him looked at them but neither spoke.

"Who dat?" the squat man said without turning around.

"Frenchy, you got a mainland connection up tonight?" Shiffman asked.

The squat man swiveled around to face them. He was a captain with a dark stubby crew cut and heavy, five-o'clock shadow on his cheeks. With his swarthy complexion, Hayes thought he could pass for either black or white. His nametag read Granville.

"Yep. Faff by faff. Howya, major?"

"I'm five by five," Shiffman said. "Want a favor, Frenchy. Sergeant Hayes here needs to talk to his girlfriend. You got much traffic?"

"Da girlfriend? Oooh, she purty?"

"Trust me Frenchy. There's more to it than you know. I wouldn't ask if it wasn't important."

"Mais oui, eh! Da traffic's light. Saturday morning back der, dem brassies all on da golf course."

"I hope you got your girl's phone number," Shiffman said.

They called Mrs. Lincoln's number, but there was no answer.

"She would have known if Gloria went to Hawaii. She must have gone out somewhere," Hayes said.

"It's a little after ten thirty Saturday morning in Detroit. You got another number we can try?" Shiffman asked.

"No, that's the only… wait, can we call information?"

Shiffman looked at Captain Granville.

"Mais oui, pourquois pas!"

"Gloria has this lawyer. If she went to Hawaii, she might have gone to him to get money. His name's Papineau."

"Dat Frenchman have a first name?" Granville asked. He connected to information as Hayes tried to remember the first name. He heard Granville asking for Detroit lawyers named Papineau. He wore a pair of fat headphones so no one else could hear the other end of the conversation. "Could he be Parker Papineau?"

"That's it!" Hayes said, remembering the name that had been on the letter with the money order he'd received. Then Hayes heard the captain telling someone to standby for Jimmy Hayes.

"Another Frenchman!" Pulling off the headphones, the captain flipped a switch and turned the microphone toward Hayes. Suddenly the bunker was filled with a staticky voice. "—name is Antoine, but he's here."

"Antoine? This is Sergeant Jimmy Hayes. I'm trying to reach Parker Papineau... unless Gloria's there."

"Yeah, wait." The static mixed with scuffling noises then another voice boomed over the speaker.

"This is Pip Papineau."

Hayes would remember the next twenty minutes as among the worst in his entire life, worse than his weeks underground and even worse than the tunnels. As Papineau outlined what he believed had happened to Gloria, his stomach churned and he almost vomited.

"I just met with one of the Detroit police homicide detectives. Between Detroit police and Wayne County Sheriffs, I expect the manhunt for Juntasa will be massive. I don't see how he can evade such a large law enforcement effort."

"He's also a pilot with military training," Shiffman said, taking the microphone from Hayes. "He was one of the first pilots in the Royal Thai Air Force to qualify as a helicopter pilot."

"We're aware he's a pilot. Police are covering private airports," Papineau said. Hayes scraped his chair closer and grabbed the microphone back from Shiffman.

"He has the nickname, "Colonel Whop Whop," because he flew helicopters, but also because he has a history of cutting people's fingers off. Whop, whop. I was told he sometimes procures white women for wealthy Asian men."

"That's actually a little encouraging," Papineau said. "He's killed four people, but it might explain why he doesn't want to hurt her."

Hayes shoulders sagged. He didn't find it encouraging at all.

The exchange had stalled, and Papineau ended the call by saying, "I have a lot to do, so unless there's anything else?"

Outside the bunker, Shiffman said, "Jesus Christ. I didn't see how it could possibly be as bad as you thought. But it's worse. I'm sorry."

"Better to know," Hayes muttered and said no more on the way back to the transient barracks. He understood that Shiffman had tried to help him, which, when he thought about it, meant a lot. He didn't think many officers in Shiffman's position would have done anything. But he was too upset to thank the major.

-50-

July, Unincorporated Wayne County

Late Monday afternoon, Antoine Dewitt sat in Susanna's rusty VW Bug watching a small, well-kept house half a block down a heavily potholed street of shabby homes, cars up on concrete blocks and ditches of dank water. The house stood less than a quarter mile from where Jettrin Juntasa had murdered the two homosexual men and kidnapped Gloria Doran.

All day Sunday and most of Monday, Antoine had checked out houses in the vicinity of the airport. Unlike the police, Antoine knew that Juntasa had a knowledge of real estate, something Antoine also knew a little about. Three times Antoine had pounded on doors so loudly that no one could have ignored him. He crossed other houses off his list because they had no for-sale signs. Foreclosed properties, their occupants evicted, constituted the bulk of the list that he'd compiled. But without a for-sale sign, Juntasa wouldn't have noticed them.

Antoine sensed that his relationship with Susanna was over and that she'd probably kick him out for good when she returned from visiting her parents. It was past time for him to leave Detroit, anyway. He had the seventy-five dollars he'd gotten by pawning the guitar, and another seventy-five Gloria had given him to ship it to her Gomer boyfriend. He still couldn't believe how easily she parted with her money. He also had the hundred he'd gotten from the Thai murderer. So he had enough money to get out of Detroit. But he'd be lucky to make it to state line in Susanna's piece-of-crap car.

After they'd finished at Papineau's office, he'd asked himself how this strange criminal from Thailand might use his knowledge of real estate. In Philadelphia after he'd finished high school, Antoine started a night school course in real estate but left home before he finished. Aware that women found him attractive, and with a smooth-talking glibness that could connect with both genders, Antoine went to college towns, which were full of attractive, and naïve, young women. Also, his revolutionary black power fervor also went over well with many white college students.

When students prepared to start another semester, Antoine would set up his apartment brokering business. First, he compiled a list of apartments for rent in college neighborhoods. Then he told students looking for apartments that he could get them a discount on the rent, typically fifteen to twenty percent, if they signed up through him. He required them to put up a first and last month rental deposit, cash only. He'd make a bunch of copies of an old key. When he got somebody to bite and give him the cash deposit, he gave them the key and told them the date they could move in. He had them sign one of the bogus leases he'd printed.

"You hafta wait till the previous tenants are finished movin' out and we clean the place. Just sign this lease agreement and you're all set."

When pressed on how he could offer the discounted rate, he'd explain that he saved the apartment owners the time and trouble of dealing with a lot of prospective tenants.

"I get them tenants and save them a lot of hassle. But if you want this deal, you gotta move on it now 'cause they're goin' fast. I only got a few left."

And he did have to move fast before people caught on. Not everyone fell for it. In fact, most didn't. He succeeded with women more often than men, sometimes scoring "a two bagger," collecting the deposit and sleeping with a young woman. He'd successfully pulled his scam in Cleveland, Iowa City, Champaign and Madison before coming to Detroit, all while keeping his eyes open for an opportunity at a bigger score.

Gloria had "big score" money. He'd already picked up some crumbs, including the money she'd given him to buy a pistol. He'd gone to the pawn shop to buy a pistol, not for Gloria — he'd long ago spent that money — but for one of his black power friends. The pawn-shop people had set him up. Antoine, the scammer, fell for their scam. The honkie bastards took his money and got him arrested. Clever.

Gloria, and her money, fascinated him. When he first met her at an anti-war rally, he'd written her off as a stupid, self-centered white chick, a fake peace-and-love, hippie flower child bent on selling her records. But he'd underestimated her. Smart in her own way, she really believed all that flower power crap. If he could find her, and that tackle box, he'd have a serious shot at a big score. Or, maybe he could get back in Susanna's good graces, Susanna being the most sexual woman he'd ever been with. Would he have a shot at Gloria too? Unlikely, but he could dream. No, he'd settle for money.

After the session at Papineau's office, Antoine went to a big real estate office where he pretended to represent an investor looking for cheap properties near the airport, primarily foreclosures. He spent a couple of hours working with a realtor who eventually grew tired of him and said he had to get back to his own work. Back at the apartment, he discovered that Susanna's brother had picked her up to visit their parents in Inkster.

"We need to have a serious talk when I get back Tuesday morning," she wrote in a note. He found the spare key to her car in a kitchen drawer.

This last house on his list, while farther from the airport than any other, had some promising features. The best-looking property in a bad neighborhood made it a difficult house to sell especially if the seller wanted top dollar.

"The owner moved out, and it's furnished," the realtor said shortly before he'd quit working with Antoine.

This house had a freshly painted, five-foot-high white wooden fence surrounding the entire property, making it hard for Antoine to see inside. The fence would attract someone wanting to hide. Antoine saw a "For Lease" sticker tacked to the bottom of the for-sale sign, a sure sign of seller desperation.

But a lockbox hanging on the front gate had excited him more than anything else. The lockbox would contain a key so realtors could show it without having to make an appointment with the seller's agent. And the lockbox looked like it had been there a long time. Lockboxes usually meant unoccupied houses, something Juntasa would likely know. Antoine had sometimes broken into and slept in lockbox houses when he had nowhere else to go.

After parking for half an hour he decided he'd better move. He didn't want to get rousted by some racist redneck. He drove to a nearby strip mall where he found a phone booth and called the telephone number he'd copied from the for sale-sign outside the house. He gave the address to the agent who answered the phone.

"Is that place still for sale?" Antoine asked.

"Sorry, it's been leased."

"Were you the one who handled it?"

"Naw, that was Becky Weinberg."

"Could I speak to her? I might have a buyer and maybe we can work something out with the lessee."

That drew a pause. "Well, I haven't seen Becky today, or yesterday for that matter. She dropped off the lease agreement last night along with the deposit, first and last month, all cash. Little unusual leavin' that cash in an envelope she slid under the door. But that's Becky. She's creative," the man sighed. "Her family has a cottage up by Traverse City, so she mighta gone up there to celebrate. That one's been on the books forever. I'm sure she'd listen to any offer to buy. Appliances are new, and the place is furnished, if that means anything to you. Best I can do is have Becky call you when she checks in."

Antoine gave the man a fake name and telephone number before hanging up. He sat on the little seat in the phone booth for a couple of minutes thinking about it. Why hadn't the realtor taken off the lockbox? He couldn't decide what to do.

Antoine realized he had to buy gas for the piece-of-crap VW. Why couldn't Susanna drive a Mustang or Camaro?

From the gas station, he crossed the street to a small hamburger stand touting "Gasper's Gargantuan Ground Round." He ordered a burger with fries and a Coke for 59 cents. What a deal.

"Business is kinda slow, eh?" Antoine said to the thin white teenage boy working the stand.

"Yeah, we mostly do a lunch business," the kid answered getting Antoine his Coke. "McDonald's is killing us with that new Big Mac."

Antoine nodded, thinking the kid had a bright future flipping burgers. Then he thought about his own future. Susanna had been a major complication for him. He'd hung around Detroit far longer than anywhere else. Could he stomach a real job? Factory work paid okay, but, Jesus, the same old, same old, day after day. He'd never handle that. But what else could he do? The Madison police had almost caught him the last time he pulled his apartment scam.

Twenty-four years old and drifting. Antoine needed to make a move but couldn't decide what move to make.

When he drove back to the house, he parked in front but hidden in the deep twilight shadows. After pulling on a dark gray sweatshirt to hide his yellow University of Michigan T-shirt, he crossed the street and slipped between an elm tree and some bushes. He crept along the white wooden fence and near the back of the house vaulted over the fence. Crouched inside the yard, he half expected someone to yell at him, but heard only crickets and the high whine of mosquitoes.

Bending almost double, he snuck around the back corner of the house where he found a long, low, black car that he hadn't been able to see from the street. Squinting, he saw it was a Lincoln Continental. His heart jumped and he felt clammy moisture in his armpits. He slunk over to the back door, looked in through the window and saw a light moving inside. A flashlight? He looked along the back of the house and saw he'd have to walk between the car and the house on loose gravel. Too noisy, so he crept around the big Lincoln. Halfway around, he stopped to look at freshly turned earth in an otherwise immaculate flower garden. Nearby, a shovel lay on the ground.

Jesus, is that the realtor, Becky?

With a shudder, he continued around the car to the far back corner of the house where he heard faint voices. Bending low, he moved around the corner and stopped underneath the only window on that side of the house. Dim light inside illuminated flowery curtains.

And through the closed window, he heard screams.

"No! No! I don't know!" Then another voice, low and guttural, said something, but Antoine could not make out the words. He heard more screams.

He froze. It sounded like Gloria. The other voice must be the Oriental man who cut off fingers.

But for all of his clever sleuthing, Antoine had made no plan about what to do if he found Gloria.

-51-

Unincorporated Wayne County

An odor of food going bad turned her stomach. Had Mrs. Lincoln left fish out on the kitchen counter? Or maybe food scraps in the trashcan under the sink had started to rot. Gloria thought she should get up and do something about it. But she had a headache so terrible that the ceiling spun and shimmered when she opened her eyes.

Slow, deep breaths steadied the ceiling, but it was the wrong ceiling. Suddenly, she awoke more fully, groaning from flashes of horrific memories. But more than anything else, she needed to pee. When she started to get out of bed, the nausea returned with a vengeance. Something restrained her ankle, and she sprawled halfway out of the bed, vomiting over her chest, and then on the floor. With both hands and one foot on the floor, she tried to free her other leg, but that only triggered an electric jolt of pain from her ankle. Twisting sideways to relieve the pain, her hip squelched into a puddle of vomit. Then her bladder released, spreading warm shameful wetness as she passed out.

Twenty minutes later

Somewhere far away, a dog barked. Nearer, birds sang quiet evening songs undercut by chirping crickets and trilling frogs. Moths attacked a window screen with soft thup, thup, thups.

When she awoke the second time Gloria saw a dimly lit room. She lay on her back in the bed. Awareness returned in fits and starts, but this time she knew that Juntasa had her. Slowly, she sorted memory fragments, the bloody images flashing into her mind. Juntasa slashing and stabbing Peanut, blood blooming on his abdomen. Benny waving his crutch until Juntasa sliced his neck. His fist clutching the knife hilt as it slammed into her head.

When she fingered her face, she jerked as her finger brushed a painful spot low on her forehead just above her nose. The light touch started her headache again but the jerk reminded her that something clasped her ankle. Now she remembered falling, vomiting, urinating. Her jeans felt wet when she touched them. So did her shirt. She recoiled at her own rank odor. Carefully, she slid a hand down her leg toward her ankle, which necessitated sitting up. She felt dizzy, her head throbbed and she sensed a tightness across her ribs on one side.

The stitches. She remembered getting stitches after Juntasa attacked Mrs. Lincoln and her. The bandage on her side didn't feel wet. Moving her hand back to her leg, she found a metal ring like a bracelet encircling her ankle. It connected to another ring that went around the metal frame at the foot of the bed. Handcuffs.

When she lay back down, her headache eased. Her mind seemed foggy and fuzzy, strange and shimmery, half in a dream, not fully awake. She wanted to close her eyes and finish sleeping.

I just want to sleep.

Sensing danger, she tried to keep thinking.

Jimmy had told her he'd learned how to unlock handcuffs with a pick. She didn't know exactly how but he'd used a large straightened paperclip. She looked around the room at the flowered wallpaper, inched her way up again. More headache, the walls shimmered, then cleared. Her eyes didn't feel right, like they wouldn't open all the way. In the brightest corner of the room, a tiny light at the top of a mirror shined down on a small vanity table.

Could she find a hairpin to use on the handcuffs? She strained but couldn't make out fine details on the cluttered vanity top. After thinking about getting out of bed placing one foot on the floor and stretching toward the vanity, she rejected the idea. She probably couldn't reach the table and might fall again.

She sagged onto her back making the bedsprings squeak. A few seconds later the door opened, and a bright light shone on her face, blinding her. Her stomach heaved as she sensed foul body odor. Then Juntasa loomed over her and she heard the squeal of the window behind her sliding shut.

"You wake now? You tell me what's in box."

"What?"

He scuffled out the door and came back a few seconds later holding the green tackle box in the beam of his flashlight.

She tried to play dumb. "I don't know. It looks like something fishermen use."

"I hit with box," he said raising the tackle box.

"No, no, I don't know!" She screamed as he swung the box at her. She tried to protect her head, and the box whacked her forearm. He raised it again.

"You say what inside."

"Safety deposit box keys and bank books."

This seemed to puzzle Juntasa. The light from his flashlight left her eyes and pointed at the floor. She heard him talking to himself in another language. Then the light wobbled around the room flashing briefly on Juntasa and revealing a dirty rag dark with old blood wrapped around his hand. She remembered biting him.

Juntasa slammed the tackle box down on the vanity. Gloria wondered if one of the safety deposit box keys could open the handcuffs.

"You tell how say-fee key work," Juntasa demanded. He snapped open a large knife. "You tell now or I cut fingers off, one by one till you tell."

"No, no, I don't know," she shouted as he waved the knife in front her face. He slashed at her, ripping the pillow and missing her face only because she rolled her head to one side. She screamed again. He pushed up her chin driving her head deep into the pillow. She thought he wanted to slash her throat.

"You scream. No one hear. I pay ten thousand 'merican dollars for you, but you no virgin like father promise." Letting go of her chin, he suddenly jabbed the knife slicing the top of her ear and her scalp.

"No! No!" She screamed louder.

"You tell how turn keys to money and I no cut off fingers. I sell you instead." He bent over with his face inches away. She smelled soy sauce and fish. Then he placed the sharp edge of the knife blade horizontally across her forehead and slowly drew it across, cutting her. She shrieked again trying to push deeper into the pillows. She felt blood run down her nose and into her eyes. She tasted the blood on her lips. "You talk or I cut off ears, and nose too." Raising the knife, he took a breath and his lip curled. "Ew! You stink like water buffalo. Nobody buy you. I just kill you."

She screamed louder than she'd ever screamed before, kept on screaming, sure she was about to die.

But he fumbled with the flashlight in his bandaged hand. The light briefly lit his laughing, sweaty face. Would it be the last thing she saw? Wild and bright, his eyes danced. Spittle dribbled from his mouth.

The realization that he would kill her jolted away the fogginess, focused her mind bringing newfound clarity.

She forced herself to speak slowly and loudly though her voice caught. "M-my stepfather br-brought keys home from trips. He-he put gold and silver coins, and bars in safety deposit boxes at banks. If you look, the k-keys have the names of the banks. You bring the key to the bank and they give you the box to open."

He took in her words, backed away and opened the tackle box. He laid the knife down on the bed by her feet. He began picking up keys while holding the flashlight awkwardly in his wounded hand. This occupied him for a couple of minutes while he muttered in another language but sometimes in English.

"Bangkok. This bank Bangkok…"

Then, someone knocked on the front door, loud crashing knocks like a hammer would make. It startled Juntasa, confused him. He stretched and turned off the light over the vanity table. Then, with the flashlight still in his bandaged hand, he picked up the tackle box in other and hurried out of the room.

Gloria sat up too quickly and almost passed out. Fumbling in the dark, she grasped the knife and hid her hand holding it under the blanket.

She couldn't see but she heard the door open followed immediately by a thunderous boom. Then she heard a heavy thud, a metallic bang and clattering rattle of the tackle box and keys spilling over the floor.

"Gloria, Gloria, are you here?"

The voice sounded familiar. She said, "In here, I'm in here."

A gray shadow shuffled into the dark room. No, two shadows because now she saw double.

"It's me, Antoine."

"Antoine?"

"Yeah, Antoine."

"What happened?"

"I shot him," his words deliberate, flat. But after a pause he seemed to feel a need for more explanation. "He shined that flashlight in my eyes. I thought he was gonna attack, so I pulled the trigger. I have my shotgun. I'm minister of defense."

He backed out of the room. She saw light from the flashlight moving around.

"Jesus, I got him right in the face."

More footsteps and the shadow, no longer double, came back into the room. With a click, the vanity light turned on. She saw Antoine starting to smile, but it quickly died.

"Oh man, you're bleeding bad, Gloria." He stood in the doorway leaning the shotgun against the wall. "Something stinks in here."

She couldn't bring herself to tell him that she'd soiled herself. "My foot's handcuffed to the bed. I, ah… I'm hurt. You better get the cops Antoine, and an ambulance."

"Yeah, okay." But Antoine shuffled closer to look at her. He pushed the bunched-up blanket that was over her handcuffed ankle to examine it. "Man, I think that stink's coming from you."

"Yeah it is, but you gotta call for help, Antoine." Her head hurt so badly it felt ready to explode. Blood from her forehead still trickled down her face and neck. She carefully spit out the blood in her mouth onto the floor. "Please, Antoine. It really hurts bad."

"Um, yeah, okay." He turned around and pointed the flashlight toward the front door. Was he looking at Juntasa's body again? He moved out of sight. She heard him sorting through the tackle box. "Man, there's a lot of them."

He came back into the room with the tackle box, looking at her. He put the tackle box down on the vanity and picked up the shotgun. He held it with the barrel pointed at the ceiling as he studied her. He took a couple of steps closer.

"I never killed anyone before. Can't believe how easy it was. Boom, and he hit the floor." He looked at her, shook his head and then the barrel of the shotgun lowered until it pointed at her face, the black hole of the end of the barrel inches away. "Sorry, Gloria, but this'll be my big score. It'll be quick. It's not gonna hurt."

The black hole in front of her face wavered a tick.

"What the fuck…"

Understanding flickered into her brain first. *He forgot to pump the shotgun after he shot Juntasa.* And she didn't think about what she did next.

Using both hands, she she summoned all her strength and with an underhand thrust, plunged the knife through Antoine's jeans into his upper inner thigh, feeling the the blade scrape against bone as it slid deep into his body.

Screaming, Antoine tried to take a step, but fell over landing hard on the knife hilt pushing the blade deeper. The shotgun thumped to the floor in the doorway. Antoine kept shrieking. If he screamed words, Gloria couldn't make them out. He kicked and wriggled on the floor. His screams weakened to crying. Still, she could hear no words. The crying grew softer then stopped. He lay still, face down in a spreading pool of blood. She heard him gasp. Then silence.

Gloria collapsed backwards. The bed squeaked. The ceiling blurred and spun above her as she closed her eyes.

-52-

Long Binh Base Camp

After an agonizing restless night on a bunk in the Long Binh transit barracks, Jimmy Hayes got up early and took another shower. He had no towel or anything to wear on his feet except his jungle boots. At least his fatigues, which had been damp with sweat the night before, had dried. He clumped to the outdoor showers in the unlaced boots, then pulled on his soiled clothing over his still damp body. The first man to enter an enlisted men's mess hall when it opened for breakfast, he got coffee but had to wait for food. Half an hour later, Delaney came in and sat down at the same table. They nodded to each other but didn't speak. Finally, Hayes asked Delaney to pass the sugar for a bowl of oatmeal he'd decided to eat. Delaney pushed the sugar bowl toward him. As the mess hall filled, other men who seemed to know each other sat down at the long table.

The courier flight to Nui Binh wouldn't leave until mid-morning so Hayes took his time drinking four cups of coffee, the last one as he watched Major Shiffman and First Sergeant McConaughey talking to each other by the mess hall entrance. He knew they were talking about him because both men kept glancing at him. Finally, Shiffman left. McConaughey poured himself a cup of coffee and sat down next to Hayes. Delaney got up and left. Two spec fours, the last of the others who had been sitting at the table decided to leave as well.

"The major told me what's going on with your girlfriend—" McConaughey began.

"Nothing anyone here can do about it," Hayes said. "I want to get back in the air as soon as I can and shoot somebody. Doesn't matter if I've been busted to spec four or a damn private—"

This time McConaughey interrupted him.

"You're still Headhunter platoon sergeant. I spoke to the CO this morning."

Hayes bit his lip. "I still wanna shoot somebody."

McConaughey's voice grew harder. "Sergeant, your first responsibility is the men in your platoon. You're in the Army, and we're at war."

Hayes opened his mouth to say he didn't want to be platoon sergeant anymore but stopped himself. McConaughey had stuck his neck out for him.

"I don't think you'll have much time to fly. For starters, be advised that Private Delaney told me this morning that he wants to resume flying as a crew chief. Says he needs the money. I told him he had to talk to you. If he's going to fly, he'll have to pass a physical, and then you'll have to clear it with the new Headhunter commander. That is, if you want to take him back."

Hayes looked around the mess hall but Delaney had left. "Delaney didn't say a word to me about this and sat right across from me for almost an hour. Shit."

Flight pay meant an extra sixty-five dollars a month, and Delaney's reduction in rank had meant a big reduction in his pay. He realized that he knew nothing about Delaney's circumstances. Was he married? Did he have a family to support? "I'm not so sure he should be flying. Can't we put him in Maintenance?"

"They don't want him, and neither do the other flight platoons. Right now he's yours. If he's not going to fly, I'll put him to work digging bunkers and filling sandbags."

Hayes sighed. "If he flies again, somebody could get killed."

"Yep." McConaughey took a long time picking up his coffee, blowing on it, sipping, blowing again before taking another sip. Finally, the first sergeant put his coffee down and looked at Hayes. "I believe the CO took a chance on you after my predecessor busted you and then tried to court-martial you. Heard you had quite the reputation. And he's given you another chance."

Hayes swallowed. "I didn't do anything wrong here, and I was never as deep into it as Delaney. All I did was smoke pot. But yeah, you're right. I'll talk to Delaney."

"He told me he wanted another chance. Tell me, was he a good crew chief?"

"Yeah, he was, always did his job. I'll give him that. I don't remember any screw-ups. But he's been a pothead ever since I've known him. I wasn't here when he got into the opium."

McConaughey nodded. "Your decision."

Back at Nui Binh, Hayes attended to his platoon sergeant duties, trying hard to keep his mind off Gloria. What could he do? He went to Operations to post a flight schedule for the next day, taking the easy way out by repeating the current lineup of crews. He'd fix it later if he had to. He was tired and tense from the constant worry, but Delaney's desire to earn flight pay sparked an idea.

"Who keeps track of guys earning flight pay?" Hayes asked, looking around the Operations bunker.

"I do. Is there a problem? Somebody not getting paid?" said a clerk.

"No problem. Just wondered if anybody kept track of guys who fly once in awhile so they can earn flight pay."

"Yeah, we're pretty loose about it."

"So you don't keep records of who's flying gunner on the courier or other odd flights?"

"Oh, yeah, we have to keep records of flight time. The Army's got regs about how many hours a month pilots can fly… not that those regs don't get busted all the time. So we have records on the courier flights and all the extra flights that come up. Hell, even when extra crew goes down to Vung Tau to fly back a new ship, we have a record. I gotta type up all that shit in triplicate. A copy for us, one for brigade and one for God knows who. The Green Machine runs on fuckin' paper."

So Hayes started combing through records. He borrowed a calendar from the clerk so he could check dates. When he finished, he felt sure he had a lot of evidence pointing to the murderer.

Why didn't I think of this before?

But out loud he said, "I'd be grateful if you didn't say anything about me looking up stuff." He knew he had to tell the clerk something. "I'm not doing anything bad or against Army regs."

"So what *are* you doing?" the clerk asked.

"It's a personal issue and a personnel issue. Somebody's not playing straight with me. It may not amount to anything," he answered. That was a very watered down version the truth.

The clerk nodded and Hayes left.

From Operations, he went to the Orderly Room to talk to the first sergeant.

"Sergeant Slobojan just brought these over," McConaughey said handing Hayes an ice-cold can of Pepsi. "You talk to Private Delaney yet?"

Hayes shook his head and took a long slow drink of the soda. "Haven't seen him since we got back. Been over in Operations."

McConaughey nodded. "He came to see me again about getting flight pay."

"I'll talk to Delaney as soon as I see him. I think he's going to you because he's afraid to ask me." Hayes took another long drink, hoping for a caffeine boost. His stomach rumbled. He'd missed lunch while looking up the flight records.

"Thanks for getting Delaney and me out of the stockade. How come you and Major Shiffman did it?"

"The CO wanted me to go down there to see if I could get you out after a sergeant at the stockade called to say they had you. Then before I left, Shiffman called to tell us. When he found I was going there, he said he wanted to come with me. Said he had to talk to you again about that spy."

Hayes finished his Pepsi, looked around the empty Orderly Room and made up his mind. "I know who the murderer is."

When he finished telling McConaughey everything he knew, the first sergeant didn't say anything for a long time. "Sit on it for another few days. I'll talk to the CO. I might be getting some more information that'll help."

"Does Kucharski's position on the general's staff give him that much control over personnel?"

"I've wondered the same thing," McConaughey said. "You know, Doc Goetz's sudden transfer to Korea looks fishy. The CO had a fit about it. We didn't have a flight surgeon for more than a week. Maybe Kucharski had something to do with it."

Back at his hooch, Hayes moped around. Gloria. Should he write to her? What would he say? Where would he send the letter? As he brooded on his bunk in the NCO hooch, Delaney showed up.

"Um, ah, could I talk to you, Hayes?"

Hayes nodded. "Okay. The first sergeant said you want to resume flying as a crew chief, right?"

"Um, yeah. I need the flight pay."

"There's something I need to talk to you about first," Hayes said.

"What?"

Hayes pulled out his wallet, opened it and held a hundred-dollar bill in front of Delaney's face. "I'll give you a hundred bucks if you tell me who replaced Kannegiesser as gunner that day you threw those villagers out of the helicopter."

Delaney looked at the money for a long time. "Somebody's gonna get killed if I tell you that. You gotta believe me."

"Don't bullshit me, Delaney. You could get killed flying for the Headhunters. It happens all the time. And you damn near died from that heroin. You don't want the hundred bucks? I thought you needed the money."

Delaney looked at the money again. Finally, he shook his head. "I can't. It's not just me. My kid brother could get killed."

"What do you mean?"

"He's in Germany. If I say anything, he'll be sent here as a grunt right away. You can't do nothin' about that."

"I don't get it," Hayes said.

"The Army doesn't usually send two brothers to 'Nam at the same time in case they both get both get killed. That's why I extended. If I say anything, he'll be sent here."

"Who says?"

"That Lieutenant Colonel Kucharski."

"Kucharski? How can he do that?

"His ol' man's some kinda bigshot general in the Pentagon. He can make stuff like that happen, and he will. He's got Moss by the balls too. My brother's infantry. He wouldn't do well here."

Hayes didn't know what to say, but Delaney kept talking.

"Kucharski's brother-in-law is a captain. You remember that day we had the big argument about rolling in on that village... when we kept Mitchell and Grugel from havin' a fight in the mess hall?"

"Yeah, I remember."

"Kucharski's brother-in-law was the commander of the grunt company. They killed a lot of civilians. Kucharski's been coverin' it up, not that the Army wants it to get out either. Kucharski's whole fuckin' family's career military. They take care of each other."

"What do the Green Berets have to do with it?

"I don't know. I think they were the ones who first said it was a VC village."

"It's the same village?"

Delaney looked confused. "What do you mean?"

"The village where you threw the villagers out of the helicopter, and the village where Mitchell got upset about killing civilians. They're the same?"

"You didn't know that?"

"No, I didn't," Hayes said, shaking his head. He thought back to the records he'd examined in Operations. The records didn't have place names. Besides, what happened in that village was now classified. "So what if it was a VC village? Most of the people were women and children and old men. At least that's what Mitchell said."

"Yeah, the stupid bastard made a big stink about it, said he was gonna tell his congressman."

"Where'd you hear that?"

"I heard Mitchell tellin' Sergeant Grugel."

"When?"

"Same day he died."

Hayes scratched his head to think, and Delaney kept talking.

"We took those two Green Berets back there 'cause they were supposed have an informant. Only, their informant wasn't there. Shit, I don't know what they were expecting 'cause it was weeks after the fact. I couldn't believe anyone still lived there. Maybe the Green Berets wanted to scare somebody into sayin' it was VC village and get it on the record. Maybe Kucharski thought it would help his brother-in-law's case. But it didn't work."

Shaking his head, Delaney stopped.

"Look, you gotta believe me, Hayes. The only thing I did was throw one guy out a few feet from the ground. Then we went up again, like five hundred meters. This kid was screaming when…"

"Did you throw him out?"

"No, I was back on my M-60, but I was lookin' right at that kid. He was younger than my little brother, didn't look old enough for junior high. This Green Beret sergeant and… I can't tell you who that gunner was but he's the one who did it. I think he caught the Green Beret sergeant by surprise too. It happened so fast. They were both holding the kid, and then he went sailin' out the door."

Hayes had to think about what Delaney said. "I know who you're talking about. Why are you so willing to tell me all about Kucharski but not the guy in the 99th?"

"Shit, you already seem to know lotsa shit about Kucharski. But I watched this other guy kill half a dozen of those villagers. I figure he killed Mitchell, maybe Grugel too. That didn't seem like an accident. And he almost killed me with that fucking heroin. He's the one that gave it to me." Delaney looked away and hung his head. Then he took a breath before continuing. "He'll kill you too, Hayes. He's got a free pass. They're not fuckin' around here. You might be next. Shit, they put both of us in LBJ."

"Yes, they did, but I got out, and got you out too. And if he comes after me, I'll put him in the fucking ground. This guy didn't just kill Mitchell and Grugel, he sabotaged my ship. So you can add Nesterenko, Donaldson and Flowers to the list."

Delaney opened his mouth. but no sound came out.

"Now, about you flying."

Delaney sat on Hayes' footlocker and took almost a full minute before he spoke. "Um, who's flyin' my ship now?"

"Not your ship anymore, but it's Higgins. Came over from Second Platoon. He's been a Headhunter since you got court-martialed. We have a couple of other new guys too."

"Are you sayin' you don't need me?"

"I'm saying I don't need a crew chief who gets high and flies that way."

Delaney colored but met Hayes' challenge head-on. "Shit, you should talk, Hayes. You hit the pipe as hard as anybody."

"Yeah, I did, but I stopped after I got busted. I quit doing that shit. Are you ready to do the same thing?"

Delaney looked down at the floor for a few moments before answering. "I really need the money. A private barely makes anything, and most of it's gettin' docked to pay the fines from my court-martial and the Article Fifteen."

"You didn't answer my question? You ready to stop smoking pot and opium?"

"C'mon, Hayes. Smokin' pot never affected me. Hell, it's not as bad as gettin' drunk. Nobody can say I didn't take good care of my ship. I'm the best mechanic in the platoon. Besides, I can't afford opium now. Hell, I can't afford pot either. So there."

"Yeah, well, I'm serious about this Delaney. I'm not saying you didn't do your job. I used to believe the same thing. I never screwed up when I was stoned. But after I got busted, I promised the CO not to smoke again. I kept my promise. If you want fly with the Headhunters again, you have to make the same promise and convince me you mean it."

"Shit, Hayes, I already told you I can't afford it."

"Yeah, what are you gonna do first time somebody's passing the pipe or offers you a hit off a joint? I don't just mean not getting high when you fly. You gotta stop altogether. You're a lot deeper in the hole than I was. You almost fucking died. Is that what you want to do? Die? 'Cause in that case, you can stay on the ground and do it where you can't hurt anyone else. Maybe you're as good a mechanic as you say, but you keep gettin' high, you'll eventually screw up."

Delaney didn't say anything. Instead, he remained on the footlocker staring at the floor. Hayes finally broke the silence. "What do you need money for anyway? I can't help thinking the real reason you want money is to buy more dope. That's what you wanted to do in LBJ."

Hayes thought he heard a muttered "Aw shit," and then Delaney said, "Okay, I promise I'll stop smoking pot and opium."

Maybe Delaney meant it, but even if Hayes had doubts, he decided to give Delaney another chance.

"Okay. No guarantee, but I'll do what I can. You gotta pass a physical, and the new Headhunter lieutenant and the CO will have to okay it. You'll probably have to make the same promise to them. There might be some resistance. In fact, I can guarantee there will be. And if I catch you, or even hear about you smoking dope, you're out."

Delaney shrugged, then shook his head and smiled. It was the first time in many months that Hayes recalled seeing Delaney smile. This might have been the longest conversation he'd ever had with him.

After he left Delaney, Hayes wandered around thinking about Delaney and the killer, more certain than ever of his conclusions. When he found himself near the officers' hooches, he decided to visit Moss again. He knew Moss wasn't flying and had the day off.

"Who's there?" Moss asked when he rapped on the door.

"Hayes."

"Whaddye want now, Hayes? I can't tell you anymore." Moss cracked opened the door with a scowl. He wore only boxer shorts, his hair still damp from a shower.

"I want to talk to you about how Colonel Kucharski has you by the balls." Hayes pushed the door all the way open and went inside without waiting for an invitation. "We're gonna need to work together if you ever want to get out from under Kucharski's thumb."

"What do you mean, we?" Moss said.

"You, me and… and Delaney."

Before Moss could say anything else, Hayes outlined how the killer had murdered Mitchell, Grugel, Nesterenko, Donaldson and Flowers and probably tried to kill Delaney. Moss might have figured some of it out, but probably not the helicopter sabotage.

"Are you sure, Hayes? You should go to the CO."

"Oh, I will, but I'm giving you a chance to do the right thing and get on board first."

Moss looked away, then grabbed a pair of civilian Bermuda shorts and put them on. "Maybe you should tell the military police. There's a detachment here in Nui Binh."

"You mean the same MPs that concocted that bullshit report on Mitchell and faked Delaney's death?"

Moss groaned.

"What kind of a man are you, Moss? You shut up about Mitchell, and probably Grugel. Are you going to keep protecting somebody who's murdered five Headhunters?"

Moss kept looking at Hayes but finally answered. "I don't wanna spend the rest of my life in the fucking stockade, or worse." he said.

"Neither do I." Tired, Hayes sat down on the extra bunk in the hooch.

They talked for a long time. Hayes didn't say the name of the killer, and neither did Moss. Hayes lost any respect he'd ever had for Moss. But he left more convinced than ever that he was right about the murders.

The Headhunters returned after everyone had gone to bed, when the lights in the hooches had turned off and Nui Binh had settled into the uneasy nocturnal rhythms of outgoing artillery shells, aircraft taking off and landing, and the clatter of tools of Maintenance night shift. Hayes lay awake, thinking about how to kill the killer. He almost got out of bed to search for a piece of rope or a wire to serve as a garrote. He had already killed somebody that way. He could do it again. He could do it that night. Easy.

And stupid. He did not want to spend the rest of his life in a military stockade any more than Moss did. The murderer had gotten away with killing five American soldiers. He had gotten away with it because he had protection from at least one senior officer. If Hayes killed the killer, even if he got away with it, Kucharski might follow through on his threats to Delaney and Moss. And what would he do to Hayes?

Thinking of murdering the murderer brought Hayes back to the people he'd killed when he'd been back in the United States. He grinned. That had been murder. And it had been easy.

Maybe I've lost my soul, but I am a badass.

A worse thought intruded.

Have I lost my soul mate?

While Hayes had been an enemy captive, he'd never given up, always believed he'd survive. Had Gloria given up? No way. Everything she'd been through, her horrible stepfather, seeing her father killed, learning her heritage, losing the baby, worrying about him.

She's gotta be a badass too.

And a little before dawn, he started believing it and fell into a fitful sleep.

-53-

Henry Ford Hospital, Detroit

Gloria lay in the hospital bed wanting to feel better. She felt safe, clean and aside from a mild, but persistent headache, not in pain. Dr. Sadowski said she'd suffered a serious concussion. A handsome resident had stitched up her ear and decided her forehead didn't need stitches. He said the scars would disappear in a few months though he refused to let her see herself in a mirror. Her forehead felt very tender, and she still couldn't open her eyes fully because of the swelling. The expressions on the faces of anyone who looked at her told her that her face looked bad.

On the morning of the second day, Pip Papineau came to visit and told her that a neighbor had heard a gunshot and called police. Two sheriff's deputies who responded noticed the open front door to the house and found her and the two dead men. Now, Wayne County homicide investigators were in the room and wanted to talk to her about what had happened.

She murmured, "Please, not yet." It was the most she'd said in twenty-four hours and she could tell it upset the detectives.

After the police left, Papineau squeezed her hand and said, "Don't talk to them unless I'm here too. I don't think there's a problem, but…" He couldn't finish and stifled his emotions with a cough. "I'm so glad you're okay."

Okay? She had no appetite, no energy. Getting out of bed and taking a few steps to the bathroom and back exhausted her. She answered questions from nurses and other medical people with grunts, weak nods or head shakes and sometimes with a reluctant word or two.

Even Dr. Sadowski could not elicit much response. "It might be better for you to talk about what happened instead of holding it in. It eats away at you."

Gloria looked at the doctor and said, "No, I'm not holding it in. I'm just too tired right now." Neither did she speak when a nurse pushed in a wheelchair with Mrs. Lincoln. Mrs. Lincoln looked at her with rheumy eyes. Tinged with gray, her skin sagged like a too large sweater. She tried to speak to Mrs. Lincoln but failed to find words. Sighing in frustration, Gloria stretched out her hand to grasp Mrs. Lincoln's hand. She loved her like a mother.

After the nurse wheeled Mrs. Lincoln away, Gloria whispered, "What's the matter with me?" to herself.

On the morning of her third day in the hospital, Susanna Quinn came to visit.

"Oh, Susanna," and then Gloria couldn't stop her tears.

Susanna countered with a laugh. "I think I told you once that I'm just plain old Susanna Quinn, I'm not Suzy Q or Oh Susanna. I hate those songs—"

Gloria cut her off with a wet sniffle, "I killed him." And then she cried out so loudly that a nurse rushed into the room.

"Maybe I better leave," a shaken Susanna said to the nurse.

"No, no," Gloria pleaded in a hiccupping squeak.

The nurse handed Gloria a tissue, then helped her drink a glass of water. Gloria gulped down the entire glass.

After refilling the glass, the nurse asked, "Better now?" When Gloria nodded, the nurse left, glancing at Susanna who had settled uneasily into a chair beside the bed.

Susanna plucked the tissue from Gloria's fingers and dabbed at the tears on Gloria's cheeks. "It's gonna be okay, Gloria."

"No, it's not, Susanna. I killed him. I killed your Antoine. I'm so sorry."

"You killed him? I heard how he died—"

"I know you loved him."

Susanna was shaking her head. "No, well, maybe once. The Antoine I loved wasn't real. I didn't know the real Antoine." Susanna dabbed at her own eyes with the tissue. "I never expected perfection. It's so tough for black men. And, God knows, I fall way short myself."

"You must hate me, Susanna. I deserve every bit of it. I'm not the loving person I thought, I was."

"I don't hate you Gloria. And we are all so relieved that you… that you're alive." When Gloria sagged back in her pillow, Susanna said, "Are you feeling sick?"

"I'm just so tired," Gloria whispered.

Susanna put a hand on Gloria's cheek. "You're a little flushed." She moved her hand to grasp Gloria's and sighed. "Antoine… You know, we never got back together. It wasn't gonna work. I went home to my parents 'cause I couldn't face telling him that it was over. Now, I've learned about Antoine, the real Antoine, mostly from your lawyer, I'm ashamed of myself. He wasn't what everyone thought. His father wasn't a rich doctor in Philadelphia. His father's in prison. His mother's on welfare. He's got two half-sisters. And the police in Madison wanted him for ripping off college students. If he'd been half of what he pretended to be, I might have taken him back." She stopped when she saw Gloria trying to speak.

"He tried to kill me." She spoke in a voice so soft that Susanna leaned in closer to hear. "He pointed that shotgun right at my face and pulled the trigger. But it didn't shoot."

"That shotgun? I found it in the closet. Told him to get rid of it. Was he working with that Asian guy?"

Gloria lay still for a few moments. "No, Antoine saved me. If he hadn't come…"

"The police think he mighta been an accomplice."

"No, I don't think so. No, Antoine found me somehow. He killed that guy. He saw the tackle box and said it was his big chance."

"The tackle box?" Susanna leaned back in the chair to think. "I can't remember if Antoine was there when we were talking about it." Gloria closed her eyes. She heard Susanna sigh. "Antoine, he always wanted to be rich." Then after a pause, "It is gonna be okay, dammit."

Gloria felt a little movement of air as somebody entered the room, then the familiar voice of Emily Sadowski. "I need to talk to Gloria about a medical issue."

"I think she's trying to sleep," Susanna said.

"Stay, Susanna," Gloria whispered. "I'm just resting my eyes."

"Okay," Sadowski said. "It's nothing bad, might be good news because it explains why you feel so tired. You *are* sick. We believe you have mononucleosis."

"She has mono? I had a friend at Wayne State who got mono." Gloria opened her eyes in time to see a glare from the doctor. And the smile that followed.

"I went back and checked when you were hospitalized before. Both times you had a fever. It wasn't high, so no one paid much attention. You probably had it then. I think the main thing is that it's made everything else that's happened worse. We expected you to recover faster, at least physically. We were getting worried that your concussion was worse than we thought, but the mononucleosis changes that assessment. Your body's doing exactly what it needs to do, which is rest. Mononucleosis is a viral infection. There's really no treatment except rest and more fluids."

Sadowski looked at Susanna. "So maybe we should both leave and let Gloria rest."

In a soft whisper, Gloria said "I had to talk to Susanna. Please tell my lawyer that I'll talk to the police about what happened now. Maybe after a nap."

And this time when she closed her eyes, she fell asleep.

-54-

Two days later

Sergeant Chris Overholzer, homicide investigator in the Detroit Police Department, and Pip Papineau ate breakfast outdoors at Eastern Market, just east of downtown Detroit. Their table in the shade and the breeze from the Detroit River made Overholzer appreciate the hot coffee. Papineau had already attacked a big omelet. He'd arrived before Overholzer and by the time the detective got his sausage and eggs, the lawyer had demolished most of the omelet.

"Sorry, but I'm starving. I missed dinner last night on account of Wayne County and Romulus."

"What's the problem? I heard everything's clear for your client."

"Yeah, clear. That's a good word. But has she ever been anything but clear? She was a victim, dammit. Wayne County was pissed because she wouldn't talk to them right away. Then that sergeant from Romulus wanted to press charges. But his chief stopped. Threatened to fire him, which he should do anyway."

"Well, she's clear with Detroit PD, though..." Overholzer didn't finish, and both men concentrated on eating. Papineau already knew that Overholzer had spoken to his good friend, the head of the organized crime unit, a Captain Lincicombe. So he already knew that several police agencies wanted to speak to Gloria Doran. As far as Lincicombe knew, none of the police thought Gloria Doran guilty of anything, only that she knew more than she'd told them. She'd told them remarkably little, largely because of Papineau.

"Though what?" Papineau said as he popped a thick slice of dark brown bread into his mouth.

"Nothin' much. There's still guys who aren't happy about Clyde Bonaventure shootin' those two cops last summer. They think she coulda told them more."

Papineau shrugged. "She could. And still can. But they wouldn't like what they'd hear. I've already provided your department with a summary of what she witnessed. Believe me, you don't want to open that can of worms."

"Hey, I'm cool with everything. I like your client. But she's been around a lot of murders."

Papineau nodded and spread strawberry jam over another bread slice. "Well, her stepfather was up to his neck in organized crime."

"Yeah, I spoke to Captain Lincicombe yesterday."

"Good man," Papineau mumbled, his mouth full of bread.

"He thinks the state police might want to talk to your client, and East Lansing PD too."

Papineau swallowed and sighed but didn't respond.

"How 'bout the boyfriend? Is he your client as well?"

Papineau looked at Overholzer. "Now that's a good question. He's never asked me to represent him. But I sent him his share of the money he and Gloria Doran earned from the record they made. And my firm reviewed the contract with the record company, and the contract includes him. So I'll call him a client."

Finished eating, Overholzer sat back and drank some coffee. "The captain—"

"Lincicombe?"

"Right. The captain suggested that I pass on anything that I thought might be helpful, so I'm lettin' you know that the Staties have developed an interest in the boyfriend regarding four bodies that were fished outta the St. Marys River in the spring. I think they're mostly interested in finding his uncle. Did you know that his uncle fought for the Nazis? Four years on the Russian Front."

"Didn't know that." A waitress refilled their coffee mugs.

"Yeah, they think the Garganos ran into more than they expected. State police have connected all four to the Garganos, even the sheriff's deputy," Overholzer said. He sipped some coffee. "You probably already know that East Lansing wants to talk to the boyfriend about Matt Doran."

Papineau took his time drinking his coffee. "Thanks. I appreciate this."

"I wouldn't worry. Nobody's shedding any tears about any of them. But I hear the boyfriend's due to come home from Vietnam shortly."

Papineau nodded and drained his coffee. "I owe you."

Overholzer shook his head. "Naw, the captain says you've been very helpful and I like stay on good terms with captains."

-55-

Nui Binh Base Camp

Four days after he told McConaughey the identity of the killer, a Red Cross representative delivered a telegram to Jimmy Hayes.

> *GLORIA DORAN IN HOSPITAL STOP NOT SERIOUS WILL RECOVER STOP JETTRIN JUNTASA AND ANTOINE DEWITT DEAD STOP WILL SEND DETAILS IN LETTER STOP PIP PAPINEAU*

Hayes started hyperventilating. He almost passed out from relief. Suddenly, he knew he had exactly nine days and a wakeup before he went home. Went home to Gloria.

But will she still love me?

The next day

Hayes sat on his bunk trying to finish a long letter to Gloria, the telegram open beside him and Eric Clapton's guitar solo on *Sunshine of Your Love* distracting him. He'd gone to the PX and bought the most expensive stereo system there and planned to ship it home. And he'd borrowed the record from Kannegiesser. When First Sergeant McConaughey appeared at the entrance to the little alcove he occupied in the NCO hooch, Hayes turned off the stereo.

"Glad I caught you," McConaughey said, eyeing the turntable as if it could hurt him. "That Major Shiffman just called the Orderly Room. He wants to see you. You know where he is?"

"I think so. Isn't he in that hooch beside the brigade operations bunker? Why's he want to see me?"

"I don't know." McConaughey leaned against the doorway and took out a pack of Winstons. Hayes knew that first sergeants didn't deliver messages so he must want something else.

"By the way, we got a new sergeant, came in this morning, gonna be your replacement," McConaughey said.

Hayes grinned. "Great. So you want me to show him the ropes?"

McConaughey laughed. "He's a brand new E-6, but yeah. Let's hope he doesn't get too goddam military on us."

His head swiveling, McConaughey looked around the hooch.

"Nobody's here except for the hooch maid and she's outside doing laundry if you want to talk." Hayes carefully lifted the turntable off his footlocker, put it on the floor and motioned for McConaughey to sit.

"I told the CO everything you told me about the murders the other day," McConaughey said.

"And?"

"And nothing. He doesn't want to do anything. Doesn't think there's enough for a court-martial."

"What?"

"Well, he's probably right about there not being enough for a court-martial. But I think there's more than enough to open a serious investigation."

"So, why doesn't the CO want to do that?"

McConaughey shook out a cigarette and offered the pack to Hayes, who declined.

"I don't think he wants to take on Lieutenant Colonel Kucharski. Maybe after Kucharski leaves, which should be soon." McConaughey said. He took several puffs from his cigarette before continuing.

"People keep saying that Kucharski's father is a general and pulls strings for him. So I wrote to my own contact in the Pentagon about it. He told me there isn't a single general in the entire United States Army named Kucharski."

"Then how's Kucharski pulling all those strings?"

"Well, he's been on General Westmoreland's staff. That's a lot of juice," McConaughey said.

"But could he send somebody to Vietnam from the States or from Germany?"

McConaughey slowly shook his head. "Maybe, but he probably couldn't do it without the general's help. And I've always heard that Westmoreland's a boy scout."

"Maybe Kucharski's bluffing. Do you think Kucharski has some kind of hold on the CO?" Hayes said.

McConaughey shook his head. "Not really. They both went to West Point, different years. But they don't like each other. The CO wasn't very happy when Kucharski put you in Long Binh Jail even though he was pissed after Kucharski told him you tried to go on R and R in Sanderson's place." Hayes started to say something but McConaughey raised his hand to stop him. "He was furious when he learned Delaney was in jail and not dead. He didn't like the report on Mitchell. Or that he was ordered to inform the entire company."

"Kucharski ordered him?"

"No, the order came from the brigade XO, Colonel Winthrop, but Kucharski was behind it. It was part of keeping the lid on what happened in that village."

"You know he's protecting his brother-in-law," Hayes said.

"What do you mean?"

"His fucking brother-in-law was the grunt company commander at that village where Mitchell said the grunts were killing civilians. A civilian massacre would hurt his fucking career. I'm talking about the brother-in-law's career." After almost a year in Vietnam Hayes was bitter about career soldiers who traded their integrity for advancement.

"You mean Captain Oregan?" McConaughey pronounced the name like the state.

"His name's O'Regan, with an apostrophe, you know, like O'Connor or O'Hara. I saw the name in some of the records I looked up in Ops. Sometimes, the apostrophe gets left out, but the correct name is O'Regan."

McConaughey leaned back, looked up at the ceiling. "That's it. That's how he does it."

"Does what?" Hayes asked.

"My friend at the Pentagon is a sergeant major. We've known each other since Korea. He's the senior NCO in the Army Personnel Directorate. The name of the brigadier general who commands the directorate is a real asshole by name of O'Regan."

"So he's not Kucharski's father, he's his father-in-law?"

"It would seem so."

Fifteen minutes later

Soon as he saw Hayes walk into his office — a real office with a door that Hayes had to knock — Major Shiffman said, "Good news for you. Your girl's okay."

"Thanks, but I already got a telegram about that."

"A telegram? Wow, I didn't know you could receive a telegram here." Shiffman stretched over his desk to hand Hayes a heavy manila envelope that had been opened. "I didn't open it, but I read the newspaper story."

It took Hayes a few minutes to read a long story from the *Detroit American*. There were two fat letters in sealed envelopes that had been in the larger envelope. Hayes tapped the envelopes on Shiffman's desk. "I'll read them later."

"Your girl's been through the wringer. She's only sixteen? And she has a hit record?" Shiffman said.

"Yeah. We made a record album together, along with our friend Roscoe. But it sounds like she wrote another song on her own." Hayes edged toward the door, wanting to read the letters by himself.

"This came in a pouch to the embassy in Saigon. I don't know how, but I have to believe that lawyer… Papineau? I think he was responsible."

"How'd you get it?" Hayes asked.

"Our good buddy Frenchy Granville. He said the embassy called him."

Hayes nodded. Anxious to leave, he felt obligated to Shiffman. "I never thanked you for getting me outta Long Binh Jail. If I can ever repay you some day…"

"No, no. Me and Colonel Kucharski don't see eye to eye."

Neither said anything for a moment until Hayes thought of something. "What's gonna happen with that spy?"

"Hell, nothing. The CIA wants her for something. I think it has to do with that Thai ex-air-force colonel, and I've heard whispers about heroin trafficking."

"Well he's dead now, and I have no doubt that she's VC," Hayes said.

"Yes, I believe that too. But she also might just be peddling information to a lot of different people."

"Jesus Christ. You believe she's a spy, right?"

"Yes, but not just for the VC."

"What do you mean?"

"The CIA, the Thais, the South Vietnamese Army and up until you spoke up, the U.S Army all used her for translation jobs. She's heard a lot of sensitive information. Information has value and she could have been trafficking in it with everyone. It's a dangerous game, but I think her bottom line is the VC." Shiffman sighed. He scraped his chair back from the desk and stood up to extend his hand to Hayes. "I owe you for exposing her.

"This whole thing led to my next assignment," Shiffman said. "I'm going to the Pentagon to work for a colonel who's not afraid to ruffle feathers. “Good luck to you, Sergeant Hayes. I hear you’re going home.”

“Eight days and a wakeup.”

-56-

Henry Ford Hospital, Detroit

Gloria recovered from her injuries and the bout with mononucleosis but feigned lingering illness because she was afraid to leave the hospital. She'd been a patient for more than a week. What would happen to her? Where would she go?

Gloria lay perfectly still on her back, her eyes closed, her hands folded on top of the covers, chords from *Locked in Love* meandering in her head. She felt someone enter the room.

"I think you're awake, Gloria," Emily Sadowski said in a low voice.

"I'm praying." Gloria said, which was only a slight untruth.

"Sorry." Dr. Sadowski started moving away.

Gloria opened her eyes. "My song wasn't finished." The revelation had surfaced suddenly, and she didn't want to lose the thought.

"Huh?" Pausing in the doorway, Sadowski looked back at Gloria.

"Nothing, I was thinking about my song."

"I thought you were praying. I can come back later."

Gloria smiled. "No, I finished praying. Last night, I heard this priest out in the hall talking to a nurse about a woman who was dying. Started me thinking about someone's soul departing this life."

"You were praying for a stranger's soul?" Sadowski nodded absently as she sat in the chair beside the bed. "The nurses tell me you're having nightmares."

Gloria shrugged. "I've always had nightmares."

"Like these?"

"Well, um, maybe not. Nightmares are always worse at first when something bad happens. But it usually gets better after I pray."

Sadowski nodded slowly. "I wanted to talk about how you pray."

"You do? I tried to explain it to Susanna once. She thought it was weird. Said God had nothing to do with it."

Sadowski's lips tugged into a smile. "Yes, I talked to Susanna. Sounds to me like you're meditating or doing a form of self-hypnosis. And that's not at odds with it being prayer. It's a good thing and you learned it on your own. I'm impressed. And you're wrong about Susanna. I overheard her telling someone that you taught her how to pray. She was… she said she was blown away. Me too."

"Really? Who'd she talk to?"

Sadowski's lip curled and then relaxed into a smile. "Logan Carlton. Susanna told him off. It was when you were missing."

"She did that? You know he used to help me a lot, and I liked him. I don't know why he doesn't trust me anymore. Maybe it's my fault."

Shaking her head, Sadowski said, "I don't think it's your fault, Gloria. He doesn't understand you. You know, he's never been married or been around children. And he's full of himself sometimes, actually, most of the time."

"You think I'm still a child?"

"No, I didn't mean to..." Sadowski suddenly snapped her fingers. "Oh, Susanna called me last night. She wanted me to tell you she's sorry she hasn't been able to visit. She got a summer internship at General Motors and has to work a lot of hours."

Gloria felt relieved. "Good for her."

"I don't think she likes it." The doctor stretched over Gloria to grab the clipboard with Gloria's chart. Sadowski studied it for a few seconds. "I am discharging you. The hospital wanted me to do it yesterday. I can't keep you in here any longer."

Gloria sank back in bed. "I don't know where I'm gonna go. Mrs. Lincoln's still in the hospital and that Logan Carlton wants to—"

"Your lawyer, Mr. Papineau, wants to meet with you. The senator's going to be there, and they asked me to attend as well."

Gloria's stomach lurched. "I-I don't have any clothes. Ah, the ones I had on were all bloody and smelly and—"

"You can wear hospital scrubs to Mrs. Lincoln's house. You have clothes there, right?"

Gloria nodded in glum silence.

"I should get some new clothes. I don't have anything good. Just old sweats and pregnancy stuff."

She started thinking about what she should bring to the meeting. Maybe she should pack a bag because the senator might send her to a school or even put her in foster care. No, she'd just bring her guitar, and maybe Jimmy's Stratocaster too.

"I'll drive you home so you can change, then I'll take you to the meeting. Mr. Papineau asked me to do that."

"Home?"

"Mrs. Lincoln's house. Don't you live there?"

"Well, I have been, but isn't that what the meeting's about? What's gonna happen to me?"

"Yes, maybe, but I think the meeting's also about your boyfriend Jimmy and the record company too. Mr. Papineau didn't tell me much. But I heard the record company wants you to do a benefit show with Zoomer Patterson to raise money for those two homosexual men who were killed, and that realtor. She had two teenage kids."

"Sure, I'd be willing to do that. But what about Jimmy? Are they gonna try to stop us from being together?"

"I don't know. However, I think Jimmy might have some problems with the police."

Gloria thought about it for a moment. "I guess that's not surprising. But do you know where I'm gonna live?"

Sadowski shrugged, and Gloria didn't say anything for a long time.

"When I was little, I thought you prayed to God for things you wanted. But I never got what I prayed for, so I'd get angry at God."

"Well, you're not a little girl anymore. Not getting everything you want is part of growing up," Sadowski said.

"I know. If you expect too much, you'll be disappointed. I'm sure Jimmy and I have lots of expectations, but we'll have disappointments too. No matter what the senator does, we might not end up together. Jimmy may not love me now. Bad things have happened to both of us. We're not the same people. But I know *I* still want to be with him."

"Well, aren't you due for a change? I mean a good change?"

Gloria shrugged with a soft laugh. "I used to be so angry. I'd feel bad and get angrier 'cause I felt so bad. But I'd feel good when I thought about how much I loved Jimmy. Anyway, the Beatles are right; all you need is love. But I heard it in church first. Jesus said love your enemies, do good to those who hate you and pray for those who persecute you. So last night I started praying for a departing soul and ended up praying for Zoomer Patterson. Now I'll add Logan Carlton. Praying for two people I don't like, but it makes me feel better. Clever, eh?"

Sadowski regarded her. "You're really growing up, Gloria."

"I'm trying. When Jimmy comes home, we'll need to be grown up."

-57-

Nui Binh Base Camp

The day after his meeting with Major Shiffman, Hayes went to the Orderly Room to ask the first sergeant for permission to go to Long Binh the next day.

"I'm gonna go over these murders with Jimmy Ray Suggs, that CID sergeant I know."

McConaughey nodded, then frowned. "Okay, but stay away from Kucharski."

Hayes shrugged. "Why shouldn't I see him? I don't want him to think he can get away with threatening Moss and Delaney."

"What are you gonna do, threaten him back?" McConaughey frowned. "He's a lieutenant colonel on his way to being a very young full colonel. He put you in the stockade once. He didn't have cause, but don't give him a chance to do it again. We might not be able to get you out next time."

"I don't care what he does. I'm gonna be a civilian in a few days and he won't have any power over me. I just signed an agreement with my girlfriend's lawyer to represent me." Hayes pulled a thick envelope from his jungle fatigue shirt pocket. "He's the head of a big law firm in Detroit. The only thing I'm gonna threaten Kucharski with is legal action."

McConaughey considered the envelope for a moment. "I don't see what a civilian lawyer could do. You got more faith in lawyers than I do."

"Got more faith in 'em than the fuckin' Army."

"Touche', but stay away from the bastard." McConaughey tilted back in his chair and stretched. "I talked to the CO again and I don't think he'll do anything about these murders. He pushed back on that report about Mitchell and got his knuckles rapped good. Maybe he doesn't want to believe us."

"Maybe he wants to be a full bird like Kucharski."

McConaughey groaned. "Blair's a good combat CO, and a good man. I like him. We might be the best assault helicopter company in this war. But somebody under his command murdering five Americans wouldn't help his advancement. So maybe you've got something."

"It's almost six murders. Stanton gave that heroin to Delaney. I've no doubt he meant to kill him."

"Stanton..." McConaughey whispered the name. He smoked his cigarette, drawing in deep breaths and tilting his head up to blow out giant clouds of smoke. Hayes caressed the Makarov in his pocket. "He's the one I wish we could nail."

"Maybe I'll just start telling everybody that Stanton murdered those guys. Talking to Delaney and Moss, I've never said his name. I pussy-footed around Ops when I looked up those records. Maybe I should just open up and tell everyone that Sergeant First Class Stanton is a murderer."

"Don't do that. He might kill you too."

"I would love for him to try because I'll put him in the fucking ground," Hayes snarled and hit the desk with his fist.

McConaughey dropped his cigarette on the concrete floor and ground it out with his foot. "Don't do it sergeant, it'll make things worse. Your other idea's better. Get your lawyer and go after him as a civilian. Apparently, the Army isn't equipped to handle problems like this."

He pushed his chair back from his desk. "I'm gonna get out in another year, go back to the Philippines. If I help my wife with her business, we'll do good, maybe expand it. She worries about me all the time. Worries too much."

George Cartwright ambled out of the back of the Orderly Room. He looked at the envelope Hayes held. "Want to mail that? I'm going to the post office in a bit."

"Type up a pass for Sergeant Hayes for Long Binh," McConaughey ordered. "Or have Conrad do it."

Cartwright had gone back to work as company clerk in the Orderly Room. Conrad, the clerk who had replaced Cartwright when he went to the gun platoon, had struggled with the job. Hayes knew that Cartwright had thought about reenlisting. He had a better shot at promotion as a clerk than as a gunner. During Hayes' long absence as a VC prisoner, he'd heard that Cartwright had had several close calls flying with the Headhunters. The thrill of flying in gunships had worn off.

The next day

The next morning, just before he went to Long Binh, Hayes called Lieutenant Colonel Kucharski's office from the Orderly Room. Sergeant First Class Bell answered the phone.

"The colonel around?" Hayes asked.

"Who wants to know?" Bell said.

"Sergeant Jimmy Hayes. I'm gonna be in Long Binh today. Thought I'd stop by to see him," Hayes said. "Wanted to thank him, and you too, for the LBJ visit. It was quite enlightening."

"Fuck you, Hayes. But feel free to stop by. We can always arrange another visit." Bell hung up.

He decided to visit Kucharski anyway. But first he went to see Staff Sergeant Jimmy Ray Suggs. He learned that Suggs had gone on R and R. He kicked himself for not calling before he came to Long Binh. But he left a sealed envelope for Suggs containing everything he knew about the murders. Then he headed for Kucharski's office.

When he arrived at the hooch he found half-packed cardboard boxes around Bell's desk. The hooch appeared empty.

"Anyone here?" he called.

A few seconds later, a disheveled Bell came out of Kucharski's office carrying a cardboard box.

"What the fuck do you want, Hayes? You got a lotta nerve showing up here."

"Cool your jets, Bell. You owe me. I never got around to telling anyone about you and that spy. Now where's the colonel?"

"He ain't around. Might be back later today, or maybe tomorrow. I gotta pack his stuff up. He's rotating back to the States." Bell bent and put the box on the floor beside the others. "I'll repeat myself, Sergeant, what do you want?"

"Tell the colonel that I know who killed five people in my company."

"You don't know shit, Hayes."

Hayes took a step forward, leaned in close to Bell who shifted to stay between Hayes and Kucharski's office. For a moment, Hayes thought Kucharski might be in there but quickly dismissed the thought. The colonel wouldn't hide from Hayes.

"I didn't know shit till the Vietcong and the North Vietnamese put me on trial. They're even worse than everyone says, but the villagers, they told the truth, at least they tried to."

"What the fuck are you talkin' about, Hayes?"

"When they were identifying me, one of those villagers said she saw herself in somebody's sunglasses and I almost told them I didn't even own any sunglasses."

"You're fuckin' crazy, Hayes."

"No, I'm not. Sergeant First Class Stanton wears these mirrored aviator sunglasses. He was the gunner you and your boss wouldn't tell me about. He's the one who threw those people off the helicopter. And it was all to save fucking Kucharski's brother-in-law's career."

Bell's shocked face confirmed Hayes' suspicion that Bell had known all along about Stanton. He still tried to downplay Hayes' allegation. "And you're basing this on the kind of sunglasses he wears?"

"Not just that. I checked our flight records and some other records too. Stanton took the courier to Long Binh the day this happened. And I think Stanton's known the colonel's father-in-law since Korea. The colonel's been protecting Stanton with the help of his father-in-law Brigadier General O'Regan because Stanton's doing some of the dirty work for him to cover up a massacre by Captain O'Regan's company. Captain O'Regan is the son of General O'Regan."

Bell looked at Hayes for a long time. "Get out of here, Hayes. That's all a fucking fantasy. Just get the fuck out of here."

-58-

Detroit

At Mrs. Lincoln's house, Gloria sat on her bed staring at the picture of her great-grandmother for almost fifteen minutes while Emily Sadowski waited downstairs. At first, the meeting at her lawyer's office had terrified her. Her future, her life. Could she trust anyone? So many bad things had happened. But the more she looked at the image of her great-grandmother, the stronger she felt. She came downstairs still wearing the faded wrinkled hospital scrubs a hospital nurse had given her at discharge.

"I want to go to Hudson's. I don't have anything nice to wear."

"You don't have to dress up. You'll be fine in jeans and a sweatshirt if that's all you've got," Sadowski said.

"I don't want to look like a kid, okay? This meeting's about my future. And Jimmy's too."

Sadowski looked at her watch. "Well, we do have time. Are you gonna go into Hudson's in those scrubs?"

"Why not? Long as I come out wearing something nice."

Sadowski offered a smile, "Okay, maybe that's good."

Twenty minutes later, Gloria, clad in the scrubs and a pair of hospital slippers, marched into Hudson's heading for women's clothing. Detroit's premier department store, and the second largest department store in the nation, Gloria knew it well. She had fond memories of shopping excursions with her stepmother Gina during her stepfather's absences. Anticipating court appearances, Pip Papineau had opened a Hudson's account for her but she hadn't used it until now.

"If you want to eat, you could get something at the dining room. It's up on the thirteenth floor," Gloria suggested to Sadowski.

"I know where it is," Sadowski said. I love the cheese soup but it's a little warm for soup today. Maybe I'll get a Maurice salad." Smiling, she headed for the bank of elevators.

As Gloria looked around at the displays wondering what kind of clothing would make her look more mature, a frowning, middle-aged man in a suit with a Hudson's badge on the breast approached.

"May I help you, miss?" He sounded more like he wanted to help her find the exit. He had a pencil moustache, a shiny red tie and smelled like cigarettes.

"Um, yes. I need something to make me look older and… professional."

He'd been about to touch Gloria's shoulder, probably to direct her toward the door, but her statement stopped him. Gloria spotted a smartly dressed young black saleswoman hovering behind him and caught her eye. The woman squeezed past the man and asked, "You going away to college? Or is this for a job interview?"

"Sylvia," the man muttered. "Let me—"

"I think I'd rather have a woman help me, if you don't mind," Gloria said smiling. "It's a woman to woman thing."

The man paused, then backed away. Her hands on her hips, the young woman appraised Gloria.

"I have an important meeting at two-thirty. I don't want to go in there looking like a teenager. And I need everything." Gloria leaned in close and whispered, "I just got out of the hospital. I don't even have underwear."

The woman nodded and took a deep breath. "My name's Sylvia, and I have to ask before we get started. Do you have a budget?"

Gloria spoke loudly enough for the man, hovering nearby, to hear. "Well, I'll pay whatever I have to. I have an account here. My name's Gloria Doran." She saw the man start to walk away. Sylvia noticed it too and chuckled.

"That'll keep him out of our hair. He's gone to check up on you. You don't have parents who are gonna rein you in, do you?"

Gloria shook her head. "I don't have any parents. The bills are paid out of my lawyer's office. And it's my money so they damn well better not try to rein me in."

The first thing she bought was underwear, a Detroit Tigers T-shirt, a pair of gym shorts and some slip-on, rubber-soled shoes. After she'd changed, she wadded up the hospital scrubs and threw them in the trash. In an hour she'd picked out an array of lingerie and nylons, two blouses and a pair of black slacks. Some of the lingerie was more than a little sexy.

This is for Jimmy. I couldn't do this if Dr. Sadowski was here.

She tried on half a dozen dresses and a few pant suits. Her favorite dress, a bright yellow summer dress with spaghetti straps and bare shoulders, had misshapen purple spots that looked psychedelic. It fitted her perfectly, maybe too perfectly. The stretchy fabric clung to her hips, and a scooped neck displayed a lot of cleavage. The dress ended high up her thighs. She absolutely loved it and found some purple shoes that matched.

"You were made for that dress but…" Sylvia had started to speak but stopped as Gloria stared at herself in the mirror.

I haven't worn a dress or a skirt since the night I met Jimmy. I'm just waiting for him to come home so I can start living again.

Shaking off her malaise, she said, "I'll get this dress and the shoes too, but it won't do for the meeting."

Finally, she settled on a summer weight woolen business suit. Worn with a matching jacket, the light blue, sleeveless, knee-length dress, with a high square neckline looked stodgy, but it did make her look older. She tried on matching pumps with low heels even though she had almost never worn heels. But she didn't think she should wear flats with the suit.

"You're not tall so adding a few inches'll make you more substantial," Sylvia said. She'd tried to persuade Gloria to get higher heels.

"I don't know. If I go much bigger, I'm afraid I might fall over," Gloria said with a giggle, embarrassed about her inexperience with high heels. But after trying on several more pairs, and encouraged by Sylvia, she settled on higher heels that she hoped she could handle, at least for the meeting.

"These are about as high as I can go," Gloria said.

"Those will work. They go with the suit, and now you don't look like a college girl. Long as you don't land on your ass."

Gloria laughed, but felt growing tension knotting her stomach. She didn't regret skipping lunch.

Sylvia talked Gloria into a matching shoulder bag and small faux-pearl earrings. "You should consider piercing your ears, but these'll do for now."

Sadowski returned. Gloria saw her point to her watch and hold up two fingers.

Maybe there's time for one final touch. And what can they do to me if we're late?

"I need to do something about my hair. I don't want to cut it. There's no time anyway. Could we pin it up?" She held handfuls of her long hair as if weighing it. Turning, she stepped toward the mirror and examined her face. "Don't I need some makeup? Maybe hide the cut on my forehead and tone down the bruises... Is there anyone available in the beauty salon who could help? It has to be right now, and fast."

"I know somebody," Sylvia chirped. "What happened to you? A traffic accident?"

"Long story," Gloria said. "Maybe it helps. Makes me look tougher. But still…"

"Gloria, I don't know if we should…" Sadowski started.

"Her name's Polly. She's working a summer job here like me so she's usually got openings, and she's fast." Sylvia continued. "I'll call up."

Less than a minute later Sylvia had packed Gloria onto the elevator for the fourteenth floor and the beauty salon. "When you're done, have Polly call me. I'll have everything boxed up and meet you at the Woodward entrance. You can sign the bill, and your friend can pick you up there. In fact, what kind of car do you have?"

"Fifty-nine Ford Falcon. It's green," Sadowski said.

"I'll get Alphonse from security. You can park at the curb in front of the door, and he'll make sure there's no trouble."

It was almost two-thirty when Polly walked Gloria to the elevator. She had swept Gloria's hair into a neat beehive and pinned it together. Makeup helped her face more than Gloria had expected, and she didn't regret the time it had taken.

Every little bit helps.

The last thing Polly did was dab some Bat-Sheba perfume on Gloria's neck and behind her ears.

"No charge. If you like it, you can come back and buy some. But it's not cheap," Polly advised. Like Sylvia, she was young, black and pretty.

On the way down in the elevator, Gloria stared at herself in the mirror, amazed but not entirely pleased at the transformation that had taken place.

The hair makes me taller, but I'm going to get rid of it as soon as the meeting's over. I don't like the suit. Probably never wear it again. Why am I so scared about this damn meeting? Or am I scared about Jimmy? What if he doesn't want me anymore? Everything he's been through. Last thing he needs are my problems.

As the elevator doors slid open, Gloria made a concerted effort to push away the stress. Her stomach felt queasy and her shoulders ached.

My lawyer and my doctor work for me. So does the record company. I write songs. I sell records. I won't let Logan Carlton push me around. And Jimmy loves me. I know he loves me. And I love him.

Trying to feel confident, she strode past the displays of jewelry, watches, toiletries, belts and handbags, her new high heels clicking on the hard floor as she wondered if her shopping spree had been worth it. Sylvia, holding two huge shopping bags loaded with boxes, waited at the entrance. Gloria plucked the bill and the pen from Sylvia's fingers and scribbled her name without looking at the numbers.

"If you could grab those boxes on the ledge over there, I'll load these in the car, and you can be on your way," Sylvia said.

"Thanks for all your help, Sylvia." Gloria picked up the three light but wide boxes and walked carefully out the door. Over the top of the boxes, she saw Sadowski opening the trunk. A few dozen feet down the street a policeman rode slowly away on a horse, hoofs clopping on the pavement.

Gloria couldn't see below her because of the boxes. As she reached the rear of the Falcon, her right foot went over the edge of the concrete curb catching her by surprise. She sprawled forward, irrationally throwing the boxes to the side to avoid landing on them. Instead, her stomach and chest smacked onto something soft on the pavement.

Horse manure, and very fresh horse manure by the smell of it.

For a few seconds Gloria lay still.

"Oh, my God!" Sylvia cried.

Gloria didn't cry. Instead, she let loose with a shrill hysterical laugh shocking both Sylvia and Dr. Sadowski.

-59-

Nui Binh Base Camp

The morning after he returned from Long Binh, Cartwright found Hayes and told him to report to the Orderly Room.

"Am I in trouble?" Hayes asked.

"You'll see," Cartwright said. "The first sergeant wants to talk to you."

Looking stern, First Sergeant McConaughey handed Hayes a sheaf of orders, then broke into a broad smile. "You got a drop. Pack your stuff right now and get out to the flight line."

"What do you mean I got a drop?" Hayes asked.

"Just what I said. You're on a flight back to the States leavin' Bien Hoa sometime tomorrow. I don't know when it leaves tomorrow, but you better get to Long Binh today. There's a ship leavin' in half an hour. They're running some Donut Dollies back to Long Binh. So get your ass in gear."

Hayes looked at the orders as McConaughey grabbed his hand. "You take care of yourself and that girl of yours."

Cartwright appeared, proffering his hand as well. Then he dropped it and hugged Hayes instead. "Stay in touch, man. You've done a lot for me. I'll pack up any stuff you want shipped home."

"I just bought a stereo," Hayes said.

"No problem, just leave me an address."

Hayes had heard about the young female Red Cross volunteers called Donut Dollies, but he'd never met or seen any of them. He'd heard that they mostly just talked to soldiers and sometimes served donuts. When he took in the skirts, blouses and lipstick, and smelled the faint flowery fragrance of soap and shampoo, he felt his world starting to change. After they landed in Long Binh, he remembered nothing about their conversation. He only thought about Gloria.

Is she still going to be there for me? Why would a peace and love hippie chick want to have anything to do with me?

He found the transient barracks, dumped his duffel bag on an empty bunk and wandered next door to the unit listed in his orders. He asked the harried sergeant where he could get a Class A uniform, which he presumed he would be wearing on the flight home.

"You wear your fatigues. You get the Class A's in the States. The bus to Bien Hoa don't leave 'till 1600 Hours tomorrow so bugger off and stop botherin' me."

That night he barely slept, thinking about Gloria and home.

The next morning as he sat in a mess hall drinking coffee and contemplating an untouched bowl of oatmeal, he overheard two soldiers at the next table.

"... heard they cut off his fuckin' head."

"Was his dick in his mouth? 'Cause the VC'll do that shit."

"Naw, they just cut off his head."

Hayes slid his chair over to the two spec fours. "What happened?"

They both looked him over before one of them replied, "They just found somebody dead outside the main gate. VC musta dumped him there last night. I work nights at Second Field Force HQ. Heard about it just before I got off this morning."

"He was beheaded?"

"Yeah, and it was a fuckin' colonel."

"Didn't you say it was a lieutenant colonel?" said the other spec four.

"Yeah, but that's still a colonel, dipshit."

"Do you know his name?" Hayes asked.

"Naw, I didn't hear a name."

With a sense of dread, Hayes hurried out of the mess hall and ran toward the gate. Three jeeps parked haphazardly around the entrance and half a dozen MPs blocked him from going further. Just beyond the gate a dozen or more men, mostly officers, stood talking in a cluster. Hayes spotted a few ARVN officers and a couple of civilians wearing sport shirts, tennis shoes and sunglasses. CIA. Then Hayes recognized Major Shiffman in the crowd. At the same time, Shiffman spotted Hayes and hurried through the gate to talk to him.

"Is it Colonel Kucharski?"

Shiffman nodded. He took Hayes by the elbow and they moved away from the crowd. "It's him, and we think Sergeant Bell might be dead too."

"Bell too! I had a feeling about Kucharski when I heard." Hayes didn't know what else to say.

"Late yesterday afternoon, Kucharski, Bell, a third man and an Asian woman drove out in a jeep. The three men were armed and wearing combat gear. The MPs are looking for the jeep, the other two men and the woman now."

"It's probably that spy, Bich" Hayes said. Shiffman nodded. "Something you should know, sir…"

"What?"

"Bell was sleepin' with that spy. I shoulda told you before, but there was a lot going on."

Hayes expected the major to be angry but the major turned to look at the crowd outside the gate. "That might explain some things, but we had a lot of evidence already that she couldn't be trusted. She should have been locked up the day you exposed her."

"I spoke to Bell yesterday morning. Talked about what happened in that village, how Kucharski's brother-in-law's company massacred those villagers. And about the villagers who got thrown out of the helicopter. I know who actually threw those villagers out of the helicopter and let him know that I knew."

"Okay," Shiffman said, now looking at him intently.

"Bell told me Kucharski wasn't around, but I had a feeling somebody might have been hiding in Kucharski's office when I was there. Could it have been Bich? Or could Bell have spoken to her later? A little pillow talk? If she found out who was really responsible… I mean, the VC were going to execute me for it."

Shiffman sighed. "Most of my ARVN contacts wanted Bich to be executed, even at the cost of upsetting us or the Thais. She must have known she wasn't going to last long."

"Why did the CIA and Kucharski still think they could trust anything she said?"

"It's complicated, but Bich grew up in the Central Highlands. Her family fled to Thailand after Dien Bien Phu. Her mother's Thai, her father's Vietnamese. Apparently, Bich not only speaks some of the indigenous tribal languages but knows a few tribal leaders."

"The Montagnards?" Hayes asked.

"Well, yes, but there's a coupla dozen different tribes, and they're not all Montagnards. You need to disabuse yourself of the notion that the Vietnamese people are one big, happy family who all want the same thing. There's the North and the South, the farmers and the city people, Buddhists and Catholics and other religions like the Cao Dai. You were a Cao Dai prisoner so you know firsthand they don't get along with the government or the Vietcong. There's all of these different groups. None of them wants to be losers. They all want to come out winners in this war. I don't know who's gonna win, but I know who's gonna lose."

"Who?" Hayes asked, though he already knew the answer.

"Us."

They were silent a few moments.

"So, where do you think Bich is now?"

Shiffman shrugged. "With the VC. I doubt we'll ever see her again."

"What about Bell and the other guy?"

"What about them? They're probably dead. We're trying to figure out who the other one might be. We don't have a report of anyone missing."

"It was probably Sergeant First Class Stanton. He's in the 99th, and he murdered five people in my company. Kucharski's been protecting him. He's the one who threw those villagers off the helicopter."

Shiffman didn't say anything. He looked down at the ground. "Dammit, I talked to your CO back when that report on Spec Five Mitchell first came out. I know he got in trouble trying to get it overturned. He was sure Mitchell was murdered. Wasn't it you and First Sergeant McConaughey who found the body?"

"Yeah, and it was definitely murder."

"You say there's four more?"

Hayes took a breath, then told Shiffman everything. He'd told the story enough times and the night before had spent several hours writing the information down for his MP friend Suggs and composing a letter to his lawyer about it, so he got through it quickly.

The major didn't interrupt, and when Hayes was done Shiffman said, "It would have ended Kucharski's career, and the collateral damage would have hurt the Army too."

"We should call the 99th to see if Sergeant Stanton's there, but I'll bet he isn't."

Shiffman nodded. "Let's go find a phone. What are you doing in Long Binh?"

"Going home. Gotta catch a bus for Bien Hoa at 1600 Hours."

"Thought you said your DEROS wasn't till next week."

"I got a drop. Didn't ask for it, but I'm not complaining."

Hayes liked Shiffman and sensed that Shiffman liked him. As they approached a bunker festooned with antennae, Hayes remembered the place.

"Are we going to see Frenchy?"

"If he's there," Shiffman said. "He probably isn't 'cause he usually works nights, but we can use a phone."

A spec four pushed a phone across the counter to Shiffman. "Help yourself, sir," he said.

Hayes made the call, and the phone made a strange noise like a fast busy signal. The operator came back on the line. "It's not connecting. Who you calling again?"

"The 99th Assault Helicopter Company Orderly Room."

"Well, their phone must be out."

"Can you try Operations? Sorry, but I don't remember the number."

After a pause, he heard the phone ringing normally and somebody picked it up on the first ring.

"Lieutenant Colonel Blair. Who am I speaking to?"

"Sergeant Hayes, sir, I have some news for you and I need to find—"

Blair interrupted. "Sergeant, I have bad news. Specialist Conrad Myers was killed about an hour ago by a rocket that hit the Orderly Room. First Sergeant McConaughey and Specialist Cartwright were wounded"

Hayes was too shocked to speak.

"Apparently, the three of them were talking to each other when the rocket hit. A big piece of shrapnel hit Myers in the head. He died instantly." Blair's voice caught, and he coughed

Hayes asked, "What happened to the first sergeant and Cartwright?"

"Top's hurt pretty bad, but he'll survive. Cartwright got some shrapnel in his arm and back. Didn't look too serious, but he's badly shaken. He hasn't been able to speak. Doc Morrison's sending him for a psych evaluation."

"Aw, man, that's terrible."

After a few moments of silence, Blair said, "I'm very busy here. You said you had news."

"Yes sir. Colonel Kucharski is dead. The VC left him outside the main gate in Long Binh. He was beheaded."

"Kucharski's dead!" The silence dragged for a long moment. Now it was Blair who was speechless.

"There's a Sergeant First Class Bell, worked in Kucharski's office. He's missing. He, Colonel Kucharski, a woman who's a lieutenant and translator in the Royal Thai Air Force, but who's that VC spy, and another soldier drove out of Long Binh in a jeep yesterday afternoon. They found Kucharski's body this morning. The woman's likely gone back to the VC, but Sergeant Bell and the other soldier are missing. I think the other guy might be –"

"Sergeant First Class Stanton, the person you think is a murderer," Blair said.

"Yeah, him."

"We'll check on Stanton, but I haven't seen him today, or yesterday either. Where can we call you?"

Looking at his watch, Hayes said, "Sir, maybe you should talk to Major Shiffman. I'm supposed to catch a bus out of here soon."

"Shouldn't take long to check, but about your DEROS being moved up? Top talked to me again last night about these murders. He convinced me to talk to CID. That's Criminal—"

"I know what it is."

"Top said I should get you outta here, that you were in danger from Stanton and maybe Colonel Kucharski. That's why you got the drop."

"Sir, thank you."

"You've done your duty, sergeant. Time for you to go home."

"No, no, not that, sir. Thank you for going to CID. I know it wasn't easy."

"Good luck to you son," Blair said.

-60-

Over the South China Sea

On a Boeing 707 jet airliner full of happy soldiers, an edgy Jimmy Hayes had convinced himself that Gloria would reject him when he got home. Out of his league, quite simply too beautiful, too talented and far too smart for someone like him. Every night he had stripped and cleaned his rifle and collection of pistols. Lying awake, he'd plotted how to murder Stanton and Kucharski too. Only the certainty of getting caught held him back. He'd fantasized about Stanton making a threatening move so he could murder him in an act of self-defense. And now he'd convinced himself that the Vietcong had not killed Stanton, that Stanton somehow had escaped and that Stanton would come after him. Irrational, but he believed it.

Am I going crazy?

He knew he'd have serious challenges adjusting to civilian life, a big topic of conversation on the airplane.

"We gotta stop sayin' fuck all the time," announced the spec five sitting beside him.

"You got that right, motherfucker," replied a soldier across the aisle.

Ecstatic about getting out of Vietnam alive, everyone seemed apprehensive. Hayes knew some of the others shared his fear about what awaited them at home.

"I see one of them fuckin' hippie protestors I'll wring his fuckin' neck," snarled somebody sitting behind Hayes. Many soldiers knew that public sentiment had turned against the war, and that many of their same-aged peers felt nothing but contempt for soldiers. Hayes resisted the attempts of his seatmate to engage him in conversation. Instead, he curled up against the window and tried to sleep. He felt like he hadn't slept for days.

The Pan Am flight stopped in Japan, then in Alaska, and he still hadn't slept. Shortly before they touched down in Oakland he thought he might have dozed off. On the short bus trip to the center where he would process out of the Army, he attempted to sleep sitting up, a skill he'd mastered in basic training. Didn't work. And for several minutes, the same seatmate he'd had on the plane sat next to him on the bus, rambling on about what he was going to eat, how much he was going to drink, the women he planned to screw, and how many times he would screw them. In the processing center, Hayes dragged himself from one station to the next like a zombie. He stood in lines, answered questions, signed papers, collected papers, listened to sergeants and officers, and immediately forgot everything they said.

At the end of a long line of soldiers, he dropped his duffel bag on the concrete floor. The bag clanked.

"Whatcha got there, Sergeant?" asked an eager young spec four.

Hayes didn't say anything.

The spec four picked up the bag and shook the contents out. Among the socks, underwear, T-shirts, boots and jungle fatigues, four pistols hit the floor.

"Jesus H. Christ, you gotta fuckin' arsenal here."

Hayes had an M1911 .45 Colt automatic that an ARVN trooper had left on his gunship, the Makarov, a Colt .38 revolver and the big antique revolver.

"Looootenant! Come see what we got here."

Hayes didn't say anything. No one had told him he couldn't bring the guns home though he knew it must be against some Army regulation. A first lieutenant appeared. He picked up the antique pistol by the barrel.

"What the fuck is this? Looks old."

Hayes said nothing.

The blond lieutenant appeared older than most men of his rank. Overweight, his belly strained the lower buttons of his khaki uniform shirt. He'd sweated enough to grow large dark patches under his arms though Hayes thought the temperature quite comfortable. The lieutenant picked up the forty-five, the thirty-eight and finally the Makarov, expertly ejecting the magazines and emptying the cylinders. He checked for chambered rounds. He examined the old revolver carefully, breaking it open, peering down the barrel and running his fingers over the old metal before laying it back down on the table.

"Where'd you get these? How much did you pay for them? I hear there's a big black market for firearms, especially enemy weapons."

"I didn't pay anything. An ARVN Ranger left the forty-five on my helicopter. I got the thirty-eight from a pilot in a trade. The other automatic's Russian, a Makarov."

"I know what it is," the lieutenant said.

"It belonged to a Vietcong or a North Vietnamese. I'm not a hundred percent sure what he was."

"I repeat, how much did you pay for these? An enemy soldier didn't just give the Makarov to you."

"No, I had to kill him first," Hayes said. Fully awake now, he understood that for the past year he'd usually carried a weapon, often more than one, except for when he'd been a prisoner.

The lieutenant said, "Sonny, smuggling firearms into the USA will get you a court-martial."

Tired, Hayes spoke without thinking. "My name's Sergeant Hayes not 'Sonny'." Then realizing he didn't want to antagonize the lieutenant, he added, "Sir."

"Specialist Radcliffe, go find that MP sergeant and bring him here," the lieutenant said. He stabbed a finger into Hayes' chest. "Sonny, you're a danger to the citizens out there."

Biting his lip, Hayes glared at the lieutenant but remained silent until the MP appeared. Hayes saw the MP's eyes narrowing as he approached. The MP was a staff sergeant and, judging by his eyes, also a combat vet.

"What is it now?" he asked the lieutenant.

"Got us a gun smuggler here. We need to lock him up." The lieutenant pointed at the four pistols. "They were in his duffel bag."

The MP glanced at the pistols but focused on Hayes nametag. "Let's see your papers." He took the wad of papers from Hayes' hand and looked through them until he found the sheet he was looking for. After reading for a few seconds he gestured to the lieutenant. "Sir, we need to talk about this."

The two walked over to a corner out of earshot. After a minute or two of animated conversation, the lieutenant walked away clearly upset.

The MP returned to Hayes and handed the paper back. "This is your DD 214. Make damn sure you hang onto it. Get copies made. It's proof you're a veteran, and it's a snapshot of your service. I told the lieutenant over there that court-martialing somebody with your decorations was stupid and a losing proposition all around. So he's backing off. But I can't let you keep those guns."

He looked at the spec four. "Pack up Sergeant Hayes' stuff." He turned to Hayes. "Keep your cool, sergeant. Sometimes there's demonstrators exercising their freedom-of-speech rights at the airport. Don't let 'em get under your skin. Just go home to your… you gotta wife, or a girl?"

"I hope so."

-61-

Detroit

"I don't know why, but I thought I'd end up in this dress," Gloria said, her first words since she had fallen. She and Emily Sadowski hurtled up the Penobscot Building in an elevator.

"Are you okay? You really scared me—" the doctor started.

"I'm okay," Gloria said with a squeaky laugh. "You don't have to keep asking. It was just a little horse manure." Gloria sucked air through her teeth and pushed back against the agitation boiling up. "But I can still smell it."

"Gloria, it only got on that suit, nothing else. The smell's in your imagination. The only thing I can smell in here is that Bat… Bat… whatever that perfume is. And it's very nice, too."

"I got this dress for Jimmy. I know it's not appropriate for this meeting."

"It's a little unbusinesslike, but it looks fantastic on you. I wish I could wear something like that."

When the elevator doors slid open with a ping, Gloria stayed inside breathing deeply and staring at her reflection in the mirror. She waited so long Sadowski had to stop the doors from closing and nudge Gloria out. "Let's go. They're waiting for us and, believe me, nothing bad's going to happen to you."

"I don't know about that," Gloria muttered.

At four minutes after three, Gloria, carrying her guitar, clicked into the conference room in her matching shoes and the yellow dress with the purple psychedelic spots. Papineau; Maxie Zimmerman, president of the record company; Zoomer and State Senator Logan Carlton sat around the big table. Carlton stubbed out a cigar in an ashtray. Most surprising, Gloria saw Mrs. Lincoln in a wheelchair sitting by the big window. Susanna Quinn stood beside her and waved encouragement. She'd drastically cut back her Afro and unsuccessfully tried to force the shorter kinky hair into a more conventional style. Wrapped in a plaid flannel blanket, Mrs. Lincoln smiled.

As Sadowski headed for an empty chair at the table, Zoomer sprung up. He wore his signature obscenely tight white pants with a red frilly shirt open to his navel.

"Sunshine, you are one gorgeous chick. Last time I saw you—"

"Sit down and shut up, Zoomer," Zimmerman said. Then all smiles, he turned to her. "You really do look fabulous, Gloria." Zimmerman's sparse mussy hair stuck out on the sides, and his nose was as red as clown's.

Gloria hurried over to Mrs. Lincoln, bent down and kissed her cheek. "I thought you had to have more surgery?"

"We decided to wait," she said in a weak but firm voice. "They want to put me in a nursing home, but I don't know… My mother went into one and never came out."

Gloria said, "I'll take care of you."

"And I'll help," Susanna added.

"Aren't you working at GM?" Gloria asked.

"Bad scene there. I quit. Tell you about it later."

Out of the corner of her eye, Gloria caught Papineau sneaking a glance at his watch. He said, "We should start. I have important matters to go over with Miss Doran in private, so let's get the rest of you on your way." He patted an empty chair next to him. "Gloria, I'm so glad you are out of the hospital and looking so well. We've all been worried."

"Sorry I'm late. I had a little problem with a horse." She gave Mrs. Lincoln's shoulder a squeeze.

"A horse?" said Carlton, resplendent in a full three-piece dark navy blue suit. He looked nervous.

As she sat, she noted Zoomer's and Carlton's eyes riveted to her chest. The low-cut dress made all the bra's she'd bought too visible, so she'd elected to go without. Maybe not a great decision.

Papineau started. "Mr. Zimmerman has asked if you would be willing to appear at a benefit concert he's organizing to raise money for—"

"Sure, I'll do it," Gloria said. "Where's it going to be? And when?"

"The Grande Ballroom, two weeks from Saturday. But in the afternoon, which is gonna be a little tough 'cause the Byrds are playin' there that night. And Zoomer's opening for that show."

"Do I have to give up the proceeds from both shows?" Zoomer asked.

Zimmerman frowned. "C'mon, Zoomer, we've been through this already."

"How big's the Grande Ballroom?" Gloria asked. It seemed to be one of the main venues for visiting rock and roll bands but she'd never been there.

"You can pack in twenty-five hundred, sometimes even three thousand. And it's got decent acoustics," Zimmerman said. "*Locked in Love*'s number one locally right now and Billboard has it in the top ten nationally, but it'll still—"

"Numero nine with a bullet. Grrroooovy," Zoomer chortled. "Sunshine, how's about givin' me another song? Make money for both of us."

Gloria looked at him, her mouth tight. "I didn't give it to you, Zoomer. You stole it."

"No, no, c'mon, sweetheart. Be nice."

"Zoomer, cool it," Zimmerman warned.

"What's done's done," Gloria said, "and I've been thinking about what you did with my song. I'm willing to give you joint songwriting credit and a third of the songwriting royalties. That doesn't mean I don't think you stole it. Just acknowledging that you improved it."

A gloating smile appeared on Zoomer's face. "Cool. No reason we can't do it again and make more bread."

"No way. Jimmy, my boyfriend's coming home soon. I'll be working with him." Looking at Zimmerman, she said, "Two weeks? Jimmy should be home. I'd like him to play the show with me. That okay?"

Zimmerman nodded enthusiastically. "Yes, yes."

She thought for a moment. "We'll probably need a bass player and a drummer. Can you help me, Mr. Zimmerman? There were two guys who used to play with Mrs. Lincoln's son, Roscoe. Jimmy and I played with them when we first met. I think their names were Lionel and Arthur. They were cousins."

"I know who you mean. Lionel Evers, good bass player, always lookin' for work. I don't know about Arthur. Hasn't been around lately."

Zoomer stretched his long frame toward Gloria. "You can sing with us, baby. You come out at the beginning of both my shows and we do *Locked in Love* together. Then at the end, for my encore, I'll give it the full Zoomer treatment, 'cause that's what they're payin' for, right? That way, you only have to do the one song. You don't have to get a band together and rehearse and all that shit." He glanced at Mrs. Lincoln. "You'll be able to take care of the old lady."

"She's not old." Gloria said, pausing to smile at Mrs. Lincoln. "No, Zoomer. Jimmy and I, and Roscoe, have an album. There are ten songs on it and we have another seven we recorded but haven't released yet."

"The more you can do, the better," Zimmerman said.

"What the fuck, I'm the one with the hit here," Zoomer said.

"Zoomer, we're talkin' about drawin' a coupla thousand kids used to payin' five bucks to hear, sometimes, three or four good bands at the Grande." Zimmerman ran his fingers through sparse hair. "On your tour, you been playin' half an hour. We gotta fill at least 90 minutes. Two hours would be better. It's true, Locked in Love's the hit. But that's the only original you got."

"So what?" Zoomer said. "All you need's the one hit to get 'em through the door. And hell, I can play two hours, easy."

"I'm gonna do a show, Zoomer," Gloria said. "I just gave you thousands of dollars in royalties. Are your pants so tight you can't do math? I could change my mind and sue you for stealing my song." She turned toward Papineau. "Right?"

"Right," Papineau said, amused.

Carlton let loose with a snorting laugh. "Careful, son, you're playing with fire."

After a tense pause, Zimmerman sighed. "Don't sue, Gloria. Zoomer'll come around." He glared at Zoomer before looking back at Gloria. "Your album's started selling again. Just a little, but it could pick up. Maybe we should release another single. If I could get something to local radio stations to promote the concert..." He sighed.

Gloria considered the idea. "How about using something from those unreleased seven? A tease for the next album?"

"Really good idea," he said. "But you know, seven songs is a little thin for an album. If you could do one or two, or even three more…"

Gloria shrugged. "Once Jimmy's back, we could do a couple more if he's…" Her voice trailed off and she shook off despairing thoughts. "You know, one of those seven unreleased songs is an instrumental jam. It's more than twelve minutes long. So an album wouldn't be as thin as you think. And I could do my own version of *Locked in Love*. Just me and my guitar with all my lyrics. Maybe they're not great, but they're not *that* bad. I could do that right away."

A slow, approving nod from Zoomer surprised her.

Zimmerman tapped his pencil on the table as he thought. "Do you listen to any FM radio?"

"Yeah, sometimes," Gloria said.

"It's really starting to take off," Zimmerman said. "High-end stereos have FM receivers, and cars are starting to get them too. It's catching on, especially with college students."

"Some of my friends listen to it all the time," Susanna said.

"There's a rock and roll FM station in town, WABX, that plays a lot of long cuts, especially at night. I could give them that twelve-minute jam. I'm sure they'd play it. Might spread to other stations too. Anyway, another way to promote the show."

Nobody said anything until Gloria finally nodded. "Let's do it."

"I'm done here," Zoomer announced. "I need a fuckin' drink." He got up and headed for the door. When he got even with Gloria he stopped for several seconds looking down her dress. "There's a party tonight. I could take ya. Mitch Ryder, Terry Knight and the Pack and a buncha Motown people gonna be there. You oughta meet 'em."

"Zoomer…" Zimmerman started.

Gloria wasn't about to go anywhere with Zoomer, but the possibility of meeting other artists intrigued her enough to think about it. Maybe Susanna could come too. She finally shook her head. "I don't think so, Zoomer, but thanks, and thanks for helping with the benefit."

With a leering grin, Zoomer departed.

Nobody said anything until Zimmerman finally rose from his seat. "I better go too. I apologize, but Zoomer's been on tour. He's tired. He's been working pretty hard. I appreciate you doing the benefit, Gloria. I'll run down Lionel and see if I can find out what happened to Arthur."

"Hang on a sec, Mr. Zimmerman, I need your help with something else, too."

"Anything, just name it."

"I need someone to fix my guitar." She picked up her guitar, one hand on the neck and the other holding the cord. "I think the pickup inside is broken. I'll need it to work on the *Locked in Love* thing. I have this fingerpicking technique where you play bass notes with your thumb and melody with your fingers. I can play lead and rhythm at the same time. Sounds harder than it is. Some players like Joan Baez and Chet Atkins do it all the time."

"I know some guitar people. I might need your guitar for a day or two, no wait, I'll get somebody to come to you," Zimmerman said before heading out the door.

Papineau checked his watch again, steepled his hands, glanced at Gloria and then focused on Logan Carlton. "Senator Carlton and I have come to an agreement on finalizing your father Clyde Bonaventure's estate. The senator has agreed to return the funds that he took from the estate. He's fired his attorney and will let my firm tidy up the remaining legal matters. I think it should all be settled in a month. And Dr. Sadowski will continue to be your physician for as long as you want."

"Like I had any fuckin' choice," Carlton said.

"Logan, watch your language," Mrs. Lincoln snapped in a surprisingly strong voice. "You're as bad as that crude young man who just left."

"Sorry, sorry. But I'm probably gonna lose the election now. Republicans are putting up serious money for this law-and-order ex-cop they dug up to run against me."

Carlton looked down at the conference table before turning to Gloria. "Clyde was my best friend. After he found out he was your father, he made me promise to take care of you if anything happened to him. He financed my first election run and said he'd finance this one too, but he died before he gave me any money. My lawyer said I was entitled to it, but I think he mighta been settin' me up. He's a damn…" He looked over at Mrs. Lincoln. "Sorry, Frances. He's a Republican."

"Your lawyer's ethics have raised questions in the past. I tried to warn you," Papineau said.

"Godammit counselor, you won your case. You don't have to rub it in." Carlton glared at Gloria while Papineau clicked his ballpoint pen like a machinegun. "I've been tryin' to do right by you. You're not grown-up. You need guidance from a responsible adult. I'm a state senator. You need to go back to school and drop this Jimmy character. Believe me, he doesn't give a... doesn't care about you. I've been in the military and I know what young soldiers are like when they're on leave. And he used to be one of those long-haired musicians just like that Zoomer character who—"

"How dare you pass judgment on Jimmy. You've never even met him. And how dare you pass judgment on me."

Gloria leaned forward, her eyes fiery and her jaw clenched. "I love Jimmy and the way you describe us hurts me. It hurts a lot. Jimmy and I both had a rough start in life. But we're going to succeed if you'll just give us a chance."

"My Roscoe thought a lot of Jimmy," Mrs. Lincoln said in a voice so soft Gloria barely heard.

"Thank you," Gloria said.

The senator hadn't finished.

"I checked your school records. You can't expect to succeed in life with only an eighth grade education. Can't you see that?"

Gloria felt her face flush with embarrassment. Unable to respond, she let herself go slack like she did when she prayed, closed her eyes, tried to call up the picture of her great grandmother. A woman born in slavery who'd made a life for herself revered by three generations of her family.

Susanna broke the silence.

"Senator, didn't you see what Gloria did a few minutes ago? She negotiated with the president of her record company and that Zoomer so that she gets equal time on stage at that concert. The Grande Ballroom is a big deal," Susanna said. "And it seems to me that splitting the songwriting credit with Zoomer made everybody happy. A lawsuit woulda made everybody unhappy. You're a politician. Isn't a good deal one that makes both parties happy?"

Then Mrs. Lincoln spoke again. "Logan, Gloria says she wants to learn about finance. Maybe we should let her do that instead of high school."

Sadowski said, "These past few months, Gloria's made giant strides growing up. Most young people Gloria's age don't know what they want to do with their lives. She not only knows what she wants to do, she's already doing it quite successfully. Going back to school could be a regression."

"Jimmy Hayes has some legal issues, but as far as I can see he's a good soldier. I'd be surprised if he's anything like you seem to think, senator," Papineau said.

Conversations sprung up around the room with everyone trying to speak and no one listening. Gloria slapped the table hard.

"Stop it," she said. "Everyone, just stop talking about me like I'm not even here."

They all stopped.

"This is my life you're talking about."

"I'm only tryin' to—"

"Shut up, senator!" Gloria glared at him, then looked around the room trying to fix on each person, one at a time. "I appreciate that you all want to help me. I really do. But this my life. I'm the one who has to live it.

"I wrote a hit record, and I'm going to play the Grande Ballroom. But you want me to give that up. Funny, I'm making a lot of money, but right now my bank account's empty and I have to beg for even a little of it. All those boys dying in Vietnam, but my Jimmy's coming home. *We* lost our baby. Not me, but *we*. Jimmy and me together. We both loved our baby. And we are going to be together no matter how hard you try to keep us apart. So get used to it.

"My life seems like a blues song. I can see sunshine all around me except for the clouds in this room."

She snapped her fingers.

"I'm gonna write a song about it and call it *Sunshine Blues.*"

Gloria looked around at everyone. "A year ago I had no friends, and now I've got all of you. I love you all, even you, senator. Everything's finally coming together for me."

"Who's going to pay all the hospital bills for me and Mrs. Lincoln? Me, that's who. It's great that I'm making enough money to do that. And it's even greater that Jimmy and I both survived.

"I had mono, and I had a concussion. Still have stitches in my body and bruises on my face. I have bad dreams at night. Jimmy was locked in a dungeon for more than a month. He has bad dreams too. I don't need to waste money on some fancy doctor because some of you think I take drugs. I need to pay Dr. Sadowski 'cause she's the one who's been helping me.

"And senator, if you want money for your re-election, get in line with everyone else.

"I'm not going to high school. I am going to play my music. And as far as Jimmy's concerned, that's my business, not yours or anyone else's.

"This is my future, and I am in charge of it. Me. Gloria. Sunshine."

There was silence in the room until Gloria heard Papineau's ballpoint pen clicking. She saw Susanna take Mrs. Lincoln's hand and pat it. The senator and Sadowski eyed each other like two rams who'd smashed heads once and might go at it again.

In the corner of the conference room on a table beside Mrs. Lincoln, a black telephone rang. Papineau sprang up like he'd received an electric shock and moved to pick up the phone.

"Yeah, yeah… okay, good… yes… of course, as soon as he gets here… yeah, right in." He dropped the phone back into the cradle and looked around the room, a smile tugging at his lips. Then he ran a hand through his silvery hair. "Nothing important. Keep going."

Looking at him, it occurred to Gloria that for the most part, Papineau had been strangely quiet.

The senator slowly looked around the room finally settling on Gloria who turned her head away.

"I can read a room as well as anybody, and I can see that you have won this room, young lady." When she looked back at him she found him smiling at her. "I once told you that you reminded me of Sally Hemings and I wish I'd kept that in mind. I lost sight of just how remarkable you are. Thomas Jefferson never freed Sally Hemings, but I am not going to make that same mistake. You have more than earned your freedom."

Before Gloria could think of a reply, the door to the conference creaked open. Sergeant Jimmy Hayes, in his Class A dress green Army uniform walked in. Mouths popped open, jaws dropped.

Gloria jumped up knocking her chair back into the wall, ran past Papineau and slammed into Jimmy's arms, knocking him back into the door jamb.

"Sunshine."

"Jimmy."

While they were kissing, unaware of everything else, Carlton shook his head.

Mrs. Lincoln said, "Logan, that's love. You oughta try it. Might improve your disposition."

Jimmy and and Gloria came up for air.

"I love you, Sunshine." Jimmy kissed her again. "You're so beautiful and you smell wonderful, kinda earthy…"

"Horse shit," she whispered.

Epilogue

A year later

Sitting at the kitchen table on a Saturday morning, Jimmy Hayes picked a letter from the pile of mail that Gloria had dropped on the table the night before. He looked at a business-sized envelope with a red and blue checked border and a complicated U.S. Army return address. The key characters that had caught his eye were "G2", which he knew denoted Intelligence. He was about to open it when Gloria, wearing the Detroit Tigers T-Shirt she'd slept in, entered the room. She looked over his shoulder at the letter.

"Does the Army want you back?" Giggling, she slid past him and sat on his lap to kiss his cheek. Then he kissed her full on the mouth for a long time.

"I can't get any of that in the Army, so I'm not going."

Arching an eyebrow, Gloria picked up the sheet of foolscap where he'd been writing lyrics for their latest song.

"The red-penciled words are my corrections from the first version," Hayes said. "The last stanza in red's better than the blue one above it. At least, I think so. Maybe we could keep both." He clicked his tongue, shook his head. "It's not there yet."

She stood and studied the words for a moment, then began singing. Hayes grabbed the guitar leaning against the kitchen table. When he started playing, he discovered she sang exactly in tune with the guitar. He'd never understood how she did that. She'd created the melody the day before. They sang and played for more than an hour, trading the guitar back and forth, tweaking words and chords, until Gloria sang the song all the way through with Hayes adding a little harmony on the chorus. They looked at each other.

"It's done," Jimmy said.

He put down the guitar and yawned. He'd gotten up early. After a nightmare, he'd lain awake for a long time, trying to shake off the terror. Finally, he'd gone down to the kitchen to work on the song.

They lived in the fine Craftsman home she'd inherited from her father. Best house he'd ever lived in. He kept a loaded .45 M1911 pistol under the bed. She tolerated it. Barely.

"Did you have another nightmare? That why you got up so early?"

Shrug. "Yeah."

"Why didn't you wake me?"

Another shrug. "You were sleeping so good, and we're both still tired from touring."

"Wanna to go back to bed?"

"It's almost noon," he said.

"Not to sleep." She pushed her breasts into his face. "Nightmare sex?"

They both suffered from nightmares. At first, Hayes had tried to wake Gloria up when she had one. Emily Sadowski counseled them to let the nightmares run their course.

Usually, Gloria thrashed around, waking Hayes during her night terrors. His often didn't wake her, and that fooled them both. They thought his nightmares weren't as bad. But she'd started improving. Gloria had told him to wake her up after he had one. He usually did. After the bad dream ended, his or hers, they talked about it. They comforted each other. They almost always ended up making love. Gloria called it "nightmare sex."

Hayes stood and stretched to pick up the Army letter with the red and blue checked border. He tore it open and shook out a photograph and a sheet of paper with a typed letter.

"Oh shit," he said, his knees suddenly weak. He slid the picture back into the envelope.

"What is it?"

"It's bad. Gruesome. Dead people."

"Let me see."

"You don't want to see this."

"Jimmy, we said no secrets."

He licked his lips, glancing at his empty coffee cup. "I don't want to make your nightmares worse."

"What about you?"

"I can't unsee it." Hayes tapped the envelope against the kitchen table. "You know, it's possible this could help."

"Then I have to see it."

"You wouldn't understand."

"Then you have to explain."

He looked at the envelope and back at Gloria. "I don't know… maybe."

"Emily said we should talk about things like this." Hayes had told her his stories from Vietnam. She'd told him what her stepfather had done to her, and about killing Antoine. It hadn't been easy for either of them. But she'd also gone with him to visit Marina Nesterenko during a break in their last tour. And on another break, they'd driven 200 miles to sing *Amazing Grace* at a tiny Baptist Church in Arkansas where the Leroy Flowers' family worshipped. She understood Vietnam better than anyone he knew who hadn't been there.

"Yeah, well okay…" He pulled the picture out of the envelope and dropped it on the table between them. It was a color photo, probably a copy of a Polaroid. It showed a dead black man and a dead white man, both dressed in jungle fatigues, sitting in chairs. A grinning Vietnamese woman stood between them, unrecognizable because she wore bright mirrored aviator sunglasses. But Hayes knew it was Bich. Behind her, barely discernable, hung a picture of Ho Chi Minh. The camera's flash starkly illuminated the three people, but every else looked dark, almost black, with a slight reddish tinge.

"The men are dead," Jimmy said as Gloria picked up the picture to look.

"They are?" She scrutinized it. "Yeah, they look like they're dead. Strange that they're sitting in chairs, but it's not gruesome. I've seen dead people before."

"That dark stuff all over their shirts, a little hard to see, but it's blood."

She looked again, lips tight. She shoot her head and pushed the picture back toward Jimmy.

"It was taken in that underground chamber where the VC condemned me to death." He continued studying it. "Oh, man… oh shit."

"What?"

"It's a black man and white man, right? Look at the faces and then look at their hands."

She picked up the picture again, swallowed hard. "Yeah, the hands are wrong." Once again, she pushed it away.

"They've been decapitated. Then the heads were switched on the bodies."

She looked away. "That's sick."

Taking his time, he told her about the two men in the picture, Sergeants First Class Stanton and Bell, and the Vietcong spy, though he'd told her much of it before.

"Her days as a VC spy were over. She would have been, should have been, executed. But she managed to pull off one final coup. She lured those three men into a trap, and the VC killed them."

He stared at the picture one last time before sliding it back into the envelope.

"I'll put that pistol away now."

The next day

Gloria and Jimmy met Mrs. Lincoln and Susanna for brunch. Susanna tried to talk all of them into going to Hawaii for a vacation. She only had a vague plan. Rent a house on the beach. Check out the cool Hawaiian music. Relax. Everyone in the band had agreed to take a month off before starting work on a new album. Mrs. Lincoln seemed intrigued by Hawaii.

"I've never been to Hawaii," Hayes said.

"We'll think about it," Gloria said. She had her own secret that she'd put off telling Jimmy.

Later that afternoon, they were back home lying in bed recovering from some inspired sex. Inspired by a copy of the *Kama Sutra* that Gloria had found in a shop in Ann Arbor. She'd actually read it while Jimmy just looked at the pictures. They'd begun to work their way through it.

"You know, I don't think that would qualify as nightmare sex," Hayes said. "Nobody had a nightmare."

"Preventative," Gloria answered. "We shouldn't take chances." She got out of bed and walked naked to the closet. Then she returned carrying a big green tackle box."

"Are we going fishing? Maybe in Hawaii?" he asked.

"Scooch over," she said, lowering the tackle box onto the bed. She climbed back in, the tackle box between them.

"Let me tell you all about this. But first, if you really want to go to Hawaii, it'll be a stop on the way to Hong Kong, or maybe Singapore or Bangkok."

"Haven't been to any of those places, but I'd just as soon avoid Bangkok, for now at least."

"Okay, we can save that one for another time."

"Should we bring the Kama Sutra?"

"Of course. We've barely started."

Then she told him about the tackle box. When she was finished, Jimmy said, "So we'll be doing some traveling."

"Yes. Don't you want to see the world?"

He turned to the next page of the Kama Sutra, looked at the picture. Smiled.

"As long as we do it together."

"All we need is love," she said.

THE END

Acknowledgments

It doesn't take an entire village to produce a novel, but perhaps a small hamlet. The point is, I had help, including some from folks who did not know they were helping.

Stories I heard at the reunions of my Vietnam unit, the 187th Assault Helicopter Company, ended up in this novel. Year after year the stories keep getting better. The line between fact and fiction blurs with the passage of time. Or maybe it's the consumption of the adult beverages.

A few years ago, my wife and I visited Vietnam and saw a beautiful country that I mostly missed the first time I was there. We saw the tunnels of Cu Chi where I staggered, bent almost double, through a tunnel that had been enlarged to accommodate bulky Western tourists. Similarly, the tunnels in *Sunshine Blues* are probably a little larger than the real ones were in 1968. For those interested in learning more about one of the Vietcong's greatest accomplishments, I recommend *The Tunnels of Cu Chi: A Remarkable Story of War* by Tom Mangold and John Penycate.

I also visited the Hanoi Hilton, which the Vietnamese call Hoa Lo Prison, and the War Remnants Museum in Ho Chi Minh City. These two museums focus largely on Communist victories, the huge suffering caused by Agent Orange, napalm, phosphorous and other explosives, and American and French atrocities. It is a different perspective than you'll find in the United States or France, and an example of the victors writing, or re-writing, history.

For almost a decade, I lived in Detroit — in the city, not the suburbs — and worked for the *Detroit Free Press* where I wrote many stories about medicine, science, crime and rock and roll. I also worked in public relations for a business conglomerate. However, my experience in Detroit was about ten years after the time frame of this story. So any discrepancies are covered by my poetic license. I look at it this way. I started in journalism where you stick to the facts. I transitioned into public relations where you stick to facts that benefit the people who are paying you. Now I write fiction and my characters tell me what the facts are. And some of those characters lie. It's a very slippery slope and I slid all the way down.

Three beta readers from Entrada Publishing found many mistakes in my manuscript and made many good suggestions. However, since Entrada doesn't identify them, I'm unable thank them by name. Anonymity allows those beta readers to be brutally honest and blunt. It only took me a week to recover, but it's so much more useful than accolades from friends and relatives. Not that I don't appreciate those.

Another person to whom I am deeply indebted is my editor Edmund Pickett. He helped me turn my perfect manuscript into a far better story. Or should I say two stories, because, as he pointed out, *Sunshine Blues* is really two stories in different genres. Working with Edmund was a humbling experience and I learned a great deal. Like all good editors, he didn't change anything. He told me what he didn't understand or what he didn't like, and why. Then he left it up to me to fix it.

My critique group partners, Danielle Ste. Just, Christina Steiner and Alan Zimmerman also provided much help, and a great deal of encouragement. We've been helping each other improve as writers for many years and having a blast doing it.

Support from the Conejo Valley Writers and the Ventura County Writers kept me sane. Writing can a lonely pursuit, especially if your characters stop talking to you. So getting together with others with similar interests is not just fun, but necessary. And my fellow writers are all so much nicer than my characters.

When you've finally given birth to a brand new story, you have to dress it in pretty clothes and present it to the world. So I turned to Debora Lewis for a great cover and her expertise in formatting the paperback and ebook editions. Thanks Debora!

Last but not least, I am eternally grateful to my wife, Cyndy, who not only put up with long hours I spent with my characters, but she volunteered to copy-edit the manuscript. That was no small job. I asked her why she wanted to do it. She said, "Well, to make a long story short…"

About the Author

Bob Calverley has been a newspaper reporter, writer, editor and public relations consultant. He is the author of a Sixties novel, Purple Sunshine: Sex & Drugs, Rock & Roll, War, Peace & Love and the murder mystery, Hyperventilated Underwater Blues. Sunshine Blues, is his third novel. He lives in Thousand Oaks, California.

Made in the USA
Monee, IL
24 March 2024

55183717R00292